ALSO BY CHRIS PAVONE

Two Nights in Lisbon

The Paris Diversion

The Travelers

The Accident

The Expats

THE DOORMAN

THE DOORMAN

A Novel

CHRIS PAVONE

MCD | FARRAR, STRAUS AND GIROUX | NEW YORK

MCD
Farrar, Straus and Giroux
120 Broadway, New York 10271

Printed in the United States of America
First edition, 2025

Library of Congress Cataloging-in-Publication Data
Names: Pavone, Chris, author.
Title: The doorman : a novel / Chris Pavone.
Description: First edition. | New York : MCD / Farrar, Straus and Giroux, 2025.
Identifiers: LCCN 2024049579 | ISBN 9780374604790 (hardcover)
Subjects: LCGFT: Thrillers (Fiction) | Novels.
Classification: LCC PS3616.A9566 D66 2025 | DDC 813/.6—dc23/eng/20241029
LC record available at https://lccn.loc.gov/2024049579

Hardcover ISBN: 978-0-374-60479-0
Canadian and International Paperback Edition ISBN: 978-0-374-61963-3

Designed by Gretchen Achilles

10 9 8 7 6 5 4 3 2 1

In memory of Johnny Irizarry

Money often costs too much.

—RALPH WALDO EMERSON

If you kept the small rules, you could break the big ones.

—GEORGE ORWELL

Prologue

TONIGHT

FRONT DOOR

Chicky Diaz stands on his little patch of the earth, the clean quiet sidewalk in front of the Bohemia Apartments, thinking: there sure are a lot of great places to kill someone in this city.

There are the sprawling industrial zones in Hunts Point and Maspeth. There are the underpasses of bridges and highways and on-ramps and off-, all those loud echoing voids littered with abandoned vans and homeless camps and piles of trash. There are the late-night-creepy canyons down in the Financial District, and the creepier step streets up in Washington Heights, the ends of elevated subway stations, underground ones too. There are hundreds of miles of waterfront with car-sized boulders and crumbling piers that jut out into the deadly currents of rivers and canals and bays and the mighty Atlantic Ocean. There's that weird-ass auto-repair shantytown out in Willets Point, a place that reminds Chicky of nothing in the States so much as that time he and his buddies took a wrong turn in Panama City. A few wrong turns.

There's all of Staten Island, probably, though in truth Chicky has never stepped foot. Just driven through that time with Julio to visit Reggie who was living rough in Rahway. But he's heard.

There are the parks, ten thousand acres of hills and woods and beaches and ponds, grass ballfields and concrete courts and golf courses and even a lawn-bowling green of all things, just a few minutes from here. The bowlers wear all white. They basically are all white.

Signs at entrances claim PARK CLOSES AT DARK but there aren't many gates that close and no attempt at enforcement. Has anyone ever been deterred by a Parks and Rec placard? It's like no spitting, no loitering, no jaywalking. The type of laws that make a mockery of the very idea of laws.

No jaywalking. What an idea.

The best place to kill someone, though? That's right at home. Away from witnesses and good Samaritans and security cameras, in environments that can be controlled and crime scenes that can be scrubbed, evidence that can be destroyed on the one hand or manufactured on the other. Behind the locked doors and closed curtains of aluminum-sided Capes in Elmhurst or Flatlands, of brownstones up in Harlem and out in Park Slope, of luxury lofts in Tribeca and shitty lofts in Bushwick, of little Tudors out in Forest Hills and huge Tudors up in Riverdale, of slums in the South Bronx and Brownsville, of the housing projects that are everywhere, in every corner of every borough, even places you'd never expect—the Alfred E. Smith Houses just a couple blocks from City Hall, or the ones practically spitting distance from right here.

Every class and every race and every religion and every sexual orientation, everybody's every body, shoulder to shoulder.

This fucking city. Eight million people.

Every one of them can be killed.

Chicky looks across to the park's dark that's broken up only by streetlamps along roadways and footpaths. To Chicky these pools of light seem to increase the menace more than lessen it, drawing attention to just how little safety is out there. Even here on fancy Central Park West with fancier Fifth Avenue on the far side, on these streets that are homes to millionaires and billionaires and the biggest museums of the greatest city in the whole wide world. Even here, danger is right over there.

This is one of the main reasons Chicky's job exists to begin with. Ensuring safety. Trying to.

Chicky has been here for twenty-eight years. Longer than anyone else on staff, longer than most of the residents too. Chicky is who comes to mind when people think of a doorman at the Bohemia, residents and visitors and regular guests, the extended families who descend each Thanksgiving to watch the parade. In all these people's mental dictionaries, the definition of doorman is Chicky Diaz in his spotless uniform and bell crown cap. He's woven into the fabric of the place.

The job suits him. Chicky is always quick with a smile or a joke or the door. He never hesitates to grab a bag or hail a cab, to gently shoo away gawkers or panhandlers, to commiserate about the Mets or the Nets or even the godforsaken Jets.

Chicky is not a particularly religious man but he does believe in god, and it's obvious that he has forsaken the Jets for some unknowable reason. It seems impossible for any sports franchise to be so bad for so long. Especially a team that plays in a major market. The major-est. And yet.

Mysterious ways, they say.

Chicky never fails to remember a resident's name or a visiting grandson or a close friend or "friend." He never calls in sick, never leaves early, never arrives late. He never complains or rolls his eyes at a ridiculous request, of which there are plenty. He is unerringly patient and unfailingly nice. He is relentlessly upbeat.

Or he was.

On the next block a tiny old woman is walking a tiny dog, both miniatures. But otherwise there's nothing but red traffic lights and red taillights and a red light at the end of an awning to beckon a yellow cab. Good luck, this day and age. Taxis don't roam like they used to.

Somewhere a car guns its engine in a way that sounds hostile. Chicky feels a tingle on the back of his clean-cut neck.

Every place to kill someone is also, obviously, a place to get killed. It can happen out on the sidewalk in a hail of automatic gunfire, the murder attempt of a coward who's sitting safely in the passenger side, random bullets hitting thighs and butts and arms but mostly trash cans and windows and innocent passersby. Sometimes little kids, babies.

It's surprising how many gunshot targets manage to survive the indiscriminate spray. Not the one well-placed bullet to the head. No one survives that. But that requires a whole different set of balls. To walk right up to a guy, maybe even look him in the eye, boom.

It can happen at any moment, anywhere, to anyone. Right here, right now. You might never know that you're about to get killed. You might never know that you're about to kill someone.

Chicky sure as fuck hadn't.

"Oh what a good girl," Mrs. Frumm coos. Her bichon frise is peeing right next to the PLEASE CURB YOUR DOG sign. "Yes you are Antoinette."

Antoinette is Mrs. Frumm's third dog since Chicky started working at the Bohemia. All three have been tiny white yappy females, much like Mrs. Frumm, four-foot-nothing with a bosom out to there. Mrs. Frumm had already seemed like an old lady back when Chicky arrived. Now he was catching up.

"Yes you are. Such a good girl."

Over the years Chicky watched Mrs. Frumm instruct dog trainers to reward her puppies for soiling the sidewalk that was Chicky's job to clean. He'd stood by and smiled at the insult.

"Have a good night, Mrs. Frumm."

"*Ungh*," she answers. Mrs. Frumm has a lot to say to her dog but not to her doormen. She scoops up Antoinette and gives the dog a kiss on the snout. "So good."

Chicky holds the door. He suspects that Mrs. Frumm makes him wait on purpose. Chicky has always tried not to let anything bother him, and for a long time he succeeded.

The truck seems to arrive out of nowhere, roaring down Central Park West. Chicky spins toward the sound, sending pain shooting through his chest. The pain is a reminder of his situation. As if he needed one.

No, Chicky tries to tell himself, it would not make any sense for someone to come at him like this. Not tonight. Not so soon, not without giving him the chance to make it right. And not here, not now. This would be too risky. This would be too stupid.

He doesn't entirely believe any of these arguments.

The truck is two blocks away.

Chicky feels his whole body responding. His training can kick in, even three decades after Parris Island. He tries to control his body's autonomic response mechanisms, to use them to heighten his situational awareness instead of compromising his judgment.

He's acutely aware of the clarity of his vision, even though five years ago his eyesight started getting blurry and he picked up some ready-readers at the Duane Reade. There's no blurriness now.

The truck's souped-up sound system is heavy on bass. Chicky can hear a dog bark and another answer, and classical music coming from the Petrocellis' living room on the second floor.

He smells the funk of the garbage that had been put out around the corner on the side street by the new guy Ernesto. That job sucks. But you can get used to almost anything.

Every muscle up and down Chicky's skeleton is engaged. Extra blood is flowing.

He can taste it too. Fear. It has a flavor.

Chicky's self-preservation instinct is telling him to get the fuck inside. But at the same time he feels the pull of duty. This is his sidewalk.

The truck has arrived at the corner and seems to be coming right at him.

Chicky has been in some shit. New York City was a dangerous place when he was a kid. Then there were the years when it was his job to carry a weapon in Panama and Saudi Arabia and Kuwait amid sniper fire and roadside bombs. Actual war zones.

So he never would've imagined that it would happen here on Central Park West, wearing a doorman's uniform with gold braiding and epaulettes.

No, not in a million fucking years.

Chicky reaches to the back of his waistband.

Epaulettes. Jesus.

Chicky doesn't want to overreact and look like a fool. Or feel like a fool. On the other hand he doesn't want to be a fool, under-commit, allow himself to get killed.

He realizes that the truck is speeding up, not slowing down. That's a good sign. No one would speed up before throwing shots.

Chicky takes a step backward and bumps against the wall. He's now partway hidden from the truck by the big potted topiary. The truck is upon him now, and Chicky's heart is hammering . . .

The truck flies by.

All the windows are tinted, even the driver's. Pennsylvania plates. No bumper stickers. No regard for speed limits or red lights. This truck is probably rushing down to Fifty-seventh Street where the police and demonstrators are clashing. None of that has anything to do with Chicky. At least not directly. At least he hopes not.

Chicky feels his phone vibrate. He's been getting a lot of calls he doesn't want and none that he does. This is another unknown number, or the same unknown number, the person he doesn't want to talk to, a conversation he simply cannot have. He hits the red button.

Now it's the growl of multiple engines rumbling from downtown, driving away from the skirmishes on Fifty-seventh. Bright headlights, driving fast but not manically like that other truck.

This can't be Chicky's problem. If El Puño comes after him it's not going to be with a whole fucking convoy.

As these vehicles get closer, Chicky can see that it's four pickups, each flying a massive flag from the tailgate. Each has a couple of guys standing out there in the bed. All of them are wearing tactical camo gear and bulletproof vests and helmets and face masks.

This looks like a police action but these aren't police. The vibe is more ISIS or Taliban or cartel than American patriot. Much more. What this looks like is a hostile invasion because that's what this is. As the trucks roll past, the drivers and passengers and thugs standing in back all stare down Chicky. He stares right back.

All the bumpers and windshields are filled with signifiers. Sports teams and military insignia and silhouettes of assault rifles and, most of all, American flags, thin-blue-line edition. The final tailgate also sports a big Confederate flag. Chicky doesn't understand how anyone can possibly believe in both things at once.

As that last truck passes the twin chimney stacks belch out thick black smoke that engulfs the whole avenue. Chicky coughs and waves away the smoke.

Rolling coal, this is called. Fucking assholes.

The traffic lights have all changed to red but the caravan doesn't stop. Breaking the law openly and repeatedly and with presumed impunity.

Terrorism, Chicky thinks. That's what this is.

A siren is wailing on the far side of the park, and another to the south. Chicky feels another tingle. Maybe the demonstration has gotten out of hand. Maybe the response to it. Maybe both.

The march began at the scene of today's shooting then headed across MLK Boulevard, pausing to rally at each corner, amassing numbers and volume and energy. The crowd was somewhere like five thousand when it turned down Park Avenue, the backbone of white privilege, headed for Fifty-seventh Street. There was plenty to be outraged about in this world and Billionaires' Row was a manifestation of so much of it. Institutional racism and police brutality and income inequality and the conspicuous display of extreme wealth. All of it, right there.

Spillover was inevitable. There are knuckleheads in every crowd. Especially a nighttime crowd that gathers to make themselves heard. A nighttime demonstration is an irresistible invitation to troublemakers and provocations and skirmishes and riots. To looting. To shooting.

There are counterprotesters too. And if anyone in this world is looking for trouble it's people who show up just to be against somebody else. That vigilante kid in Wisconsin was acquitted, so where's the disincentive?

What a fucked-up world we live in, Chicky thinks, that people hate each other so much.

The previous march, a few weeks ago, was a protest against the DA's failure to indict a white guy who'd choke-held a Black man to death on the subway. He'd supposedly been menacing, the dead man. What he'd mainly been was a very unwell person having a psychotic episode. That march had infuriated the law-and-order MAGA-capped dudes, the stand-your-grounders, all over cable news after the fact. Chicky suspected that what pissed them off most was that they hadn't been prepared to counter. They'd missed a golden opportunity to gear up, kick some ass. There weren't nearly enough situations when those guys could take the sorts of action they'd trained for.

Which was probably why rolling coal existed. Thin-blue-line flags too. Shooting deer. All stand-ins.

This time they were not going to miss out.

Chicky hears more sirens. Louder sirens. Closer sirens.

Park Avenue, Fifth Avenue, Fifty-seventh Street: those are all far away psychologically but not geographically. It can take as little as one minute to drive to the Bohemia from Park Avenue or Columbus Circle. Especially if you're not obeying traffic lights.

Hopefully that shit won't make its way here. Chicky does not want to have to be that guy. Not ever. But especially not with tonight's protest, with the lines that are being drawn. Chicky does not want to be forced to choose a side.

The subway rumbles past then everything is quiet again except for those sirens.

Central Park West is almost entirely residential, one fancy apartment house after another interrupted by a few town houses and churches and a school and the sprawling Museum of Natural History. Chicky hasn't stepped foot in there since fifth grade, but he still has clear memories of the lunchroom, the whale, the brontosaurus, those dioramas. On any weekday it seemed like half the fourth-graders in New York were at the Natural History. Kids from the suburbs too. You could always tell who they were.

That whale had scared the shit out of Chicky. It was just too big.

Now Chicky's idea of a cultural expedition is getting to Citi Field early enough to watch batting practice.

Up near Harlem a few blocks are zoned for business, but that's miles away. Down here there's nothing. No bars or pizza parlors or liquor stores or twenty-four-hour delis. None of the busy business you find along other subway lines. Central Park West is unsullied by neon lights or idling taxis or packs of shrieking screenagers.

It's a peaceful street. Which means there's not much deterrence to mischief, to crime. Especially as midnight approaches, and traffic thins to almost but not quite nothing, just a few people straggling or staggering home, doormen pulling doors tight for the night, depositing the last guests into backseats to speed up or down the avenue, or across to Fifth

Avenue's mirror image of exactly the same sort of fanciness on the far side of the park: the dangerous sort.

Chicky is a big guy. In his youth he lived in a world that rewarded being intimidating. So for a few years he tried to make himself bigger. He lifted weights and drank protein shakes and wore big shit-kicking boots. If someone had been asked to describe twenty-one-year-old Chicky in one word that word would have been: big.

When he started working at the Bohemia, Chicky realized that intimidating was not always a good thing. Not usually. He started to make himself smaller. He refocused his workouts on reps and endurance. He started running and cycling instead of lifting. He tilted his head forward and down, rolled his shoulders forward too. He spoke softer. He smiled more. In fact he smiled almost nonstop.

Now that one word would be: nice.

Chicky is still a big guy. But only when he needs to be.

The Bohemia is ringed by a dry moat that's ten feet below street level. This moat is protected by a waist-high stone wall that's topped with a wrought-iron fence crowned with gold-painted spikes. The whole building looks like a Middle Ages castle, but with twenty-first-century floodlights and security cameras, plus doormen twenty-four seven. Everything about the Bohemia warns that if you're looking to do some crime, this is a place that's going to be very hard to penetrate, plus you're going to be videotaped in bright light, you're going to get caught, you're going to get convicted, and you're going to go to prison. So take your bullshit somewhere else.

This time of night is when the rats come out in full force, swishing their tails through the cracks between the cobblestones in the dappled light of streetlamps through tree branches. Chicky can see a big one right now, and he suppresses a shudder. Everyone is creeped out by rats, but just because something sucks for everyone doesn't mean it doesn't suck for you.

Last year Mrs. Frumm saw a rat climb *out of her toilet* and scamper down the hall, leaving a trail of water to her stove. This is the worst thing Chicky has ever heard, a nightmare that will haunt him until his dying breath. And Chicky was in an actual *war*. He saw guys *die*.

Mrs. Frumm claimed that the rat was as big as Antoinette the bichon frise. Now Mrs. Frumm keeps the lids closed on her toilets, always. Everyone should. But management chose not to publicize this incident. They didn't want everyone to be constantly worried about rats climbing out of the toilets.

"Does that happen a lot?" Chicky had asked Olek.

The super shrugged. "Who knows?"

This was not the answer Chicky had hoped for.

Olek's cabinets contain plenty of traps and poisons for rats and mice and cockroaches. People who live in apartment houses like the Bohemia want to imagine that their wealth insulates them from these problems. But the whole city is connected underground, and vermin don't recognize the distinctions of street addresses or socioeconomic classes. There are just as many rats here on Central Park West as in those projects a few blocks away. Maybe even more. But at the Bohemia every effort is made to exterminate them, to solve problems instead of pretending they don't exist. To try to make the world more perfect, or to look that way.

But that doesn't mean the rats aren't here.

Bzzz.

Chicky glances into the lobby before he grabs his phone. Canarius as usual has his head buried in a textbook. This spring Canarius will finish his MBA after six years of part-time schooling. Then these doorman years will become a character-building tale of grit and sacrifice and determination that he'll tell in boardrooms and banker bars. He'll probably move into a full-service building himself where the staff will call him sir, and Mr. Taylor. Chicky hopes that Canarius won't turn out to be a guy who uses his origin story as an excuse to be an asshole. But you never know. Evolution isn't always the same as improvement.

Chicky will be the one who organizes Canarius's send-off. This is one of Chicky's roles here, like a team captain. He's the one who passes the hat for the ailing or the grieving, for wedding presents and bottles of booze.

He organizes every event. Sometimes it's just shift-straddling donuts in the break room. Sometimes it's a rowdy affair off-site. His cousin Junior waives the buy-out deposit for the private room as long as Chicky guarantees a minimum. Junior is generous but only to the point where it might cost him something.

Bzzz.

The rules of the job prohibit talking on your phone, and Chicky is not a rule-breaker. But he is and will always be a parent, and now a single one. Though his girls are mostly grown and flown, still he worries. Still his heart skips when the phone rings late at night. Maybe a hospital or police or some boyfriend calling with terrible news, a tragic accident. Chicky's imagination can run pretty fucking wild in the skipping heartbeat it takes to answer a phone.

It's not just talking on the phone that's prohibited. You're also not allowed to listen to music or play games or watch videos. Anything with a screen or headphones.

Chicky hits decline, again.

It's also forbidden to sit. And, of course, to carry a weapon. A rule that Chicky had obeyed for all of his twenty-eight years at the Bohemia.

Until tonight.

From somewhere on the East Side—or maybe down on Fifty-seventh, hard to tell—Chicky hears a *pop-pop* like gunshots. Then all the noises fall away again and Chicky's surroundings slip into one of those narrow windows where for a second or two it doesn't sound like a city at all. It doesn't sound like anything. Just Chicky's breath and the beating of his heart. *Bump-bump. Bump-bump. Bump-bump.*

A barking dog breaks the spell.

Chicky hears an engine accelerating. Shifting into a higher gear. The sound seems to be coming from uptown but he can't see it.

He glances downtown and sees a couple of men walking up the block. They're both wearing all black including face masks. In the depths of the pandemic those masks would have meant one thing. Now they mean something completely different. The opposite.

Chicky turns back uptown where suddenly another pair of men has appeared. These two are also in black with masks. This cannot be a coincidence.

Then squealing tires and a giant black SUV tearing around the corner and fishtailing onto Central Park West—

"Fuck."

Chicky almost reaches for his gun but realizes it's already too late. Drawing will only get him shot. Whatever's going down, he's not going to prevail in a shoot-out. Not against four men. At least four. All these black-clad guys have now put on reflective glasses to cover the parts of their faces that weren't already hidden by the masks. Chicky sees that all these guys are holding things in their right hands.

The truck is pulling to a stop.

They're all holding guns.

Part One

THIS MORNING

CHAPTER 1

APARTMENT 11C-D

Emily Longworth had not knowingly married a villain, of course. And yet.

"Children!"

She called out loudly enough that the kids could hear, but not loudly enough to be a yell. Emily Grace Merriweather Longworth did not yell at her children. She did not yell, period. She did not swear, she did not chew gum, she did not wear athleisure in public, she did not drink anything through a straw except a milkshake, and drinking a milkshake was almost entirely theoretical. She had one sip per year, maybe two.

"Time to go!"

Emily did not lose control of her emotions. Or if she did, she did not let it show, and though that may not be the same exact thing, it's awfully close.

She stood in the entry gallery with arms crossed, trying to project both patience and impatience toward the bedroom wing. If Whit happened to glance this way, Emily wanted him to see a wife who was not eager to talk. If her children looked, Emily wanted them to see a loving mom whose patience was wearing thin. It was, like everything, a delicate balance.

Whit had awoken in a horrible mood, which was understandable. But Emily didn't want his snit to be directed at her, and she didn't want to argue about it. She was, as a matter of deliberate policy, nonconfrontational. So at this moment what she wanted was to avoid her husband entirely. And not just at this moment.

In hindsight, there'd been signs. The borderline-insane lawsuit against the super-tall tower's developer, which Whit had passed off as mostly a joke. Also his evasiveness about his business, which Emily chose to dismiss as run-of-the-mill sexist condescension. And his compunction to place his hands around her neck during sex; that one, she's not quite sure how she justified.

Now Emily understood that she'd turned a blind eye. Because through her other eye she saw Whit's chiseled jaw, his Stanford law, and above all his nearly incomprehensible wealth. She'd seen what she'd wanted to see. She had no one to blame except herself.

She made a micro-adjustment to the alignment of the Hopper. Choosing art for this spot had been a challenge. This would be the first thing guests saw, and it ought to be identifiable to anyone who knew anything, but not hackneyed. Emily had a well-earned reputation as an expert, if no longer a professional, so she wanted something at least a little unconventional. Not edgy—she cringed when people like her pretended to be edgy—but something less expected than an Old Master or an Impressionist, of which there were plenty hanging around this town. Around this building.

The Hirst was so obvious it was practically a shrug. Also the Richter, the Kelly, things you recognize from postcards.

Emily heard rustling that sounded a lot like a backpack being pulled on. She patted her blazer, looking for the reassuring heft, finding it.

The Kiefer would have been perfect, if only it weren't so macabre. No one wants to confront that mood immediately, it would put a damper on the whole evening.

When the renovations were finally on the cusp of being finished, Emily had stood in this white box of an entry gallery, scrolling through images of her collection—no, and no, and no.

Then she'd placed a call.

"You're not going to believe this," she'd said. "I've been standing here, staring at the wall, for a half hour, and I finally realized: I have nothing for the entry. *Nothing!*"

He'd laughed that laugh of his, which often seemed to be a tiny bit at your expense, but not in a mean way. It was like a lover's tease. Did he laugh this way with all women? Emily hoped not, but suspected so. He was a man who loved women, though she didn't know if that meant he was a ladies' man.

"Oh dear," he'd said. "I'll come, right away."

That was how it began.

After college Emily moved out of her parents' suburban center-hall colonial to a studio in Yorkville, a tiny apartment that she shared with mice and roaches and a nonadjustable radiator and unreliable hot water. She got her MFA at the Institute, taking the crosstown bus to class, to the museum, to everything.

The moment felt a few generations too late. Emily had missed out on the New York of the fifties and sixties, the Abstract Expressionists, the Ninth Street women, the drunken fistfights at the Cedar Tavern. She'd missed out too on the grittier seventies, and the dramatically dangerous eighties—crack, AIDS, rampant murder. Some of those artists were still relevant, but they were now sober and richer, or they were dead. Young artists were no longer living in illegal lofts and cold-water flats in SoHo and Alphabet City, because there was no such thing anymore. That scene had moved to Berlin, Los Angeles, São Paolo, Detroit. People no longer flocked to New York to make art.

But they did come here to buy it. With her newly minted MFA Emily secured a gallery internship, then became an artist's assistant, then gallery girl. While her college cohorts were spending credit-card debt or discretionary income or trust funds on red-soled shoes and strawberry-mint mojitos, Emily was in the back row at Doyle's, she was at estate sales, she was sipping complimentary Thursday-night pinot grigio on West Twenty-second.

She made one mistake with an older artist, boastful and indiscreet. Emily called it a fling but he apparently used the phrase *one-night stand.* After that she became exceedingly careful. New York was a big place, yes, but every community within was small, and she needed to guard her reputation. Very few men made it into that studio, fewer still into her pants.

Emily's mother had always nudged her in the direction of rich boys, then rich men, and raised her daughter with all the prerequisites to become a rich woman—she could ski, she could sail, she could speak French. But this had pushed Emily the other way. She had an irrepressible desire to be independent, and refused any help from her parents, even when a hundred dollars would have gone a long way.

Emily had been plenty familiar with normal rich, like her parents' version—law-firm-partner rich, country-club rich, four-vacations-per-year rich. No real worries about day-to-day money, about housing, about food, about clothes or cars or healthcare or education or retirement. The off-the-rack version of responsible, hardworking rich, of maximizing employer contributions, of life insurance held in trusts, the lifelong everyday endeavor of generating and maintaining wealth. That just didn't look worth the hassle, the hustle. For what? Nice hotel rooms in Anguilla?

She'd been given a massive head start. She could make it the rest of the way on her own, and she would. She sat there at night, watching reruns of Mary Tyler Moore, the theme song like a daily incantation, a mantra.

But as her twenties came to a close, Emily began to grow tired of the broke artists and pretentious curators and venal gallerists, of the unabashed strivers and hopeless losers, the premature ejaculators and incompetent cunnilinguists, all those pathetic young hipsters and more pathetic older ones, the suffocating neediness of men whose self-esteem was measured in the price tags of their latest canvases. Little by little, she became willing to try other types of men, those who might be completely unfamiliar with Bushwick, who'd never worn any type of facial hair nor tattoos nor piercings. Maybe men with law degrees or—god help her—MBAs, maybe even both.

Men with money.

It was becoming hard to trust her memory of their courtship, how relentlessly Whit had pursued her. She'd been flattered, intrigued. She'd let him kiss her on their second date, and on their third she'd accepted his invitation for a nightcap, even though she wasn't much of a drinker.

Before they left the restaurant, Whit excused himself to the restroom. Years later, Emily became convinced that he'd deliberately left the table while the check presenter was about to arrive, knowing she'd peek. Back then such deviousness wouldn't have occurred to her.

Just a few weeks earlier, Emily had burst into tears after realizing she'd purchased an unnecessary red onion, wasting ninety cents. That redundant onion was rolling across her kitchen linoleum, which was separated by a postage-stamp countertop from her living room, which was separated from her bedroom by nothing except imagination. Emily's oven was used exclusively for shoe storage; she'd removed the racks to accommodate boots. The apartment had no room for a Christmas tree, but every December she bought a wreath from the guy on First Avenue, lugged it home, and strung it with drugstore lights. The optimism!

It ran out. She'd been living in those four hundred square feet for eight years. Her thirtieth birthday had come and gone, and she was still price-sensitive on the question of a second onion. This precariousness was beginning to look permanent.

Was she, really, going to make it after all?

It wasn't that the ninety cents mattered so much. It was that it mattered at all.

So there was something hugely appealing about Whit Longworth's lifestyle. Something that, despite herself, was even arousing, which made her feel a little dirty.

As they walked out of that restaurant, Emily still wasn't completely sold on the idea of Whit, and she definitely wasn't going to spend the night, but at his well-appointed apartment she mustered the enthusiasm to go down on him, which turned out to be a briefer endeavor than expected. Another red flag.

"Oh god," he panted. "Can I come in your mouth?"

Although she didn't care for it, she didn't want to be the type who doesn't swallow.

"Of course," she said, taking a beat, a breath. "I'm no philistine," then finished him off with a flourish she didn't know was in her, like a soloist who reaches deep to hit the high C, bringing down the house.

"Christ." Whit's head was lolled back. Waves of bravas were washing across the concert hall.

She took a sip of Dom to wash out her mouth, discreetly. It was the '96 rosé, a nice wine. Emily's art consultancy was not a steady business, but she consorted with a crowd of wealthy people who were always buying Champagne.

The dinner bill had been a thousand dollars. The check came with a little gift bag, chocolates and cookies, puff pastries for tomorrow's breakfast, everything tied with a satin ribbon.

"That was the best blow job of my life."

Emily doubted Whit's honesty, and although she appreciated the thoughtfulness of bothering to lie, she was also a little affronted by the idea of a ranking of blow jobs. A spreadsheet.

"Gee," she said, "thanks."

Emily can still remember wondering, in that moment: was Whit's the last cock she'd ever suck? Suddenly she believed it was, and hoped she was right.

She was wrong.

CHAPTER 2

APARTMENT 11C-D

Whitaker Hamilton Longworth was a man whose features were in all the right proportions, he had straight white teeth and meticulous haircuts, well-tended skin and a well-tailored wardrobe. Anything that money could buy, he'd bought. Whit was, at first glance, handsome. But what was missing was a spark, and for their first months together Emily struggled to remember his eye color. It might have been harder for her to pick his face out of a lineup than his prick. It leaned right, as did his politics, though neither inclination was obvious unless you knew him intimately. Emily made sure he was pro-choice, but that was just the bare minimum. Otherwise they didn't really get into it.

He was intelligent, ambitious, responsible. He was often funny, and usually charming. He seemed kind, sort of, maybe. He was interested in art, or at least interested in being seen to be interested in art, which was close enough.

But the main thing that defined Whit was his wealth. He didn't think twice about the cost of first class, because he owned a plane. This had never occurred to Emily as a lifestyle option, not for people who went to the same parties as you, who flirted with you, who asked you out to dinner. An option for people like you.

It didn't take long for Emily to become accustomed to the fine dining, the chauffeured cars, the luxurious apartment, the extravagant travel. The plane!

Emily hadn't expected Whit to propose, certainly not so soon, but there he was, on one knee, proffering a diamond of outlandish proportions, hard to resist. Impossible, apparently. Because being immensely wealthy would make her happy, wouldn't it? It would make anyone happy, that's the promise of America, the premise.

Okay, she reasoned with herself: so you suspect he might be a bit of a jerk. Maybe more than a bit. But you can have *anything*. Not just any pair of shoes, any baubles. You can travel anywhere, live anywhere, buy anything, do anything. You can have children who themselves will never want for anything. You can give away fortunes to charities of your choosing, you can help innumerable people, exert influence in whatever sphere you want.

Isn't all that worth it? Everyone makes compromises.

What would you do?

Don't kid yourself.

Emily turned toward the front parlor's windows, the park ablaze in autumn foliage under a brilliant blue sky reflected in the sparkling mirror of the lake. A million-dollar view. Or more accurately thirty-two million, plus another seven in renovations, but who was counting? She'd have thought Whit would be counting. She'd have been wrong.

"Hud!" she called out. "Bitsy!"

Front parlor. Such a resonant pair of words, suggesting so much, but without needing to say so, or to offer a tour. Emily was more than happy to give house tours, but she would never be the one to suggest it, especially these days. There's so much that has become out of the question.

They've lived at the Bohemia only a couple of years. Their previous apartment had been on a street that some people call Billionaires' Row, both derisively and triumphantly. That apartment had been a thousand feet in the sky, and its view was, obviously, more jaw-dropping. This eleventh floor was a fraction as high. But the super-tall had made Emily nauseated—the altitude, the floor-to-ceiling windows, the clouds scuttling beneath the ninety-third floor, it could be like standing in a glass airplane. And the swaying! Even when the building wasn't actually swaying, it could seem like it was. Plus Emily had been pregnant for a good portion of the time they'd lived there, which contributed to the nausea. Also, she was not unfamiliar with Sartre.

The prospectus had promised unlimited views, but in real life those views were regularly limited by the clouds up there. And the ninety-third floor, it turned out, was an arbitrary number. The building's residential floors began at thirty-two, and the space from sidewalk to what was called the thirty-second floor was definitely not equivalent to thirty-two levels.

This disparity was part of Whit's lawsuit, albeit an oxymoronic one. The defense countered: So was the apartment too high? Or not high enough?

Both, was Whit's allegation.

"I hate living here," Emily had finally admitted. She didn't like being surrounded exclusively by immensely rich businessmen and their trophy wives. She didn't want to be seen as one of them. She didn't want to be one of them.

Emily had long coveted the Bohemia, seeing the celebrities on TV, the entertainment magazines, the mystique of the place, artists and musicians and actors, and not the poor downtown versions with their drug problems and their rent parties, but the successful uptown types with retrospectives at the Whitney, platinum records, Tony awards. She'd been alerted to 11C-D by a wily real-estate agent before the unit was on the market, an estate sale that would need a full-scale gut renovation, an expensive and complicated proposition that most buyers didn't have the stomach for. Emily did.

"The *West Side*?" Whit had asked. "Really?"

"It's not a tenement on Amsterdam. It's one of the most famous buildings in the world."

Maybe the wedding hadn't made the money hers, but bearing the children had. She'd won that battle. At the time she hadn't realized she'd been in one. Not until Whit exacted his revenge.

Emily especially loved the view this time of year. She loved the low angle of the sunlight, she loved the chilly nights, red wine in front of a roaring fire, blazer weather, scarves. Autumn was like mainlining nostalgia, just the feel of a crisp morning transported her back to school, reading Dickinson and Austen on quads blanketed in red and gold maple leaves, French seminars debating Proust, rushing home from the dining hall in the season's first flurries, staid chaperoned teas and unsupervised parties that raged late into the night, waking on a Sunday suffused with the satisfaction of knowing you were doing exactly the right thing, in exactly the right place, with exactly the right people.

Autumn weather was Emily's petite madeleine.

The season had always felt like the beginning of something, not the end; it felt to Emily like hope. Every autumn was a season when her life could get better.

"My lawyer insists," Whit had announced, as if he had no say in the matter. This was just a couple of weeks after she'd started wearing that garish engagement ring.

"Oh." Emily was leafing through the sheaf of charts, tables, it was like an amortization schedule. She didn't know what she was looking for. Nothing. She was just buying time. "I see."

Whit rested a hand on her shoulder. "This isn't a surprise, is it?"

It was, though it shouldn't have been. Emily continued to not look up at the man she'd begun referring to as her fiancé.

"For anyone in my, um, situation . . ."

She could tell that Whit wanted her to interrupt with "Sure I understand" or "Of course"; to let him off the hook. But she wanted him to feel bad about it.

"You know how much I love you, Emmie." This was back when he used to call her by that nickname. Now he barely called her anything at all. "It's just that no one like me would ever dream of getting married without a prenup."

"Well, *obviously*," Emily's mother said later, then called a friend who provided a referral to an oily outer-borough attorney who always made Emily feel as if she needed a shower. She dug in her heels on only one issue.

"Morals clause?" The attorney had smirked.

"If he behaves in a way that makes it impossible for me to stay mar—"

"You mean, infidelity?"

"No, I—"

"Kinky bedroom stuff?"

"If you'd let me finish."

The smirk grew. "Sure."

Emily had given this a lot of thought: what was the thing she most wanted to avoid?

"If he engages in behavior that humiliates me in public."

"Humiliates you? That's sorta hard to quantify, isn't it? Or to prove."

Emily's lawyer and Whit's conducted a brief negotiation that came to a rapid conclusion: a half-million dollars per year for herself, plus all childcare expenses—tuition and tutors, vacations and wardrobes, whatevers—up to two hundred thousand dollars per year per kid.

"I'm sorry," the lawyer had said, after supposedly looking into it, "there's no enforceable morals clause we can include. Humiliation is not a provable fact."

At the time, the financial arrangement seemed so generous. Now, though, Emily saw that it was impossible. There was absolutely no way that she and her children could live on nine hundred thousand dollars per year.

CHAPTER 3

APARTMENT 11C-D

"Kids!" A little louder. Emily was running out of patience. "Now!"

Tatiana the housekeeper was in the living room, dusting unobtrusively, giving Mrs. the space to be a mother. It would be Yolanda the nanny who'd collect the children from school, but in the mornings it was Emily who brought them, even in the most foul weather, in the darkest depths of winter. There were plenty of valid reasons for not picking up kids, moms were well within their rights to be doing other things at three P.M., even those who didn't work paying jobs, which was most of the mothers at this school. Emily herself was often otherwise engaged, sometimes doing things that were undeniably selfish. But the only reason for someone like Emily to not show up for drop-off was laziness. You don't get to be Mrs. Whitaker Longworth by being lazy.

"Thirty seconds!"

It was an absolute requirement for Emily to entertain on a regular basis, to throw parties, to volunteer all over town, and in particular for the school's parents' association—to fundraise, to hold positions of real responsibility, meaningful commitments. This was not a hardship for her. Emily had always been a joiner, model congress and yearbook, sorority and ski club, eager to take responsibility—class parent, social chair, committee head, yes, absolutely, love to.

"Twenty!"

Some of Emily's volunteer work was admittedly the high-end sort—arts fundraising, library support, club committees, meetings that were social occasions as much as anything, hobnobbing with other board housewives. But she also made it a point to help in soup kitchens and food pantries, cleaning up the park, good works when no one was looking. No one she knew.

She even picked up garbage along the side of the highway a few times, like in a chain gang. Wearing one of those fluorescent vests.

Some of this work thrust her into deep dejection, especially at New Hope.

"Then quit." This was what Whit had counseled the only time she'd been completely honest after a horrid day, when a young mother had been dragged out kicking and screaming—literally—while her small children looked on, a trauma for all of them, including Emily. "Nobody's forcing you to spoon out slop to illegal immigrants."

"They're undocumented, not illegal." But this wasn't even her third most important objection. "And I don't want to quit, Whit. In fact it's days like today that remind me why I need to do this. I'm just telling you that it can sometimes be difficult."

Whit snorted, whose meaning Emily understood clearly: no, sweetheart, difficult is running a multibillion-dollar multinational, not volunteering your unskilled labor for eight hours per week.

"I get that," Whit said, though Emily knew he didn't, and he probably knew it too. "But if you're going to complain—"

"I'm not complaining," she interrupted, gently. "This is not me complaining. This is me sharing why I'm not always in a terrific mood on New Hope days. That's all."

This was back when she'd still expected compassion from her husband. Back when he occasionally gave it, or at least did a passable job of pretending.

Emily had accepted that marriage would include known unknowns, plus unknown unknowns, in the immortal words of the immoral Donald Rumsfeld. And one of those unknown unknowns has turned out to be that there'd come a point when Emily was pretty sure that her husband hated her, and absolutely positive that she hated him.

Whit had even come close to hitting her, she'd seen the rage in his eyes. That would have made things straightforward: she'd have taken photos, called the police, gone to the emergency room, gotten in touch with that lawyer who'd handled the prenup, which she'd signed back when she was so young, so naïve.

A decade on, she was neither, just another middle-aged woman who couldn't sleep, and had the eye twitch to prove it. Over the years Emily had tried many different sleep aids. All of them, really, except narcotics. NyQuil, melatonin, THC, Ativan, Lunesta, et cetera. Each worked, incrementally, briefly, until it didn't. Her problems could not be solved by pharmaceuticals.

She examined herself in the massive gilt mirror, one of the many things she'd purchased during a very satisfying spree at the Paris flea market. The eye twitch was barely visible, and only if you were looking for it.

"Children? *Now.*"

This entry gallery, with Emily posed right here in front of this Hopper, had been the opening photograph in the magazine feature. She'd hoped that the story would be a celebration of her diverse and eclectic collection, which she'd assembled not simply by throwing around money at auctions, but as a purposeful mix of classic and modern and contemporary pieces in conversation with one another, a sophisticated curation, cleverly arranged.

That wasn't the magazine's agenda, and Emily had allowed the shoot to get away from her, she hadn't mustered the courage to say no to the photographer, to the journalist, sorry, I'm not comfortable with this. She'd even agreed to a wardrobe suggestion, something that would go better with the Pollock.

In the end, the images focused on the blockbusters, on the apartment's decor, on Emily's figure. The dress with the Pollock was very flattering.

Emily hated the article, but Whit loved it. Whit didn't have any genuine taste of his own, so what he craved was external validation, he wanted to be the owner of iconic, instantly recognizable art, the sorts of pieces that were reproduced on posters and T-shirts and coffee mugs. This was what Whit wanted out of everything—his home, his car, his clothes, his wife. When the real-estate agent asked if Whit minded if the details of their Bohemia purchase "leaked"—she actually used air quotes—he'd laughed. "Of course not," he said.

Whit's philanthropy was never, ever anonymous.

The magazine feature did turn out to be a coronation, just not the sort that Emily wanted. "You look gorgeous," school moms told her. "The apartment," others said, "is amazing." People asked about the dress, and the other dress, they asked about the drapes. Emily tried to be grateful for these compliments. But she did not want to be known as well-dressed, she did not want to be known as a rich woman who'd hired a competent interior designer to hang nice wallpaper. She did not want to be seen as frivolous. She wanted to be seen as a serious person, because that's what she believed she was.

"Have you seen this month's issue?" For a while this was something Whit asked everyone, strewing copies everywhere—office, apartment, beach house, that summer's yacht. Sometimes this made Emily deeply uncomfortable; sometimes it made her afraid. Whit did business with some unsavory characters, with whom it seemed unwise to highlight his wealth. Especially the reprehensible Justin Pugh, who'd come from up-island with his unconscionable wife.

"Cool." Justin was not remotely interested in art, but he was very interested in money.

The magazine's twelve-page spread could almost serve as a guide for someone who wanted to rob the Longworths' apartment. You could see which paintings were too huge, which you could tuck under your arm and carry out the door, which had cost what.

"That's a couple hundred million worth of art," Whit pointed out.

The corrosive thing about New York is that there's always someone with more—more money, more fame, more power, more respect. It's hard to ever feel as if you've truly made it, hard to stop striving, hard to not show off.

"No shit?" Pugh kept his lips pressed together and pushed out in defiance, imitating the *Sopranos* imitating the *Godfather* imitating some Little Italy guys from the 1960s.

"Ooh, lemme see," Kayleigh Pugh said as she polished off another Aperol spritz. This was years after that summer when everyone was drinking spritzes. Kayleigh was the type of woman who chose her trendiness from reality television, at least a year or two out of date.

"Some of our neighbors have substantial collections too," Whit continued. "The building is littered with Picassos, Chagalls, Renoirs. It's practically a museum."

"Whit, please." Emily felt like she was going to throw up. "Justin and Kayleigh don't want to hear about any of this." She stood. The crew-to-guest ratio was two-to-one, but Emily always made at least a token effort. "Who's ready for dessert?"

Pugh's conversation had followed a predictable path: personal responsibility, welfare state, national debt, tax burdens, governmental overreach. Conservative talking points, half the country felt that way. Even if Emily wasn't one of them, she accepted that these were largely matters of opinion.

Then: wokeness, pronouns, liberal media. Sure, Emily heard these complaints from plenty of people who were not unreasonable. Even she had to admit that the media she consumed was tending toward advocacy. But so was the media she didn't consume. Everything had become partisan.

Then Pugh continued: stolen elections, fake news, witch hunts.

Then: suspending civil rights, arresting political enemies, canceling elections.

Then: seizing state houses.

"They're trying to away take our country," he asserted, with the borderline-comical seriousness of an inebriated and not especially intelligent man. He was drinking yet another glass of the Pappy twenty-year-old. He probably had no idea. "We cannot let that happen."

"Well," Emily said, smiling, rising again to put an end to another unpalatable topic. "I'm afraid I'm turning into a pumpkin! But please don't let my exhaustion end your evening."

That summer's boat resembled a James Bond villain's, docked at a prominent slip in the middle of Sag's harbor, where everybody on the South Fork would notice it, which was Whit's goal. "That's Longworth's boat," he hoped people would say. "Wow," he hoped others would answer.

"Whit." Emily looked at her husband in the mirror as she brushed her hair. "I know that you're a loyal person. And I know that Justin was hugely supportive, way back when."

Justin Pugh's military contracting business had been one of Whit's earliest customers, and Pugh's contacts had been invaluable in generating international business for Liberty Logistics. But over the past few years Delta Canopy had begun to engage in activities that looked illegal, and a lot like treason, or at least treason-adjacent, and Whit had finally agreed to put some distance between the two companies, and the two men. Which was why Pugh had dragged his unconscionable wife out from the South Shore, hoping that the couples might bond over sunset lobster in Gardiners Bay, and rekindle the romance. Emily had been a little afraid that he'd propose wife-swapping.

From three staterooms away Emily could hear that woman moaning and screaming. Kayleigh Pugh learned what to drink from Bravo, and how to have sex from pornography. Her breasts were not even remotely credible.

"I freely admit that I don't know anything about business." Emily turned around to face her husband. "But I'm not completely unfamiliar with the way the world works. And you simply cannot continue to do business with that awful human being. You see that, don't you?"

From the tone of Whit's groan Emily could tell he knew she was right. At that point she still didn't know about the full roster of Whit's clients—the warlords, the fundamentalists. She didn't know what deplorable company Delta Canopy kept. She thought Pugh was the problematic one.

"Even if you could somehow discount his revolting politics—which: *can* you, Whit?—the way he's parading himself around is a PR fiasco just waiting to happen. In fact, not even waiting. He's actively courting it, as if it's a business strategy. That cap? My lord."

"What cap?"

"The one he was wearing when they arrived. You don't know what that means? 6MWE?"

Whit returned a blank look.

"Six million wasn't enough."

Whit closed his eyes as if in physical pain. There's a lightbulb moment when you realize you're dealing with a psychopath, and many questions have a newly obvious answer.

"That's the sort of lunatic, Whit."

Emily knew what it meant to get into bed with someone, literally and figuratively. She knew the sorts of things you can tell yourself, the deals you can make. Oh he's not so bad, there are plenty worse. I'm just doing what it takes to survive, to get by, I'm just doing my job, just following orders, trying to get ahead, to earn a living, to provide for my family.

It's up to everyone to draw a line, and hold it. If you keep pushing that line further, and further, eventually you're storming the Capitol, you're opening fire on protesters, you're shoving people into gas chambers. Or you're admiring those who did. Or you're selling them body armor.

Or you're getting into bed with the person who's selling them body armor.

Is evil transitive? That was one of the questions that kept Emily awake at night.

A few weeks after that dreadful evening, Whit found the fortitude to publicly cut ties with Justin Pugh and Delta Canopy. It was done the way everything is done these days, on social media.

The threats started immediately.

The thing about getting into bed with a lunatic is it can be impossible to kick him out, and very difficult to leave. Sometimes the only thing you can do is set the bed on fire.

CHAPTER 4

APARTMENT 2A

Julian Sonnenberg stepped out to the warm glow of the morning sunshine streaming through the leaves of the trees in the park. This was when Central Park West was at its very best. A sunny autumn morning could still, occasionally, trick Julian into being hopeful.

As soon as he entered the park, Julian unclipped his old dog's leash. Gilgamesh no longer ran, but the little guy still loved to root around in the undergrowth, to sniff at the bases of benches, lampposts, garbage cans, anything that another dog might have peed upon. But if Gillie got too far ahead of Julian, he'd stop, turn back, and wag his tail, waiting for his dad, or mom, or sister, or brother. He loved his family so much.

Man and dog walked down the hill, away from the Imagine mosaic in the middle of Strawberry Fields, where a busker was strumming. There were always buskers at the John Lennon memorial. There was always an audience.

"You're such a good boy, Gillie." Julian knelt to pat the dog, and his chest filled up. "So good." He planted a kiss on Gillie's snout, and was rewarded with a big lick on the chin. "Thank you, Gillie. I appreciate that."

Julian stood, and saw a familiar woman walking toward him with a long-haired dachshund.

"I saw that," she said, with a smile. "That was sweet."

"Thanks." Julian couldn't place her. She wore the leggings and running shoes and sweatshirt of the morning dog-walker, and a smile that suggested more than mere politeness.

"Who's that?" she asked.

"Gillie. Short for Gilgamesh."

"Gilgamesh the Brave?"

Gilgamesh was the possibly fictional king of Mesopotamia who may have lived somewhere between three and four thousand years before Christ. This king had been defined by his bravery; this dog was the meekest creature imaginable. The name was in the same spirit as Tiny for a basketball center. You saw some dogs losing their minds at the sight of a squirrel, and you could clearly understand the evolutionary link to wolves. With dogs like Gillie, it was much harder.

"Wow," Julian said, "that's right. How'd you know?"

She shrugged and pulled a faux-modest face, then laughed at herself, and he did too.

"You don't remember me, do you?" she asked.

The dogs, too, were sniffing each other.

"I'm sorry," Julian said, and then his phone was ringing: an unfamiliar number. He was pretty sure who this was. "I'm so sorry, I have to get this."

She gave him another smile, this one tinged with regret. "See you around."

"Yeah," then, "Hello?" He watched her walk away. Who the hell was she?

"Mr. Sonnenberg? Hi, it's Dr. Ramirez. Sorry for not getting back to you yesterday."

Julian was trying to read the tone of this throat-clearing. He didn't like that the doctor was apologizing. He didn't like that this call was happening before business hours.

"So I've looked over your scans. I'm afraid they're not what we were hoping for."

Anguish struck like a violent blow. Julian couldn't move.

"I suggest we have the surgery sooner rather than later."

Gilgamesh was now staring up at his dad, tail down.

"Is next week possible?"

Next week?

"Mr. Sonnenberg?"

Julian tried to speak, but there was nothing there. He cleared his throat. "Yes?"

"This is not a death sentence."

It sure as hell felt that way.

Julian stood there in the park, phone in hand, stunned, strangers streaming by him. He took a deep breath, but that didn't help, in fact it made it worse, and he said, "Come on, Gillie," and stepped off the path, and hid behind a tree, so no one would see him cry.

The busker was still singing the same song.

Julian felt like he'd grown up in Central Park. His earliest vague memories were of playgroup on the Great Lawn, and class trips to the zoo, to the Met. Then firmer recollections of Little League in the North Meadow, rambling in the Ramble to get high-school high, summer picnics in the Sheep Meadow with the Sunday *Times*, bagels from H&H, lox from Zabar's, wine coolers, Camel Lights.

And his kids too, every year of their lives, every season. The same zoo but now smaller and cuter, the carousel, the castle, preschooler birthday parties in the marionette theater. Feeding the ducks in the lake, and spring expeditions to look for ducklings. The little-kid playgrounds of sandpits and slides, graduating to the Diana Ross Playground, and finally to the Adventure down past the Heckscher fields, then Asher's baseball, Oona's softball, skating at Wollman Rink, pulling laces tight on rented skates with a borrowed key, the musty smell of those old insoles, cold noses, hot chocolate.

Yesterday.

Julian took another deep breath, trying to fight back his despair. He couldn't hide behind a tree all day, feeling sorry for himself. But maybe just another minute.

A few tourists were gathered in front of the Bohemia, phones aloft. One of them turned her lens toward Julian, then squinted, trying to figure out if he was worth it.

For the first century of its existence, the Bohemia had been inhabited by the famous much more than the rich, by stage actors and opera singers, celebrated artists and prize-winning academics, European nobility and old-moneyed public servants and, for a few years, Joe DiMaggio. As with everything else in New York, the cultural class was being replaced with financiers, with guys—almost always guys—who worked in hedge funds and private equity, investment banks and venture capital, tech. Every recent apartment sale was from the old sort of family to the new, accompanied by increasingly outrageous prices.

Paparazzi used to camp out front, autograph seekers, tourists gazing up at the fabled gables and wrought-iron railings of Juliet balconies, hoping to catch a glimpse of the recluse screen star, the network news anchor. Sometimes they didn't even know why they were looking, whom they hoped to see, just the generalized idea that here dwelt fame. But no one wanted an autograph from a financier. Nor, for that matter, from a gallerist like Julian. Maybe he was kidding himself that there was any real difference. Maybe he was just another capitalist, only far less rich.

Many people in the world would consider Julian Sonnenberg wealthy. He did not. This may not have been the root of every single one of his problems, but it wasn't far off.

Although the Bohemia was nearly rid of famous inhabitants, still the tourists came. The building was a monument as much as a residence, it was featured in guidebooks, tour-bus itineraries, self-guided walking tours, the pedicab guides who were all somehow African men. The New York labor market featured surprising ethnic specializations.

"Morning, Mr. Sonnenberg," Zaire said, staring straight ahead as he held the door. Zaire rarely made eye contact.

"Thanks, Zaire. Good morning."

Julian missed having Chicky on day shifts, especially this time of year, with the baseball pennant races, the football season. Julian didn't care about sports, but he relished how much Chicky cared; the doorman's enthusiasm had always made Julian feel a little more alive himself. He could've used that today, instead of Zaire's aloofness.

This marble-floored lobby had long been a hotbed of dinner-party invitations and extramarital flirtations and rumors of every sort—social, political, financial, cultural, all the gossip that smooths the gears, keeps the city humming. Corporations were founded, business deals finalized, films conceived, marriages begun, and ended. For more than a century the Bohemia had functioned more like a club than a mere collection of apartments, with a full-service kitchen and dining room, dumbwaiters to transport meals up to residences and dirty dishes down, an in-house tailor, a shoeshine. All of that was gone, although some of the old dumbwaiter hardware was still around. Like many of the building's older residents, and their entire way of life, the world they'd known: extinct, but still around.

Maybe like Julian himself.

He turned toward the elevator, and his precarious heart did a somersault when he saw Emily Longworth getting off. She noticed him too, and she smiled—god, that smile—and walked in his direction, with an adorable kid on either side.

"Jules," she said. "Good morning."

He did his best to smile, but it was a poor effort, and Emily noticed. She cocked her head with the question, but she wouldn't ask anything aloud, not with her kids here, not with Gio a few feet away at the desk.

"Good morning," Julian managed. "Hello Hudson. Hello Bitsy."

"Hi Mr. Sonnenberg."

All three of these Longworths looked, as always, perfect. Too perfect. Julian needed to get away from them before he humiliated himself by falling apart.

"Have a great day," he said, and stepped past Emily just in time. The tears were flowing again before he pressed the elevator button. The busker's song was still ringing in his ears.

He stood at the bathroom sink, naked but for a towel around his waist. He placed three fingertips against the inside of his pectoral, as close to his heart as possible, or where he thought his heart was. He knew it wasn't possible to feel the problem in there, but he couldn't help trying, and failing.

Julian let the towel drop, and examined himself. He definitely had less hair where he wanted it, more where he didn't. His hearing was failing in his right ear, possibly his left, hard to say. He was on his third escalation of reading glasses, and probably should get another, but you don't replace the wipers on a car that needs a new engine.

But he was in good shape, strong and lean. Not bad, he thought, especially considering the inevitable qualifier: for his age.

Fifty, of all the bitter pills.

"If I start wearing Skechers," he told his family a few months ago, "please put me out of my misery." Then he blew out the single candle; no one wants to deal with fifty. The cake was, of course, gluten-free.

These bodies are temperamental machines, prone to constant breakdown, requiring outrageous levels of maintenance and repair, the doctors and dentists, the exercise, all the damn food—a constant supply of fuel in one end and waste out the other, every few hours for a lifetime, a full third of which is spent powered down. These machines were designed to operate for twenty or at most thirty years, but modern medicine has extended that to eighty, ninety years, a hundred. Like driving a car two million miles, three, four. What do you expect?

After a certain age, nothing ever gets better, not really. It's just different speeds of getting worse and, ultimately, futile. No one gets out alive.

For most of his life, Julian had felt like a big bright painting hanging over New York City. Maybe not everyone loved it, but they all knew it was there, like Times Square. Then a few years ago he began to feel washed out by time, by exposure to the elements, his vibrant colors bleeding away, the lines softening, blurring, leaving behind a faint outline, like an old ad painted on the side of a building for a business that no longer existed, in an extinct industry—typewriter repair, VHS rentals. Eventually he'd be entirely erased, an old man with saggy jowls and ear hair, telling insufferable stories about the way things used to be, back in his day, when everything was better.

But he'd thought he'd have more time. A lot more.

Despite any friendly flirty women he might run into in Central Park—and, much more so, despite Emily Longworth—Julian felt himself becoming irrelevant. Irrelevant to his wife, who barely noticed him, a relationship that consisted largely of coordinating logistics, as if they were cordial colleagues whose fortunes were tied together on the success or failure of executing clearly demarcated responsibilities on the Sonnenberg account. Irrelevant to his kids, Asher off to college next year, Oona the following, both of them barely giving their dad the time of day. Irrelevant to his business partner, who no longer relied on Julian, and was possibly no longer willing to carry him through another downturn. Irrelevant to the world at large, a man with no real skills or expertise other than a broad social network among people who collected art.

Julian went to cocktail parties for a living. His main qualification for his career was taste, and what could be more subjective? More subject to dismissal? Julian felt as if he was on the verge of cancellation, for no offense other than his irrelevance.

There was just one part of his life that made him feel supremely relevant. Only a few hours per week, but those hours were the sole thing Julian truly looked forward to, maybe in his whole life. Which also made it the biggest problem he'd ever faced.

He rubbed crème into his washed and conditioned hair. He flossed, brushed his teeth, shaved, aftershaved. He massaged lotion onto chapped hands, analgesic gel to his wonky shoulder, anti-inflammatory cream to his tendonitis-afflicted ankle, CBD balm to his osteoarthritic wrist, a recent and deeply discouraging diagnosis, though far from the worst of them, obviously.

He clambered down to stretch his back, with his forehead planted on a High Atlas rug that he'd purchased in the Marrakesh souk a million years ago, back when he did things like go rug-shopping in Morocco.

He took ibuprofen to encompass aches and pains generally, a tablet to manage blood pressure, another for cholesterol, two fish-oil capsules for reasons he didn't remember—someone had suggested it, possibly Chicky, whose advice Julian was game to entertain; they were the same age, and Chicky was in enviable shape. Julian took a multivitamin supposedly formulated for men aged fifty-plus, a fiftieth birthday present from his kids, a half joke whose other half was not at all funny, even in the moment of the gluten-free cake.

He shoehorned into black wingtips, ten years old but resoled and shined, fresh laces too, good as new, or close enough, or that's what he told himself. Julian wore business suits the same way that maître d's do, or hotel managers: to show respect to his clientele. His suits shouldn't be too fine, his ties not showy. He didn't want clients to think he was making too much money, because that would be possible only by exploiting them.

He closed the button of his jacket and examined himself again. No, he thought, not bad at all. Is this really a person who might be dead in a week?

CHAPTER 5

APARTMENT 2A

"Good morning, darling," Julian said.

At the sound of her dad's voice Oona practically jumped out of her skin. "Jesus," she said, "don't sneak up on me like that." She was busy choosing an apple from a bowl. Julian's daughter was gluten-free voluntarily and vegan insufferably. His eighteen-year-old son was a carnivore-carboholic who ate five meals per day with unlimited calories and a maximum volume of red meat. His wife cycled through one punitively restrictive diet after another. Family meals were a minefield.

As Oona turned from the counter, Julian's eyes fell immediately to the rips at the knees of her jeans, which were obscenely tight even in the context of skinny jeans.

"Don't," she said.

"Don't what?"

Oona rolled her eyes.

Julian knew he shouldn't pursue this, but he couldn't stop himself. "I can't understand why you want to dress like that."

"You mean, um, dress like everyone else my age?" She squinted as if confused. Oona's default setting was sarcasm. "You're saying, what, you can't understand why I want to do that?"

"Why do you want to look like you've been slashed? I want to understand, Oons."

Oona chewed, swallowed. "Okay boomer."

"I'm not a boomer!"

She took another bite, without dignifying his objection with a response.

The matter of teenaged fashion was an unwinnable battle, always had been. Like a parenting Afghanistan: the graveyard of empires. Julian should just push past it. "You home for dinner tonight?"

"Nope. Field hockey, musical rehearsal, study group for AP chem." All those activities that could be all-consuming before they ended forever, memories in yearbook photos, a commemorative T-shirt tucked in the back of an inconvenient shelf. Are you better off knowing you're at the end of something? Or would that only ruin the last enjoyment? Julian had recently become obsessed with this question. He was afraid he was at the end of many things. Everything.

"You'll eat dinner?"

"I'll grab a salad." Always with the salads, the juices, as if she were trying to lose weight that didn't exist.

"Well, have a good time." Julian kissed his daughter on the top of her head. "I probably won't see you till tomorrow. I have a thing tonight."

Oona nodded in a way that seemed like a shrug. "Bye, Dad."

She swiped up her backpack, and left through the kitchen door. Oona preferred bounding down the two flights of service stairs to riding the elevator. Julian suspected she didn't want to risk being trapped in the elevator with grown-ups.

One evening last week he'd heard noise coming from that stairwell, which sounded like the exact type of pleading a girl does when she's saying no to a boy who won't stop. Julian opened the door slowly, quietly, not wanting to be caught eavesdropping, but also not wanting to stand by idly if his daughter were being assaulted. With the door ajar he could tell she was a half floor below, and alone, on the phone. Julian was tempted to eavesdrop, but he didn't want to be that type of asshole. He didn't want to be any type of asshole. But he knew he was, and it pained him immensely.

"You're the best boy ever," Julian said, and in response Gillie thwacked his tail, a couple of times, and lifted his head, a couple of inches. The dog was on his last legs, and his next illness would likely be his last, and then the whole family was going to fall to pieces. Julian had already begun. He'd pick up the skinny little spaniel and carry him to a sofa, where the dog would harumph and spin and settle into a ball, and Julian would lie beside him and stroke his silky hair.

Mortality is a contagious thing to confront.

And now heart surgery? Jesus.

Way back in pre-K, Oona had claimed to her teacher that she had two brothers. "My older brother is Asher," she'd asserted. "My younger brother is Gilgamesh. He's my brown brother."

This comment had provoked a rapid-response panic at school, as if NORAD had detected intercontinental ballistic missiles incoming over the Bering Strait.

"Yes, I know he's a *dog*," Oona acknowledged to the hastily assembled meeting of her mother and father and both of her classroom teachers plus a so-called learning specialist as well as the head of school. All hands on deck.

"But that doesn't mean he's not my *brother*."

Even at age four, Oona had a firm command of the double negative. All the grown-ups paused to make sure they understood the sentence correctly, then the learning specialist arranged her face into an extra-condescending smile, and said, "Yes, Oona, it does mean that," in contradiction to everything that had ever been uttered in the Sonnenberg household.

"No," Julian said, "it doesn't." Everyone in the room was squinting at what was maybe a quadruple-negative divvied up between two speakers. "Gilgamesh is absolutely your brother, Oons. And now we should go home to him. Thank you all for your time."

This became known as the brown-brother episode, and now that brother was old, he was deaf and lame and mostly blind and occasionally incontinent, and spent his days on a threadbare bed under the kitchen window, shifting to follow the sun. For years Julian had paid a walker to take Gillie for a midday walk, but the dog had lost interest, so they saved that fifty dollars per week.

Julian left a small pile of cash on the counter for Silvia, next to the jumble of newsprint with which he covered the kitchen island every morning—the *Journal*, the *Times*, even the *Post*. The Sonnenbergs' was the only *New York Post* subscription in the building; a porter confirmed it. There were a dozen *Posts* from Washington.

For years Silvia had cleaned weekly, but at an especially low moment on Julian's financial roller coaster, he'd recognized that they could scale back here; he also looked for a cheaper garage, suspended a club membership, it all added up when stacked against mortgage and maintenance and tuition and health insurance and 529s and 401(k)s. He started buying meat on sale, and stopped replacing his phone until the old one stopped working entirely. The current device was getting close; it rarely made it to bedtime without dying.

The cheapest parking garage in the neighborhood, a half mile away, was eight hundred dollars per month. This city was brutal.

It had seemed uncaring to take away Silvia's wages, so Julian had found another family who wanted biweekly cleaning, and he raised her wages incrementally to go with her halved hours. Everybody won. The apartment was marginally less clean, but not in a way that mattered, especially now that everyone was home so infrequently. The kids were always busy, on their way to becoming part-time seasonal residents, and Jen was scarcer than ever.

Julian's wife had always been an early riser, early departure, early to the office. For years, early mornings had been when Julian could expect sex. "This is my time," Jen had said early in their relationship, climbing atop. There'd been uncountable dawns when he'd been barely alert, his wife grinding atop his morning erection until she orgasmed, reliably as clockwork.

These days he didn't expect to see Jen in the morning. Julian had at times wondered if his wife was rushing out to collect her morning orgasm courtesy of someone else's erection. Would he mind? Not much. Maybe they were both pretending not to know things, willful ignorance for the sake of propriety, for the sake of the children. When Oona left for college, though? That was less than two years away, which seemed both excruciatingly long and heartbreakingly short.

Everyone is always running out of time. As soon as you become aware of the possibility of something ending, it is. High school graduation is just around the corner, college is over almost as soon as it starts, your twenties are slipping away and you still haven't accomplished anything. By fifty it seems like you've been running out of time for decades. And then you do.

Julian and Jen had this conversation before they were married: she definitely wanted children, but she was not willing to sacrifice her career to raise them. She was a corporate lawyer, her workdays began by eight at the latest. Julian's days at the gallery skewed later, so he would need to take morning duty, getting the kids clothed and fed and off to school.

"Are you up for that?" she'd asked.

"I am."

And he was. Some of it was tedious as hell; Julian didn't pretend it wasn't. But he also loved it. He loved their tiny fingers reaching into tiny bowls for tiny Cheerios. He loved strapping a kid to his chest in a Björn, pushing a stroller, walking down the sidewalk with one warm little hand in each of his.

Julian wanted his kids to grow up not just confident and content, but competent. So when each kid hit fourth grade, Julian began regimens of independence training, dispatching first Asher and the next year Oona on increasingly far-flung missions—to the corner for a quart of milk, across Columbus to the pharmacy, take the dog to the park, here's a hundred for new sneakers at Tip Top. During those two Septembers and Octobers he'd follow the fledgling kid, wearing sunglasses and a hat pulled low, peeking around corners, hiding behind lampposts, like an inept spy in a comic-action movie. The kids were nine years old, ten, easy to fool.

By each kid's fourth-grade November, Julian would be finished with the spying. By middle school, each would be fixing their own breakfast, folding laundry, navigating the city on buses and subways, flying as unaccompanied minors to Jen's parents in Vero Beach.

Julian had known, of course, what was coming next: the children began to pull away. At first it felt like a reprieve, he had so much more time, so much less to keep track of, to worry about. Then it began to feel like a loss, he was no longer doing the best thing he'd ever done, and would ever do. This loss was momentous, and irreversible, and ongoing; it was only going to get worse.

To compensate, Julian began to work more, but this was the same moment when work was becoming less enjoyable. Which meant he'd replaced something he loved with something he didn't. This was the opposite of how life was supposed to work, and it made him wonder: what's the point?

When Oona was four years old, she'd asked, "Daddy, what are people for?"

Julian had been blindsided. As with most very deep questions from very small people, it had seemingly come out of nowhere. He was unprepared, and couldn't think of a good answer before she followed up with: "What am *I* for?"

Now this was something he asked every fucking day. What am I for?

Julian glanced at the painting in his foyer, a *Last Supper*–like arrangement of characters from the *Great Day in Harlem* photo. This oil was for sale. Almost all the art in 2A was for sale, always. Julian hung everything with symmetrical space on all sides, picture hooks in the dead centers of walls, making it easy to swap out anything with no measuring, no yanking out old hooks or hammering home new ones. Here in the foyer was where Julian hung whatever he thought was most saleable, or most profitable. He really wanted to sell this picture. He needed to.

His finances were teetering. His kids were leaving. His marriage was withering. His career was, quite possibly, ending, and so was he. Someday he'll need to deal with all these problems, but today was not that day. Though you never know.

He couldn't stop hearing the busker's song.

I'm not half the man I used to be.

CHAPTER 6

APARTMENT 11C-D

"Mommy?"

Bitsy had been saying something about the Lenape, a subject that seemed to be taught in every single grade of school. Again and again with the Lenape. But Emily had been distracted by that odd lobby interaction with Julian, and she'd stopped paying attention to Bitsy, and had now been caught.

"Mommy?"

"Yes, Bits, I'm so sorry." Emily looked down at her daughter. "What did you ask?"

"I asked, *Mommy*, if we should start doing a *land* acknowledgment at home. Before *dinner*."

"A what now?"

"A *land* acknowledgment. To acknowledge that this land"—Bitsy swept her hand across Central Park West—"was *stolen* from ingenious peoples."

"Indigenous?"

"Who were *slaughtered* in a holocaust."

"Goodness. Who told you that?"

"Mix Gonzalez-Fetterman. At *grade* meeting." This was the teacher who'd worn a TAX THE RICH tee shirt to Parents' Day, at a school where nearly all the parents were rich, which would've been admirable if it weren't so obnoxious. "Mix Gonzalez-Fetterman is the director of community, um . . . *community*."

"Community community?"

"No, just community, I think. They used to be *mister*, but now they is *mix*. They and them and their are their pronouns."

"Are you sure that's the right, um . . ." What was this? "Verb agreement?"

"Huh?"

"They *is*? That doesn't sound right to me."

Bitsy shrugged. School was definitely going to be the most authoritative source on any pronoun question, but little Bitsy Longworth here was not necessarily the most reliable conduit, and this was a perilous game of telephone. Emily would need to research the subject herself.

A trio of teenaged girls were coming up the block, in animated conversation, all three of them tall and beautiful and dressed in those jailbaity plaid skirts. Emily couldn't believe these uniforms still existed, anachronistic with everything else about New York City education.

"He was with some girl who goes to *Chapin*," one of these girls said, and another answered, "Ugh," shaking her head in utter disgust.

"Mommy?"

"Yes, Hud?"

"This morning I weighed my poop!"

Oh Jesus, Emily thought. "Oh my," she said, terrified what the boy might mean. "How'd you do that, exactly?"

"I weighed myself before I pooped, then I pooped, then I weighed myself after I pooped!"

Well, thank goodness for that. Small mercies.

"My poop weighed eight pounds!"

Parenting was much more scatological than Emily had expected. Hudson referred to diarrhea—a word he did not know—as poop juice, which was that special combination of disgusting with brilliant that Emily thought was the superpower of six-year-olds.

"Wow. Are you sure, Hud? Eight pounds seems like a lot. Especially for someone who weighs—what are you now? Forty pounds?"

"Forty-three!"

There were many ways that Emily could explain how an eight-pound defecation was not possible, but she couldn't choose among them. "Well," she said, "aren't you clever."

"Mommy?" Bitsy wanted to redirect the conversation back to herself. "*Mom*my?"

"Yes, sweetie?"

"The land acknowledgment?" The children were encouraged to bring their whole selves to school, and little Elizabeth Parker Longworth's whole self included a generous helping of sanctimony. Kids can be awfully pious, even when their moral outrage is secondhand. Being outraged on behalf of other people—or other species—was practically Bitsy's hobby. Don't let her get started on octopuses.

"Oh, I don't know, Bits." But that was disingenuous. Whit was already in a hot lather about what he called the Great Awokening, instigated by the WWW—the Woke White Women. There was no way he'd countenance a predinner land acknowledgment, like saying grace.

"It's . . . um . . . it's an interesting idea. We'll discuss it."

"Tonight?"

"No, not tonight, I'm afraid. Remember you'll be on a sleepover with Nana and Pop-Pop?"

Tomorrow was a curriculum day, no classes, so the kids were going to spend the night at Emily's parents' pied-à-terre, then first thing in the morning they'd go straightaway to see the Bronx Zoo's gorillas. Hudson called them bodrillas, and they were his favorite thing in the world. His favorite TV show was *Curious George*, though in truth he didn't seem to enjoy watching it, because he needed to leave the room every time the mischievous monkey did something that might get him in trouble, which happened in every single episode, it was like the misunderstandings that underpinned *Three's Company*. Hud would hide in the hall, then creep back when he hoped that the danger had passed, peeking around the corner. It was one of the funniest things Emily ever saw, but she was always careful not to show it. She didn't want her son to think she was laughing at him.

"So tonight is no good, Bits. I'm sorry."

Hudson called Curious George's human the Yellow Man in the Hat, instead of the Man in the Yellow Hat. It always made Emily want to squeeze him.

"Oh." Bitsy wanted resolution of this land-acknowledgment thing. She always wanted swift resolutions. "No or yes?" she used to ask, whenever either parent hesitated for even a second to answer one of her requests. "Tomorrow?"

"Maybe," Emily said. "We'll see."

Bitsy accepted her mother's goodbye kiss dutifully but with a tinge of resentment, then marched away, elbows out, ready to take on any comers. If there was one thing Emily wanted from the world, it was that her daughter's spirit never be defeated, as Emily's had been.

This was the main reason why Emily was staying in her marriage, as well as the main reason she wanted to leave it. An irreconcilable tension.

Emily had never in her life voted for a candidate who wasn't a Democrat, except the one time she voted for a Socialist because he was cute, and she was nineteen. Emily was in favor of progressive taxes, a safety net, public works, civil rights, affirmative action, choice, the separation between church and state. She believed in relativism, and context; she respected other points of view; she'd read Marx. Emily was, as far as she was concerned, a liberal.

But these days many so-called liberals assumed not only that everyone was liberal, but that everyone agreed on what exactly that meant, on every issue, with no acceptable variance. To Emily this looked like the opposite of liberal. This seemed a lot more like fascism than democracy.

There was no way to say this aloud to almost anyone. There was no way to say a lot.

Emily had been trying, she really had. She'd been hyper-attentive during the special assembly on microaggressions, and at the roundtable on combatting institutional racism, and on the task force about decolonializing the curriculum, adding units on pre-Columbian cultures and African kingdoms, replacing Hemingway and Fitzgerald with Morrison and Cisneros, centering the contributions of women of color, amplifying the voices of the repressed and the underrepresented and the marginalized. Yes, yes, yes, absolutely.

It wasn't only the institution and the curriculum, Emily knew, it was interpersonal too, racism and privilege needed to be confronted in the way everyone did everything, and she accepted her responsibility to take action, to have uncomfortable conversations. She'd been the one to intercede during the chitchat portion of the PA meeting: "Listen, after break, maybe we shouldn't all come back in here talking about our ski trips."

"Hmm?" Morgan Lipschitz had cocked her head, alert.

"Personally, I *love* getting everyone's reports from the slopes." She didn't. "But I can't help but worry that maybe, for some people, it can feel exclusionary? Maybe unkind?"

"Oh please." Morgan had already had more than enough of inclusion before DEI even got off the ground. "You're going to talk to me about exclusion?"

Morgan's stepson Seth had been excluded from Dartmouth early admission, along with the other half dozen kids who'd applied early, in what instantly became known as the Dartmouth Bloodbath. Panic set in. Self-medication exploded. Kids were staying up all hours, "demonstrating interest" by taking virtual tours, working on supplemental essays. Why Is a Diverse Student Body Important to You? Describe a Moment That Heightened Your Awareness of Privilege.

"We did *everything* right," Morgan had complained, repeatedly. This gaping wound was still fresh. "There's Jerry's legacy, and his consistent giving, and a *very* compelling support letter from a *huge* donor. Seth has *impeccable* grades, *perfect* essays, *all* the extracurrics. It's not like we just thought of this! We hired the college adviser back in *ninth* grade."

A college application was something that could be purchased: grades from tutors, essays from outside advisers, athletics from private coaches and travel teams and summer camps and tournaments in far-flung locations. Internships, language proficiency, community service: every line of an application was a thing that can be bought.

"Yes," Emily had said, "you certainly took the initiative."

"I mean, he's now thinking about Trinity." Morgan believed that paying for Seth's spot at Dartmouth was not altogether different from purchasing anything else, and she wasn't ashamed. She owned it. "*Trinity.* I mean."

"Trinity is a great school," Emily countered, and Morgan scoffed. Morgan had the unquestioned reverence for the Ivy League that's peculiar to those who'd gone elsewhere. "Anyway," Emily pivoted, "I don't think it would kill us if we skipped the ski talk with people who probably don't ski. Would it?"

Morgan rolled her eyes.

Some steps were small, but that didn't mean they weren't uncomfortable.

"Bye-bye Mommy!" Hudson called over his shoulder, running to join his friends. Is there anything cuter than a little boy in wide-wale corduroys? "Love you!"

The vast majority of the drop-off crowd were women. Some of the small assortment of men wore business suits, some sweatpants, some in between. Nearly all the men scrammed promptly after shooing kids inside, except a couple who were clearly on the make, and a few others who were obviously bored—the unemployed, the underemployed, the never-employed househusbands. Plus the dad called Scrubs, because that's all he wore. No one knew his name. Everyone preferred it that way.

"My god, Emily"—Morgan was upon her—"those boots!" Morgan crossed her hands over her chest, to protect her heart from breaking at the sheer beauty of Emily's suede boots. "I mean."

For a while Morgan used to say "Stop," or "Shut up," then transitioned to "I can't even," later truncated to "I can't," recently replaced with "I mean." Morgan had vibes and she had mood and she had all the feels, she was here for it, she was living for it, she was all about it, she was obsessed, crushing it, killing it. Morgan's dialect was like the local radio's traffic-and-transit report, "NJT is on or close": lingo that makes sense only to the initiated.

Morgan was one of the many women on the West Side who wore leggings and sneakers whenever they took to the streets, while some of the men tried even less. Like this one here, in plaid flannel pajama bottoms and a Michigan sweatshirt and Crocs. If an East Side dad came to drop-off in pajamas, moms would bombard his wife with questions about his mental health, while other dads would stand around in their Barbours and their Burberrys, shaking their heads, pity what happened to that guy, he used to be such an *animal.*

New Jersey Transit trains are running on schedule, or close to it.

Pajamas. On the *street*. And what's with these Michigan alums? They're like a cult.

"Oh lord," Morgan said sotto voce, her eye caught by something. "Look out."

Frida Yarborough was approaching with her preschooler Jendayi. "Hi Emily, hi Morgan, nice to see you, how *are* you?"

"Awesome!" Morgan said this with so much enthusiasm that Emily hoped it might cover her too, then Frida was gone, always running late, in a rush, things are *so crazy*. Frida wielded the frenetic activity of her political activism as a cudgel, an excuse to be not only sanctimonious but also rude, substituting the performance of being good for actually being good.

"Did you see what that child is wearing today?" Morgan asked. "I mean, can you imagine if I brought Brett to school in a White Boy Magic shirt?"

Emily didn't think this was a parallel, but she didn't want to argue.

"I'd be canceled *on the spot*. I'd be *lynched*."

"Oh Morgan. You can't use that word, not about yourself."

Morgan waved off the objection. "I heard"—Morgan glanced around, leaned closer—"that *Frida* was the one who chose the name Jendayi. Do you know what that child's birth name was?"

Emily did, but she didn't want to ruin the story for Morgan. "No."

"Karen. Can you believe it? *Karen!* I mean, really."

Frida's Long Island parents had named her Stacey; at Oberlin she discovered one of her great-grandparents had been Mexican, and promptly changed her name to Frida. It seemed to be a hobby of hers, changing names to make statements.

"Who does she think she is? And that sweatshirt?" Now that people wore their politics on their sleeves, sometimes literally, it was getting hard to remain friends with—or married to—people with whom you disagreed, because they were constantly telling you about it.

"Maybe she's wearing that because of what happened over the weekend?"

It was a TRAYVON hoodie.

"What weekend? Last weekend?"

"You know, that man getting shot."

"What happened? We were out east." As if it was simply not possible to get local New York City news out there in the wilds of Westhampton, seventy miles away.

"A Black man was killed by the cops. In the lobby of a building on Fifty-seventh Street."

"Oh god. How horrible." Morgan waited a beat before asking, "Which building?"

"The Park Spire."

"Well that's too bad," Morgan acceded. "Obviously." Morgan was probably thinking about whom she could call in the Spire to get the scoop. Morgan was extremely good at typing into her phone. "But it's *every* day with the slogan shirts, Insta, tweets, petitions. Did you see her *gushing* about that unwatchable Spike Lee movie? And the way she went on about Faith Ringgold. I mean, right?"

These days it was much better to not answer many questions. Instead Emily tended to smile, and people could read into it whatever they wanted, but wouldn't be able to quote her. Which was exactly what she did now, and waited for Morgan to fill the silence. People abhor silence.

"Oh god," Morgan muttered. "Now this one? I am *not* here for it."

"Good morning Emily," QR Code said. "Morgan."

QR's job title was director of the department of diversity, equity, inclusion, and—last year's supplement—belonging. There was no actual department. The expansive title was more of a signal of the school's commitment than a fact. Plus it wasn't called a school anymore, it was a learning community. Teachers were educators, books were texts, populations were communities, people were folks. And, as of last spring, women were—at least occasionally—humans who menstruate.

"I mean, we're not allowed to say *mom* anymore?" This had been the straw that had broken the back of Morgan's civility with QR Code. "I just can't with her."

For years Lianne Quisenberry-Roth had tried to get students to call her Quiz. But then she'd led a schoolwide workshop on code switching, and that was the death knell for Quiz.

"I hope we'll see you both at tomorrow's meeting?" QR asked.

Emily smiled. "I'll do my best."

This meeting was going to be another in the long-term fallout from last year's lūau debacle, which someone had put on the calendar for AAPI

Awareness Month before anyone had taken the time to discover that the only Pacific Islander affiliated in any way with the school was a lone part-time kitchen worker, who didn't want to be involved for a host of reasons that were too obvious to enumerate, and the ensuing debate about appropriation and representation and inclusion and tokenizing and exoticizing and othering and even diacritical marks consumed the PA in heated debate for the better part of the year, leading to a community-wide survey of everyone's self-identification along racial, religious, ethnic, gender, and sexuality lines. The results were the subject of tomorrow's meeting, which was going to be a real doozy.

A culprit for the lūau misstep was never publicly identified, a failure that many suspected was due to a cover-up of Watergate proportions, and that the perpetrator was QR herself.

Emily thought that a Pulitzer Prize should be awarded to whichever middle-schooler came up with the nickname QR Code. It was brilliant on so many levels.

These issues weren't specific to this school. It was practically every educational institution in New York City that purported to be progressive, which was what most parents wanted, or claimed they wanted, at least in the abstract, or at least ten years ago, and especially after George Floyd. But recently the mood had shifted. Some parents were now wondering if there wasn't possibly a little too much social-justice awareness at the expense of, you know, *math* awareness. And wouldn't all these no-grades policies make it harder to get into Brown?

It was the dads in particular who wondered if standardized tests were *really* so evil? These were all guys who themselves had scored in the ninety-ninth percentile. They expected that standardized test scores were inheritable. They weren't wrong, but it wasn't because of genetics.

At a certain level of wealth in this city, it was nearly unthinkable to not be a Democrat. But at the wealthiest levels, many people started referring to themselves as independents, which Emily believed usually meant Republicans who didn't want to be aligned with the increasingly berserk national party. "I don't agree with Hannity, of course, but it's important to be exposed to all points of view." To Emily this sounded like the guys who'd once claimed to read *Playboy* for the articles. Sure, dude. Whatever.

Morgan was one of those who claimed to vote for the candidate, not the party. She was married to a man who was twenty-five years older than her, and played golf with Trump. A lot of the men with much younger wives golfed together.

"I'll be momming hard today," Morgan said, "but wanna grab a matcha?"

"Oh," Emily said, smiling, "I wish I could. I'm sorry."

"What are you doing now?"

Yet another question Emily didn't want to answer. It wasn't that she was ashamed, not of this, it was that she didn't want to appear too proud, not of this. There was an awful lot of performative progressivism swirling around her, relentless virtue signaling, loud screaming that made Emily want to keep extra quiet.

"Maybe tomorrow?" she offered.

"Absolutely!"

As Emily walked away, she noticed Bitsy in animated conversation with a couple of other girls.

The ingenious Lenape, Emily thought, and smiled.

CHAPTER 7

FRONT DOOR

Bzzz!

Chicky's eyes popped open at the sound of the doorbell. This noise in no way resembled a ringing bell. It was more like a short-circuit of a large machine that was thinking about exploding.

Bzzzzzzzzzz!

"The fuck." He threw his legs over the side of the bed too quickly and pain shot up his side. "Ow. Fuck."

Chicky was not unaccustomed to waking in pain. Softball can look mostly like a bunch of guys standing around, jawing. But sprinting and diving and lunging and swinging and throwing, those are all movements that maybe don't hurt when you're a teenager or twenty-five. But when you're fifty-one years old they take a toll. Monday mornings can be brutal. Tuesdays worse.

For fifteen years Chicky has played short and managed the team sponsored by Junior's Bar & Grille. The league's permit was over in Riverside Park with the bridge out there past right, day games on Sundays and night games on Thursdays and a cold beer after the final out, maybe two beers, home to Tiffani by the girls' bedtime or near enough.

Most teams in this league were very near equal in ability. Management of a squad like this was not about athletics. It was about organization and attendance and camaraderie and teamwork and most of all it was about attitude. Attitude was Chicky's specialty. His team had won four championships in a row.

If he were born to another life, Chicky thought, he'd be CEO of a large organization. He'd sit at the head of a conference table in a sharp suit and shined shoes. He'd listen intently to what his people were saying and he'd take notes and he'd ask incisive questions and he'd make decisions that everyone respected. Every year his bonus would grow. Car-sized bonuses. House-sized bonuses.

But he was born to this life. At the end of each season his guys treated him to dinner with all he could drink even though he barely drank. He took home the trophy, which more often than not was a piece of hardware he'd chosen and fronted the money for and gotten engraved and picked up and lugged to the back room at Junior's. That's how it works in the life he actually has.

This week's pains were not just from a ball game. This week's pains were psychic in addition to physical. This week's pains were existential.

The first steps of the day were the worst. Which could probably be said about almost anything. Chicky limped to the shoddy plastic intercom in a color of beige that should be called dinge. He couldn't imagine why anyone would design anything in this color unless the goal was to be depressing. He pressed the half of the TALK button that hadn't cracked off. "Yeah?"

"FedEx."

"For Diaz?"

"No. Gutierrez."

"That ain't me. Next door."

"No answer next door."

As a rule Chicky was happy to do a solid but he did not want to get involved in Alberto Gutierrez's deliveries. "How's that my problem?"

"Come on bruh. Just need a signature."

Chicky closed his eyes and shook his head before answering, "Okay. Gimme a minute though. You woke me up." He held DOOR long enough for the guy to get through the front door and vestibule and inner door. Both doors had the potential to stick.

The FedEx guy was built like a cornerback and wearing a uniform nearly as tight along with the dreadlocks that nearly all D-backs sported.

No one was going to fuck with this FedEx guy. Chicky watched football year in and year out and no announcer ever seemed to mention that one hundred percent of the starting cornerbacks in the NFL were Black while eighty percent of starting centers were white.

"Sign here please."

Chicky squinted but that didn't do it. He obviously needed to see an ophthalmologist but he just did not want to start another medical relationship. He was already so tired of it all. Tired by Tiffani's decline. Tired by his own bouts with this and that. Once you start you never stop. It's one doctor after another with appointments more frequent and problems more serious and solutions more drastic until one day there are no more solutions. That's the only way it ends.

"Thanks bruh."

Only one percent of the NFL was Hispanic in a country that's nineteen percent Hispanic. *One percent.* How was that possible?

The package was smaller than a shoebox but light. The return label was all a blur. Chicky pulled the box closer and squinted and pushed it farther and moved to better light until he could make out at least one word: MEXICO.

This fucking guy.

Chicky took a few steps to his neighbor's door and banged with the side of his fist—*bang bang bang*, wait a few seconds, *bang bang bang.*

"Yo! Alberto!" *Bang bang bang.*

Chicky put his ear to the door and didn't hear any sign of life. No music and no TV and no footsteps. He hefted the package and shook it. Nothing rattled. Nothing seemed to move in there. Whatever was inside was very light and packed very tight.

Lightweight. From Mexico. Shit.

"Yo!" *Bang bang bang.* Chicky was standing out in the hallway in his boxers. "'Berto!"

He couldn't just leave this package on Alberto's doorstep. Someone might swipe it and Alberto would find out that it was Chicky who'd signed so it would be Chicky's mistake that cost Alberto however many thousands of dollars these drugs were worth. Who knew.

Fucking Alberto.

Chicky needed to hide this box. You never know when you're going to get burgled or when police are going to show up. The girls' rooms were mostly empty but didn't have any good hiding places, just obvious spots like dresser drawers and under the bed. Chicky opened the coat closet and pulled out the duffel filled with rubber cleats and fielder's mitts and catcher's gear. He had a whole separate bag for bats.

"Yeah," he assured himself. He tucked Alberto's package between shin guards and buckled the pads around each other. The result looked like an amputated leg. Or no, not amputated. What it looked like was a leg that had been blown the fuck off. Like Reggie's leg lying there in the dust outside Kuwait City. Poor fucker.

Chicky should give that guy a call. It had been a while. Too long. Maybe tomorrow. Or next week.

Though maybe not. Chicky wasn't in any position to cheer up anyone.

It was only a few months after their youngest left for college when Tiffani was diagnosed with lymphoma not treatable enough to survive but not terminal enough to be a no-brainer of giving up. Tiffani was a nurse in an old folks' home in White Plains taking care of other people's parents and grandparents. Rich old white people. Meanwhile Tiffani's own mom spent her last years with dementia by herself in the projects. Tiffani visited every Sunday to clean up the worst of the messes—domestic and physical and financial and emotional, every type of mess. Then Tiffani would come home and take care of her own three children and husband. She'd spent most of a decade going to night school to train to take care of other people all day every day.

Tiffani was dead within a year.

Instead of a life-insurance death benefit she bequeathed a death punishment: two hundred grand in bills that were at various stages of unpaid or disputed or unreimbursed or what-the-fuck-ever. The processes were circular and the paperwork impenetrable. As if the doctors and hospitals and insurance companies were all conspiring to overwhelm you with such an avalanche of conflicting and confusing information that you'd just give up. But even after you give up: what do you do then?

Tiffani also left Chicky with five more years of aggregate college tuition plus the probability of graduate school for at least Mariella, who wanted to be a lawyer. The girls received financial aid but there were plenty of gaps so they also worked part-time jobs while studying full-time. Not to mention the student loans they'd be paying back for who knows how long. Sometimes the whole setup didn't look like financial aid so much as financial entrapment. A system that existed mainly to create loans to generate interest and defaults and fees. Maybe college was just another way to trick poor people into a lifetime of consumer debt. To redistribute income upward.

Once you started looking for reverse redistribution schemes, they were everywhere.

Tiffani also left behind a husband who'd never in his fifty years lived alone. Not for a single week of his life. Chicky had moved from his parents' to Parris Island to bases in Panama and Saudi Arabia. Then after the Corps he shared a dump with his younger brother. Then he moved to his first marital apartment and then this bigger one. Chicky's life had been a half century of uninterrupted cohabitation, almost all of it with his immediate family in this neighborhood, a place filled with other people who'd also grown up here. An old-fashioned neighborhood. An old-fashioned life.

Chicky told himself he was still adjusting. Still adjusting to Tiffani's death. Still adjusting to his kids' departure. Still adjusting to the new schedule.

He hated having no one to talk to when he was washing dishes and folding laundry and eating breakfast and watching ball games. He found himself cheering aloud and mocking the stupid shit that announcers said and second-guessing the managers' and GMs' and owners' decisions and cursing out umpires—

"Yo Chick." Alberto had knocked on the door a month ago. "You good?"

"Yeah yeah. Why? What's up?"

Alberto was craning his neck to look past Chicky. "Just that I heard some yelling up in here."

"Aw that was just"—Chicky half turned to half point at the TV, an ad for erectile dysfunction meds. The same old-man products at every commercial break, light beer and car insurance and dick pills. This was one of the depressing parts about watching ball games. There were a few.

"The fucking Mets. They just blew another lead. Can you believe it? The bullpen, man."

"Oh okay." Alberto's tone was unmistakable I-don't-give-a-shit. Young guys like Alberto weren't into baseball. For them it was all hoops or football if anything. Many didn't care about any sports at all, which would have been unthinkable when Chicky was young. Back before video games were acceptable and back before any kid would admit to being gay: it was an absolute requirement to have a favorite team for baseball and basketball and football. Favorite players too.

Not hockey though. Hockey was strictly for white people. In high school Domingo Alvarez had played hockey and everyone gave him shit. Like, daily. *Everyone.* Even younger girls made fun of his ass.

Alberto was peering around. It seemed like he was trying to decide whether to broach a subject. Then he made the leap. "So, um, you doing okay, Chick?"

It took Chicky a second to realize what Alberto was asking.

"Oh, me?" Chicky felt his eyes cut away involuntarily. Then he forced himself to look at Alberto and to meet the question though not honestly. "Yeah, you know. It's getting better. As they say, one day at a time." Chicky gave Alberto a weak smile. "Am I right?"

The guy looked unconvinced. Chicky didn't blame him.

"You want a beer, Chick? I got—"

"Oh thanks man," Chicky cut him off. Those days it didn't take much for Chicky to spiral into a pit of self-pity so deep it seemed insurmountable. He needed to keep away from alcohol. He had at least that level of self-awareness even if he didn't recognize that he wasn't relating to televised sports like a non-crazy person.

"I gotta be up early. You know how it is." In truth Chicky doubted that Alberto did know. It was possible that the guy had never needed to be up early a single day in his whole lazy-ass life.

"You sure Chick?"

"Yeah yeah. But hey man thanks for asking. Really."

Alberto had stood there probably debating whether to leave or to insist on keeping Chicky company. These days everybody was a psychiatrist. Athletes and performers and so-called content creators all popping off about mental health. About prioritizing emotional well-being. About self-care isn't selfish. Blah blah fucking blah. Granting permission to everyone else to pretend that they were experts too. It was obvious to Chicky that no one knew what the fuck they were talking about.

Self-love. What a thing to boast about.

"You sure Chick? I'd be happy to watch some of the, uh . . . what is it, the Mets?"

Until that moment Chicky had never much liked Alberto. The guy seemed like half a punk who never did anything besides smoke weed and play video games. Chicky very specifically did not want to know how Alberto made rent. Sooner or later someone was going to come asking—a gangster, a girlfriend, the police—and Chicky wanted to be able to say with complete honesty, "I have no idea what that dude does in there. I mind my own goddamned business."

But Alberto's concern made Chicky feel like crying. It could come on just like that.

"I appreciate it Alberto." Chicky swallowed back the tears. "Another time? I'd like that."

The ball game had resumed. Chicky could hear the announcers and the hum of the crowd. Runners on second and third and nobody out.

"But I'm good, really. And"—he thumbed backward—"I should hit the sack."

The Mets weren't playoff-bound. This was a meaningless late-season game of a hopeless team. Still Chicky felt like it was his responsibility to watch till the very end. To root. To hope. That's what it means to be a fan.

Also what it means to be a husband. Chicky had been at the hospital every day. Even there at the end when there was nothing left to hope for and nothing left to do except hold his dying wife's brittle hand. He had to stick around for the final out.

"All right then Chick. You take care of yourself."

For years Chicky had felt his life narrowing. At first little by little and then massively, removing this, removing that. People leaving. People dying. And now what was it that Chicky could look forward to? Walking his daughters down the aisle? Maybe. Playing with grandchildren, okay. A day game, Mets win, a nice nap. Is that enough?

Back in his beat-up BarcaLounger Chicky could no longer pay attention to the TV. He didn't notice when the inning ended.

For a few minutes there he didn't realize the game was over.

Chicky had told almost no one about his wife's death. At work all the guys had heard, of course, and they'd all come to the service except those on duty. But they'd also accepted that Chicky didn't want to discuss it. So most days Chicky could almost pretend—almost—that no one knew his wife had died. Maybe he could even pretend for a second or two that it hadn't really happened. This was one of the things Chicky appreciated about going to work.

Many of the residents didn't even know that Chicky had a wife to begin with, much less one who'd died. Tiffani had been only forty-eight years old, a young woman whose dye job was still credible, who looked foxy that last time she wore her fancy purple dress. People don't expect your forty-eight-year-old wife to have died. You don't expect it.

The only resident Chicky had told was Mr. Sonnenberg. They'd known each other since they were kids on opposing teams in the same Little League. Julian's Upper West Side team was mostly Jewish private-school kids with new gear and moms who brought donuts to games. Chicky's was the Spanish Harlem squad of Puerto Ricans and Dominicans. Mrs. Lopez came to the park with giant bags of Doritos or Lay's with the neon-bright SALE sticker. You could see that sticker from out in left field. Everybody on the other team could see it too.

After Mr. Sonnenberg moved into the Bohemia, once or twice a year the two men would go to the batting cages over in the basement of Apple Bank. They'd try fast-pitch for the fun of it, fouling off a couple, whooping it up if either managed to square up eighty-five. But mostly it was medium hardball then slow hardball. Now it's been years since they'd swung at anything other than softballs.

He went to see the super the very next morning after Alberto's visit.

"Chicky my friend," Oleksander said. "Please come in."

The super's office was crammed. A draftsman's table dominated the middle of the room flanked by giant flat files for floor plans and architectural renderings and renovation blueprints. Oak filing cabinets held permits and contracts and correspondence and meeting minutes and fire-safety plans and personnel records. One entire wall was floor-to-ceiling cabinets and drawers for plumbing joints and electrical switches and window hardware and spare doorknobs and dozens of different sizes of brass hinges. It was like the Home Depot Museum with supplies dating from 150 years ago up to today. The drawers had little windows and neat labels that had all been hand-redrawn by the old super. Tommy O'Sullivan often had a half-pint of rye in his back pocket and he was borderline illiterate but his handwriting was like a wedding invitation. Say what you want about those old Catholic schools but nobody has penmanship like that anymore.

"How you are doing Chicky?"

Oleksander was one of the few people Chicky had told about Tiffani's passing. Not because the two men were especially close but because Chicky needed to take some days and the schedule needed to be rejiggered. He'd had no choice.

"I'm good, thanks Boss." He'd barely slept. "Getting better. I appreciate you asking."

Olek was also the only person at the Bohemia who knew Chicky's real first name but Chicky had begged him to keep it quiet, though this was obviously unnecessary. Olek kept secrets like he was KGB. Which was what some of the guys thought he might have actually been before coming to New York. It was a hobby around here to speculate about Olek's history.

"Listen Olek, I was thinking—and I don't want to be presumptuous—but maybe it's time to give one of the younger guys a chance to work days."

Olek raised one of his immense eyebrows. Those things were like two small mammals had crawled onto his forehead and fallen asleep, end to end. They were not symmetrical, those eyebrows, but more like parallelograms. As if whoever constructed Olek had a vague idea of what a face should look like but didn't grasp all the conventions. The eyebrows weren't his only asymmetrical feature.

"You want have a seat Chicky? Please."

Chicky didn't. But he didn't want to be impolite. He sat.

"So Boss. With my kids at college and my wife, you know"—Chicky held out his arms, there-you-go—"I don't *need* days anymore. But Pascal has little kids. Zaire too. I'm sure those guys would *love* to see their families more."

For most of his time at the Bohemia Chicky had worked weekday-days, civilized hours that allowed a guy to have a normal life, wife and kids, birthday parties and Sunday suppers. Maybe you sacrificed some tips because you were never around to help with weekend luggage and shopping sprees and all the random shit that comes up when all the residents are in and out. A twenty here, a twenty there, the occasional fifty. By the end of a Saturday day a guy could go home with a few hundred in cash.

But every year Chicky made up for it with the Christmas envelopes. Everyone loved Chicky Diaz.

And he didn't need big nights anyway. Chicky ate dinner at home. He got to see his girls grow up. He went to school plays and music recitals and middle-school basketball games. All that shit.

"It's your call Boss. Obviously. I'm just saying I'd be good with it. If you shifted some things around. If you shifted me."

Olek blinked slowly before nodding curtly. "Okay Chicky. Sure." The super turned to the magnetic board that everyone called the Master, a schematic of every shift for a half dozen different responsibilities that required personnel at nights and weekends as well as weekdays. It's not as if plumbing problems arise only during business hours. Every employee was represented by a little magnet with a name and phone number laser-cut plus stick-on colored dots for the guy's trades or skills: yellow for electrician and blue for plumbing and green for handyman and red for first aid. Everyone was aware that Olek possessed all these competencies and many others besides.

Actually not everyone called it the Master. Zaire refused. He made a big political point of it.

"*Master?* Nah fuck that plantation slave shit." Zaire made a big political point of everything and he didn't hide his frustration with guys like Chicky who didn't.

"You want night shift, yes Chicky? Not overnight?" The night shift was four till midnight. The overnight was midnight till eight A.M. There was a world of difference.

"Oh no"—Chicky held up his hands—"honestly I hope to never work an overnight again. But nights?" Chicky gave his biggest smile. "Nights would be awesome."

The super had messy Cyrillic tattoos on his arms that no one had the nerve to ask about, stick-and-pokes that suggested prison. Ukrainian prison, Russian prison, who knew.

"You are sure about this Chicky?"

Chicky should not continue to yell at the TV every night in his empty apartment with the smell of skunk seeping through Alberto's walls and the corner store's refrigerators beckoning with their cold bottles and the dealers on the stoops beckoning with their everything and the bars and the clubs and all the trouble a guy could find, especially a lonely single guy who didn't have much to look forward to. Chicky wasn't going to see any of his daughters again until Thanksgiving. Even the baseball season was ending. He needed a different way to spend his nights.

"Most definitely Boss."

"You got it Chicky. Let me talk to the guys. We will figure it out."

Although Chicky was asking the super for a favor, he was also doing one too, giving Olek the opportunity to give another guy something he wanted, and that other guy would owe Olek and owe Chicky too. Management of a staff like the Bohemia's was heavily reliant on giving favors and getting favors and banking favors and redeeming favors. Everyone knows whom they owe and who owes them and how much. The softball team worked this way too.

"Thanks so much Boss." They shook hands. "I really appreciate it."

At least on nights Chicky would have someone to talk to, sometimes. Even if some shifts it wasn't more than "Welcome home Mr. Goff" and "Let me get that bag for you Mrs. Frumm."

Even if sometimes they didn't bother to answer.

CHAPTER 8

APARTMENT 2A

Julian tried to push away his spinning worries, tried to force his attention back to a conversation that had been deteriorating and now was heading toward combustible. Seven members of the co-op board were gathered in the meeting room, a space that had once been part of the building's kitchen. Another part of that kitchen was now the gym. But otherwise the Bohemia had resisted faddish amenities: no wine vaults, lap pools, multipurpose rooms, screening rooms, roof deck.

The Bohemia was luxurious, and famous, but also tasteful, and even somehow modest. The address wasn't visible anywhere, nor the name. If you know you know, and nearly everyone knows, except delivery guys who are new to the neighborhood—new to the country—and for them locating the Bohemia was the least of their problems. Those guys were mostly undocumented immigrants who spoke little or no English, now employed largely by tech companies with anonymous remote bosses, bombing around city streets at forty miles per hour on electronic bikes that could spontaneously burst into flames. These workers were delivering more, faster, while making less, risking serious injury and, increasingly, death, while their Silicon Valley CMOs were buying Gulfstreams and pied-à-terres on Billionaires' Row, or at the Bohemia.

"He's not a good *cultural* fit!" Mrs. Frumm half screamed, as she did everything.

Julian was the youngest person on the board, and Isabel Reed was the only other member under seventy. The Bohemia was like a NORC.

Mrs. Klein leaned toward Gareth Blankenship, whose wrist was bandaged. "What happened to your wrist?" She probably thought she was whispering. Mrs. Klein was one of the chief contributors to the Naturally Occurring Retirement Community ambience.

"Torn ligament."

She pointed at her own head. "Concussion."

"*Mmm*," Blankenship said. "Explains a lot."

"I agree with Ethel," Art Onderdonk pronounced. "Some people are just not good cultural fits." *Good cultural fit* was impossible to argue with: there was no fact to dispute. The only evident fact was that this was racist. Julian had to be careful here.

"I mean, his name is *Amir*!" Mrs. Frumm added. Amir Jackson had just signed with the Knicks for twelve million dollars per year. He wanted to buy 5D for ten percent over asking in cash. If this deal went through, Amir's would be the building's only Black family, out of ninety-four units.

"What's the problem with his name?" Julian asked. He was president of this board, a position that bore much more in common with being a servant than being the boss. He needed to deal with this issue before it got out of hand. Before it got illegal.

"Oh please! You know!"

Julian counted to five before responding. "I think," he began. He didn't want to be the one to say this, but no one else would. "I think we need to consider anti-bias training."

"*Anti-racist?!* You mean *anti-white*!"

"No, Mrs. Frumm, neither anti-racist nor anti-white."

People tossed around *anti-racism* like a grenade, which they then counterattacked with machine-gun-fire accusations of Critical Race Theory. Only a tiny percentage of anyone understood what any of these phrases meant, and Ethel Frumm was definitely not one of them.

"Anti-*bias* training is not about dismantling institutional racism—"

She rolled her eyes.

"—but about helping us recognize our biases. Racial, cultural, sexual."

"Sexual biases?" Art Onderdonk asked. "What are you talking about?"

"Biases against women, Art. Or gay people, or trans people." Julian saw Onderdonk glance at Gareth Blankenship, the only gay person on the board. It was well known that Gareth had recently been canceled, and he no longer said anything at meetings. His wrist bandage looked much more like a suicide attempt than a torn ligament.

"We've never had a tranny prospective buyer." Onderdonk scoffed. "Have we?"

Julian stifled the urge to correct the language. He didn't want to be accused of being a woke scold or the PC police. He didn't want to pick unnecessary fights in addition to the necessary ones.

"I'm going to have to push back," Tucker Goff said. Goff had been CEO and chief shareholder of the second-largest bubble-wrap manufacturer in America. When the company was sold to a conglomerate, Tuck took in a bit more than a half-billion dollars. And *a bit* meant thirty million. Julian never stops being amazed by the myriad ways that people get rich in this country.

"We can reject any buyer for any reason, or for no reason," Goff continued. He was convinced that his immense liquidity event had rendered him an expert in all subjects, bar none. "That's the value prop of the co-op model."

This guy didn't even use his lingo correctly. Goff couldn't get through almost any conversation without throwing out pivot or best practices or core competencies or optimization or onboarding or, of course, supply chain. He practically leaped out of his chair at the chance, like a middle-school boy with a newly acquired vulgarism for vagina.

"You know that's not true," Isabel interjected, thank goodness. "We can't reject people for *illegal* reasons. And one of those, I'm sure you know, is discrimination based on race."

Isabel was the most reasonable person on the board, or at least the most aligned with Julian; he admittedly had a hard time telling the difference. She was, like Julian, the owner of a small business, an experience that created a specific type of vigilance.

"But we've never discriminated!" Onderdonk had gone from zero to livid with mind-boggling speed. It was hard to imagine how this guy had ever functioned as an attorney. He'd been retired for at least a couple of years but still wore suits, leather-soled shoes, bow ties.

"Are you sure about that, Art?" Julian asked.

"Name one! Just one! We're Jews!"

This had long been part of the Bohemia's identity while the peer buildings on the other side of the park maintained unapologetic antisemitism. New York City was home to a million Jewish people—as many as Jerusalem and Tel Aviv combined—which didn't even include the suburbs, the Great Necks and Livingstons, the Scarsdales and Five Towns, the exurban enclaves up in Rockland that were so Orthodox they might as well be Settlements. Which, in a way, they were. New York was the largest Jewish metropolis in the history of the world.

Julian's family was emblematic of the old-guard old–New York Jewish aristocracy, Our Crowd schooled at Horace Mann or Riverdale before Harvard or Yale—but not Princeton, which even for the WASP-iest of Jews was usually a bridge too far south—before careers on Wall Street, or white-shoe law, or noblesse oblige work in the arts or civil service, evenings of opera subscriptions and Shakespeare in the Park, taxis down to Chinatown for dumplings and Peking duck on Christmas Day while Gentiles busied themselves worshipping the birth of a Jew.

Here on the West Side the best addresses had names—the Langham and Beresford, the Prasada and Dakota, the two-towered triumvirate of Majestic and Eldorado and San Remo, the Bohemia. Over on the East Side, none did. Julian once overheard a man who lived at 740 Park talking to a guy who lived at 834 Fifth—addresses that mean nothing except to people for whom they mean everything—"Naming your apartment building?" Sip of gin, shake of head. This was at the Union Club, or maybe it was the Knick. "That's a *Jewish* thing, isn't it?" They both laughed.

Although Julian could feel the sting of antisemitism, what he'd never felt was any attachment to Judaism itself. Julian Sonnenberg was an avowed atheist, and he visited temple very rarely, and very reluctantly. The Sonnenbergs' dumplings were fried pork, except when they were pork-and-crab soup dumplings. Not merely un-kosher, but anti-kosher.

For a couple years, almost every weekend one or the other of Julian's kids had attended a bar or bat mitzvah whose parties were held in catering halls or dance clubs or bespoke candy shops, or ballrooms at the Plaza or the Pierre, commandeering the top floor of the St. Regis where a hip-hop star performed four songs in exchange for a million dollars while thirteen-year-olds jumped up and down with neckties around their foreheads, hopped-up on unlimited sugar and all-you-can-drink alcohol that they'd snuck from their parents' abandoned glasses. Julian had a hard time believeing this was what any god had in mind.

Schools needed to maintain sign-up sheets, posted years in advance, to reserve your Saturday night. There were rigid policies about invite lists.

Asher once pointed to a slender cloud hanging low in the sky, its long concave underside hovering just above the convex top of a ski mountain in Utah. "Look," the kid had said, "a yarmucloud." That was now what Julian thought whenever he saw a yarmulke: a yarmucloud. He had never in his life put on a yarmulke.

Those middle-school years were the last when Julian knew for certain where his kids were at eleven on a Saturday. It's a brief window when kids are old enough to be out at night yet young enough that the parents know where. One year? Two? Then you have to let go. Or maybe you don't have to, exactly, but you do.

"We've been discriminated against for *millennia*!" Onderdonk concluded in a red-faced tizzy of self-righteous indignation.

Yarmucloud was one of Julian's favorite things.

"Look at, um, Harmon!" Goff offered. The guy's name was Skip Hardiman, and he'd served two terms on the board, one as treasurer, and had lived in the building for a quarter century before downsizing to a downtown pied-à-terre and a mansion in Oak Bluffs. Yet Goff couldn't remember his only Black neighbor's name. You didn't need to look any further for proof of Goff's racism.

"Well," Julian said, "just because we didn't discriminate against that one particular Black person doesn't mean we don't discriminate against others. This is not a theoretical issue, nor ethical. Just practical. We're exposed, legally. If we don't take action, it's just a matter of time and luck before we face serious, expensive problems."

Now everyone was paying a different sort of attention.

"I'm sure our hearts are in the right place, and I don't think anyone here is racist." These were out-and-out lies. There were plenty of hearts in plenty of wrong places, and at least a few obvious racists here, plus a couple of less overt ones. Art was using the existence of antisemitism to excuse his own racism. But that wasn't an argument Julian could win. No one holds a grudge quite like a racist old man who has been accused of racism.

"If we volunteer for training, we'll be demonstrating a proactive attempt to solve a problem *before it even occurs*. This will bolster our defense if—*when*—a disagreement does arise."

Julian could see a few heads of steam building up.

"Well I'm not going to do it!" Ethel threw up her hands, shaking her head in disgust, as if Mengele himself had been let off on a technicality. Chain of custody, maybe—I did not have possession of those Jews!

"I will not sit here and be accused of racism!" It was only recently that Ethel had finally stopped referring to Black people as coloreds. "The nerve of these people!"

Half the board looked down at the table, at their papers, at their hands. Onderdonk, though, was nodding along with Ethel's outburst. He wasn't the only one.

That was when everyone looked up at the sound of knocking on the door.

CHAPTER 9

APARTMENT 2A

"I'm sorry to interrupt," Oleksander Ponomarenko said, "is now good for me to join?"

"Now's great," Julian said. "Come on in."

The super shut the door behind him, but did not sit. Olek never sat unless told to; he never entered a room without invitation.

"Please have a seat."

"So," Olek said, "is everyone aware of the incident over the weekend?"

"What incident?" Art Onderdonk asked. "You mean that man getting shot?"

"*Shot!*" Frumm actually screamed this. "Who was shot?!"

"A Black man was killed by the police, Mrs. Frumm. On Fifth-seventh Street."

"Oh." She was clearly relieved. Just a Black man. "That."

"There is a demonstration planned for tonight," Olek said. "I am being told that it is expected to be large. So the immediate question is: do we want to hire additional security—"

"*Absolutely!*" Mrs. Frumm leaped in before the guy had even finished his question.

"—for tonight?"

"Not so fast, Ethel," Onderdonk interjected. "How much would this cost?" Onderdonk could always be relied upon to keep his eye on his money. Most people wasted everyone's time pretending they were concerned with other things, when really it was just their money.

"My understanding is that the rate is currently seven."

"Seven *thousand* dollars?" This was a guy who spent thirty thousand per year on club dues.

"Wait, wait, wait," Julian said. "What are we talking about?"

"A team of armed guards to supplement the doormen."

"To protect us! Against *rioting*!"

What a horrible idea.

"What makes you think there will be rioting?" Julian asked.

Olek shrugged in a way that somehow suggested a very strong hunch, plus inside dope. "There is a limited supply of security firms that is not elastic in the very short term."

Goff was obviously impressed at this reference to short-term inelastic supplies.

"The demand will increase over the course of the day. Our neighbors are flying in a team from North Carolina."

Julian was shaking his head.

"What, Sonnenberg?" Onderdonk was squinting. "This too *racist* for you to contemplate?"

"As a matter of fact, yes. Since when does a protest equal rioting?"

"*Of course* there will be rioting!"

Julian tried to stay calm. "Do we really want to be those people?"

"*Those people?* We already *are* those people, Sonnenberg. Even if you're too *woke* to admit it. Or maybe it's just that you don't have as much to lose as some of us."

Oh what a jackass.

"I'm not dismissing your concerns about safety," Julian said, trying hard to rise above it. "You think I'm in favor of—what?—defunding the police? *Shooting* the police? I believe in the rule of law. But I also believe that Black men should have the right to not get killed by the police. I also believe that we—all of us—have the right to protest, especially against abuses of power. Not just the right, the obligation."

Ethel rolled her eyes, while Julian felt the momentum of his own argument gathering.

"And I believe that as Americans—as humans—we have the obligation to support protesters, and to support their right to protest. Hiring armed security sends the opposite signal. The signal that not only don't we support the protest, but we don't trust it. That we're afraid of it."

"But we *are* afraid of it!"

"I'm not. If you're that afraid of your neighbors, Ethel, maybe you shouldn't live here."

"Maybe you shouldn't!"

"Please." Isabel was trying to be conciliatory. "Let's everyone calm down."

"Can we double-click for a sec: what's the downside of extra security? Specifically?"

"Specifically? I'm worried that we'd be hiring coked-up dishonorable discharges who think of themselves as hammers, to whom every Black man will look like a nail. Maybe one of those nails says something, in passing. Everyone is on edge, everyone overreacts, and suddenly a bunch of white guys gun down some unarmed Black men, on our sidewalk, which we *paid them to do*."

"Oh come on now."

"Is that scenario impossible, Art? You know it isn't. Even if nothing dramatic happens, it very well may become public that the Bohemia hired armed police to mete out extrajudicial vigilantism during a protest against the abuse of power by armed police."

"How will that become public?"

"Are you kidding? Hundreds of people are here every day, snapping photos. All it takes is one suspicious person to start asking questions, and in very short order we'd be humiliated."

"Who'd be humiliated, Sonnenberg?"

"Me, Art. I'd be humiliated. And so would anyone else who isn't a racist."

"Ex*cuse* me?"

Olek's phone chimed. He looked down. "The security firm is now asking ten thousand."

"We should've hired them at seven," Goff said. "I knew it."

"No, we shouldn't have," Julian said decisively. "We're not hiring them at any price."

Onderdonk puffed himself up to deliver an oration. "If things get bad out there, you know the police are going to have other priorities. If the *whole city* is burning, the NYPD is not going to be rushing to the Bohemia to save us. They have never been particularly *keen* to protect our people."

Oh good lord, Julian thought, here we go again. "What do you mean, *our people*?"

"The Irish have always *hated* Jews!"

"The Irish?" Jesus. "Even if that were true, what does it have to do with anything?"

"The Irish run the police!"

Julian thought his head might explode from the hypocrisy. There'd been a moment—a long moment, which lasted a couple of years—when Mrs. Frumm regularly asserted her suspicion that Olek was antisemitic, based on nothing other than the well-publicized existence of neo-Nazis in Ukraine, where he'd grown up. Julian had been unable to make her see the insanity. Then Russia invaded Ukraine, and Putin was more provably antisemitic, so her allegiance shifted on a dime. "I stand with Ukraine," she posted on Facebook, where she had sixty friends, most of them relatives.

Julian took another pause before responding to this outburst about the Irish. "In my experience, the police have always been extremely responsive to our concerns; some might say disproportionately responsive. And what is it you're worried about? A rock through a window?"

"Well, they could overpower our doormen," Onderdonk interjected, as if it were the most obvious thing in the world. Which, in a way, it was. "Just come *rushing* in here."

"I have *many* valuables!" Mrs. Frumm collected French furniture, English porcelain, Flemish oils. "Precious stones!" Abe Frumm had been a saint; Julian couldn't imagine how he'd lived with this woman. "Furs!"

Everyone fumed for a few seconds. This was no longer productive.

"Well," Julian said, "thank you all for coming."

"That's it?!" Mrs. Frumm shouted. "That's *all* you're going to do?!"

"What else do you think we should do, Mrs. Frumm?"

"*I* don't know. That's *his* job." She was pointing at Olek, who was doing the heroic work of remaining impassive. That guy had one hard job.

"Yes, it is, Mrs. Frumm. Thank you."

"Maybe we should just *leave town*," Onderdonk said, shaking his head, shuffling out.

"I *can't*! I'm renovating Hampton Bays!"

While everyone else filed out, Julian remained seated. The super took the hint, stayed too.

"Olek?"

"Yes, Mr. Sonnenberg?"

"You don't happen to own a gun, do you?"

"I served in the military for a number of years. I have training in such situations."

Julian supposed that this nonanswer was plenty of answer. "There are worse things than a little property damage, you know."

"Yes," Olek agreed. "There are."

Julian felt the strong pull of responsibility. "The building has ample insurance, you know. Windows can easily be replaced. Lives can't."

"I understand," Olek said, but that didn't mean he agreed. Olek kept his cards closer to his chest than anyone Julian had ever met. It seemed like the guy's whole life was a secret.

A few months ago, leaving an event late at night in Chelsea, Julian had noticed Olek rushing down the far side of the street, and couldn't resist the impulse to follow. The street was dark, empty. Olek was moving abnormally fast, as if fleeing something, and glanced back over his shoulder at the corner; maybe he'd heard footsteps. Julian's stomach churned at the idea of getting caught, so he slowed, and by the time he arrived to that corner there was no sign of Olek. Julian was left with the sense that Olek had been hiding something there on West Twenty-fourth Street.

But everyone is entitled to keep their own secrets. Lord knows Julian has plenty of his own.

And maybe his suspicion of Olek, like Mrs. Frumm's baseless presumption of antisemitism, was nothing more than a prejudice. There are a lot of different types.

"Thanks, Olek," Julian said. "Please let me know if you hear anything important."

Just outside the conference room, Julian practically crashed into Zaire. "Oh, hey Zaire."

"Excuse me, Mr. Sonnenberg."

"You waiting to see Olek?"

"Me? Nah. Just passing." This was an obvious lie. The conference room was not a passage to anywhere. And Zaire knew that Julian knew this was a lie. Zaire had been eavesdropping, and he was unashamed for Julian to know it.

"Ah, okay," Julian said. "See you later, Zaire."

"Have a good day, Mr. Sonnenberg."

Ha, Julian thought. If only.

Despite his protestations in the meeting room, Julian was fully aware that tonight's demonstration was a powder keg. Not just broadly out there in the city at large, but narrowly in here at the Bohemia.

The question was if anyone was going to light the match. If anyone was going to be the match.

CHAPTER 10

APARTMENT 2A

Julian saw Whit Longworth's car double-parked at a fire hydrant directly in front of the building, with the driver-bodyguard waiting behind the wheel.

"You see my guy?" Whit had asked Julian one evening last year, back when they were on more pleasant terms. "Ex-SEAL. Licensed and carrying a Sig Sauer."

Whit was determined for Julian to know that DeMarquis was not just another gig-economy side hustler. The car was at the fire hydrant then too. The car was always at the fire hydrant, as if this public emergency facility were Whit's private parking space.

Julian and Whit were waiting for their wives at the front door, sparkling glass and shiny brass. A porter spent a shift every week polishing the Bohemia's brass. After all the hundreds of bits were polished, it was time to start again, a cycle that had been repeating ceaselessly for more than a century.

"DeMarquis convinced me that I should have one too." Whit inhaled sharply through his nostrils, like all pricks do when boasting about something repugnant. "You can't be too careful."

Julian had known Whit for a long time, they'd been doing business together for years, and Julian had always quietly despised him. But as a matter of policy Julian didn't tell anyone whom he hated. Until recently.

"*Mmm,*" Julian answered.

There was an obvious hierarchy at the Bohemia. The least luxurious units were on the lowest floors facing the side streets; the most luxurious on the highest floors facing the park. Julian's 2A had no view of anything, and barely any natural light, it was just a normal three-bedroom apartment in an abnormally posh building, for which the Sonnenbergs had paid one and a half million dollars with twenty percent down on a thirty-year fixed-rate mortgage. Most of their net worth was equity in that apartment.

On the other hand, Whit had purchased 11C-D for thirty-two million, in cash, which represented perhaps three percent of his net worth, an expenditure he could earn back in one decent quarter. Even a single great day could do it. After making the most expensive purchase in the Bohemia's history, the Longworths undertook the building's most expensive renovation. It became famous. Infamous.

Their purchase application with supporting documents was five hundred pages long. Julian had skimmed through the whole thing. So he knew that Whit owed his fortune to defense contracts, and the guy liked to bat around military lingo, but he'd never gone anywhere near service. Whitaker Longworth had trod a well-worn path from prep school to Ivy League to law school to investment bank to private equity, where he'd spearheaded a big stake in a small lab that had invented a high-density synthetic polymer—i.e., plastic—that could absorb high-velocity projectiles—i.e., bullets—even in a very thin—i.e., wearable—layer. Which is to say: a new type of body armor, dubbed Liberty Shield, patented in 1999, just in time for the post-9/11 gold rush, which was an especially deep lode for Liberty Logistics, where Whit got himself installed as CEO just after his college roommate was lured out of the private sector into a high-ranking position in DoD procurement.

That's how Whit had gotten obscenely rich: by exploiting somebody else's invention, using connections from an expensive education financed by inherited wealth, to redirect taxpayer dollars from the working class into his own bank account. Whit had talked himself into being proud of this.

Liberty became one of the most profitable defense contractors in the world, supplying both sides of many armed conflicts, as such companies do. Within a couple of years, Whit's net worth was twenty million dollars;

after another few, a hundred million; a half decade later, a quarter billion. And that was when he met the beautiful young art consultant Emily Merriweather.

"Wow!" A woman was in front of Julian, with a giant phone. "I'm a *huge* fan. Could I get a photo?"

This happened regularly in front of the Bohemia, where people were expecting to see celebrities, so that's what they saw.

"That's very kind," Julian said. "Who do you think I am?"

At the corner some guys were climbing out of a van, all of them wearing paint-splattered jeans and sweatshirts and work boots, carrying nylon backpacks and Husky tool bags, names Sharpie'd onto the dusty sides. They were all Hispanic.

"Um, Richard Gere?"

Last week Tucker Goff had been accused of being Bill Gates, much to both his joy and his chagrin; Emily Longworth was regularly mistaken for Alexandra Daddario. But the actual famous people were almost never recognized, because they were much older than their images in the public memory. The Tony-winning actor shuffled his beagle to the park in peace; no one tried to peer behind the disco icon's sunglasses. If what you want is anonymity, nothing succeeds like aging.

"Well, I appreciate it," Julian said. "Richard Gere is a good-looking guy. But he's a couple of decades older than me? At least."

The woman walked away without saying thanks, or sorry to bother you, anything. Now that Julian was no longer famous, she was no longer polite.

Julian's heart sank when he saw the screen of his ringing phone. Of all the goddamned people, of all the goddamned problems.

"Whit! Good morning."

"Don't give me that bullshit. It's six million dollars, asshole." Whit was one of those upper-class pansies who thought using profanity made him tough.

As in the board meeting, Julian forced himself to take a few beats before responding. Today, more than ever, he was in danger of losing his shit, and making his problems worse.

"You know I feel terrible, Whit. Which is why I'm refunding my fee."

"Your *fee*? I don't give a shit about your *fee*. And it's not even about the money."

When someone says it's not about the money, it's always about the money.

"I'm sorry, Whit. I am." Julian didn't love the genuflection in his voice. He knew he shouldn't apologize excessively, nor offer too many concessions; both could be construed as admissions of wrongdoing. Julian hadn't done anything wrong, not really, he'd done exactly what a client had asked him to do, despite explicit warnings and disclaimers. But Whit was not necessarily a rational player. He'd sued the developer of his previous apartment over the *weather*.

"What does sorry get me?"

"First of all, we don't know that the painting is, um . . ." Julian didn't want to say it aloud. He wouldn't be surprised if Whit were recording this call. "That's just a stray allegation—not even an allegation, just a stab in the dark, by someone who—to be frank—is not reliable." Julian had procured the painting for Whit fifteen years ago, but it was only with that recent article in the glossy magazine that anyone was questioning its provenance.

"Secondly, and let's be completely honest here: do you *really* care?"

"Of course I care!"

Julian knew that the painting's authenticity was the least of Whit Longworth's current concerns. But maybe that was precisely why the guy was calling: because this was the problem Whit thought he might solve, because Julian was the antagonist whom he was in the best position to yell at. Like any other bully, Whit was always aware of vulnerable targets.

"But you love the picture, Whit. I know you do. You love the colors, the energy, the—" Julian stopped himself before he said "the size," though that was obviously the chief attraction for Whit. This guy's previous apartment was in a needle-thin tower on Billionaires' Row, the tallest penises in America. Of course Whit Longworth cared about size.

"You love the *feel* of it, Whit. This picture is not an *investment* vehicle for you—"

"Not anymore!"

"—and so, what, now you won't bequeath it to a museum in exchange for a plaque? What you want from this canvas—from this *monumental* painting—is to bask in this painting's glow as you sit there sipping Château Margaux in your exquisite home." Julian felt a self-destructive impulse to add "with your exquisite wife," but held back. "That's the point of art, isn't it? *Enjoying* it."

Whit was silent for a beat, and Julian could tell that his point had hit home. It was time to parachute out of this conversation when this minor advantage might prevent him from crashing. Whit could very easily engulf Julian's gallery in ruinous litigation and bad press, and he had plenty of reasons to want to, even if he wasn't fully aware of all of them, at least not yet.

"I have a very low bar for litigation," Whit had once told Julian, in a tone that suggested he was proud of this instead of ashamed. More than suggested.

"Listen, Whit, I have to jump. Thank you *so much* for your time." As if Julian were the one who'd called. He felt like a lackey. "I do appreciate it."

During some of those years when Whit Longworth's fortune had risen steadily, Julian Sonnenberg's had fallen precipitously. The financial crisis hit very fast, and very hard. Julian had assumed that 1929 had led to reforms and oversight and regulations that would prevent this thing from ever happening again, but no. The collapse happened not just to greedy real-estate developers and shady bankers and the poor souls who'd been swindled into adjustable-rate mortgages for overvalued spec houses in Jacksonville and Phoenix; the collapse was not merely a generalized economic miasma. No, it was something that happened specifically to him, Julian Sonnenberg, who'd never even heard of subprime mortgages until they nearly ruined him.

Fine art is an easy expense to pull back on; the easiest. Your friends might notice if you stop NetJetting to Mustique or ordering prestige Barolos from the bottoms of leather-bound wine lists. But no one noticed if you slow your pace of art acquisition. Except your art dealer.

The art market had looked so rosy for so long that it seemed as if there were only one possible direction. So Julian had bought a family-sized apartment in this famous building, and his household's burn rate began to evoke nuclear fission. He managed to avoid disaster only narrowly, by doing a few questionable things, on behalf of a couple of questionable clients.

Once you've compromised yourself the first time, it's not that hard to justify doing it a second time, a third. Once you're guilty, you can never again be innocent. You never know when the guilt is going to catch up to you.

Their business relationship had been mutually beneficial for years, though never what Julian would call pleasurable. It was ending now, not amicably, and Julian needed to mitigate the degree of unpleasantness. Not only was Whit proud of his litigiousness, he was also a demonstrably horrible person, plus he bragged about owning a gun. He was dangerous in all sorts of ways.

Julian didn't want to believe he lived in a world where men shot each other over things like business transactions, but of course they did. Money, women, honor, betrayal, resentment, plain old antipathy—any of these could be reasons, and Julian and Whit shared all of them. Every single one.

On the one hand it seemed ludicrous, like a sensationalist plot device out of an old movie. On the other hand it also seemed obvious: Of course Whit might murder Julian. Or the other way around. Julian loathed Whit. But he would never admit that aloud, not to anyone. Though he did come awfully close, just last week.

"What?" she'd asked.

He hadn't answered.

"What?"

"I like looking at you."

She blushed. "But that's not what I asked."

"I'm sorry, what did you ask? I was too distracted by how beautiful you are. I can't focus."

She blushed more. "I asked what you hate. You never admit to hating anything."

"Oh I hate plenty of things."

"Name one," she said. "Just one."

"Well, I hate being fifty."

She rolled her eyes; her eye roll was next-level. "Of course you do. But it's better than the alternative, isn't it?"

That was before his most recent scan. Back when he thought the scan was a formality.

"What else?"

"I guess I hate my whole generation, X: we're solipsistic, greedy, hypocritical."

"Yes, you people are horrid."

"I also, of course, hate Millennials."

"I'm a Millennial."

"I make the occasional exception."

"Gee, thanks."

"I hate when people say, 'I'm based in New York,' or, 'My background is in strategy.' But as you might imagine, I come across a lot of people who say both. People who are based in New York, whose background is in strategy, are big consumers of contemporary art."

"You're on a roll. What else?"

"I'll tell you a secret."

She leaned forward. "Goody."

"I *abhor* when people order food or drinks by saying, 'I'll do.' Oh, you'll *do* an oat-milk matcha latte? Fuck you. But I can't hate all the people who say it, or there'd be almost no one left."

"I'd be left."

Under the cover of the table, her foot nuzzled against his ankle.

"I know. It was the very first thing I noticed about you."

She laughed.

"I hate social posts that begin *When you* or *This* or *You guys*. Also *partnerships*. Or *challenges*."

"So it turns out that there are plenty of things you hate, secretly."

This was when he felt the self-destructive urge to be completely honest. "Can I tell you what I hate most of all?"

"Please," she said.

He knew it was a terrible idea, but still he almost did it. Then he didn't.

"I hate social selfies in front of artwork," he said instead. "They make me apoplectic. Sometimes I think my hatred is wildly out of proportion. But at other times I'm certain that these posts signify an inversion of the very idea of art, and the demise of empathy, of humility, of dignity, of perspective—basically, a collapse of everything decent."

"The end of civilization, is what you're saying."

"Yes!" He smiled. "Yes, that's exactly what I'm saying. I'm so lucky you understand me."

She rubbed her foot against him. "Yes," she said, "you sure are."

Sometimes it was hard to tell how real this was. If they hadn't both been married to other people, it would be obvious that this was as real as anything. But they were, so it wasn't.

"If not for videos of dogs, I'd delete my accounts. Videos of dogs with kids keep me on social media. There's nothing I love more on the internet than videos of puppies with babies."

"And what else do you love?" She poked the very tip of her tongue between her teeth, which drove him crazy. "That drives me crazy," he'd once told her. "I know," she'd said.

He smiled. "Are you *fishing*?"

This was a game they played, even though they both knew it was dangerous.

"You know I am."

They were at a secluded booth in a generic bistro in Hell's Kitchen, far from the orbits of their lives. But still, New York could be awfully small, and they needed to be careful. So he leaned forward, and said it quietly, this loudest thing that anyone ever says.

CHAPTER 11

FRONT DOOR

Chicky pulled the disintegrating shirt over his head. He touched his black-and-blue rib cage with the tips of two fingers.

"Ow," he muttered, probing the bruise's contours. "Fuck."

Chicky was always getting conked by something hard. In ball games and minor cycling accidents and even at work, his shins banged by groceries and ski-boot bags and small pieces of furniture he was carrying out of someone's trunk, knuckles scraped, elbows funny-boned. But this was the first time in forever that he'd been subjected to another person striking him with the intent to do serious harm. A big strong brutal person.

His side hurt like fuck. Bruises get worse before they get better as blood continues to pool and swelling increases. Chicky suspected he also had a cracked rib, maybe more than one. But there's really no treatment for a cracked rib so no sense wasting time and money seeing a doctor.

He reached for the canister with Tiffani's name and the warning about controlled substance and habit-forming. He pushed the cap and twisted and shook out a pill. He let it sit in his palm.

Chicky had seen more than one guy start off with an Oxy or two for pain like this and before you know it they're hollowed-out junkies who live mostly at Rikers before dying. This was well known. So what Chicky really ought to do with these pills was flush them down the toilet. But he couldn't bring himself to. And he couldn't bring himself to confront why not.

But he didn't need to make any permanent choices now. He just needed to make this one choice. He dropped the pill back into its amber plastic and instead tumbled out three generic ibuprofen from a price-club tub that he no longer bothered to cover. He'd thrown away the cap.

Chicky pushed his shoulders back and chest out. He heard nitrogen bubbles popping along his spine. Satisfying, definitely. But bodies are probably not supposed to make noises like that.

He checked his phone for the first time today and found the sort of message he never wanted to see from Junior: *Yo Chicky come see me.* For a second Chicky pretended to himself that he didn't know what this was about but he was full of shit.

Be there in 30.

Chicky showered quickly and dressed quickly and ate quickly. He almost left his dirty bowl in the sink but he was constitutionally unable. Chicky rarely used the dishwasher anymore because it would take two weeks to fill and he didn't want to run half loads. So every day he used the same breakfast mug and bowl and spoon and glass. One each sitting in the drying rack. He never put them away.

On his way out Chicky checked himself in the mirror. He did not love what he saw. A middle-aged man with puffy eyes and big bags beneath and a notable shiner on his left cheek.

"Fuck," he said to himself, about himself.

It was a dozen years ago when his oldest asked Chicky to get a big mirror for the front door, to make last-minute adjustments on her way out. The habit was copied by the middle kid and then the youngest and for one chaotic year all three girls would jockey for positioning, like battling for a rebound.

Chicky had been outnumbered by four females. Lip gloss everywhere and feminine hygiene cramming the cabinets and bras drying on the shower rod. He'd pretended to be put out by the mess. But in truth he'd loved it.

His life used to be filled with things he'd loved. It could all change so fast.

Chicky double-locked his door and trotted down the stairs. Ever since Kuwait he'd suffered from mild claustrophobia so he didn't ride the small creaky stinky elevator. Someone got stuck every month. And it was only two flights. The day Chicky needed an elevator to go down two flights would be a sad-ass day indeed. Sadder-ass.

"Hey Chicky hold up."

"Oh hey Nestor." Fuck. "What's up?"

Tenements like this did not have a lobby. Just a first-floor hallway with mailboxes mounted into the walls and some taped-up legal notices that no one paid any attention to. There wasn't any room for Chicky to maneuver past his landlord-super-neighbor.

"*What's up?* You know what's up Chicky."

He did. "I'm sorry man."

"Yeah," Nestor said, "I'm sure you are. But sorry don't pay the mortgage. Sorry don't pay the taxes. Sorry don't feed my kids."

Chicky owed his landlord at least thirty thousand dollars in back rent. He'd lost track of the exact amount. He owed somewhere like forty thousand to the oncological practice and thirty-seven to one hospital and fourteen to another. Twelve on credit cards. He'd borrowed seventy against his pension. The total was more than two hundred thousand in official debt. If that were the sum of it maybe he could file for bankruptcy and run out the clock with shitty credit. Shittier.

But wait there's more. There was his kids' future schooling. Plus the thirty he owed to the loan shark that Junior had referred. That loan had begun as sixteen. Consumer debt from credit cards was famously horrible but not compared to loan sharks. To their collections protocols.

Not to mention the question of Chicky's own surgery in the future. Without which he was apparently going to *die*.

So no. Bankruptcy was not a solution. What Chicky needed was three hundred thousand dollars.

Apartments at the Bohemia cost in excess of twenty-five hundred dollars per square foot. That was for the unrenovated units that people referred to as estate sales or total guts. Three hundred thousand dollars bought a closet. An unrenovated closet.

Chicky had once overheard Mr. Longworth on a call as he was walking through the door that Chicky was holding. "It's what," Mr. Longworth was saying, "eighty million dollars? Ninety? Whatever. It's nothing."

Nothing. Longworth didn't even glance in Chicky's direction much less thank him for holding the door.

Chicky had not yet played the dead-wife card and he wasn't going to start with his landlord. Nestor himself had gout and three kids under ten and a shut-in wife who weighed four hundred pounds. In a small owner-occupied building you learn a lot about each other. Nestor knew that Tiffani had died and he'd given Chicky a long grace period. Bringing it up now would be an insult.

"I'm sorry Nestor. I really am. I'm trying."

Nestor's family lived in what would be called a garden apartment on the Upper West Side. Chicky had also heard the word *maisonette* for these units. Up here in Spanish Harlem it was called the basement.

"You know it's a process, right? Eviction?"

Chicky wished he could reassure the guy that he'd pay soon. But he couldn't. So he nodded.

"I'm very sorry Chicky. I gotta start that process."

Some guys worked at the Bohemia as a sort of holding pattern until they figured out other careers or landed in a trade or started their own business. These guys kept their heads down and banked their paychecks and lived with their parents. They were trading their youth for the promise of something in the future. But for some guys this was a lie they told themselves.

Not Chicky. He was a lifer. This was a job you could do until you retired. Or died. That was Chicky's plan. As far as he had a plan.

Chicky had never asked for much and he still didn't. His has been a life of modest expectations and modest pleasures. A good life. One that Chicky could never have imagined back when he was a young knucklehead. A life that maybe he didn't wholly deserve. Which was why he'd tried so damned hard, for so damned long, to keep it.

As each of his girls left for college his apartment grew bigger and tidier and lonelier and lonelier. On the other hand his girls also left him bursting with pride. Chicky couldn't stop telling everyone—umpires and bartenders and strangers on the subway. "My youngest"—getting out his phone, swiping through photos of young women in party dresses and graduation robes. "Ivy League. Can you believe it?" Chicky was always ready to share this pleasure on the flimsiest of excuses. Or none at all.

But not with the residents. This was a line you didn't cross. You didn't want them to think for one second that you were trying to be one of them, Hey maybe I'll see you on Parents' Day. It was an unspoken line but everyone on either side knew it was there.

You could know what these people were proud of. You could know their shameful secrets too, the dirty details of their most private problems. But you could not let them know yours. Little things? Sure. Stiff knee, bad weather, tough loss. But these people didn't want to hear about your past-due rent or your mother-in-law's Alzheimer's. And they certainly didn't want to hear about your dead wife. Because if you were a human who was as full and as real as they were, then why were you holding their doors and carrying their bags and collecting their dry-cleaned dresses and takeout Chinese and the stinking steaming piles of their dogs' shit?

No one wanted to ask those questions or everything fell apart.

Absolutely everything.

CHAPTER 12

APARTMENT 2A

There are many different New Yorks, with many different centers, for many different people. Julian's center has mostly been right here at the Bethesda Fountain, equidistant from Fifth Avenue and Central Park West where he has lived for nearly his entire life, except for college then that year in Paris then his sojourn down in SoHo, back when everyone in the art world seemed to live downtown, he was always running into people at Jerry's and Raoul's, beer and burgers at Fanelli's, coffee at Dean & Deluca, foreign films at the Angelika and classics at Film Forum, gallery openings on Greene Street and Wooster and over in gritty shitty Alphabet City, live music at Pianos and the Knitting Factory, late nights at Lucky Strike and later nights at Max Fish, staggering home at four-thirty, hangovers that seemed to last a week, but worth it.

Julian loved those years, the excitement of being young and single, the possibility of meeting someone who'd put him in a good mood for a week, a month, a year. But the flip side was a dateless Saturday, or no one on New Year's Eve, parties he wasn't invited to, the pernicious suspicion that tonight was a precursor to permanence, alone forever.

All the best things in life come with a lot that isn't. Maybe that's what makes them the best.

His fourth-floor walk-up—seventy-four stairs—was an illegal sublet of an illegal loft, and you'd have thought that the doubly illegal would make the rent cheaper, but Julian was barely getting by. Barely getting by was, for a while, cool.

Cool is nothing if not ephemeral, and for Julian SoHo lost it when the rag trade invaded, the same luxury boutiques as uptown on Madison, on rue Saint-Honoré or via Condotti, places where the same people did the same things for the same reason: because they couldn't think of anything better to do with their time, or their money. Hundred-dollar socks, thousand-dollar scarves.

This was the same moment when Julian felt the flower of youth slipping away. He'd done his time, he'd worn his New Republic, he'd climbed countless flights of interminable stairs to unfinished lofts with exposed pipes and kitchen bathtubs, everyone wearing all black all the time, chain-smoking, professing that exercise was unbearably bourgeois, "I never go above Fourteenth Street," an especially widespread refrain among recent transplants, trying with the fervor of the newly converted to prove how much they belonged, importing their provincialism from the provinces, pretending it was cosmopolitan.

Julian moved back to the uptown world of doormen and dry cleaners and weekly dinners with his parents, the everyday serenity of the park's dewy footpaths on mornings like this, everything in autumnal splendor, perfect.

He missed all those open doors of youth. This was one of the main reasons he'd been doing what he'd been doing, despite vowing that he never would.

You have no idea, when you're young, what it's going to be like when you're not.

At the bandshell, preschoolers were arrayed in a semicircle around a guitar-playing man and a woman who was holding up cue cards with lyrics. Each kid stood in front of a stroller, each stroller flanked by a nanny, every kid was white, every caregiver a woman of color.

Ellington was perched on the edge of a bench, looking impatient.

"Morning," Julian said. The partners have a long-standing meeting on Tuesday mornings, away from the gallery, the ringing phones, the perked-up ears of the gallery girl, usually over breakfast at an Upper East Side hotel, a public place, surrounded by clients or potential clients, an opportunity to see people, to be seen.

"Why are we here, El?"

"Murray called last night." Even here in the park, Ellington glanced around to make sure there were no eavesdroppers. "He's worried about Whit Longworth."

"Murray is a lawyer, it's his job to worry."

"Are you saying you're *not* worried?"

Julian gave an exaggerated shrug—yes, of course, but what can you do? There are always going to be lunatics.

Ellington raised his eyebrows. "Longworth is one litigious, vindictive, and insane motherfucker, and he's furious at you, Julie. For, I might add, *good reason.* And do I remember correctly that you rejected this guy's renovation plans in your co-op?"

El didn't know much about white-glove co-ops. He'd never bought an apartment, which Julian suspected was because he was afraid of getting rejected. El had grown up in St. Louis, and had never stepped foot in New York until Julian brought him home for freshman Thanksgiving. That Wednesday night they'd gone to watch the balloons get inflated, along with thousands of other people who were themselves getting inflated, joints and one-hitters and half-pints of Bacardi mixed into bottles of Coke. All college students were home for the holiday, so it was like a group reunion for private schools, kids Julian had known his whole life, teammates and rivals, first kisses and lost virginity. It seemed like all of them were there outside the Museum of Natural History.

"Jesus," Ellington had said, looking around. "I thought college was white."

They spent the rest of that weekend at the Whitney and the MoMA and the Met, at underage-friendly bars in the East Village and Morningside Heights, a Saturday-night party in Gramercy where Julian bought an eighth from the brother of an ex-girlfriend, a guy who'd been selling drugs since middle school while also getting straight As at elite educational institutions.

At one A.M., walking through Washington Square, someone called out "Hey." Julian turned to see two uniformed cops, nightsticks dangling, pointing at the joint his hand. "Put that out."

Julian glanced at the joint as if its appearance was a mystery. "Yes sir." He carefully scraped the ember against the pavement as the cops walked away.

"We're from different planets," Ellington said. Julian was tucking his illegal substance into the cellophane of a pack of cigarettes. This was decades before legalization. "I have no idea how gravity works on this one."

Ellington was paying for college with scholarships and student loans and work-study jobs in the dining halls. He was one of the kids wearing aprons and hairnets serving classmates on the other side of the sneezeguard, the other side of the class divide.

"You know if it was me holding that joint, I'd have gotten arrested."

Julian wasn't so sure. Washington Square had always been like Amsterdam. But the legal reality didn't matter as much as what El believed. Discrimination was his reality, selective enforcement, incarceration. He spent every day aware that his life could be ruined, over nothing, just because he was Black. They were eighteen, and Julian was a little drunk and more than a little high, when he decided what he was going to do with his life. And he never really changed his mind.

Three decades later, the divide had narrowed perhaps, and definitely shifted its axis. But it was still obviously there, you could see it right over there at the bandshell playgroup. Everywhere, if you looked closely enough.

"It wasn't me who rejected Longworth's plans," Julian said. "It was the board. That's one of the points of co-ops: to prevent shareholders from making irresponsible decisions."

Cooperatives had a lot of rules. But not condominiums, which was why the highest-end new construction in Manhattan were all condos. Elsewhere in America, condo was a disparagement. In Manhattan, condos were where billionaires could do whatever the fuck they wanted.

"Can you hear yourself, Julie? You didn't want to let this guy tinker in your little club, yet you still take his money?"

"I wouldn't describe our relationship as me taking his money."

"I'd sure hate you. And you say that our lawyer is *overreacting*?"

"Of course I'm worried. But I'm trying to project calm—to Murray, Longworth, his lawyers, *you*—because I think the way out of this problem is to treat the situation as if it's routine."

"Routine?"

"I warned the guy that proceeding would be at his own risk. He was adamant that he wanted to take it. Plenty of people make the same decision. Feigning ignorance now is bullshit. Whit Longworth is far from the only reckless collector, and he's not even that reckless. Just aggressive."

Julian could tell that Ellington wasn't buying this.

"If you ski expert terrain," Julian continued, "and then you go beyond the trail boundaries—if you bomb right past the warnings that you're leaving the ski area—if you do all that, then break your leg? You can't sue, can you? These are the inherent risks of skiing."

Ski mountains were among the many places where Ellington often found himself the only Black man. Ski mountains especially. Every winter El blew an exorbitant sum to spend a day riding helicopters to empty mountaintops specifically to do this exact thing: be an aggressive, risky skier.

"Would it surprise you that every year forty thousand people in America get injured skiing off-trail?" Julian asked.

El shrugged.

"Neither would I, but I just made up that number. There's no way to find out, just as there's no way to know how many people engage in risky art acquisitions. Longworth was very specific about what he wanted, and I told him, many times, that it's not always possible to find exactly what you want. Of course it is, he said. Everything is possible. It's just a question of price."

This was something that rich guys said all the time. Ellington had heard it too.

"You can talk sense into people about some things, but there's no way to talk anyone out of a whole worldview like that. Longworth was fully aware of the risks."

"Was he though? *Really?*"

"Someone else would have said yes, El."

"Maybe. Then this would be their problem, Julie, not ours. Not"—Ellington glared—"*mine.*"

"You're right. This was my mistake, and I'm sorry, I am. But let's remember that I didn't make this deal for personal gain. I did this to keep our business afloat. And anyway, here we are."

"Here *you* are."

Julian recoiled. "Yes. Here I am." He wondered, not for the first time, if the end of their partnership was imminent. "Listen, El, I'm not going to insult you with empty optimism. But I do believe this will blow over. Longworth will be appeased by a return of our—*my*—fee. He'll be reluctant to bring this into the open of lawsuits, because the publicity would make him look like a sap. This guy has a billion dollars. He's willing to eat six million to preserve his reputation. Plus his wall is still adorned with a great painting. Which might very well be genuine."

"You don't believe that, do you?"

"It's not impossible. And as long as Longworth keeps the canvas hung, no one will know one way or the other. It won't ever make a difference."

"That's a pretty casual attitude about a pretty substantial crime."

Julian had a sudden worry that Ellington was recording this conversation, that he'd pretended to worry about eavesdroppers only as a smoke screen. They'd been best friends since college, but Julian knew that it was the strongest love that could turn into the most intense hate.

"You're right, El, I'm just trying to be cute. It *would* make a difference. I *am* concerned. I *do* apologize. But let me ask you, in all seriousness: what is it you think I should do about it?"

"I honestly don't know, Julie. But I don't think it would be fair if my career—my whole life—got sucked down into the vortex of your fuckup with your frenemy."

"I won't let that happen."

Ellington held Julian's eye for a few seconds, maybe waiting for more explanation, maybe assessing what was already there.

"I promise," Julian added, and, in the moment, he almost believed it.

Ellington glanced at his watch. "We should get going."

Julian stood, buttoned his jacket.

"Are you okay?" Ellington asked. "Physically?"

"Yeah, why?"

"You just made a noise that sounded like pain."

Julian was no longer always aware of the involuntary noises that emanated from him when he arose from a chair, when he bent to tie his shoe, when he did anything, really. Sometimes he noticed his groans, and thought, who the fuck is this old man? Oh, right: it's me.

♦ ♦ ♦

They walked beneath the towering canopy of American elms, the largest grove in the world. These trees had evaded Dutch elm disease thanks solely to their isolation in the center of the largest city in America, buffered by the expanse of concrete jungle that's inhospitable to the beetles that transmit the fungus that killed sixty million trees. Sometimes what looks like a problem is the solution.

Ellington's vintage Jaguar was waiting at a metered parking space. Last year, when he was shopping for a classic car, El had asked Julian to accompany him up to Scarsdale to scout the Jaguar.

"But I don't know anything about cars," Julian had said. "Literally nothing. People throw around these phrases, cylinders, V-whatevers. I have no idea what they're referring to. Rack-and-pinion steering, I used to hear that all the time. Is that still a thing?"

Ellington had chuckled, but hadn't answered. He probably didn't know either.

"So if you're looking for someone to ask questions about fuel injection and whatnot, I'm going to disappoint you. Sorely."

"No, Jules. I just need a ride."

"Come on, El. That's not true."

"You're right. What I need is to show up with an unthreatening white guy."

They took Julian's Volvo wagon, which he leased so he could trade in his cars every three years, before any problems arose. When they pulled up to the house, the widow who was selling the car was out front with her arms crossed, looking dubious. She glanced from Julian to Ellington and back again, then chose to direct her question to the white man. "Are you that guy who's interested in my husband's old car?"

"No," Ellington piped up, with his biggest, most ingratiating smile. Julian knew how much that smile hurt. How much it cost. "I am."

The Jaguar was a thoroughly impractical car that required constant and expensive maintenance. And it was spectacularly ostentatious, everybody on the street noticed it, all the time. They noticed the people who were in it.

So maybe the car wasn't impractical, after all. It depended on what you were trying to accomplish.

CHAPTER 13

APARTMENT 11C-D

Emily descended from the sunny leafy street to the dank subway, the comingling of mold and marijuana and stagnant water. She waited up against the wall, away from the platform edge. Someone could push you onto the tracks just because they didn't like the way you looked, just because they were crazy. Emily also never sat on the subway, never wore earphones, never let down her alertness.

As she waited for the train, she scrolled through her phone, bestowing positivity—*Lovely! Fabulous! Adorable!* From the advent of social media it had been obvious to Emily that she should friend everyone, like everything. She wanted to be liked, and this was how you got there: you told other people you liked them, you nodded at what they said, you smiled, touched their arms, fire-emoji'd their posts. It wasn't rocket science. The tech evolved quickly to facilitate passive enthusiasm, and soon Emily barely needed to use words, or her brain, she could just thumbs-up and heart while exercising, watching TV. Emojis streamlined the whole operation.

Some people used social media for the opposite: to tell the world what they hated. Like Justin Pugh here, posting a video of using an assault rifle to shoot up a political poster. Emily did not want to go through the world looking for things to be scared of, but with Pugh she had to worry that it was personal, and specific. She had to keep an eye on that monster.

The train's arrival was preceded by a gust of stale air, rattling tracks and a swelling roar, a million pounds hurtling through the concrete tunnel. Sometimes at night, in her bedroom nearly two hundred feet above the tracks, she could feel the vibration. Like an earthquake.

If you listened to public radio, if you read *The New York Times*, maybe you weren't exposed to stories about street crime. But the *Daily News*, the *Post*, local TV, the business press: those were full of horror stories, nowhere in this city was safe, no one immune from being stabbed, shot, shoved in front of a train. If you were out in this urban world, you were at risk. And it wasn't just the media, it was a gathering panic in the school-mom echo chamber, in which plenty of people responded by bunkering inside their privilege.

Were the crime fears overblown? Or underestimated? The statistics seemed to be headed in the wrong direction, but numbers were easy to manipulate, no longer the same types of facts they used to be. There was no such thing anymore as an incontestable fact. Plus numbers don't matter, not really. One in a million are low odds, sure. But not if you're the one.

She dropped her scarf and sunglasses into her tote, tucked her hair under a Yankees cap, checked her reflection in the window. Yes, it would be hard to recognize this person as Emily Longworth.

When Emily decided to wear a cap up here, she realized that the ones in her closet were all unacceptable—Aspen, the US Open, a hotel in the south of France where the bill had come to nine thousand dollars per night. So she'd purchased this one from a sidewalk vendor. The Mets seemed like too much of a fan allegiance, but the Yankees meant nothing more than you needed a hat.

It's not as if she were famous, not in the contemporary sense of celebrity—she wasn't an influencer, a performer, a public personality. But she appeared regularly in society pages on red carpets, step-and-repeats, even video clips on the local news. Emily was the type of New York society woman who was universally known within her tribe, and to the sorts of outsiders who paged through the party pictures in *Town & Country*.

None of these people were likely to be on this C train, but you never know. After all, Emily was here. She imagined she was the exception, but that's probably what everyone thinks, isn't it? I'm exceptional.

The door at the end of the car slammed open.

Just the sound itself made Emily's adrenaline surge, her heart race, her breath catch.

Anyone who goes careening between cars is, de facto, a threat. All dozen passengers turned in unison. Was anyone surprised by what they saw? Emily wasn't.

The woman staggering through the door was draped in an unseasonably heavy coat that was holey and filthy. She wore a single beat-up boot with no laces. Her other foot was bare, grimy, scabbed-over, and actively bleeding. She paused, swayed, and took a drag from a tiny stub of cigarette.

Emily wished she would have noticed all those details before she noticed the color of the woman's skin. But that's the first thing everyone always sees, isn't it? About everyone, everywhere, all the time. That's everyone's first identity—before gender, before age, before anything.

"Help me," this woman said, trying to meet the eyes of passengers, failing. Everyone knew the rules: do not make eye contact, do not engage, do not antagonize. But also: do not show fear, do not make yourself a target. Similar to how to avoid bear attacks: do not look like prey.

Emily felt in her pocket for the reassuring heft, the lethality of it.

"Please, help me." This woman exuded a miasma of tobacco and urine and feces, the particular pungency of living on the street. She was sobbing.

Emily kept her eyes forward and down, not looking at this woman directly but also not looking away, affording herself plenty of peripheral vision. Emily's heart was beating like mad.

"Won't anybody please, *please* help me?" Seeking out one averted eye after another.

Emily wrapped her hand around the smooth cool metal. It had long been illegal to carry a box cutter on the subway, unless you were traveling to or from employment where you needed the tool; a very specific circumstance. Box cutters also couldn't be displayed openly in stores, couldn't be sold to anyone under twenty-one. Box cutters were more regulated in New York City than firearms were in most of America. It was not illegal to make your own a machine gun.

"*Please!*" Much louder than a normal plea, startling all the passengers.

Emily held her breath against the aroma, and the fear. This was one of the rare times when she almost wished she'd accepted her husband's gun. Almost.

"Why won't anybody *help me*? *FUCK!*"

Last week, in Midtown, a man had wielded a machete. A *machete*.

Emily put her thumb on the knife's switch as the woman lurched by, bawling.

"PLEASE!"

Then she was five feet past, ten, and Emily exhaled, and moved her thumb. Emily's emotion switched from fright to sympathy, her concern from herself to this poor woman. Self-preservation was an instinct, not a matter of choice, but still Emily felt guilty for being afraid.

At the far end of the car, the woman slumped against a door, and turned to face the other passengers. She banged the side of her head against the door's window, loud, violent, terrifying. Everyone glanced up at the noise, then quickly turned their eyes away. No one wanted to see this.

"Help me."

She banged again, more brutally.

"Help me."

This thud was yet louder, a cracking sound too, and one of the passengers gasped.

She started rhythmically banging, as if trying to break the window, or her head, or both. Tears were streaming down her face, carving glistening paths through her ashen skin.

These days there was a lot of evident distress in New York City, but this was exceptionally dire. Emily felt actual pain course through her.

The subway came to a stop, the doors opened. A few people glanced toward the woman, now that it was possible to escape.

"*FUCK Y'ALL!*" So loud that it felt like a physical attack. Everyone flinched, or gasped. A middle-aged man stood up, but didn't go anywhere. Just getting ready.

"Fuck every single motherfucking one of you motherfuckers!"

She lurched out, and the doors closed, and the subway started moving, and everyone looked down. Everyone was ashamed, of everything.

At the far end of the station, it looked like someone was bundled up in a sleeping bag, surrounded by plastic shopping bags. Emily sidestepped what appeared to be human feces on the platform. "Oh god," she muttered. Sometimes it was hard to feel sympathy. Those were probably the times when it was most important to try.

Emily climbed out of the subway into what seemed like a different New York, just a few miles north of her own, up past the gentrified parts of Harlem. The architecture up here was different, the people, the shops, the churches, the languages.

When Emily had come to her very first shift, she'd taken a taxi. She'd felt herself being watched as the taxi pulled to the Frederick Douglass Boulevard curb, as she walked across the sidewalk, breezed through the pantry's door in front of dozens of people out in the January bluster, waiting to collect donated food so they wouldn't starve. Emily could see women leaning in, *Look at this woman, who does she think she is, arriving to a food pantry in a motherfucking taxi?* Emily had never appreciated just how shameful luxury could be. Even the small luxury of a taxi. Thank god she'd resisted Whit's suggestion to take the Maybach and driver.

The next time, Emily considered asking a taxi to drop her nearby. But if you have to lie about it, you shouldn't be doing it. This was one of Emily's guiding principles. Though in one discrete area—discreet too—she'd been breaking this rule regularly, which made her a hypocrite. But this bit of hypocrisy was the only thing keeping her sane the past year.

Although: was this sane? Maybe sanity wasn't the operative consideration. What this hypocrisy had made her was happy. Or less unhappy.

Emily worried that her unhappiness was a weakness, a neediness, a selfishness, an indulgence. And unhappiness about her marriage, that was a betrayal on top of everything, and an ingratitude. Ungrateful was at the top of the list of things Emily didn't want people to think of her. So she never told anyone. Not her oldest friend Skye, not her mother, not anyone.

She'd never realized how oppressive it was to keep this secret, not until she finally unburdened herself.

There were a lot of ways in which Emily was betraying her husband, and she was astounded at how little guilt she felt. This in itself occasionally made her feel bad—guilty for not feeling guilty. But not very guilty, and not very often.

She was, after all, married to a villain.

"Here," Whit had said, after she'd admitted that she'd been riding the subway. "Take this."

"Oh for the love of god, Whit." Emily raised her hand to push the gun away, but held back. She didn't want to even touch it.

"Please. Do it for me."

"Are you out of your *mind*?"

"This city is going to hell. Crime is skyrocketing. The police are more worried about being accused of racism than preventing crime. We need to take personal responsibility for our safety."

Whit had gotten fond of the phrase *personal responsibility* during the pandemic. Although he'd been pro-vaccine, he'd been very anti-mandate.

"What scenario are you picturing with that thing? Do you think an intruder is going to show up here, and you're going to—what?—hear him coming, and race back to the office, and unlock the safe, and load the ammunition, and race back out here and . . . and what, Whit?"

She could see his jaw twitching.

"Are you going to *open fire*? Put a bullet through the wall, get rid of Gareth once and for all?"

They certainly didn't need any more square footage in this apartment, but still Whit fantasized about swallowing Gareth Blankenship's adjoining 11B, for no reason other than expansion in the abstract, manifest destiny. Whit had internalized the fiction that everything needed to expand to survive, a pseudo-capitalist principle that he believed applied not just to his company but to his own real-estate holdings, the size of his family, everything. More is more. He'd wanted a third kid, maybe a fourth too, but Emily had let him down.

"I'm prepared to protect my wife and children. My property."

She came very close to laughing at him, but resisted. It can be a dangerous mistake to laugh at a man's ridiculousness. Whit thought of himself as a tough guy, he talked admiringly about tough guys. But the only peril Whit had ever faced had been self-imposed choices along the lines of drunk driving and off-piste skiing. He'd never been in a violent altercation, he'd never been worried about his physical safety, not in a serious way, just a wimpy one. Flu shots, double-black-diamonds: these were the sorts of obstacles Whit had confronted.

Emily didn't mind this, per se. She didn't assign much value to physical bravery. In fact she thought physical bravery often corresponded with stupidity. What infuriated her wasn't that Whit was not tough, it was that he pretended he was.

"Well," she'd said, "I hope we never learn how that works out. But regardless, I've told you before that I'm never going to touch that thing, so please don't bring it up again. It makes me feel like you're not listening to me. And promise me, Whit, that you'll keep it in the safe. *All* the time."

He rolled his eyes as he swiped up the weapon. This was back during Whit's flirtation with macho, and weaponry, back when he was still doing business with Justin Pugh, before the guy became an undeniable liability. Pugh felt squeezed by resentments from either side: he was against billionaires, but only to the extent that he couldn't be one; he was against the American poor who didn't look like him, the Hispanics and Asians and Africans—Africans!—who were invading his swath of exurb, taking good jobs—*good* jobs?—while driving up the cost of living, the cost of labor, the cost of healthcare, the cost of hamburgers. Any problem that could be blamed on someone else.

Pugh's limited success in the world had been predicated on his willingness to do anything, to risk his neck, to look like a fool. This willingness could be an asset, and it definitely had been, for Pugh himself and for Whit too. But it could also be a liability, for Pugh, and for his allies, and of course for his enemies. Whit had recently become one those enemies.

"Whit. *Promise.*"

Emily watched her husband march away like a sulking boy, and couldn't help but wonder what Whit was really trying to accomplish with the weapon. Why was he trying to get his wife to carry a gun? How was he envisaging it would be used? And who was it who'd get shot?

Fifty people were waiting out on the sidewalk for the doors to open. The pantry's selections were best in the morning, so that's when attendance was best. Half the people were elderly, many of them leaning on shopping carts, others carrying plastic bags. There were also young mothers clutching small children, or standing behind strollers that they'd need to wrestle up and down the stairs. Emily had seen these strollers in the corner store, eighteen bucks. The last stroller Emily purchased had cost two thousand dollars, it was made in Italy, hand-stitched leather. She'd eventually donated it to a Long Island charity that helped the immigrants who labored as landscapers and contractors, and on farms and vineyards.

"*Buenos días, Mathias,*" Emily said to the security guard, who held the metal-cage door open.

"*Buenos días,*" he said.

Emily had taken eleven school years' French, and a couple of semesters of Italian for her year of gazing at *Madonna e bambino*s in Florence. But French and Italian were not especially practical in New York City. Emily had picked up a little Spanish along the way, by osmosis, then she learned more when she started volunteering here, at first forms of politeness, and numbers, foods. Then she'd hired a tutor.

She walked back to the meeting room—plastic table, folding chairs, fluorescent lights, a wall lined with metal lockers that were dinged and dented, evidence of attacks with hammers, crowbars. A single window with grimy chicken-wire glass and rusty security bars faced a rubbish-strewn courtyard that was ringed by concertina wire. Everything contributed to a penitentiary aura.

Emily took off the suede boots that made Morgan swoon, put on canvas tennis shoes from a chic boutique in Palais-Royal, the type of brand that wouldn't be recognized by anyone who did not actually shop in Paris. She looked dorky now, wearing a skirt with sneakers. But dorky was fine. What she did not want to look was glamorous.

She deposited her blazer and boots into a relatively intact locker, pushed closed her Master lock, tugged, tugged again. For a while Emily also stowed her jewelry in a locker, but the jewelry had made her extra-uncomfortable on the subway, and out on the streets, so she'd stopped wearing jewelry altogether, as well as anything with any logos. Emily didn't own any handbags that cost less than five thousand dollars, so she'd sifted through her collection of giveaway totes—WNYC, *The New Yorker*, MoMA—before settling on a bag emblazoned with Joan Didion smoking a cigarette.

She plucked a dingy canvas apron from a wall peg, and affixed a sticky-backed ID tag on which she wrote GRACE. Emily used her middle name here. None of the clients or staff would recognize her from the society pages, or the magazine features, no one would know which boards she sat on, which exhibitions and scholarships she sponsored, how much money she'd donated to what foundations, which designer she wore to which gala. But with the other volunteers, you never knew. Her life's details could be collected in mere seconds, all you needed was a first name and a willingness to wade through search results. But you needed more than her middle name.

Emily was conflicted about the evasiveness of hiding her identity. She was conflicted about everything here, it was always a complex mixture, it was heartwarming and heartbreaking, uplifting and depressing, exuberantly hopeful and unbearably sad, it made Emily proud but also ashamed, grateful and humble but also superior and patronizing, she almost always felt like crying, and sometimes couldn't prevent it—the addled old man who couldn't understand the point system, the teenage mom of two tiny kids who had to forgo the milk so she could keep the dried beans.

On the worst days Emily would go home, open her calfskin checkbook, and use a nine-hundred-dollar pen to make a fresh donation, even while she knew this wasn't going to cure anyone's dementia, it wasn't going to pay anyone's rent. It was just going to make Emily's own self feel a tiny bit better, which in itself could make her feel worse.

If you have essentially unlimited money, charity is not an actual sacrifice. But what else was there? Emily was doing what she could. Sometimes she managed to convince herself that she was making the world a better place, but she also never forgot that her household was definitely making it worse. Another irreconcilable tension. Which could very well describe every single facet of her life.

The title of her memoirs: *Irreconcilable Tensions*.

Emily's children had never been on a commercial flight. Not one. A couple of years ago, the day before spring break, one of the kids turned to Emily. "Mrs. Longworth?" Dahlia asked. Her sisters were Rose and Lily. "Are you going to Colorado tomorrow?"

"Yes dear. We are."

"When's your wheels-up?"

Emily could see one of the scholarship moms raise an eyebrow. That was a low point.

Today's day-tripping volunteers were a corporate team in matching T-shirts on their "Giving Back" day, young people with brand-name MBAs and brand-name khakis who'd work the morning in the pantry, the afternoon in a Spanish Harlem elementary school, then migrate en masse to bars in Yorkville or Murray Hill to get expensively drunk, and by ten P.M. they'd be eating sushi, or scrolling through Tinder, or both at once, self-satisfied that they'd done their bit to help the less fortunate, and tomorrow could return to their regularly scheduled programming of generating wealth for the already wealthy.

"I trade bonds," one of these guys said to Emily, checking her out. His name tag identified him as Buckley, and she could tell just by looking at him that he'd attended Wharton.

Emily didn't begrudge the token volunteerism. It certainly didn't matter to the clients. No one cared what motivated Emily to be here instead of with the other school moms, drinking skinny lattes and debating international vacations and household decorations and college applications, giving each other advice about architects in the Hamptons and chiropractors in Manhattan, about juice cleanses and Pilates instructors, resorts on the Mayan Riviera and safaris in Kenya, interspersed with lamentations about the disappointing service, the aggressive panhandlers, the difficulty of getting an appointment with the dermatologist everyone goes to, who accepts no health insurance and has a personal net worth of two hundred million dollars.

No one cared why Emily was here. It was the work that mattered.

That's what she told herself.

CHAPTER 14

FRONT DOOR

The streets of El Barrio were buzzing. Music was streaming from portable speakers on benches in the projects and through the windows of kitchens and blasting from systems in the trunks of souped-up Hondas with guys leaning on hoods, bass thumping so low you could feel it through the pavement.

Delivery workers were everywhere. There were the lone wolves from FedEx and UPS and USPS but mostly it was Amazon teams. They reminded Chicky of the crack dealers who were everywhere in the eighties when that was the job if you had zero experience and minimal skills. At some point or another almost everyone had been tempted to deal or use or both. Today's version was feeding different addictions. If college was good for anything it was for getting out of the way of the irreversible bad choices. The sorts that many of Chicky's friends made back in the day, that Chicky flirted with till he got wise. Though it was never too late to make bad irreversible choices.

At Junior's the riot gate was still down but the doorway cutout was open. Chicky rapped and waited. It was one thing to be impatient with deadbeat Alberto. Junior was another story.

C.C. opened the door.

"What's good C.C." Chicky's nerves were vibrating. Being summoned meant trouble.

"He's in back."

Chicky walked past the kid who mops in the mornings, Richie or Rico or something else that means rich. A fucked-up name for a kid who mops floors instead of going to eleventh grade.

"My man." Chicky held up his fist for a bump. The kid obliged.

There was rarely a moment when people weren't working at Junior's. On Fridays and Saturdays the after-hours business stretched till dawn. By the time the night's final customers were leaving the next day's employees were arriving to take deliveries and prep food and scrub surfaces. Junior was a stickler for hygiene.

"Tomás!" Chicky called as he passed the kitchen pass. The prep cook chopped a hundred pounds of onions seven mornings per week fifty weeks per year. *"Qué pasa?"*

Tomás waved his knife in reply.

Then Chicky was in the back room's doorway. This was the room that smelled the least like beer.

"Hey Boss." Chicky waited for permission to enter. Junior may be Chicky's cousin out there in the world at ball games and christenings and family barbecues. But in here he was the Boss. At the Bohemia Oleksander was the Boss. At home Tiffani had been the Boss.

"Chicky. *Ven aquí.*" Junior was a large man with a large jowly face and large puffy lips and large fingers like chorizos. Even Junior's ears were large in a way that bothered Chicky. The lobes especially. Chicky tried not to look at Junior's ears. *"Siéntate."*

In front of Junior was a pile of receipts and another of cash and some marble notebooks bound with thick red rubber bands that he recycled from bunches of carrots or celery. For a guy with money Junior was one frugal motherfucker. He was owner or part-owner or active investor or silent partner in dozens of enterprises. None encouraged credit cards or did much in the way of official bookkeeping with spreadsheets or software. That's what these Meads were for.

"Shit," Junior had explained to Chicky years ago, "the president *brags* about avoiding taxes. But my Puerto Rican ass is supposed to pay full retail to the IR-fucking-S? Fuck no, uh-uh."

Chicky had never declared his tips but didn't have a choice about wages. "Tax avoidance," Canarius had explained, "is one of many privileges accessible to people who don't need them."

"You doing okay these days Chicky?"

"Yeah." No one ever wanted an honest answer to that question. "You know."

Junior nodded. He'd had his own experience of loss. Though not a wife. That's different.

"Money okay?"

"Yeah," Chicky lied. "All right." He nodded vigorously. Money was obviously not okay. That was why he was here. Being a bouncer wasn't a fucking hobby. But Junior didn't probe. Another thing no one wanted to hear about was anyone else's financial problems. Especially not when they were in positions to help but wouldn't. Giving Chicky a job was as far out on a limb as Junior would crawl. Which wasn't very far. It wasn't even a limb.

"Chicky." Junior's tone shifted. "I hear you got into it Saturday night." Junior had been away for a long weekend in San Juan. "I can see it too." He waved his meaty paw at Chicky's cheek.

"Not a big deal. I been hit worse." Chicky added a smile for emphasis.

Junior nodded but with no smile. Chicky's bad vibe was getting worse.

"You know who that was?"

"The guy that hit me? Nah. You?"

"Yeah Chick." Junior leveled a serious look at Chicky. "That was El Puño."

"Fuck. I didn't know." That explained the surprising force of those punches. The Fist had boxed Golden Gloves before he put his hands to work as an enforcer. Then he became a dealer himself. There were still plenty of drug addictions that could be fed for much more profit than delivering for Amazon.

"You know him, Boss?"

"We're not friends if that's what you asking. I know him to nod to. Not to intervene."

One thing Chicky had always appreciated about Junior was that he never left shit open to interpretation. Junior wasn't necessarily nice but he was clear.

"What can I do Boss?"

"How'd it go down?"

"What have you heard?"

"Don't matter what I heard. Just you tell me what happened."

"Okay." Chicky nodded. "The dude's hands were all over waitresses.

And not just a little side brush of a titty. He was making a *spectacle*. Practically begging to be tossed. *Begging*, Boss."

Junior continued counting out twenties. He never wanted to hear excuses.

"So Anna comes to me to complain and *while* she's talking to me I watch this dude grab a fistful of Layla's ass. It would have been funny if it weren't so fucked-up. What could I do? I walk over and tell this guy politely that he's being rude. He tells me to fuck off. So I ask him—politely—to leave. He repeats that I should fuck off."

Junior didn't respond. He put the twenties in an envelope and started another count.

"So I take his arm and just like that"—snapped his fingers—"he hooks me in the ribs and then again to the ribs and then jab to the face—*pop*—and I stumble backward. Those were solid punches and I'm a little dazed and before I know it a bunch of people jump between us. One of his boys pulls a piece and waves it around for everyone to see. People start screaming and hiding behind furniture and shit. The whole crew bounces. Cursing me all the way out the door like it was *me* who was the asshole."

Chicky was hoping for Junior to jump in to commiserate. But no.

"So this crew busts out to the sidewalk and wouldn't you know it right into a couple cops. Twirling their nightsticks and shit like it's the nineteen-fucking-fifties. I mean *right into* them."

Junior was failing to see the humor.

"I follow them out to be a, y'know, a witness. As soon as I step out I can see that one of these boys is still holding his piece. So the cops freak the fuck out and draw down. Now people are yelling their asses off, scattering. The cops are calling for backup. It's mayhem."

Junior closed his eyes and dropped his head.

"Two of the crew are shoved into a squad car. The others are let go." All the while the guy who turned out to be El Puño stood out there glaring at Chicky. Chicky chooses not to share this additional detail with Junior.

"Is it possible that anyone could have a different interpretation of the events?"

"All due respect Boss? No. Anyone who says different is lying. Is anyone saying different?"

"All's I heard is that there were words and punches and you threw El

Puño out of my bar and he's pissed." Junior stuffed another envelope and started another stack.

Chicky had hoped that bouncer would be a natural extension of doorman. Both required a type of concentration to be polite even to assholes. To appear friendly and happy when you were neither. To defuse volatile situations. To de-escalate. To manage conflicts and protect property without doing either in an obvious way. To convince troublemakers that it wasn't worth it—not this trouble, not here.

The biggest difference was going to be confrontations. Because there was no such thing as an apartment-house doorman winning a fight. If you were fighting you'd already lost. A bouncer though needed to be willing to stand up to anyone, to fight, and to win. It was hard to maintain this balance of accommodating and threatening energy for hours on end. Standing out there alone in the nighttime chill while hundreds of people were inside having a good time. Loud music taunting you. Women in short skirts tempting you.

Maybe that was part of it.

Maybe it was because he was exhausted. Aching from that ill-advised slide into third. He was missing his daughters and his wife. He was lonely. He was sick of watching gangsters and wannabes drive up in their tricked-out SUVs. He was having trouble focusing on the meaningful things hidden beneath all the crap. It was hard when they were hundreds of miles away. Harder still when they were years gone and never coming back. Hard to remember they even exist. Existed.

For so long he'd lived a life completely removed from all the bullshit. Now look.

Chicky could make plenty of excuses. He was sick and tired and he was very, very angry. At the whole goddamned world.

Maybe Chicky had known at some level that he was putting his hands on the wrong punk-ass motherfucker. Maybe he'd done this on purpose. Maybe he was trying to reclaim some measure of dignity. Because what was more humiliating than asking your half-a-gangster cousin for a degrading job you hadn't earned and didn't deserve and didn't want?

Maybe it was Chicky's failure to do anything about that beat-up girl Hailey a few months ago. About the man who'd beat on her.

Maybe it was all the shit that Chicky had been swallowing on the regular for so long.

Maybe it was all those things.

Though maybe it was none of them. Maybe it was just a momentary lapse in judgment. Nothing to overanalyze. And maybe that one slip was going to get Chicky beat the fuck down. Maybe a beatdown wasn't even the worst of it.

Chicky had just known that somehow this job was going to turn out shitty. "What should I do Boss? Tell me what to do."

"Apologize Chicky. You need to apologize."

"Most definitely. But how exactly?"

Junior gave a what-do-you-want-from-me half shrug.

"Should I try to find the dude on the street and say, Excuse me Señor Puño I deeply regret putting my hands on you, please accept my most sincere apologies?"

"This ain't no joke Chicky."

"Yeah." Chicky leaned forward. "I ain't joking. I'm asking. How can I fix it Boss?"

Junior contemplated this in a way that looked to Chicky like bullshit.

"One idea," Junior said as if it had just come to him. "But I don't think you're gonna like it."

He didn't.

CHAPTER 15

APARTMENT 11C-D

Emily was using her knife to break down cartons of a completely unfamiliar brand of pasta. All the regular volunteers brought their own box cutters, name-labeled with masking tape. Emily never put hers down anywhere except her pocket. It was easy to lose a box cutter to carelessness, or thievery.

She would never admit it, but carrying the blade made her feel safer. Less unsafe.

There was so much she would never admit, and the list was growing.

Garvey emerged from the kitchen, wiping his hands on his apron, and began sifting through the apple bin. This was a perk for volunteers: two pieces of fruit per shift. Emily suspected that some days these overripe bananas and bruised apples were all Garvey ate. He worked in the kitchen almost every day, or was scheduled to. Sometimes he didn't show up.

"Good morning, Garvey." Emily used to have a good relationship with Garvey, but at some point she'd slighted him somehow, something had gone wrong, she didn't know what. Now he barely acknowledged her.

He'd been named for Marcus Garvey. "You know who that was?" he'd asked her, years ago. The name had been familiar to Emily, probably from school, maybe something to do with civil rights? Civil rights leaders accounted for at least half the Black people on the school curriculum in Greenwich. When Emily was growing up she had zero real friends who were Black, then one in college, and none since. She regretted this. But she didn't think she could go out and try to force her friendship on people of color to fill a quota. That seemed much worse.

Both options were bad.

"I'm sorry," Emily had answered. "The name is familiar, but I don't know who he was."

"A Black nationalist."

"Ah," Emily had said. That hadn't clarified much, though she was very aware of white nationalists. That night she fell down an internet rabbit hole into Marcus Garvey, which led to Black nationalism, which led to the Nation of Islam. If you follow any movement far enough, eventually you arrive at the same sort of problem.

Garvey had good days, when he was all smiles and jokes, and Emily could hear his laughter ringing through the prep kitchen's swinging doors. He also had bad days, when his eyes darted around, his limbs twitched erratically, his whole body took on the mien of exactly the stereotype of young Black man who terrified Emily out on the street, her heart accelerating as she tried to locate escape routes, to find the pepper spray in her bag, to grip it firmly. Or the utility knife.

She knew that Garvey ran with a rough crowd; she'd see him outside with other guys, and she'd nod from afar. She didn't want to put him in the position of needing to be polite to her.

Emily rarely knew for certain which exact problems people faced at New Hope, and she'd been discouraged from asking. But it was clear that Garvey was homeless, at least some of the time.

"No, not homeless," Camila had corrected. "He's a person who's currently experiencing homelessness. Someone who's unhoused." At first this distinction seemed meaningless, but Emily came to understand. She'd learned a lot at New Hope that adjusted her worldview, including the logic behind the language that her husband mocked—unhoused, BIPOC, Latinx, TERF, pronouns, LGBTQIA+, terms that drove Whit up a tree. "*Justice-involved?* Come on, Em. You know I'm not saying that." She regretted mentioning it to begin with. It wasn't worth his scorn.

"You're not a therapist, Grace," Camila told her. "People aren't here for you to pry into their problems. Into their shame."

"Understood."

"You're also not an ATM. Clients are one hundred percent forbidden from asking you for money. And volunteers are one hundred percent forbidden from giving it. Do you understand?"

"I do."

"Dignity is such an important part of this. Can you imagine how hard it must be to stand out there in front of the whole neighborhood—your cousins, your old schoolteachers, your neighbors, their children—to collect free food to keep your kids from starving? It's a situation with no dignity. None. And to do this with not only the whole neighborhood's eyes on you, but the volunteers' too? People like you? To feel their *pity* on you, their *judgment* . . ."

It sounded as if Camila was speaking from firsthand experience.

"Try to imagine you're here to feed your own kids. Try to resonate with that."

Emily felt the compunction to correct Camila's misuse of *resonate*, but that's counterproductive, always. She held her tongue. Holding her tongue was a way of life.

Every shift began with a flurry as the people who'd been waiting outside made their way through the shelves and freezers, collecting unblemished fruit, packets of hamburger, orange juice concentrate. All the good stuff was gone by mid-shift. The crowd thinned, and Emily reorganized shelves, swept the floor, broke down cartons, chatted with colleagues. Usually that was Camila, who'd led such a different life that it didn't seem wholly credible that these two women lived only a few miles apart, in the same moment in history, sharing this space, both stocking the same shelves with the same ziti, beans, breakfast cereals.

It wasn't just her jewelry that Emily left at home. She'd also stopped wearing her perfume, after Camila had remarked on it. "That smells nice. What is it?"

"Oh I don't know. Something my daughter bought me."

Which was partially true, but extremely misleading. The scent had been custom-made at an atelier in Grasse, a birthday present purportedly from Bitsy that had been conceived and arranged and paid for by Skye. Emily and Bitsy had made a morning of it, driving up from the hotel while Whit stayed behind with Hudson and the nanny, an activity he later referred to as babysitting.

"No, Whit, when it's your own kid it's not called babysitting, it's *parenting*. Especially when you also have an actual professional babysitter there with you on the Riviera."

The perfume was one of many truths that Emily couldn't admit to Camila. Sometimes it seemed as if her shifts at New Hope were an exercise in stripping away one aspect of her life after another, like taking a house down to the studs.

Camila's office reeked from one of those plug-ins, a treacly so-called deodorant, really a re-odorant. Even scents were a matter of class. Every single thing.

Emily never succeeded in putting herself in those shoes, a level of deprivation she could not conjure. Maybe a better person might succeed, a more genuinely generous person. But failing was okay, she thought, or hoped. It was trying that really mattered.

"Hi, Mrs. Walters," she said. "Nice to see you again."

Many of the clients came to the pantry on a regular schedule—the Tuesday crowd, the Thursday crowd. The soup-kitchen clients upstairs were different from pantry clients downstairs, who came with shopping bags or carts; they lived in places with kitchens. Upstairs people often didn't. Downstairs was easier for Emily, more satisfying. She'd studied the Spanish words for canned vegetables and dried legumes, bags of rice and bottles of juice, and produce items that had never entered her own kitchen—plantains, tomatillos, cassava. She'd even learned how to cook some of these things, and could dispense basic advice—soak, peel, chop, fry, roast.

The groceries were disbursed according to a complex point system, a calculus that depended on the size of the households, and the number of children, of what age. Emily had plenty of experience explaining to people why they couldn't take an item. Too much experience.

"No, Señora Hernandez, lo siento, pero la leche es tres puntas, y tú tienes dos puntas solamente." She always repeated that she was sorry, and looked people in the eye to say it. *"Lo siento."*

It pained her to tell clients that they couldn't have the quart of milk, or the bag of apples, not unless they put back the frozen scrod, the can of lima beans. Sometimes she didn't have the heart, and would let someone go with thirty-four points' worth of food who was entitled to only thirty.

"You can't do that, Grace," Camila had scolded, more than once. Camila was the only person at New Hope who knew Emily's real name, but accepted without question that Emily wanted to be called something else. Camila didn't pry.

"But I'm more than happy to pay for it."

"If we don't enforce the rules, everyone is going to break them, and we'd get shut down. Then where would these people get food?"

"I'm sorry, Camila. It won't happen again."

They both knew Emily was lying. This was a situation when lying was not only what both parties wanted, it was also the right thing.

"I hope not," Camila lied too. Emily had once believed that lying was universally wrong. Not anymore. Now she lied all the time.

Emily had heard so many stories about the mistakes people make. It's rarely life's good choices that are obvious, but you could usually see clearly where you took a wrong turn, how one bad decision led to another led to prison led to here. That liquor-store holdup, the first hit of heroin, getting behind that wheel, unsafe intercourse.

Most mistakes boiled down to the same thing: trusting the wrong person. Emily's takeaway was that no one could be trusted, not fully, not forever. Love turned to hate, loyalty to treachery, friend to foe. It could happen just like that. Emily didn't enjoy having this knowledge, but she did take a measure of comfort in the insight. If you didn't fully trust anyone, you couldn't be betrayed.

"You're a nice person, Grace. And some of these people—I'm not saying *most*, but some of them? They will rob you blind if they have the chance. Do not give them the chance."

Emily had been subjected to plenty of hostility here, especially working lunch upstairs, sweating under the hairnet and nitrile gloves, filling a hundred plates in twenty minutes, ladling out potato-heavy stews and rice-dominated soups, spraying down surfaces with disinfectant, trying to maintain order on the line with what she hoped was good cheer. During every one of those shifts, something bad happened. Usually it was someone complaining that Emily had shortchanged a plate—small pork chop, stingy scoop of rice—but sometimes the complaint was an expression of pure animus—"What the fuck you lookin' at?" Escalation happened with astounding speed, mere seconds between peace and screaming, throwing utensils, being manhandled by a security guard, warned about a ban, or the police, empty threats made because something needed to be said, though not done. Emily heard the phrase "white bitch" with disturbing frequency.

She tried not to take it personally; she was just a type, an available target for anger, frustration, prejudice. But she hated working upstairs, which was why she did it rarely. Also why she did it at all.

Garvey tossed his core toward a compost bin filled with boxes of moldy grapes and a sack of rotting onions oozing stinky juice; donated food was unreliable. He missed. He bent to retrieve the core, and his shirt rode up, and Emily saw a gun handle tucked into the back of his jeans. She gasped, and Garvey glared.

Emily wished she knew what she'd done to offend, so she could apologize. But she was scared to ask, scared of the answer. She was, in truth, scared of Garvey.

"Just because bad things happen to you," Camila had cautioned, "that doesn't make you a good person. Sympathy is admirable, Grace. But be careful not to take it too far."

The lunch line was at least thirty people already. Across the street, in front of a liquor store, Garvey stood with two young men, all of them facing New Hope. Facing Emily. She could see Garvey say something, and the other guys looked over at her. She felt herself tense with fear. That gun.

Off to the side she felt a commotion, and looked past the end of the queue, where a couple of uniformed policemen were standing with an agitated man. One cop was holding his nightstick, the other had a hand on his gun. The weapon was still holstered, but that seemed temporary.

"Just calm down," the nightsticked cop said. "We just wanna ask some questions."

Emily couldn't hear the answer, but she could see the man gesticulate effusively. Dangerously.

"Why don't you just come down to the station? We can talk about it there."

More gesticulating, too much of it, and another response Emily couldn't make out, but the tone was definitely hostile. The man was Black. The two cops were white. Everyone on the queue was watching. Passersby had stopped.

Camila was now beside her. "The fuck is this?"

"I don't know," Emily said, which was true in a specific sense, but not a general one.

"Is there a reason we *should* be arresting you?"

A squad car arrived with a *bloop-bloop*, lights flashing, pulling to the curb fast and at an angle, doors flying open, and everything was happening all at once—an old woman on the soup-kitchen line yelled at the cops, and somewhere glass shattered, and all the cops spun, and the man used this distraction as an opportunity to bolt, and Emily recognized him from upstairs, he was one of the clients who had all the problems—mental illness, addiction, incarceration, homelessness.

Two cops hopped back into their car while the other two pursued on foot, though at no great speed. They had no hope of catching this guy; maybe they weren't trying. Maybe they were fleeing as much as chasing, running away from the gathered crowd—the soup-kitchen line plus the food-pantry customers plus volunteers plus passersby plus Garvey and his pals and another similar group of men, there were at least fifty people out here, some now yelling at the cops while a handful held up phones, the ever-present brigade of citizen-documentarians. The fleeing police were probably relieved that whatever had been happening here could go happen somewhere else. Somewhere with fewer witnesses. Preferably none.

Camila said, "This is some fucked-up shit."

Emily knew that Camila assumed the cops were in the wrong, because Camila always thought the cops were in the wrong. Emily didn't agree, but she definitely did not want to debate it.

"Hmm," she said. "I'm sorry, but I have to go. See you on Thursday."

Emily felt her eye drawn across the street again. Garvey was looking in the direction of the disappearing cops, and so was one of his companions.

The other, though, was staring straight at Emily. A shiver ran down her spine.

It was just a few minutes' walk to the subway. Before she descended the stairs she glanced backward, and saw no one behind her, and she felt her body slump in relief, her shoulders fall. Then she lifted her chin high, and tried to gather her composure, and took one step down—

That was when the first shot rang out.

Part Two

THIS AFTERNOON

CHAPTER 16

FRONT DOOR

Pop!

Chicky flinched. Though the gunshot had come from far away, a bullet fired at the right angle can travel more than a mile if nothing gets in its way.

Pop-pop!

The wrong angle.

A hush fell over the busy midday sidewalk. Everyone stopped everything.

Pop-pop-pop-pop!

"Oh shit," a man said. "Someone got *got*."

Pop!

Chicky looked toward the noise but couldn't see anything except that no one was moving. Ten seconds went by. Twenty. Chicky felt the neighborhood exhale. Or maybe that was just himself.

He resumed walking. He passed the community garden where some moms were spreading mulch. Chicky recognized these women from the schoolyard and the street fairs and Sundays at the public pool. They were the people who kept the peace. They cajoled the drug dealers into moving away from the charter school and the firemen into opening hydrants and the shopkeepers into donating food. They organized the block parties and the graduation celebrations and the candlelight vigils when someone got shot who didn't deserve it but not for the people who did.

"Hey Chicky!" Marisol called out. "How are you?" Marisol had been one of the first to come by with condolences and a pot of *ropa vieja* and a bright red blouse with a plunging neckline.

"You know. Another day, Marisol. Another day."

She made her way to the chain-link fence with razor wire on top. "What's up with your face Chicky? I thought your brawling days were behind you."

"Nah." He forced a smile. "Just softball," he lied. "Not as bad as it looks."

"You should come by and let me feed you. Anytime." Marisol tossed her hair, and her hoop earrings swayed. "Whatever you want."

"Thank you," he said, "that's very nice of you. I'll do that soon."

"I can't wait."

He didn't know when would be long enough. But he did know that it was not yet.

In the playground a bunch of older dudes were playing paddleball or waiting for nexts. Almost all these guys had beer bellies and skinny old-man calves and wrist braces but when they hit the ball it sounded like a cannon. These old fucks could really smack those balls. Chicky had never gotten into paddleball or handball and now it seemed too late to start anything new.

He walked by one small business after another. The barbershop and hairdresser and hairweaving and eyebrow-threading. The tattoos and botanica and laundromat and jeweler. Payday lender and international calling cards. A well-fortified drugstore and a better-fortified liquor store. Burgers and a fried-chicken joint and a fried-everything joint. National-chain pizza and 99-cent pizza and an old-school pizza parlor named for some Guinea who last stepped foot in Harlem in maybe the eighties. Chicky used to come here on his way home from PS 441 usually for an Italian ice. You ordered by color. Red or blue or green or sometimes swirl. But never pink. Pink was for girls.

Down by the Bohemia it was all French bistros and Italian trattorias and Indian and Vietnamese and ramen and falafel and green juices. At the fast-food places down there you got salads. There was practically no lunch for under ten bucks except hot dogs, which Chicky could not abide. He'd seen a *60 Minutes* that had horrified him. Or maybe *Dateline*. Thirty years ago? More.

There were also no junkies down there. Nor any of these junk characters like these two jokers sitting here on milk crates in front of the corner store. Both of them fifty going on seventy with loose Newports tucked behind their ears. Both ogling a curvy woman who was walking up the street.

"That's my girl right there. You doin' good baby?"

"Hey Willie," said the girl in question, who was a fully grown adult woman. She wore her most tolerant face and her most indulgent smile. She didn't want to antagonize these bums.

"You definitely lookin' good."

Their portable speaker was playing Rick James. These guys were always listening to eighties R&B. Chaka Khan and Peabo Bryson and Teddy Pendergrass. They even dressed like it in tracksuits and Kangols. As if they'd looked around when they were kids and thought, All right, yeah, that's what it means to be a man. Guess I'll do that when I grow up.

"*Mmm!*" Willie said in appreciation of her receding ass.

"Got that right," seconded Tito, who then noticed Chicky. "Yo Chicky *qué pasa*?"

Chicky's daughters were themselves grown curvy women. He felt like punching these bums in their faces. But he said, "Tito my man," and held up his fist. "Willie." Fist-bumps instead of palm-slaps were the only concession that this wasn't the eighties. Plus Bluetooth instead of a boom box. The menthol cigarettes and malt-liquor forties and blunts hand-rolled from Garcia y Vegas.

"You guys behaving yourselves?"

"Always Chicky. Always."

"I don't believe you. Not for one second!" Chicky didn't like Tito or Willie even the slightest but he kept that to himself. Not just with these bums but always. Chicky did not bad-mouth anyone. He did not make unnecessary enemies. Corner guys might seem jolly and unthreatening but the things that kept their asses glued to milk crates all day every day were the same things that could turn them into lethal motherfuckers. They had nothing. Which is the same as nothing to lose.

For Chicky's first half century he'd been unable to relate. Now nothing made more sense.

"Hello?" Chicky answered his phone.

There was no immediate response and Chicky allowed himself to hope that it was spam. Someone from India saying that the warranty was expiring on the car he didn't own. Or the IRS wanted back taxes he didn't owe. Or that woman yammering in Chinese whose scam was a mystery.

"Good afternoon Mr. Diaz. I'm calling from Kingsbridge Oncological Associates. Again."

Not exactly a surprise but still: fuck.

"Your bill is ninety days past. We have no choice but to turn this over to a collections agency. I'm very sorry."

"I don't know what to tell you. I don't have the forty grand."

"The balance is forty-three thou—"

Chicky laughed then stopped. "I'm sorry for laughing. This isn't funny. I appreciate that you have a job to do. But your company's bill? It's for my wife's care and she's dead. She left behind nothing except bills. I rent my apartment. I don't own a car. So you want me to, what, hock my bicycle? It's an old bike but I keep it up. I could probably get fifty bucks for it? Good day, sixty."

He was trying to sound lighthearted but he was feeling awfully heavy.

"No Mr. Diaz. No one wants you to sell your bicycle."

"Then what do you want from me? In all seriousness. What am I supposed to do?"

Sometimes the feeling came on suddenly that he couldn't go on, and shouldn't. Sure his kids would miss him. But he hasn't seen them since summer and barely spoke on the phone. The girls were busy living their lives with classes and jobs and boyfriends and parties. It's only once that you get to be young. Chicky didn't want to drag them down.

"Can I make a suggestion Mr. Diaz? Maybe you should speak with an attorney."

When the unpaid bills started to pile up the first thing Chicky did was go to Olek to ask for a raise. He explained about his sick wife and his past-due rent and his girls' tuition. He spit it all out in a rush while Olek listened with those crazy-ass eyebrows furrowed.

"I cannot do that Chicky. I am very sorry."

Chicky hated asking anyone for anything. The very idea made his stomach ache.

"Union rules." Olek looked tortured. "Pay increases are, how do you say? Very *regimented*."

So what could he do? Chicky went out and got a moonlighting gig. Literally moonlighting.

"Honestly this is not a hard job," the head of security explained during the interview. It was clear that the job was Chicky's if he wanted it. The main requirement was being an upstanding citizen. Maybe the only requirement.

"There are hotels that attract a sleezy clientele," Bazzini continued. "This ain't one. Our rooms start at eight hundred a night. Our guests are rich. Lots of Europeans here for Broadway and shopping and whatever. Museums I guess. But they ain't throwing bachelor parties. They ain't rock stars wrecking their rooms. They ain't showing up with dangerous animals."

"Dangerous animals? That happens?"

"You'd be surprised. People are fuckin' crazy. But here our main challenge is, believe it or not, loud sex. Other guests call to complain. Then the front desk calls the room to ask the offender—politely—to be considerate. Some people take that as a sorta challenge. Then if a second complaint comes that's when we gotta send someone up to knock on the door. That would be you."

"Gotcha."

"No one is happy to see you. Some drunk guy with a towel wrapped around his hard-on?"

Chicky smiled.

"So you got any questions?"

"I don't think so Boss."

"The most important thing to remember is that our guests are fancy. I'm sure you know what I'm talking about?" Bazzini was impressed with the Bohemia. Everyone was impressed with the Bohemia. "They want to be treated like fancy people. Especially those who ain't. But whatever the issue no one wants police. If you think someone's life is in danger? Sure, call nine-one-one. Anything less? Call me instead. The NYPD ain't been here in more than a year and it's my job to keep it that way. Yours too."

"When the police were here, what was that for?"

"A robbery. Allegedly."

"Allegedly?"

"I'm always suspicious of robberies." Bazzini had been a cop. Hotel security was what he was doing in his so-called retirement. "You never know what the fuck has gone on."

As promised the hardest part of the job was staying awake. Chicky started to run a long-term sleep deficit that didn't do his health any favors. Nor his mood. Nor his performance at his day job nor as a human. So he would've needed to quit even if nothing had happened. But something did.

"Diaz?" It was the front desk in his ear around midnight. "People on twenty-seven are complaining. Two calls. Not music. Maybe sex? This call said it sounded like a woman screaming."

Chicky picked up his pace. "Room number?"

"Maybe twenty-seven twelve but they don't answer. Somewhere on that end."

The elevator's padded leather walls were inset with mirrors. This was what Chicky imagined a private jet was like. Which could've been said about the hotel's whole vibe. Smooth but overwhelming luxury. Staff trained to be so deferential it was practically a parody. This level of insincerity was like a prostitute, something Chicky had indulged a few times in the Corps. He'd never truly enjoyed it. He couldn't ignore that this woman was being paid to tell him what a nice dick he had, you feel so good, that's it don't stop. The better looking the hooker the less Chicky could suspend disbelief. One of those girls was a real knockout and he could barely get it up.

"What's wrong baby? You don't like me?" She'd sounded sincerely wounded. Chicky knew even that was fake. That was his last time.

So he couldn't understand a place like this where the level of ass-kissing was not remotely credible. Though maybe for these guests believing or not believing wasn't an issue. And in truth maybe this wasn't all that different from living at the Bohemia.

Chicky stepped off onto 27's plush carpet. He waited for the elevator to whoosh away so he could tune his ears to the sounds. From the left he heard the indistinct hum of a TV. From the right the thumping of a bass at a volume too low to identify even the music genre. What he didn't hear was anyone fucking loudly.

The rooms that ended in 12 were suites and 27 was a high floor in a low neighborhood. The views from 2712 would be great. And at two grand per night what are you paying for? It's not really a nice king-sized bed. And what else are you willing to pay too much for? Everything. Anything.

Chicky paused at each door. He heard nothing and more nothing and then what sounded like an Indian TV announcer maybe reading the news.

Then: sobbing. Chicky broke into a jog but he'd taken only a couple of steps when the door at the end flew open.

A man strode out of 2712 while pulling a ballcap low. This guy walked quickly but not rushed with long confident strides and his face angled toward the floor. He seemed like a man running away from trouble but trying to look like he wasn't.

Chicky slowed to buy himself time. When the two men were just a few steps from each other Chicky stopped. The guy still did not glance up, which itself was an admission of guilt. Chicky could see the guy's jaw muscles twitching. He was wearing one of the plain ballcaps with no insignia that all rich guys seemed to wear these days.

Something seemed familiar about this guy but his face was mostly hidden and out of context. He was clearly fleeing bad behavior. How bad? What was Chicky's responsibility here? He turned and saw that the man was almost at the elevator.

"Hey," Chicky said. He had to do something. "Excuse me."

The man pressed the call button.

"Mister." Chicky started walking toward him. "Excuse me," more firmly.

The elevator dinged. To stop this guy Chicky would need to break into a sprint. Sprinting at someone was a serious escalation. Something he'd have a very hard time walking back.

The elevator opened. The man stepped inside. Over the years Chicky had come to appreciate the value of being able to walk things back. So he rushed but did not sprint. He was still a few steps from the elevator when it closed.

Chicky immediately felt the shame of cowardice. But there was still something to do. He hustled to the end of the hall. At 2712 he could hear the woman sobbing.

"Hello?" he said.

The crying stopped.

"Hello?" Chicky waited a few seconds. "Excuse me? This is Mr. Diaz with hotel security."

After another few seconds she answered. "It's okay."

Chicky could tell she was standing just on the far side of the closed door.

"Everything's okay."

Chicky knew that it wasn't. "Could I ask you to open the door ma'am? Please?" He spoke as softly as possible while still being heard through the door. "I don't want to disturb the other guests."

"I'm okay," she said. "Really."

"I'm sorry ma'am but I need to see for myself. I can use my pass key? If you prefer?"

Chicky heard her mutter, "Fuck," then the door opened halfway.

No surprise: a gorgeous woman wearing nothing but lingerie and a busted lip.

"Jesus," Chicky said. He hustled inside and to the closet where he yanked a robe off its padded hanger and draped it around her shoulders.

"You okay?" He instantly felt stupid. "I mean are you hurt? Or is it just—" He pointed at her lip. "Sorry I don't mean *just.* Do you have any injury besides the lip? Any physical injury?"

"No." She tied the robe's belt. "I'm fine."

"Could I ask your name?" He noticed marks around her neck. It looked like imprints of thumbs on both sides of her trachea and fingers around the back.

"Um, sure. It's Hailey." She said it in a way that suggested it wasn't her real name. Chicky couldn't have cared less. All he wanted was to be able to have a conversation. To be polite.

Hailey's blond hair was pinned tight to her head. Chicky looked around at the discarded clothes and wine bucket and Champagne flutes, one with lipstick. All the things you'd expect.

"Should I get a doctor, Hailey?"

He didn't see any drug paraphernalia or upended furniture or ripped clothing. There'd been no brawl here. This was not an extended bender.

"I don't mean nine-one-one," Chicky assured her. He picked up the cork's metal cover, gold script against a black background: Dom Pérignon. "The hotel has someone on call. It can be very private."

"No I'm good." She was examining herself in the mirror. "Really. This is, like, no big deal."

That's when Chicky saw the explanation for the pinned hair. "You were wearing that wig?"

Hailey followed Chicky's eyes. As if she needed to check which wig. She didn't answer.

Chicky looked back at her full cheeks and bright blue eyes and thin waist and full bust. "I thought gentlemen preferred blondes."

Hailey crossed her arms.

"Maybe this is none of my business. But do lots of men want you to wear a wig?"

She looked to the door and back at Chicky. This was a woman who knew she was in a vulnerable position. She needed to play along with this security guard, whatever questions he had.

"He told my service he wanted a girl who looked like someone particular? He sent a picture. I was the closest match. Except for the hair? So I got a wig."

Now Chicky realized who the guy had been. Fuck. "Was this your first time with him?"

"No. This was our, like, third date? Fourth."

"Has he done this before?"

"This?"

"Hit you."

She hesitated.

"Ma'am if this is a guy who goes around beating on wom—"

"No, not . . . um . . ." Hailey took a deep breath. "So here's the thing? He likes to put his hands around my neck? *As if* he's choking me? And he likes for me to pretend to, um . . . *pass out*? That's how he, y'know . . ."

"No," Chicky says. "I'm sorry. I don't know."

"Comes. That's how he comes."

Jesus. What a fucked-up fantasy.

"But he never *really* did it before? Actually choke me. I tried to tell him to stop. But I, like, couldn't get any words out? I was sorta having trouble breathing. So I kinda kneed him—not too hard—and that's when . . ." She pointed at her lip. "We had a little . . ." Hailey walked over to a chair and retrieved her dress. "Scuffle."

She continued to the bathroom but left the door open.

"You know this guy's name?"

"I know the name he, like, *uses*? But I wouldn't bet a nickel it's his real name."

She emerged from the bathroom wearing the little black dress, which was very little indeed.

"So you don't know who this guy is. But your service does?"

"I guess? They have, like, credit card info. Our clients are *vetted*." She mocked that last word.

Chicky noticed the cash on the bureau. Hailey noticed him notice. She walked over and took the money. "He pays very well."

"Hey I'm not judging you."

"Yes you are."

"I'm not. I promise. I'm sorry I made you feel that way. My bad."

"Listen." She walked toward Chicky, still holding the cash. "You're not going to call the cops, right?"

"Not unless you want me to."

She snorted. She peeled off a couple of bills and extended them toward Chicky.

"No." He put his hands up. "Absolutely not."

"I *really* don't want any cops. I have a *career*."

"I'm not involving the police."

"I'm a dancer. And not a, like, *exotic* dancer. *Broadway*."

"I promise. Really."

Hailey nodded and dropped the cash into a giant handbag. You could fit a small child in there. Chicky knew that bags like that can go for thousands of dollars. Tens of thousands. If they're genuine. He hopes this one isn't genuine. He hates the idea that she would do this for that.

"Are you sure you don't want a doctor?"

She shook her head. "I just need to put on some makeup."

Chicky didn't know if he wanted to confirm this next thing. "You mind if I see that picture? Of the girl he wanted someone to look like."

Hailey hesitated again before she scrolled, then handed her device to Chicky. He looked down at the screen, muttered, "Fuck."

"What?"

He couldn't explain the situation to Hailey. Instead he said, "Same dress, huh."

The photo was of a beautiful raven-haired woman wearing a little black dress.

"Probably not," Hailey said. "But I tried."

The photo was in an album entitled WORK.

The woman was Emily Longworth.

CHAPTER 17

APARTMENT 11C-D

Emily was still vibrating when she got home. She'd never in her life been so close to gunfire; she'd never been anywhere near it. She'd had no idea what an effect it could have.

And suddenly Tatiana was standing there. "Miss? Your guests are downstairs."

"Thank you, Tattie. I'll show them in myself." Emily thought it was tacky to have the housekeeper do it. She'd been resisting the insidious creep of paying people to do too much. First it's carrying heavy packages, then light packages, then changing lightbulbs, and next thing you're thinking you're royalty.

The doorbell was a soothing *ding-dong*, suggesting a Sunday-afternoon nap in a hammock. Emily had spent a whole morning researching doorbells. Sometimes it seemed as if her life consisted mostly of making tasteful decisions. Job title: homemaker. Chief responsibilities: raising children; hiring and supervising household help; managing $4MM annual budget; buying tasteful things.

"Welcome," she said, managing her most hostessy smile. Roland and Amy entered with the tight grins of people who were uncomfortable, and knew it was going to get worse. "Please come on through to the front parlor." Today the phrase gave her no joy.

"Oh, Emily," Amy said, "your home is beautiful."

Amy was standing in the pocket doorway between the entry gallery and the parlor. All the woodwork and hardware were original, mahogany and brass buffed and polished to rich warm shines. This doorway was one of the chief elements that had convinced the board to reject Whit's plan. He wanted to move the doorway, to create a bigger wall, so that damn Rothko would fit here.

"Thank you," Emily said. "The renovation was more complicated than anyone wanted." She gave her most self-deprecating smile. She assumed that everyone knew about the renovation's cost, delays, lawsuits; it was even mentioned in the *Post*. Emily hoped this little smile could acknowledge the debacle, and apologize for it, but not too much. That was asking a lot out of one smile.

Emily offered her guests the seats that faced the windows, as well as coffee or tea or water, a platter of pastries. She didn't expect anyone to eat a croissant here at midday on a Tuesday, but there was no way she wasn't going to have something on offer.

"In the end, we're pleased with how it turned out." In truth, Emily would always be furious.

Whit had sprung the surprise attack during one of their date nights, back when they used to do such a thing. "I've hired Meyerowitz," he'd said, offhandedly, dismissively, an opening volley launched across the crisp white tablecloth, over appetizers. They were living in that hateful tower. The Bohemia was Emily's idea, and Meyerowitz was Whit's retort.

"*Ira* Meyerowitz? You're joking." Meyerowitz had redone Whit's headquarters in a modernist Midtown building, all right angles and clean lines, glossy whites, glass and chrome and black leather and nothing else, no ornamentation, even the doorknobs were little chrome nubs of nothing. As if color were outlawed. Curves too. Meyerowitz's aesthetic was diametrically opposed to everything about the Bohemia's Art Nouveau, an effusion of flowing lines and organic forms, intricate century-old millwork and marble fireplaces, parquet floors and wedding-cake moldings.

"Joking? Why would you think that?"

Emily watched her husband take a bite of diver scallop topped with a dollop of lobster-bisquey sauce and a sprinkle of caviar, a tiny seafood sundae. Fine-dining restaurants seemed to be engaged in an arms race of esoteric and exorbitant ingredients—beluga and bottarga, truffles and foie gras, Kobe beef and Ibérico ham and, if all else fails to impress, edible gold leaf. Gilding lilies.

"Because it doesn't make sense to impose minimalism on the Bohemia."

The waiter had mentioned something about black-footed pigs that had, for their entire lives, eaten nothing but acorns. Could that be true?

Whit met her eye as he chewed, swallowed, took a sip of wine, replaced his glass to its doily with excessive deliberativeness. This spectacle of challenge was a power display, heaped on top of the preposterous choice of architect. Whit was not an idiot. He knew that Ira was the last person who should do a Bohemia job. And Whit knew that Emily knew that he knew. He was asserting his supremacy, and making the power imbalance all the more glaring because of the absurdity.

"That," he said, "is what makes it clever."

"Do you really think so?" This was the sort of conventional idea that passed for cleverness among extremely conventional people. Like wearing sneakers with a tuxedo, or ordering in fried chicken for a fancy party. The opposite of the expected thing wasn't clever. It was just as predictable, and obnoxious to boot.

Whit took another sip, another few seconds of thinly veiled aggression. The sommelier had enumerated a half dozen grape varietals, the last of which constituted one percent. Such an overload of information that it was anti-informative.

"Yes," Whit said, "I do." Go ahead, call my bluff.

Emily shaved off a sliver of scallop, giving herself a moment to think. Whit had to know—he *had* to—that she would object. Which meant he wanted to pick a fight. This fight. With her.

She'd believed that her marriage was a relatively smooth river, but whitewater rapids had just appeared out of nowhere. Sure, she had complaints. About Whit, about their dynamics, about the way they were conducting their lives, raising children. It would be unreasonable to presume that Whit didn't have his own complaints. The kids were little, difficult. Newlywed romance had given way to three-A.M. feedings and bleary-eyed mornings, tantrums and discipline and an infinite succession of soiled diapers. Hence date night. Two hours per week in a restaurant wasn't going to solve everything, but it was something. They were trying.

Maybe this starchitect gambit was the opposite. Maybe Meyerowitz was Whit's opening move in a campaign to end their marriage. Emily remembered the advice from their garishly handsome rafting guide in New Zealand: if you fall into rapids, resist the urge to plant your feet. You're unlikely to find solid footing down there, and more likely to get a foot stuck between rocks. Then you'll be unable to move your feet, and unable to get your face out of the water because the current will be pushing you forward. This was the most common way people died on whitewater, and it happened by obeying your instincts.

Was Emily's husband shoving her off their raft? Here in this Michelin star off Madison?

The thing to do was counterintuitive: throw your feet up toward the water's surface, downriver; drop backward, head aimed upriver, face toward the sky; let your life jacket float you to safety. Not dissimilar to a riptide: go with the flow, wait out the worst. Fighting only makes it worse.

Emily swallowed her scallop, resisted the urge to plant her feet.

"I've always liked Ira." The architect was a rock in a riverbed, shiny and innocuous until it snags you into a lethal foot entrapment. "I look forward to working with him."

"I hope you know," Roland began, "how much we appreciate everything you've done."

Emily crossed her legs at the ankle. She did not cross her legs at the knee. She did not slouch. She did not let more than twenty-four hours elapse before answering emails or texts, or writing thank-you notes or bread-and-butter notes, or returning phone calls, except on those very rare occasions when she was avoiding someone deliberately, as she was dodging Skye these days. Which made her feel awful. But she didn't think she had a choice.

"Not just your board service, and your volunteer work, and your remarkable generosity—*so* important—but for your expertise, right? *So* cherished. And above all for your *passion*." Roland's face was draped in patronizing concern, a tilt of the head. "All of which makes this so difficult."

Emily felt her eye twitch, her jaw too. Her dentist had recently instructed her to use a night retainer, to prevent her from grinding away all her enamel.

"I'm sure you're aware that all of us are under a powerful microscope right now, right? Which can magnify any little speck of disagreement into a full-blown hot war. And these recent revelations about your husband? They're reverberating very loudly through our halls, right? Very loudly."

The faint drumbeat had begun a few weeks ago, when an internal memo about Liberty's earnings leaked. At first it was the sorts of professional lefties who'll protest anything, with their placards and patchouli. Then some influencer grabbed ahold and spewed predictably simplistic outrage. The next day the sidewalk at Whit's office was choked, a critical mass that drew the attention of a few alternative-media outlets, which in turn drew the mainstream media. No one wanted to get scooped.

"It's all over the media, Emily."

It had happened so fast. None of this came as a surprise; the opposite. This was how the world worked these days. It could be counted on.

"Oh come on, Roland. It's the *Daily News*."

"Yes but last night I got a call from the *Times*." He said this in a reverential near-hush. For a certain type of New Yorker, *The New York Times* was god. "And on social media? I'm sure you know that a mob has gathered, hoisting pitchforks."

"It's social media, the mob is always gathered, and always casting about for fresh victims."

"Unfortunately, Emily, this mob includes some of our own."

"Our own? Not the *board*?"

"Oh god no, of course not. I mean staff. Especially the younger ones, right?"

Everyone everywhere was terrified of the assistants. Except in finance, apparently. Those were the kids who still revered capitalism, who respected hierarchy, maybe even patriarchy. The finance kids were a self-selecting group who weren't complaining to HR about dirty jokes, weren't trying to erase the founder's name. In culture, though, the self-selection was the opposite.

"But they're always up in arms about *something*, Roland. I've sat in those meetings. I've heard the grievances about queer representation.

About sexism and the wealth gap and institutional racism and the tyranny of heteronormative patriarchy."

Was Emily sounding like Whit? Maybe a little too much.

"Don't get me wrong: these are all voices that need to be heard. Conversations we need to have. Work"—air quotes—"we need to do. But does *doing the work* mean canceling anyone who isn't a full-time social-justice warrior?"

Emily's phone rang, Camila calling, which was very unusual, and worrying. All their business was handled in-person or email. Emily turned her screen down, turned back to Roland.

"The only way cultural institutions survive is through the generosity of people of means." Whit had not wanted to make the big donation to the museum, but had done it for Emily. Maybe not for her, precisely, but it was part of their bargain. "And all substantial wealth has been acquired in ways that someone is going to find . . . I think the term is *problematic*? That's what people say these days when they don't like something, isn't it? Banking, pharmaceuticals, energy, real estate—everything is problematic to someone."

She knew that the decision had already been made; Roland and Amy weren't here to debate anything. But Emily also knew that this conversation would be reported, dissected, so it was essential for her to try. She wanted Roland to feel bad; she wanted him to need to explain to the board: "How'd she take it? How do you think? She was pretty goddamned upset."

"Emily. He's an arms dealer."

Her instinct was a nearly physical urge to distance herself from her husband, from his business, from this accusation. But she had to defend him, didn't she, she couldn't sit here and throw her husband under the bus, not yet. It would look bad if she bailed at the first sign of trouble. Maybe suspicious.

"Not true. Whit is a *businessman*. An *entrepreneur*. He's never done anything illegal."

This was not, technically, true. It wasn't even true in spirit. But today Emily needed to support Whit with all the fierceness she could marshal, no matter how much it nauseated her. This was another part of their bargain.

"But he sells arms to our enemies, right?"

Emily missed the days when filled pauses were *um* and *uh*, which at least didn't demand that you agree. Today *right* seemed to be intoned constantly by everyone in academia, the arts, education, the media; it was somehow a badge of liberalism. Emily tried not to disagree with people just because they demanded that she agree with them, but it was hard.

"*Our* enemies?" Emily might as well get everything off her chest; there were precious few opportunities to speak the truth these days, and it felt good. Great. "Since when does a museum have a foreign policy? Liberty makes *body armor*. Defensive material that protects American soldiers."

"Liberty's products protect anyone who has the means, including authoritarian regimes. Including known terrorist groups."

Emily was getting angrier, but not at Roland. The person she was angry at was Whit. He'd never been completely forthright, he'd emphasized the nonmilitary applications, and he'd never mentioned any contracts with the DoD, much less with the Kingdom of Saudi Arabia, or Syria, or Yemen. The details he'd omitted had been pretty damned important.

"Do I really need to explain capitalism to you?" Emily continued. The net profit last year had been three billion dollars, which hadn't been public information until the reporters started snooping, urged on by the social-media agitators. It was an awful lot of profit.

"Surely you can see why people might object to this expression of the free market?"

"Are you one of those people, Roland?"

"Listen. I don't want to argue about the shortcomings of unfettered capitalism. I don't want to argue with you about anything, right? I have tremendous admiration and fondness for you. I deeply value our friendship, I really do, you're one of my favorite people. And everyone on the board—"

Amy cleared her throat, and both Roland and Emily looked over.

"Yes, Amy?" Emily asked.

Amy was a lawyer, or used to be, before she "stepped back" to "focus on family" and "do board work." Here, apparently, was that board work: making sure this conversation stayed on track, and ensuring that there could be no future disagreement about what transpired.

Roland took her cue to move on. "We can't ignore the concerns of these passionate, vocal members of our community. One of these young women has seventy thousand followers. *Seventy thousand.* Do you know what that means?"

"It means you're being bullied. Do you think this mob won't eventually come for you, Roland? Or you, Amy?" Roland's family wealth was derived from Southern real estate; Amy's career had been litigating on behalf of mining conglomerates. The only reason these two had been spared was because no one gave a damn, yet.

"And after Saturday night?" Roland asked.

"Saturday night?" Was Emily really being held accountable because a cop had shot an unarmed Black man? "What in god's name does that have to do with my family?"

"On the one hand, nothing."

"There's another hand?"

"The other hand is intersectionality."

"Intersectionality? Since when are you throwing around language like that?"

"Everything has to do with everything else, Emily, and it all has to do with everyone. Any instance of any injustice is a call to arms for every sort of justice. And today the calls are very, very loud."

"You've lost your mind, Roland. Or you've lost the capacity for autonomous thought."

Emily could see him make a valiant attempt to not be taken aback, and almost succeed. Then he forced a smile, and pressed on. "In my day, things were different, right? The generosity of people like you and Whit would *never* have been questioned because of politics. We would *never* be having this conversation, right? But now? To the world at large, you and your husband are not distinct from each other, nor from his company, nor from its very worst customers."

Roland stood. "I can't tell you how sorry we all are." He wanted to make a quick getaway after he'd said what he'd come to say. "I'm afraid we have to ask you step down."

When the Bohemia was built in the nineteenth century, people kept their clothes in armoires, and chests of drawers, big heavy brown furniture.

Back then, architects hadn't anticipated the demand for walk-in closets. So now every renovation added big walk-ins, along with so-called chef's kitchens and en suite bathrooms, these architectural equivalents of Suburbans or Escalades, de rigueur.

Ira Meyerowitz had transformed what had once been a decent-sized bedroom into a lavishly proportioned dressing room, with big sub-closets within the immense super-closet, there was even furniture in here—slipper chairs, a vanity table, an antique valet stand, which had been one of Emily's more valiant attempts at birthday-gifting, bought from a Nouveau specialist during that spree in Clignancourt.

She shut this dressing-room door and walked to the far corner, where an extra-tall section of racks held extra-long items—gowns, dresses, full-length coats, padded hangers, protective bags. She pushed aside these hangers. An electrical outlet was mounted in the baseboard, and a charging lead plugged in. Emily's fingers followed the cord's path to a patch pocket of a big puffer. She reached into that pocket, and pulled out a disposable phone, which like her Yankees cap was something she'd purchased in Harlem, from a street vendor, in cash. She'd bought two of these phones.

Emily powered up this one, which had only ever been used for one purpose. One person. She knew she shouldn't do this, but today had already been too awful, and it was barely noon. She needed it. She hit CALL.

"Well hello. What a wonderful surprise."

"Yes," Emily said, "I'm sorry."

"Don't apologize. Please. Is everything okay?"

"Not really," she said. "You don't happen to have time today, do you?"

Pause.

"Of course," he said. "Of course I do."

CHAPTER 18

FRONT DOOR

The yard of the Luisa Moreno Leaders of the Future School was filled with kids screaming their heads off. Chicky paused at the fence and tried to absorb some of this joy before he realized it might look bad. A middle-aged man with no child. He kept walking.

When Chicky himself had attended this very school it had been plain old Public School 441. All elementary and middle schools had numbers only, PS, IS, MS. Most high schools were named for dead white guys except trade schools. Like Westinghouse Tech in Brooklyn and Aviation out in Queens where a few of Chicky's friends went before getting jobs at LaGuardia. Tiffani went to Clara Barton High School for Health Professions, which Chicky supposed meant any healthcare profession except doctor.

At Automotive in Williamsburg the motto engraved over the front door was MANHOOD SERVICE LABOR CITIZENSHIP. Manhood, what a promise. Literally etched in stone.

Trade school used to be a thing guidance counselors pushed. Telling you about good union jobs, about pensions, when you're eleven, twelve, your bookbag filled with beat-up textbooks that you had to cover in cut-up brown shopping bags. Chicky's moms was a pro at this. His friends would bring over their books every September. "Please Mrs. Diaz? *Please?*" She pretended she didn't want to do it but she loved being asked. Everyone loved being needed.

Back then everybody on the block knew whose moms and pops were good at what. Fix a bike tire, pitch stickball, make sancocho. Everybody also knew which grown-ups had which problems with drugs or alcohol or temper or domestic violence. Everybody was in everybody's business.

During Chicky's graduation from PS 441 the songs played were "Ain't No Stoppin' Us Now" and George Benson's "Greatest Love of All." George believed the children are our future. This didn't fool young Chicky. He suspected it didn't fool anyone else. Not the kids and not their parents and definitely not the teachers. It was just the type of shit grown-ups said.

Years later in Saudi Reggie claimed that McFadden & Whitehead had not been singing about Black pride. "Ain't No Stoppin' Us Now" wasn't a protest song about civil rights or whatever. The band was declaring independence from a record label. The song was a greed anthem. Everybody had heard something they'd wanted to hear. Something more uplifting.

But who knew if that were true. Reggie was one deeply cynical motherfucker. A few weeks later he got his leg blown off. Reggie had plenty reason to be cynical.

Luisa Moreno was so overcrowded that mobile trailers served as classrooms. These temporary rooms had been in the schoolyard for so long they'd fallen apart and been replaced with less shitty models. A permanent stopgap. The school needed to stagger arrivals and departures and lunchtimes so everyone would fit. The fifth-graders, the oldest, were presumably the most flexible about when they ate their sloppy joes. These ten-year-olds went down to lunch at 10:20 A.M.

Ain't no stoppin' us now.

But each of Chicky's girls did end up at elite universities. None of Chicky's friends went away to college. Zero. It never even crossed Chicky's mind for one second.

So maybe the current system wasn't so fucked-up. Maybe it was the old system that had been fucked-up. Or maybe both were different types of fucked-up.

After the hotel incident Chicky knew it was out of the question to go to the police. And there was no way Chicky would confront Mr. Longworth.

Chicky assumed that Longworth would pretend nothing had happened. Nothing to explain and nothing to deny. This would take any decision-making out of Chicky's hands. Or at least one of the decisions.

But Chicky had to consider whether to say something to Mrs. Longworth. Not about the adultery and the hooker. Discretion was a big part of Chicky's job. But Mr. Longworth apparently got his rocks off by fantasizing about choking his wife. *To death.* And not just idly fantasizing but paying hookers to enact that fantasy. Practicing. This was a whole different level of disturbing that made Chicky worry Mrs. Longworth might be in danger.

But one choice Chicky didn't have was to continue working at the hotel.

"This has nothing to do with what happened the other night?" Bazzini asked.

"Not at all Boss." Chicky didn't want to heap lies upon lies when this single unverifiable lie would suffice. And it wasn't even really a lie. "I just can't handle the schedule. I'm sorry."

"It's been a pleasure having you around. Come back whenever you want."

Bazzini had retired from the NYPD at forty-six with full pension and benefits. Now that was a good union job.

The following weekend Chicky went to see Junior. All he was looking for was one shift on Friday nights or Saturdays. A place like Junior's could always use extra muscle and guys weren't lining up to work weekends till four A.M. Chicky hoped this could be an extra couple hundred per week hidden from the IRS and collectors. Easy money. But there's no such thing except for those who don't need it. Like those Bohemia residents raking in hundreds of thousands in one day just by letting investments appreciate. Millions.

At least that's what Canarius had told him. "Let's say you have a hundred million dollars," Canarius explained. "Which plenty of these people have, right?"

"I don't know. Do they?"

Canarius looked at Chicky like he was an idiot. They were at Pascal's apartment for his kid's christening. The security gates were pushed open so people could go out to the fire escape to smoke. Marta no longer allowed smoking inside because of the baby.

"So that hundred mil will generate five to ten per year. On average."

"Five to ten what?" Chicky asked. "Million? Dollars?"

"Managing this money is not altogether different from owning a business that does five to ten million in net profit. It needs a manager. You either do it yourself or you pay someone to do it."

Chicky had never owned any stock nor any shares in any fund. He never maintained any awareness if the market was up or down. He didn't even really know what the market was. It was just an abstraction. Except the idea that it was a specific place.

"Nah," Canarius had disabused him, "most finance firms are in Midtown. Not Wall Street."

So the only thing Chicky thought he knew about the financial markets? That was wrong.

"What are you doing working as a doorman, Canarius? You should be running a bank."

"Yeah that's the plan." Canarius was as straight-arrow as they come. He felt guilty about taking the *Journal* and growing a beard. He was the last to do it after the prohibition was finally dropped.

"It's like the Yankees here," Tommy O'Sullivan had explained during Chicky's first interview. Tommy was old-school Irish back when nearly every super in the city was Irish. Tommy was at the time younger than Chicky was now. "You wanna work at the Bohemia? No beards. No ponytails. No, whaddyacallit, rastaman dreadlocks." Tommy rolled his eyes at the ridiculousness. "A little mustache, fine. But nothing more. That gonna be a problem for you?"

"No sir." Chicky had been out of the Marines just a few months. Shave every morning and buzzcut every two weeks. Chicky didn't want any facial hair and he didn't give a shit if his workplace forbade it. What he cared about was a good union job. A pension.

"Also: *Chicky*. That a name you're attached to?"

Chicky didn't understand what he was being asked. He later learned the plumber Joe had one of those Polish names with like all the consonants mashed up together, and Tommy had demanded that the guy go by something else. "Less ethnic," Tommy had said. As if Irish wasn't an ethnicity. "How about Joe?"

"Well," Chicky said, "it's what everyone calls me Boss. My whole life."

He really did not want to use his birth-certificate name. Especially not to be introduced to a hundred people all at once.

"Hmm," Tommy said. "Yeah I guess it's okay." It wasn't that *Chicky* was hard to pronounce. Just that to Tommy it sounded undignified. And to Chicky *Tommy* sounded like the name of a four-year-old.

Ten years later Irish Tommy O'Sullivan died of emphysema. Two packs a day since he was fourteen. Tommy was replaced by Ino from Malta who was replaced by Yevgeny from Russia who was replaced by Oleksander from Ukraine. All these live-in superintendents were very different individuals. But they were also one white guy after another. Different types of white guys but still.

In the meantime basically all the staff became Hispanic. When Chicky started he'd been one of a few while almost everyone was Irish or Italian. Like the police. But now there were no more Irish guys working here and no Italians. And it wasn't just the Bohemia. It seemed like it was the whole city or maybe the whole country whose working class was Hispanic. Everywhere you go, every blue-collar job, men and women both, every busboy and dishwasher and housecleaner and porter.

Over the past couple of decades a lot of Hispanic guys had gotten jobs at the Bohemia thanks to Chicky. Mexican guys from his block and Dominican guys from his softball team and Puerto Rican guys from his extended family, friends of friends, then kids of friends. That's how building staff works all over the city. That's why at some buildings all the guys are from Montenegro and at others from the South Bronx. The new guy Ernesto is the nephew of Chicky's third baseman.

"Hispanic?" Olek asked last year. "I am told we should be saying Latino. Or Latin*x*."

"Oh yeah Boss? Who told you that?"

Olek wasn't going to rat anyone out.

When Chicky was growing up he had a friend Pablo whose family came from Puebla and everyone called him a wetback. *To his face.* Chinese people were Chinks and Chinese food was the Chinks' and Vietnamese were Gooks. Whites were honkies except when they were Micks or Guidos or Guineas or Polacks or Ivans. Chicky's mom used to take her kids back-to-school shopping on the Lower East Side where all the stores were owned by Orthodox Jews. "Don't forget," Chicky's pops would advise, "you gotta Jew them down."

"Not me Boss. I'm Hispanic." Chicky didn't know anyone who used the word *Latinx.*

Facial hair was another matter. It was soon after George Floyd when the grumbling began.

"Who the fuck are they," Zaire had said, "to tell us we can't have beards?"

Zaire had been raised in a Black Liberation Theology household and he'd been kept down long enough before he was even born. It was obvious to Chicky that Zaire was ill-suited to a job that was largely about being subservient to rich white people. The guy was putting himself in the path of his own righteous anger every single day. As if he worked at the Bohemia to spite himself. Like a Soviet mole buried deep in a society he despised, waiting to rise up and destroy the system.

But no one knew for sure if moles were real. Canarius had told Chicky that the very word had been completely made up by a British novelist.

Zaire was also putting himself in the path of suspicions, accusations, allegations.

"What are we, chattel?" Zaire organized the petition and took it to the super who took it to the managing agent who took it to the board who took it to the lawyer who debated it with colleagues then advised the board to accede to the request to eliminate restrictions on the staff's grooming as long as those choices did not negatively impact hygiene or job performance.

"*Job performance?* How the fuck can a beard impact job performance?"

"I think that means," Oleksander said, "if residents complain."

"Shit." Zaire sucked his teeth. "Fuck those motherfuckers."

"Do you think this is unreasonable, Zaire?" As far as Olek knew, Zaire meant nothing more than this guy's name. By the time Olek learned English the country had long been rechristened the Democratic Republic of the Congo. Olek's education did not extend to the English-language translations of obsolete national names of Central Africa. "And it does not matter. If the board tells me fire Zaire"—Olek shrugged—"I fire Zaire.

And there is nothing you can do about it. Unless you are fired for protected reason."

"Protected reason? You mean like organizing a labor action?"

Everyone on staff was union except Oleksander. His official title was resident manager and he was management. In other types of buildings this job was called super and that's what everyone called Olek.

"You are sure you want to be doing this, Zaire?"

"Oh fuck yeah."

Chicky knew that it wasn't only about beards. It wasn't really about beards at all.

After another couple of months of debate the policy was dropped with no restrictions. Half the guys promptly grew facial hair along predictable ethnic lines with different shapes for African-Americans and Mexicans and Dominicans and Puerto Ricans.

Chicky had occasionally gone a few days without shaving but then his face would start to itch like a motherfucker. So he shaved every morning except Sundays. But he still did his push-ups and his sit-ups. He still did his six miles.

No Hispanics lived in the Bohemia. Back in the nineties there'd been an Argentinian polo player who was the king of Spain's cousin. That Hispanic hadn't gone to kindergarten in a trailer parked in a schoolyard surrounded by NYCHA projects and his moms didn't have a sancocho recipe. That guy had like eight names and Chicky was never quite sure what to call him. He lived at the Bohemia for a week at a time for a few weeks per year.

Mr. Hardiman had been the only Black person until he moved out last year.

There were a handful of Asians. One each of Korean and Japanese and Chinese and Indian and Pakistani. Like they'd been chosen from a menu. Bizarrely most of these families were mixed. As was Mr. Hardiman's. This didn't seem like a coincidence.

Canarius did eventually grow a beard but he kept it tidy. Everything about Canarius was neat.

If an inside job ever went down Zaire would probably be arrested automatically.

Canarius would be very near the bottom of the list of suspects. But not the very bottom. That, everyone knew, would be Chicky.

Everyone trusted Chicky Diaz.

CHAPTER 19

APARTMENT 2A

Julian used to feel a surge of pride every time he approached the gallery, but these days it was mostly dread. Ellington parked in front of the gleaming plate-glass window, in which a single piece of modestly sized art was always hung, something small enough that passersby needed to get close to see it, at which point they'd peer past to the rest of the room. Large-scale obvious art was easy to ignore if you didn't like what you saw at first glance.

"Hi Jazmyn," Julian said.

"*Mmm*," she answered, with barely contained hostility. Jazmyn had opened up the gallery, triaged messages, arranged the week's deli flowers, and settled into her main workday activity: seething resentment. Jazmyn seemed to speak with her mother every hour, apparently to complain about everything. *Snowflake* didn't begin to cover it.

Julian didn't think the girl was necessarily wrong. Capitalism does suck, hierarchy too, the commodification of everything. Sure. But could Julian be held responsible for everything?

He plopped into his desk chair, and contemplated how he was going to deal with today. He hated Tuesdays. The gallery was closed on Mondays, so Tuesdays were devoted to the weekly meeting with El followed by admin—suppliers, vendors, subcontractors of every sort, artists and collectors and random buyers, or potential buyers, all the everyday detritus of a small business, largely unchanged in the quarter century since they'd spawned the idea, as many of the best ideas are hatched, at two A.M., in a bar.

"You'll attract the uptown collectors," Ellington had said, shouting over the crowded bar and Nirvana. "People who'd never dream of opening their checkbooks or their living rooms to some *shvartza* from St. Louis." El had appropriated some Yiddish from Jules, back before anyone was saying anything about cultural appropriation. Back when a racial epithet could be called benign. "Me, I'll attract the artists who don't want any part of any Upper West Side Ivy League Jew."

Ellington took a drag of his cigarette, exhaled through his nostrils. El smoked in the same way that he did everything: suavely. "You can see it, Julie, can't you?"

"Yup." Julian took an unnecessary sip of a superfluous drink. The evening had begun nine hours earlier when El had come to the barbershop where Julian was getting a trim, carrying a shaker of martinis and chilled glasses, a jar of olives. Then a cocktail party. Then a diner dinner. Then a big anarchic party. Then a chic bar. Finally this grungy bar. A not-uncommon progression to the type of inebriation that makes it possible to have unusually honest conversations. This one was a scheme to use each other, willingly, deliberately. Exploitation does not preclude affection.

"Yeah," Julian agreed, "I see it very clearly." What he saw was this: as the millennium approached its turn, there were plenty of Black creators—actors, musicians, visual artists—but very few arbiters of culture. Producers, publishers, gallerists: almost none were people of color. These gatekeeper careers were still reserved in something like a whites-only section, where Julian had admission as a birthright. What they were talking about was getting a seat for Ellington.

Julian had majored in pre-Renaissance art, a field of study that repudiated the very idea of practical employment, while all around him kids were studying economics, engineering, prelaw, premed. El had tried desperately to be interested in finance, but failed, then moved to New York with cheap luggage and lofty ambitions. This was why everyone came, especially back when Julian was a kid, the bankrupt crime-ridden version of New York, the Bronx burning; that had taken real nerve.

It was the born-and-bred natives who were often shiftless, people whose parents or grandparents or great-grandparents had been the ambitious ones, who'd made it here. But ambition isn't inheritable, and possibly the opposite. Half the people Julian grew up with never figured out what to do, or why, and drifted through graduate schools and non-careers and New Mexico and ultimately Palm Beach, whose primary endeavors were spending money and avoiding taxes.

All great fortunes were built on the backs of misery. Real-estate money, railroad money, farming money, mining money, banking money: if you traced it back far enough, you'd find the same foul source, which over the centuries had been scrubbed clean through the laundries of finance and industry, transformed into silver service and piano lessons, private schools and trust funds and town houses, the multigenerational superstructures that enabled people to go out and supposedly make their own way in the world. This made Julian awfully grateful that his parents' modest little nest egg wasn't ultimately derived from owning Black people.

"But Julie, I have to ask: is this *really* what you want to be known for?"

A pair of women walked by, giving Julian and Ellington the eye. Everyone was young and single and drunk, and it was almost time to go home, and no one particularly wanted to do it alone.

"When people talk about you, is this what you want them to say?"

"Absolutely." Julian took a drag. Everyone was smoking, even people who didn't smoke.

One of the women smiled at Ellington, the other at Julian. Back in those days El would occasionally sleep with a woman, as something like a survival mechanism, giving himself chance after hopeless chance to be hetero. The AIDS crisis had many effects.

"Are we going to regret this in the morning?" Ellington asked.

It's not only the best ideas that are spawned at two A.M. in bars.

"What?" Julian asked. "This business idea? Or those women?"

Ellington put out his cigarette. "Both."

The gallery's division of labor sorted itself organically. Ellington was responsible for the artists, the people who had something to say, who were inventing new ways to say it. El scoured the city for grad students and studio assistants and street artists, from Harlem and the South Bronx to East Flatbush and beyond to Baltimore, Chicago, Atlanta.

Julian raised the original capital from his parents and a few other private investors, so he was the de facto capitalist, responsible for business affairs, staff, collectors, math. He flitted around galas and dinners and cocktail parties, private clubs and lavish ballrooms and the parlor floors of sumptuous mansions, handing out letterpressed business cards from Dempsey & Carroll. It wasn't a showy card, that was the point. Ellington was the showy one, with his velvet suits and his pocket squares. Julian was the one who gave every appearance of prudence.

The Sonnenberg-Toussaint Project was a Black-owned business before the term had any currency. Back then the trendy virtues were green and sustainable and independent. No one was centering Black creators or hashtagging the so-whiteness of anything, there was no such a thing as a chief diversity officer nor any diversity officer, no such thing as a hashtag. No one was sorting restaurants on apps by the ethnic self-identification of the owners. By their sexual orientation.

Julian cultivated a reputation for progressivism, which he knew was risky. Although plenty of progressives collected art, plenty of conservatives did too, and no one wanted to feel judged, especially not by the help, and for some of these people Julian was clearly the help. Plus conservatives had more money, which was primarily what made them conservatives; the flipside was what motivated many progressives. People liked to pretend that their politics were philosophical, but Julian was convinced that they were almost always personal.

There was no doubt that politics had cost the gallery some potential collectors. But Julian hoped that it attracted more, especially in the space in which the gallery specialized. Conservatives tended to collect conservative art, and Jules and El didn't traffic in any eighteenth-century portraits of European nobility posing with their horses, their houses.

It was impossible to assess the efficacy of this bargain, of sacrificing one group of potential collectors for a smaller, less wealthy, but possibly more passionate group. In a way, though, it hadn't been a bargain. What Julian had chosen to be was, simply, himself. That's the opposite of a bargain.

When they were young, having young-people discussions, Julian and Ellington used to debate this all the time: were your beliefs a choice? Religion, philosophy, love—we act as if these life-defining traits are not matters of choice. They're simply who we are, like our eye color, our height, out of our control.

But maybe not. Maybe we believe what we choose to believe. Maybe we love whom we choose to love. Maybe we are what we choose to be.

The woman Julian met at two A.M. in that bar was Jennifer. He made the two most important choices of his life in one night. He was thirty years old.

Jennifer was a corporate lawyer, working eighty hours per week in mergers and acquisitions, big companies getting bigger, rich people getting richer, and she was conflicted about all of it except the paycheck. She'd borrowed a ton of money to go to college, tons more for law school, and she wanted to live in New York City, so she didn't have much of a choice.

Julian Sonnenberg, he had a choice. And Jen loved what he was doing with it: trying to do good in the world, in art. Plus he was good-looking, good to her, good in bed. A no-brainer.

"So what do you think happened?" her therapist asked.

"Well I don't know, entirely. That's why I'm here, I guess."

It took five years before Julian was able to orchestrate the cover story, which was like the Sonnenberg-Toussaint Project's breakout album. They'd been doing the equivalent of playing five-dollar-cover clubs for years, and now they were selling out arenas. Overnight success almost never is.

The gallery was buoyed by a rising tide, with sold-out shows, bidding wars, record profits. Then the backlash to America's first Black president created an exponential swell of racial reckoning, and engendered new priorities for the cultural crowd. Black-centric culture was pulled in from the margins with astonishing urgency. They'd barely survived the lethal undertow of the financial crisis in '08, but this new tide seemed so entrenched that they were confident to expand, signing long-term leases for new galleries, hiring new staff, incurring new expenses. Ellington bought a house in Harlem, and that Jaguar. Julian spent a million dollars on private schooling for his children.

Meanwhile the entire art market had begun to feel to Julian like just another portfolio diversification—bonds, limited partnerships, infrastructure funds, real estate, contemporary Black art, whatever. Assets qua assets, deployed and redeployed, capital gains and tax implications, ugh. The fun days had become fewer and farther between, and were less fun. It was now a good day if nothing awful happened. Nobody enjoyed playing for a tie.

Tides are not controllable. The one that had lifted the gallery shifted, and Julian felt himself being pulled away from the safe harbor of his intentions, out toward treacherous waters. He'd assumed that his partnership with Ellington would be a reliable lifeboat, but he wasn't so sure anymore. The gallery wasn't even officially a Black-owned business. Ellington owned fifty percent, which for a good long while had seemed fair. It was, after all, equitable. But the concept of equity had shifted with the tide, and was no longer a matter of objective math.

Over the years the Sonnenberg-Toussaint Project had employed dozens of assistants, every one of them Black. The gallery had fostered the careers of hundreds of Black artists, had facilitated the transfer of hundreds of millions of dollars of wealth from white households to Black ones. What more was Julian supposed to give? To whom? Was he supposed to dismantle himself out of existence?

Julian didn't know how he fit into the new paradigm. He didn't know how he fit into anything. Which was why he'd been overjoyed to find something new, where he did fit in. Someone. This was what had pulled him out of his pit of despair. But he was increasingly aware that it was temporary, that it might end at any moment. And then what? He didn't think he could handle it.

But of course it might not even matter. He might not make it that far.

Ellington was standing in the doorway, holding his phone. "Did you see this?"

Julian looked up from the spreadsheet. Expenses.

"Another Black man was just killed by the police."

"Oh fuck." Julian turned back to his screen, and opened a new window, and found the news, a man-on-the-street interview, an earlier video clip from an unsteady camera lens, not a great angle, a man running by, the police rushing after, the car zooming—

Something caught Julian's eye, but he didn't know what. Something gnawing at his brain.

He watched again, and that's when he saw.

"Oh," he said, leaning away from the computer. That explains it. "Oh shit."

Julian had already known that tonight was going to be hard. This was going to make it worse. This might make it unbearable.

CHAPTER 20

FRONT DOOR

Chicky walked past an Amazon team bivouacked behind their double-parked truck. They'd set up cones in the street to cordon off a private rent-free storefront. An argument had broken out between two of the guys and seemed headed toward violence. None of the others were intervening. Chicky wished he could be one of the spectators but he didn't have time.

With the matching uniforms and piles of materiel, the setup reminded Chicky of a war zone's staging area. And every single person on this team was Black. Chicky wondered if each of these units had a captain. Someone needed to be in charge even when no one wanted to be. Especially then.

An obese woman was sitting in the middle of the stoop scowling at a phone decorated with stickers of unicorns and butterflies and rainbows. All that shit.

"Excuse me," Chicky said.

She raised her eyes and stared at Chicky then sucked her teeth dramatically. As if out of nowhere he'd asked her to donate a kidney. She leaned slightly on one massive butt cheek to allow him another couple of inches to squeeze by. "You're welcome!" she screamed.

Rainbows indeed.

This doorbell sounded almost exactly the same as his own intercom's horrible noise.

"Yeah?"

"Hector? I called about that thing."

"Yeah okay."

This was another unreliable-looking elevator. Chicky knew what he was getting himself into with 5B but opted for stairs anyway. He was working with extra adrenaline. As soon as he entered the stairwell he could hear people up there. Guys. He reconsidered but claustrophobia was powerful.

As he approached the third floor Chicky heard one guy say, "Yo I got *all* my warrants cleared." When Chicky rounded the landing three young men turned in unison. Two were sitting and the third leaning against the banister.

"Excuse me," Chicky said. These guys were maybe twenty years old. The age when knuckleheads are at their very stupidest. One passed the joint to another. They were blocking Chicky's path.

"I don't want to inconvenience you," Chicky continued. "Just need to get by."

"Yeah?" The guy took a hit and held the smoke and blew it onto Chicky. "Where you going?"

These kids didn't look hard but these days a lot of soft motherfuckers had guns to make themselves feel hard. Especially if they found an excuse to squeeze one off. Chicky didn't want to be that excuse. But he also didn't want to back down. He'd been backing down way too much.

"Excuse me," he repeated more firmly. Chicky met the eye of one of the seated guys and then the other and then the standing one. His smile wasn't meant to look sincere.

The impasse held for a beat before the standing guy said, "Yo let this old motherfucker by."

He was the one in charge.

Chicky didn't think he'd need to ring the doorbell. Just unnecessary noise. So he waited at the door, which was reinforced with metal plates and four locks. Two or three was normal. Four was a statement.

The door opened a couple of inches before catching on a security chain. "Show me some ID," Hector said through the narrow opening.

"Really? Um . . ." Chicky found his license. He hadn't driven a car in years. The guy snapped a picture with his phone. "Gimme a minute." He shut the door.

Chicky looked around. The mosaic floor had cracked tiles and stained ones and missing ones but was spotless. One of the apartment doors was decorated with crosses and beads and whatnot. Another with a purple banner, A LUISA MORENO HONOR STUDENT LIVES HERE. There wasn't a place where people didn't give a shit.

The elevator door had a little window with little bars to protect the glass. Like a tiny jail cell. For a squirrel maybe. Chicky never stopped being amazed that tourists took photos of squirrels like they're wildlife. Maybe they didn't have squirrels where they were from but still. Rats with bushy tails.

Hector's chain jangled. "You said your name was Chicky. Ain't what your license says."

"If that was your name wouldn't you go by something else?"

"Maybe. But *Chicky*?"

"Yeah I know. I didn't choose it. That's how nicknames work."

Hector took note of Chicky's bruised face and decided not to mention it. Chicky guessed that plenty of Hector's customers had something like a bruised face. That's why they were here.

"You alone?" Hector asked as he leaned out and looked around.

"Yeah."

Hector cocked his head to listen to the voices from the landing. He obviously recognized the sound of knuckleheads getting high midday in a stairwell. He opened the door fully. That was when Chicky noticed the automatic in the guy's hand.

This apartment was like the apartment of nearly everyone Chicky knew. Rooms too small and a TV too big and a low ceiling and the smell of garlic. Not garlic that had been cooked here but ordered-in Chinese-food garlic. Security-gated windows that faced a fire escape. Almost every living room resembled a cage. If it wasn't the living room it was the kitchen or the master bedroom. Somewhere, there was a cage.

At the Bohemia every apartment had a main entrance and a service entrance. So there were no fire escapes needed to satisfy fire code, no window gates, no security bars.

Hector went to a bookcase that held zero books. Instead there was a

Mary with Jesus and trophies and candles and a plastic bin. A nylon US ARMY flag push-pinned to the wall.

"You served?" Chicky asked.

"Nah." Hector pulled a pair of work gloves from the bin and rummaged around. "My boy."

"He still in?"

Chicky recognized the six-by-nine area rug from Target. He had the same rug.

"Sorta." Hector snorted. "Sing Sing past couple years. Possession with intent."

For some guys the military was a road to the straight and narrow. But for plenty of others it was just a brief detour that made the dangerous curves all the more attractive. Chicky himself had enlisted because he couldn't think of anything better to do plus his Pops had pretty much insisted on it. Manny Diaz had come home from Vietnam with PTSD and expertise in mechanics. He worked his way up to super of an apartment house where he raised his family. Manny liked neither the military nor his career but that didn't stop him from railroading his son into both.

Maybe some guys enlisted because of patriotism. Some certainly made this claim. But in Chicky's experience most of these were white dudes who also happened to be the most gun-happy motherfuckers he'd ever come across. This uniformity made it impossible to believe it was coincidence. Chicky suspected that patriotism was often just an excuse to do fucked-up shit.

Hector fished a key out of the bin. He squatted at a sofa upholstered in a color that might be called vomit. He reached under for a metal box. He took a seat and put the box in his lap and used the key to unlock it. Then he put on the gloves and opened the box and pulled out a gun.

"Huh," Chicky said. "A revolver."

"This here is a Smith & Wesson forty-four magnum with a four-inch barrel."

"Yeah." Chicky nodded. "I've mostly handled semi-auto. You got anything else in there?"

Hector turned the box around and showed Chicky: nothing but a cardboard carton of ammo.

"The advantages to this weapon? First is reliability. Second? Reliability. Third?"

"Reliability?"

"Easy to conceal." Hector slipped the gun into his pocket. Chicky wouldn't exactly call that concealed. And he worried that if he needed any shots he'd need more than six and he'd need them fast.

"Fourth: this is an extremely powerful handgun with a large-caliber bullet. This can do *damage*. The flipside though is kickback. You have experience?"

Chicky nodded. Hector nodded back.

"Fifth? And I don't know how important this is to you. But this is the weapon you can walk away with *today*. I can get something else but I'd need time. What's your, uh, event horizon?"

Chicky didn't want to burden Hector with unnecessary information. "May I?"

"May I. This guy. Polite huh?"

"I try."

Hector opened the barrel and checked it was empty. Fair enough. Chicky hefted the thing in his palm. It had been a long time since he'd held any sort of firearm. He'd been hoping that the long time would turn out to be forever.

"You got a license?"

"I showed you my license."

"I mean for the gun."

"Oh that? Nah. Not yet."

Guns made Chicky a type of uneasy he wasn't ashamed of. He was also squeamish in titty bars, where since he'd become the father of daughters he felt actual physical distress. The absence of guns and strippers was probably a good measure of a good life. Though Chicky knew plenty of guys believed the opposite. Chicky had now gone maybe twenty years without watching a woman get paid to be naked. But his long stretch of gun-free was coming to an end.

"How'd your parents choose that name anyway?" Hector asked.

"Guy who saved my dad's life in Nam. Literally saved his fucking life. Plus things were different back then, you know? It was the president's name."

Hector chuckled. "So you went with something that rhymed, huh?"

"Yeah. As I said, not my choice." Chicky inclined his chin in the direction of the semiautomatic tucked into Hector's pants. "What about that one?"

"That's my personal piece. Not for sale."

Chicky knew that everything was for sale, for the right price. But he also knew that he didn't have the money to change anyone's mind about anything. He felt the revolver's weight. Familiar but not comfortable.

Sometimes you know you're making a mistake even as you're doing it. Sometimes you don't have any real choice.

"How much?"

CHAPTER 21

APARTMENT 11C-D

Camila was calling, again, and this time Emily answered. "Hi Camila."

"Sorry to bother you, Grace. Do you know what happened to Santiago?"

Santiago, that was the guy's name.

"I saw the police questioning him, then he ran."

"Uh-huh. And did you hear the gunshots?"

Emily didn't want to tell the truth, and didn't want to lie. "Gunshots?"

"The cops shot him, Grace. Santiago is dead."

"Oh my god."

That hung there for a few seconds, then Camila got to the point. "Grace, you know I'm not one to suggest that anyone talk to the police. But you're a little different, right? So you might want to think about going to the station, making a statement? That's up to you. I'm just saying."

"I understand."

"You saw what was going on, right? White cops, Black man." These days a lot of presumptions of racism were flying around, accusations.

"I'll do what I can, Camila." That wasn't going to be much; that wasn't going to be anything. Emily needed to stay away from this. "Thanks for calling."

Emily hung up, and sat in a daze.

"Miss? Are you all right?" Tatiana was standing in the doorway, concern etched across her forehead. Emily wanted to unburden herself—

something horrible had happened around her, and something bad to her—but no, it couldn't be the housekeeper she told first. Emily could not be a woman whose confidantes were people she paid. Like purchasing friends.

"Yes, Tattie. Thank you for asking."

Emily wished she had the type of marriage in which she wouldn't need to think twice, she'd already have been on the phone with her husband more than once, discussing these horrible events. Instead she had the type of marriage where she could barely discuss anything.

This was not how Emily had imagined marriage worked, back when she didn't know a damn thing about how marriage worked. Another lesson that's impossible to learn until it's too late.

Emily had never lied to herself that she'd been in love with Whit, not really. But she'd believed he was in love with her, and she'd hoped that would be enough. She still had no idea what had made him so averse to her. Trying for a third child had been important to him, for some reason she couldn't understand. It was one thing to want a third, but who *needed* it? No one.

It took a half year for her to get pregnant again, then she miscarried. Then she miscarried again. Her body was telling her something, and she needed to listen. Parenting was hard. Two children were more than enough.

"No," she said. "I don't think it's a great idea to continue to try. I don't think I can do it." She'd expended a lot of emotional energy to say this.

"I'm sorry," Whit had answered, and for the briefest moment Emily felt relief, until he added, "that you feel that way," and walked out of the room.

They hadn't been fighting, no major arguments. But once this arctic front came through, the disagreements started to mount in a way that felt relentless, and irreversible.

"You know that having children is your actual job?" he'd eventually said. This was a particularly low moment in her life, and her husband chose to make it lower. If Emily had to pinpoint the source of their demise, that choice of his would be it. For weeks afterward she'd barely been able to look at him, and she'd wondered if this was the end. With two kids, one in diapers.

Plenty of couples went forth into the world and bickered. They bickered in restaurants, at dinner parties, just walking down the sidewalk disagreeably, disputing the other's recollections, anything. Emily would not air dirty laundry like that. She made damn sure that the Whitaker Longworths hated each other quietly, privately, while in public they continued to look like a happy couple. That was another one of her responsibilities.

Whit had often put his hands around her neck during sex. For a while it didn't bother her, didn't seem weird, or at least not too weird. Emily had given him the benefit of the doubt. Many doubts.

Then a few months after she declined to try to get pregnant again, he started applying more pressure. At first Emily had thought—hoped—it was involuntary, his grip tightening as he got closer, an involuntary reaction, biology. But then he applied more pressure, and more, and she worried that it was the other way around: the choking was triggering the orgasm. She tried not to be judgmental, but that was definitely weird. That, she thought, was sick. That was the first proclivity she'd encountered that made her feel truly icky. All her previous sexual partners had tastes that largely aligned with her own. She didn't know how to handle this. She didn't want to deny her husband his pleasure, and she didn't want to judge him for it.

But then it began to hurt. "Hey," she said, "that hurts."

"*Ungh,*" he grunted, and sped up his thrusting, tightened his grip.

"Whit. *Ow.*"

"Okay, okay." He released his hands. "No big deal." But it was, apparently. He rolled off her, his penis pointing toward the ceiling, shiny and red and furious looking. Emily knew what he wanted her to do. She didn't do it.

The wildly inappropriate starchitect had been the first obviously purposeful humiliation. The second, a year later, was far more degrading, by orders of magnitude.

"I'm going out for a bit," Whit had said at ten o'clock on a Tuesday night.

"Out?" There were plenty of people in New York who left home at ten at night, but Whit Longworth was not one of them. "Where?"

"Meeting a friend for a drink. Don't wait up."

Two hours later he came back smelling unmistakably of sex. He hadn't even bothered to wash off his dick. He was taking her dignity, and challenging her to object. She was too stunned to do anything except move farther across the bed. That was one of the times when she came close to crying, but didn't want to give him that victory.

He made this a habit, once a month, twice. Call me on it, he was saying. I dare you.

Neither of them was going to be the one to end the marriage. A stalemate.

Running their household wasn't completely unlike running a business, of which Emily was chief—and only—executive. Whit was perhaps chairman, an emeritus type of position. Personnel was not the largest expenditure, but it was the biggest challenge. The housekeeper and nanny were the only full-time employees, augmented by a legion of part-time and contract and seasonal workers.

Many of these people were for the children's care or enrichment—language tutors, general academic tutors, weekend babysitters, athletic coaches—baseball for Hudson, riding for Bitsy, tennis and golf and skiing for both.

Then there was the broad umbrella of real-estate personnel, mostly on Long Island: property manager, gardener, lawn guy, specialists for pool and tennis court and trees and pests. Interior designers in city and country, general contractors. The masseuse, personal shopper, concierge-medicine GP, travel agent, pilot, three private chefs in different zip codes, caterers. The Aspen contingent was disproportionate for what amounted to—what?—eight days per year of skiing? If Longworth Inc. ever needed to trim expenses, Aspen would be the place to start.

Last year Emily paid out a million dollars to fifty individuals and companies for services.

Then there were charitable contributions—twenty dollars for this bake sale, fifty there, a thousand for any cause if a friend asked, a hundred thousand if Emily really cared, the occasional million when someone needed to step up.

Plus all the capital expenditures, and the taxes, and all the *things*, so much stuff that Emily purchased for herself, her kids, her friends, her homes.

Emily was not careful about spending money, but she did keep careful track. Last year, the grand total was over four million dollars.

At first, Whit had looked over her shoulder, but he gradually stopped caring, or started trusting her, or both. He stopped paying close attention, then any attention. What he wanted in exchange for this freedom was one hundred percent responsibility and accountability. Whit didn't want to deal with any of it, he didn't want to hear about problems, didn't want to find solutions.

"I understand," Emily had agreed heartily. This was when they used to have weekly catchups, a glass of wine at the monstrous kitchen island in the super-tall. When Whit started having his assistant schedule these meetings, Emily was taken aback. By the time he decreased the frequency to monthly, she'd lost the capacity to be surprised. Emily had now been managing their finances for years, all the day-to-day, the renovations too. Whit no longer had any real idea what almost anything cost.

She began tentatively, modestly, experimentally: small amounts skimmed from cash withdrawals, ad hoc, cash in an actual shoebox. A passive endeavor. Then she became more active, started to manufacture opportunities, testing the limits of Whit's obliviousness, which were apparently boundless. He didn't notice when one year their life became ten percent more expensive, then fifteen, twenty. His income was doubling every year, and it was of no consequence how much they spent.

Emily was emboldened. Everyday expenses generated smaller margins; seasonal maintenance was larger. Contractor work was easiest, because everyone was already shaving off covert cuts on top of overt fees and expenses. Emily became one of them—the bathroom renovation, the pool-house expansion, the barn rehab. Twenty thousand, seventy thousand, a quarter-million dollars.

This didn't feel different from wearing a life jacket for rafting: prudent protection against unlikely but not impossible misfortune. Then as their relationship deteriorated, Emily became more and more convinced that capsizing was not at all unlikely; on the contrary. The question was how prepared she'd be when Whit pushed her off into the rapids.

She acquired a driver's license in the name of Carolyn Wilson, a Yonkers woman of roughly Emily's age who'd died in a car crash. Emily used that license to open a checking account into which she deposited the purloined funds, mostly a few thousand here and there, sometimes butting up against the IRS's reporting requirement at ten grand. On a regular basis she transferred money to a numbered account in the Caymans. For the hell of it, she bought some crypto. When that investment had tripled, she got nervous—what *was* crypto, anyway?—and sold all of it.

Over the years Emily had redirected more than five million dollars, which thanks largely to the crypto insanity had appreciated to eight. This principal wouldn't generate the type of income to support her lifestyle. But with the prenup's disbursements, it would suffice. Sort of.

When it became clear that Whit was going to be cheating routinely, she called her matrimonial attorney. "We say family law these days," he'd corrected. "And infidelity isn't something that can be proscribed. I'm sorry." He wasn't, of course, sorry. If it weren't for infidelity, this guy wouldn't have much of a job. Emily got the feeling that although this lawyer wasn't necessarily expecting a divorce, he was definitely rooting for it.

Her phone dinged with the alert: *Another Black Man Dead at the Hands of Police.*

"Oh god," she muttered, her heart sinking.

You don't expect the news to be personal. Maybe the market is tanking and you've just lost two percent of your net worth; maybe a hurricane is coming, you should stock up on canned goods, fill the tub with water. But not something like this.

Emily read the first paragraph while switching on the television, then the second paragraph, the man pronounced dead from multiple gunshot wounds, name not yet released.

The video footage of the sidewalk scene was familiar but also not, because of the angle, the lens somewhere Emily would never be, in front of that liquor store across the street from the pantry. The footage was poor, from a shaky, nervous hand. A hectic streetscape, a crowd of Black and Hispanic faces and one white woman, a very familiar-looking person wearing a Yankees cap pulled low.

"Oh," she said. "Oh dear."

"Hi Zaire," Emily said, as cheerfully as possible. Zaire was the least friendly of the doormen, so it was with him that Emily tried to be the most. "Beautiful day, isn't it?"

"Mrs. Longworth. Get you a taxi?"

"No thanks, Zaire." She has failed, again. With some people there's no succeeding. "Have a good day."

She crossed to the park side and walked on the cobbled sidewalk alongside the stone wall to the gate. Inside the park, she took the bridle path until she turned off on a footpath that rose the small hill that provided the view over the oblong field.

The grass was filled with forty children, all in navy gym shorts and maroon tee shirts. The kids were divided into groups for different sports.

It usually took Emily a minute to definitively identify Hudson. Nearly all these kids were the same age and size, and white, and they were all moving, and she was far away, peeking from behind a tree trunk. What she was doing was strongly discouraged, but today she needed it. This was something she did on the slopes too. In fact the main thing she did on ski mountains was cruise around trying to spy on her children. She could identify Hudson from a quarter mile away just by the way he held his elbows out to the side; he really took to heart the instruction to carry a lunch tray. And Bitsy by her hips, always steady, while everything below leaned and bent and pivoted. Emily's children were both excellent skiers, in their own ways.

She scanned . . . squinted . . .

There. Emily watched her son running for the ball, those little elbows pumping. She was too far away to see his furrowed brow, but she saw it in her mind, which was where she could also see the tongue out of the corner of his mouth. She could see this whole scene with her eyes closed.

Hudson lunged, and fell, tumbled, and Emily felt her whole body tense, she heard herself say, "Oh," and her hands were on her chest, her breath held—

The boy got up immediately, and continued running, and Emily exhaled, and dropped her arms. It could come on so fast and strong, fear for your child. And the relief was so powerful.

She checked her watch, and pulled herself away. She started walking downtown, beginning her transformation from one expression of a woman to another. It was sometimes hard to reconcile that both were the same person.

CHAPTER 22

APARTMENT 2A

Julian didn't think he'd be able to make it through this lunch, but it was almost over, thank god.

"I'll do an oat milk matcha latte," Cole said, and Julian laughed before he could stop himself.

"What's so funny?"

"Oh, sorry, nothing," Julian said, which Cole accepted, eager to return to his disquisition on international travel—the world's longest commercial air route, lie-flat in Cathay vs. Emirates, jet-lag strategies, five-star hotels. Cole believed that complicated and expensive logistics meant that his life was difficult, and his triumphs that he's shrewd.

A waitress was crossing the room, young and lithe, with the body and movements of a dancer. There seemed to be an infinite number of these women serving food in Manhattan, a renewable human resource, fresh ones arriving constantly with their Degas posters and their Pier 1 rattan, meal kits from Trader Joe's. You saw the older ones in the Theater District, wearing leg warmers, feet in third position as they took your order. The younger ones filled Julian with hope; the older with despair. The space between the two wasn't a lot of years.

"There's big money in sales," Cole asserted, apropos of who knows. Julian had stopped paying attention.

"You don't say."

Even the guy's name seemed designed for efficiency, with no time wasted on unnecessary syllables. Cole Dodd was a semiretired arbitrageur, an Arc'teryx guy with a too-aggressive handshake and a twenty-eight-inch waist, an Apple watch and an Oura ring and those Topsider-y shoes that cost seven hundred dollars. According to the wife who'd introduced them, Cole needed some *quality* art for his *massive* new home office with the panty-dropper views—her phrase. Briony had initially suggested an interior designer, but Cole rejected that idea as too gay, a phrase she repeated gleefully. Briony was convinced that Julian and Cole would love each other, despite the obvious impossibility. Many women were deluded about the likability of their husbands. She was, after all, the one who'd dropped her panties.

"Can my guy bring you somewhere?" Cole asked when they were out on the sidewalk, nodding in the direction of the expected SUV. The Meatpacking District was littered with hulking black cars waiting for their shiny white passengers to emerge from the Whitney, from the hotels, the restaurants. It was hard to believe that meatpacking used to happen here, not long ago. Now the shops were indistinguishable from Madison Avenue's, which was exactly why Julian's gallery had moved from Madison Avenue. This depressed the shit out of him.

"No, but thanks so much." Julian would rather crawl across hot coals. "I'll be in touch."

He couldn't get away from this douchebag fast enough to check his voicemail, which turned out to be from the accountant: "Sorry to be calling with bad news. So, yeah, the IRS decided to move forward with the audit. It's time to start gathering receipts. Let's meet next week?"

Next week, Julian almost laughed at the idea. He didn't return the call.

"When people with your condition get to fifty, okay," Dr. Ramirez had said, a year and a half ago, "something needs to be done about it."

"Something needs to be done? Meaning what?"

"Because of the anomaly, your aortic valve has been under an unusual degree of pressure, okay, for your entire life. As time passes, this condition elevates the risk of valve failure."

"And what's the result of valve failure?"

"Well, that can be fatal. Usually, fatal. Almost always, in fact. Instantaneously."

Julian's mouth fell open.

"I'm not saying that valve failure is *inevitable*, okay? But it's increasingly *possible*, especially after fifty. And certainly by your midfifties, the valve should be taken care of."

"Taken care of?" Julian could barely formulate the question: "This is open-heart surgery we're talking about?"

"It's a *very* commonplace procedure, Mr. Sonnenberg. Very safe."

"And I need this *now*?"

"No."

Julian felt himself exhale, but it was a short-lived relief.

"Not necessarily. But now you should start getting an annual scan. And it's time to become careful about strain. Do you run?"

"You mean jogging? Sometimes."

"Do you sprint?"

"I do interval training."

"Well, you should stop, okay? The sprinting. Light jogging is fine. What about weights?"

"Um." Julian's routine alternated cardio and strength, upper-body and lower, core. "Yes."

"That's fine, but not heavy." The cardiologist was shuffling through folders, then handed Julian a one-sheet about weights, running, heart rate. This seemed to be a mimeograph handout from the 1980s.

"And sex?"

Julian actually laughed. "Are you asking if I have sex?" This was getting worse by the second. "Not a lot, but more than never."

"Have you tried it on your side? It's safer. And better for your back. For your wife too. How's her back?"

His wife's back, Christ. This visit had really gone off the rails. "Fine, I guess."

"Well, you should think about it."

"Hmm," Julian agreed, or didn't agree, it didn't matter, he and Jen were barely having sex. Her desire had been waning for years, a slow-motion cessation that arrived at a hard stop when she got cancer. Sooner or later, almost everyone will come down with some cancer, unless something else kills us first. Like being in a car accident—some variation happens to everyone. Whether a fender bender or a head-on collision, your chances are best if you're driving below the speed limit, wearing your seat belt, ensconced in an expensive car.

Jen's was all of those: caught early by a hypervigilant patient, beaten into submission by top-flight care. Jen dove into treatment the way she dove into everything, career and parenthood and Pilates and Mediterranean cooking; Jen puréed her own hummus. Even into Julian himself, back when he'd been her passion project. Jen was all-in, albeit carefully, she was data-driven, she was aggressive and conservative at the same time. Her homemade falafel were baked, not deep-fried.

Her cancer came and went within a year. Now it'd been three years of clean scans.

Not coincidentally, it's been four since they had sex aside from extremely rare alcohol-aided outliers. The cancer and its treatment exacerbated a preexisting trend, providing the excuse that Julian suspected his wife wanted. Not that they'd ever argue about it, nor even discuss it. The excuse, like so many other things in their marriage, was implicit.

And now this catastrophic-valve-failure thing? Jesus. Julian's entire corporeal experience was collapsing with alarming speed.

"Wait. Are you saying . . . ?" Julian closed his eyes. "Are you saying that sex could *kill* me?"

Dr. Ramirez sighed, as if his patient's life-or-death questions were tiresome.

"Life is risky, okay? You could get hit by a bus, a stray bullet. Some activities are riskier than others. Some people are at greater risk. Risks evolve. Your congenital anomaly increases the risk of *any* activity that elevates your heart rate to over eighty percent of max. There, look: it's on the flip side of that page."

Julian turned over the paper, a graph of age against heart rate. He'd seen this graph plenty, it was on basically every piece of cardio equipment in the world. He'd never paid it any attention.

"And by any activity, I mean *any* activity, okay? It doesn't matter whether it's for exercise, or for enjoyment, or just an autonomic response to stimuli."

"Autonomic? Are you saying I could get *scared to death*?"

Julian had already accepted that after his kids left for college, he'd begin to feel old; he'd begin to *be* old. This wasn't reversible, nor avoidable. The best you could hope for was a slow demise. But even within that pessimistic context, this instant-death possibility was a showstopper.

There were, Julian knew, many reasons why he was doing what he was doing.

Julian looked around the subway car, an everyday miracle of diversity—East Asians and South Asians, North Africans and West Africans, a panoply of Latin Americans, a Hassidic man poring over his Torah who was sharing a bench with a woman in a hijab, an all-blond family with a teenager in a University of Iowa sweatshirt, the five of them huddled together, consulting the map again and again, clearly concerned that they might be on the wrong train, going to the wrong place, with the wrong people.

"Due to an injured passenger," the PA announced, "all trains will be running express."

Julian exited to a crowded platform, plenty of cops, nearly all of them looking bored, staring at phones. "You know what happened?" Julian asked the one who seemed to be paying any attention.

"Homeless woman threw herself onto the tracks. Up in Harlem."

"Oh god. That's horrible."

"Yeah. But someone jumped down to pull her out of the way of the train."

Julian climbed out to Columbus Circle. When he was a kid, this intersection had been dominated by the much-maligned New York Coliseum, which was eventually relegated to the trash heap of history when the Javits Center was built. The site then lay fallow while one redevelopment deal after another fell apart in the face of stock-market dips and community opposition and lawsuits, a quagmire of Mort Zuckerman and Rudy Giuliani and Salomon Brothers. The sidewalk was ceded to drug dealers and prostitutes and homeless people.

Eventually Time Warner steamrolled over all obstacles to build mixed-use glass towers—condominiums, offices, luxury hotel, shopping mall. The uses that were mixed were different manifestations of wealth. The views were magnificent, the staff obsequious, and there was a shopping mall! Plus restaurants with tasting menus, wine vaults, caviar, gold-leafed desserts.

The Time Warner Center was proof of the concept that immensely tall apartment towers could attract the jet set if they could buy their units through LLCs, anonymously, without passing the requirements of snotty co-ops, not subject to occupancy regulations, or sublet regulations, or renovation regulations, or almost any other regulations, an asset that could be swapped for questionably begotten fortunes generated in more nakedly corrupt economies, tangible American property that would be unseizable no matter how the political, economic, or legal winds shifted in China, Russia, Africa, the Middle East.

The concept was proven. Billionaires' Row was born, grew, thrived. The financiers and profiteers and plutocrats and kleptocrats gobbled up condos for twenty, fifty, a hundred million dollars, then barely moved in. These apartments were more like vaults than residences. One sold for two hundred and twenty million dollars, a figure equivalent to spending nearly a thousand dollars per day, every day, for six hundred years. A scale that proved just how much was wrong with the world.

The Time Warner Center had at some point become the Deutsche Bank Center. And Time Warner itself acknowledged that it was a thoroughly reviled brand, and decided to simply change its name, hoping that customers would just forget their virulent antipathy. Julian laughed at the possibility that this scheme could ever work. "How stupid do they think we are?" he'd asked Ellington, who'd answered, "Not nearly as stupid as we actually are."

El, it turned out, had been right.

Sometimes a solution to a problem was just a matter of calling it something else.

Julian knew he was an extremely fortunate person. For a good chunk of his life, he'd also been a happy one. Things deteriorated. First because of the financial crisis, and the measures he'd taken to stay solvent. Then the erosion of his marriage, drifting into different orbits. Professionally too, where he felt less and less valuable, something he could've anticipated from the very inception. The premise of the Sonnenberg-Toussaint Project was to make Julian the embodiment of planned obsolescence. He hadn't necessarily expected it to work, but it had.

Following that horrific cardiologist appointment, Julian could barely get out of bed. This was a busy time for Jen, working such long hours that it may have qualified as torture under UN guidelines. Jen didn't notice that her husband was depressed, which depressed him yet more. His kids were self-absorbed teenagers who barely acknowledged his existence, on their way to becoming people he speaks to on the phone occasionally, who meet him for duck and dumplings on Christmas. People about whom he knows only what they choose to share.

Maybe everyone is, at heart, a stranger. Even your kids, your spouse. Maybe neither he nor Jen would really know the whole truth about the other, ever again. Maybe they never really had.

The only one in the household who greeted him joyfully was Gillie, but barely. And soon the old dog would be dead.

So it was that in the middle of middle age, Julian found himself greeting each dawn with pessimism, and each evening reaping the dubious reward of having proved himself correct. Each day he felt less and less valued, more and more irrelevant, a progression that looked inexorable.

It crossed his mind, every day, that his problems would be solved if he died. He wouldn't have called this suicidal ideation; he wasn't envisaging himself committing any acts, he wasn't making plans. He was just aware of the practicality of it. He even hunted down their T&E file, and checked the policy he'd taken out when Asher was born, a two-million-dollar death benefit. Seventeen years later, two million wasn't what it used to be, which was, he supposed, the foundation of the insurance business. But still, two million was a lot more than nothing, which was a possibility.

Julian asked himself: what do I still want to do before I die? This was another thing that depressed him: he didn't really have any answer.

During that long sad winter, Julian skipped all optional social events. But his job required openings, galas, dinners, meetings; he needed to be out in the world, wearing a fake smile.

His mood was lifted whenever he ran into Emily Longworth. Julian had always been flirtatious, he'd enjoyed lavishing attention on women, and he liked to believe they enjoyed receiving it, at least some of them.

His intention had never been more than playful. But he now realized he was basing his willingness to attend events on the likelihood that another man's wife would be there. Julian paid closer attention to his wardrobe. He arrived earlier. He stayed later.

So he invited her for coffee; they had fun. He invited her for lunch; they had more fun. He didn't believe that an affair was in the offing, it was just a fantasy, a way to make masturbation better. Their anodyne lunches were nothing anyone needed to hide, so they met in plain sight, two people in the art world who lived in the same building, ran with the same crowd, they were friends. It made eminent sense for them to socialize, with their spouses, without, whatever. It was faultless.

But from the very first invitation he extended, Julian knew he was doing something wrong. His proof was that he never mentioned these dates to Ellington. And certainly not Jennifer.

Julian didn't know if Emily flirted as a matter of course. Maybe she was a woman who never stopped using her sexuality to gain advantage—touching your elbow, tossing around compliments and hair indiscriminately, none of it meant anything. Or was she flirting with Julian specifically? If so, did she actually want him? Or did she just want to be wanted? There was a huge difference, and in the gap was an opportunity for profound humiliation. And if she did want Julian, did she want to do anything about it? There was another huge gap.

He had a hard time believing that such an exquisite woman could want him. Emily was a type of beautiful that was like a virus, infecting everything—her clothes, the set of her shoulders, the sway of her gait, you could tell just from the way she walked that she was beautiful, you could see it in the tilt of her neck, in the beautiful smile creeping up her beautiful mouth, those beautiful lips parting to reveal those perfect teeth. And her eyes! The blue was inhuman, like an empire butterfly, a peacock's feathers, the Ionian Sea off some Greek isle, people would come from the world over to glimpse it, snap photos that they'd disclaim didn't do justice, you wouldn't believe the color.

The more time Julian spent with Emily, he began to see that she was far more than beautiful. She was funny, and charming, and intelligent, and sexy as hell. Everything.

That dire assessment from the cardiologist, instead of making Julian more cautious, made him confront that life was getting shorter. Doors were closing that might never open again.

One morning, in the fallow hour between a co-op meeting and a lunch, he received what a different person—a religious person—might have considered a sign from god, albeit a very odd god.

It was easy to find pictures of Emily, she was heavily documented in society pages, consumer magazines, paparazzi websites. Julian reclined in bed with his laptop, his screen maximized to a photo of Emily wearing a tight little dress, which he was imagining peeling off—he was in the very act of picturing her naked breasts, and that wasn't the only act he was in the middle of—when his phone rang.

His laptop received incoming voice calls, so the pop-up announced "Call from Emily Longworth" as an intrusion over a picture of Emily Longworth. Julian didn't even need to release the grip on his dick to answer, though first he did double-check that it wasn't video. Then he triple-checked. No one was ever going to remember that legal analyst for anything else. Julian had seen the guy out on the street recently, and he'd rarely felt so sorry for someone.

"Hello?"

"You're not going to believe this," she launched right in. Emily had a habit of beginning a conversation midstride, as if an ongoing dialogue had not ended, just paused. It was one of the things about her he adored. There were many.

"I've been standing here, staring at the wall, for a half hour, and I finally realized: I have nothing for the entry. *Nothing!*"

Julian couldn't help but laugh.

"Oh dear," he said. "I'll come, right away."

And he did.

CHAPTER 23

FRONT DOOR

Chicky could tell that the building he was going to was the one with two goons out front. They were standing next to a Navigator with blacked-out windows and custom rims and a license-plate shield. A vehicle so criminal it might as well be wearing a prison jumpsuit.

He slowed his roll. Chicky didn't want to seem like he was trying to rush up on anyone. That's how people got shot. The muscle eyed him. Both of Chicky's hands were in his pockets. His left was balled into a tense fist and his right was wrapped around the new revolver. Hands in pockets were also something that could get you shot. Chicky took them out.

The more gigantic goon asked, "The fuck you lookin' at?"

"Hey, my apologies, no disrespect." Chicky smiled. "Here to see El Puño."

"The fuck are you?"

"My name's Chicky Diaz. I'm a bouncer over at Junior's?"

"The fuck you want with my man?"

"I, um. I wanted to apologize."

"The fuck for?"

"We had a"—bigger smile—"misunderstanding the other night."

Some guys are scary because they look like they don't give a shit. Some are scary because it's obvious they're strapped. Some are scary because they're the size of a tree. This guy glaring at Chicky was all those. Plus his silent companion was just as scary plus so stupid-looking it was almost funny. Almost. In Chicky's experience stupid guys were the ones to worry about. This particular guy also had job-killer tattoos all over his neck and face. This person had no intention of ever having real workingman's employment in his life. That may be the scariest type of stupid person.

"So you think I could maybe get a minute?"

The Tree sucked his teeth as if his intelligence had been insulted. "Fuck no."

One hundred percent of this guy's sentences contained the word *fuck*. It was impressive.

"Just a minute?" Chicky didn't know if begging would be useful or the opposite. Sometimes it was hard to tell if groveling would be seen as respect or weakness. "One minute's all I need."

The big guy sucked his teeth again. He couldn't be bothered to entertain the stupid-ass idea, not for one second. Just then El Puño emerged from the iron-and-glass door and glared down from the top of the stoop. He took one step down and another until he was looming right above Chicky.

"You that bouncer, huh."

Chicky was penned in by the henchmen. He resisted the urge to reach into his pocket. That might become necessary a few seconds from now but not yet. His heart was racing.

"Yes I am. I just wan—"

"The fuck was you thinkin' *puto*?"

Chicky tried not to react to the put-down. "I wasn't thinking. I'm sorry."

"You can't be puttin' your hands on people. On *me*."

Chicky had been plenty justified. He knew it. El Puño knew it. Everyone at the bar knew it. His flunkies knew it too. This had nothing to do with justified. Or justice.

"I apologize. Sincerely."

"You tryin' to make me look like a *pussy*? Up in the *bar*?" El Puño shook his head. A damn crying shame. "You got my boys *arrested*, motherfucker."

"I'm very sorry Boss." Chicky was going to keep apologizing. Even though he was the one with the busted face and maybe cracked ribs. "I really am."

"Yeah. You said that. But I lost twenty Gs bail 'cause a your stupid ass."

Chicky wanted to object that this wasn't how bail worked. But he also didn't want to dignify this line of reasoning. And he certainly wasn't going to get into an argument about it.

El Puño looked him up and down again even more slowly. The look itself was a practiced challenge. A taunt. "So how you gonna make it up to me, *puto*?"

Face Tattoo responded to the shift in Puño's energy by taking a step closer to Chicky.

"I don't know Boss. What did you have in mind?"

Chicky would grovel. Chicky would apologize. Those cost him nothing. But Chicky would not accept a beatdown. This fucking thug had already hit Chicky for the last time. Maybe that meant Chicky was going to die on this sidewalk today. So be it. We all need to go sooner or later and Chicky had already accepted that for him it might be sooner. It certainly had been for his wife.

"I heard you work in that building. What's it called?"

Chicky's heart was lifted by the realization that this was what the guy wanted. But then it plummeted. Because there was no way in hell that El Puño had heard this intel out on the street. Chicky's employment was not a detail that had any currency in Harlem-gangster circles.

"The Bohemia," Chicky supplied.

"Uh-huh, yeah."

The only way El Puño knew where Chicky worked was if Junior had told him. Which meant that Junior had been lying to Chicky that he didn't know El Puño. And lying that he didn't know what El Puño wanted. Because Junior was the backstabbing motherfucker who'd suggested it.

Maybe Chicky shouldn't have been surprised. He'd never trusted his cousin. But Christ.

The most successful people all seemed to be the most shameless liars.

"Yeah I heard they got some motherfuckers livin' large up in there."

People were always asking Chicky to reveal confidences. Everyone wanted to hear if some celebrity was an asshole. Or what car does she drive. How many bodyguards. How does he tip? She's cheap, right? Right? Come on man you can tell me.

But gossip wasn't what El Puño wanted. The guy hocked up a big gob of spit and hurled it just past Chicky's feet. Another taunt.

"Yeah." Better to get out in front of this. "I've definitely thought about it."

How could you not? Out there on the sidewalk killing time. You have to wonder. It's not like the Bohemia was a military installation or an armory or a police station or a bank or a mint. It was just an old apartment house. It wouldn't be hard to breach.

"But the security?" Chicky didn't want to continue to look this guy in the eye but he also didn't want to insult him by looking away. "Cameras *everywhere*. Every unit has unpickable locks and reinforced doors. Plus the alarms? All hardwired to private companies who respond with armed personnel *within minutes*. And I don't mean some rent-a-cop with a .38 special and an alcohol problem. I mean professional SWAT teams with assault rifles."

In reality Chicky was astounded at how little security existed.

"These people? They're not fucking around."

No, getting in would not be hard. The real challenge would be not getting caught afterward.

"Uh-huh," El Puño said.

And choosing the right apartment to rob beforehand. An apartment filled with portable valuables. An apartment where you wouldn't get shot.

"But still."

CHAPTER 24

APARTMENT 11C-D

Emily walked alongside the lake, paused to take in the perfection. Her phone rang, Skye again, and Emily declined again. This time Skye left a message: *"Hey Emmie, just hoping to catch up. And wondering why you're not answering my calls?"*

She took the final sip of green juice, ninety calories. Green juice was Emily's lunch once or twice per week, pretty much whenever she wasn't meeting someone. No-meat Mondays had evolved into no-solid-food Mondays and then Wednesdays too and occasionally Fridays, plus—or minus?—no red meat, ever, nor pasta nor bread, then no potatoes, no sugar, no dessert obviously. In essence nothing white, except wine and the occasional parsnip.

"Or returning them? Did I do something wrong?"

It wasn't easy to limit calories to fifteen hundred every day of every month of every year, with success measured by the distance between your thighs.

"Whatever it is, let's talk about it, okay? I miss you."

Occasionally for lunch Emily had an Altoid and sparkling water, maybe an antacid. A couple of Tums was not a completely unsatisfying meal. She was removing one food after another, on her way to something like Soylent Green, plus rice cakes, which Whit referred to as her cardboard.

"Why do you mock me for eating this, Whit? You want me to be thin, don't you?"

"I want you to be happy."

"Please. You want me to be happy as a size two. But if I were a happy two hundred pounds? I don't eat this because I enjoy it, Whit. I eat this so I can be thin without actually starving to death."

Today's juice was from PWRPLNT, the vegetable-forward grab-and-go owned by Morgan and her much older husband, Jerry, a serial entrepreneur. Both Lipschitzes threw around phrases like *purpose-driven lifestyle brand*, of which *narrative storytelling* was a *core attribute*.

PWRPLNT was the chain's second name, after consumers were bewildered by RwFd + Jūs, which suggested a chemical equation composed by someone who'd only ever glanced at a periodic table briefly, from very far away, and didn't understand it at all. The Lipschitzes had fallen precipitously in Emily's esteem with that *ū*, then more when she saw PWRPLNT's walls painted with imaginary raves that included redacted profanity—"the best f***ing acai bowl on the planet"—with no attributions whatsoever, the sort of canard that evoked Donald Trump's charade of being his own publicist, a level of shamelessness that suggested clinical insanity. And adding the indefensible macron in *ū* while omitting the useful cedilla for *açai*, that made it hard for Emily to continue to look Morgan in the eye.

"I really just do it for the fun," Morgan had claimed about her CMO position, eager to dispel any possible misunderstanding that she might actually need to earn money.

Morgan wasn't the only dilettante entrepreneur in Emily's group of school moms. There was also an organization expert, a feng shui consultant, a career adviser, interior designers plural, and a fashion stylist whose website claimed she wasn't taking on any new clients, "Please sign up for our waiting list." You could put together a team representing every discipline of the finance-wife life from these women, whose primary if not only qualification was leading their daily existences.

Emily was almost positive that the stylist's business had never taken on any new clients—never, not once—but that the entire endeavor was a ploy to secure invitations to fashion shows. It had apparently worked. Emily wasn't sure if she respected this or despised it.

"Sorry!" Emily typed to Skye. "Crazy days. Will call soon!"

♦ ♦ ♦

Some women had always planned to be stay-at-home moms. Not Emily.

It wasn't until midway through her first pregnancy when it became clear that Whit assumed Emily wouldn't be returning to work. She'd assumed nothing of the sort. In fact Emily had been enjoying work much more since it was no longer strictly necessary to turn a profit. She could ditch despicable clients, set boundaries, worry less.

Then one day Whit was talking about her living in Southampton full-time for the summer; he'd be in the city four days per week. "It's what everyone does." Whit himself would be commuting by helicopter. Surely not everyone did that?

Emily hadn't thought of herself as one of those everyones. She'd spent a decade of summers sweltering in Manhattan. And while she was now being chauffeured around by her husband's driver instead of the crosstown bus, she was still a working person. So she'd been planning to take off three months for the baby, four tops, and hope that her clients wouldn't necessarily notice.

As she explained all this to Whit, he wore a half smile.

"And I guess Southampton could be good," she'd concluded. She was imagining bringing clients around to the East End galleries. "There are interesting things happening in Riverhead, of all places." Some pioneers were trying to establish an artistic bulkhead in Long Island's sweaty, seedy armpit.

"Oh," Whit said, at this piece of specificity. "You're serious?"

Emily didn't know how to respond.

"Em." He could imbue one syllable with a lot. "Don't get me wrong. It's *adorable* that you want to continue to work. But do you really think it's practical?"

"Practical?" She actually laughed. "Of course it's practical."

"Okay." He nodded. "Sure."

All these years later, one thing Emily was still sure about: whatever Whit's many faults, he was not stupid. He knew how to win an argument without even making one.

Emily and the baby moved to Southampton for the summer, along with most of the other moms Emily knew, amid tennis coaches and golf pros and European au pairs and Latino landscapers and a bottomless glass of rosé. Emily never spent another summer in the city.

As a young woman, Emily had pitied those middle-aged women who were constantly reminding you of their ex-careers—when I was at Morgan, when I worked with the DA, when I was in grad school, asking to be respected for a career she'd had for just a few years, decades ago, and were still clutching like life preservers of their identities.

Then Emily became one of them. She'd been gainfully employed for nine years of her life, and in all likelihood she would never again work for money. She will probably live to be—what?—ninety, ninety-five years old. In the end, her career will have occupied ten percent of her years. She still fantasized occasionally about rebooting her consultancy. But at a certain level of wealth you can't possibly undertake for anyone to pay you for anything. It would be unseemly.

Meanwhile Whit had become a man who worked all the time. Even when he wasn't working working, he was watching Fox Business, reading the *Journal* or *FT*, listening to podcasts about leadership, or innovation, or execution, or some other mumbo jumbo pseudo-macho crap. What her husband was really doing was avoiding parenting by pretending to be earning money. Doing what he wanted, and not what he didn't, and claiming it was a sacrifice, when it was the opposite.

Skye and Emily had only ever had one serious falling-out, a few months after Em's lavish wedding. Over lunch—crisp linens, tuna tartare—Emily said something dismissive about Whit's business, and Skye retorted, "Yeah, but that's what's keeping you in Loro Piana and Park Avenue, isn't it?"

Skye had been a working single woman, struggling. Emily no longer was, but she wasn't yet ready to acknowledge what she'd transformed into during the brief two years since the red-onion episode, nor what she was on the verge of becoming. The truth of Skye's comment stung.

That lunch was when Emily began picking up the check, always. Skye had been a classics major who'd ended up in the book-publishing business. She had no money.

"Please"—hand atop Skye's—"let me do this."

Emily had found a way to make peace with the bargain she'd struck. She and Skye had gotten past that spat. Emily wasn't avoiding her best friend now due to any argument. It was because Emily had never been able to lie to Skye with any conviction, and she could not risk telling her the truth.

Emily exited the park at Columbus Circle, which seemed ripe for renaming. Columbus Avenue too. Christopher Columbus was clearly just one committed activist away from erasure. Like beef.

She walked past the hotel she'd used a few times, thinking that a luxury hotel atop a shopping mall was brilliant, everyone had an excuse to be here—meeting a friend, buying housewares, gifts, groceries, a drink, restaurants galore. This was perhaps the most explainable hotel in the city, is what Emily thought. She eventually lost no small amount of sleep over this choice.

Lenape Circle, it would be rechristened. Lenape, Ohio. Lenapia, South Carolina.

She walked west, and the neighborhood changed quickly to inexpensive Asian restaurants, repair shops, dealerships, warehouses. She stopped at the battered steel door of a squat structure between a chaotic garage and Indian takeout, and glanced back up the street. She didn't see anyone she recognized, nor any stranger watching. But of course the stranger would be a pro, practiced at the art of observing, unobserved. So the only thing this backward glance accomplished was to possibly make her look guilty, despite the immense effort she'd expended to look innocent.

There are many ways to be self-destructive when you think you're doing the opposite.

Emily opened the front door to a short dark hall that led to a large open space. The roof was dominated by a huge skylight whose grimy plastic did nothing to diminish the fantastic light. The room was strewn with painting supplies and stretched blank canvases. Finished paintings leaned against walls, large and small and in between, all of them abstract compositions of color blocks, wavy lines, dots. Experimentation.

Back in school Emily had loved art studio as much as the classroom, but she hadn't had the nerve to attempt a career as an artist. She still didn't.

What she was doing here was completely private.

Emily had purchased this sofa at a floor-sample sale. The style hadn't been important to her, the color, the fabric, none of that had mattered, even though it was practically Emily's job to be particular about such details. For this sofa, her only requirements were a queen-sized convertible with a comfortable mattress, available for immediate delivery.

She deaccessioned a set of the Mille Fleur pattern from the linen closet, something Whit would never notice had gone missing. This was a man who never passed up a chance to brag about his business acumen. "This is what I *do*," he liked to say. As if he'd invented the entire idea of business, or currency.

Whit didn't know where their linen closet was.

Emily had no idea it was possible to hate someone so much.

Back when they were dating, Emily and Whit never discussed politics, not in a meaningful way. She didn't want to go looking for obstacles, and he probably felt the same, both of them hoping it would never matter. Maybe if the world had remained the same, that could've worked. But in the current climate, everything was political, and this negligence now seemed like courtship malpractice.

Whit's professional villainy, like his sexual villainy and his political villainy, revealed itself gradually. He'd been well-raised, well-hidden behind manners and degrees and philanthropy, and above all behind the type of prodigious wealth that made people reluctant to peek behind it. These days, though, wealth like Whit's was the opposite: it practically demanded investigation.

Emily had accepted that she was making a deal, a compromise. But then she'd been bait-and-switched. Maybe not purposefully, maybe Whit had evolved unintentionally, a victim of the times, swayed by a president who wallowed in immorality, who cheated on his taxes, cheated in business, cheated on his wives, cheated in politics, cheated the public health in a pandemic, and even bragged about all this cheating, making dishonesty into a core personality trait—*the* core. If it was acceptable for POTUS to boast about a lifetime hobby of sexual assault, it was hard to imagine what behavior was unacceptable. Whatever's the worst thing about you? *Own* it.

That's what Whit had done: coaxed the worst of himself out of the shadows. His favorite television show was *Succession* but he thought it was instructional.

Whit's lies about work had mostly been omission. His business was industrial manufacturing, is what he'd explained. This sounded vaguely sinister, reminiscent of Dow and Vietnam, but Emily didn't press. Synthetic polymers, he'd said. Plastics, to be most simplistic. *The Graduate.*

"Our most important customer is the US government." This was perhaps true, but also definitely not. The US government had never been Liberty's biggest customer nor its most profitable. But maybe the government had truly been most important, because that's what justified the others. This evoked "I did not have sexual relations with that woman"—the type of deliberately constructed lie that's so much more malevolent than the reflexive self-defensive sort.

Back when he was four, Hudson had spurted out "I didn't touch anything" when Emily came upon him standing beside a broken lamp: that was just instinct, not malice. She didn't blame the kid for that lie. But she sure as hell blamed Whit. "International entities," he claimed, with a dismissive shrug. "We do a lot of business in Switzerland," implying that he was maybe helping the Red Cross. Emily eventually discovered that none of Liberty's customers were Swiss, they were not based in Switzerland, the only thing Swiss about them was their bank accounts. Most of Liberty's customers were in the Mideast and Africa; Whit did business with the Pentagon as basically a loss-leader. Though in typical defense-contractor fashion, even the loss leader was immensely profitable.

Emily didn't learn any of this because Whit told her. She learned it because she'd gotten curious, then suspicious, then she'd gone looking.

At least Whit had the sense to finally end his relationship with Justin Pugh, whose participation in anti-government activities was becoming increasingly frequent, and possibly illegal. Unsurprisingly, Pugh didn't take Whit's breakup well. He made senseless financial demands, then threatened public disclosures. He hired a lawyer, who was no match for the legal army at Whit's disposal. Not only did Pugh's legal remedy go nowhere, it got him investigated by the IRS, and now Delta Canopy was on the brink of bankruptcy, and Pugh on the edge of insanity.

"You have no idea," Pugh warned Whit's voicemail, "what I'm capable of."

Whit may have had an army of lawyers, but Pugh commanded an actual army.

In the powder room Emily removed her blazer, set it on a hanger, placed the hanger on a hook on the back of the door, next to a paint-spattered canvas jumpsuit. She unbuttoned her blouse, slipped out of it. Unzipped her skirt, let that fall to the floor. She picked up her clothes, placed them on hangers, hung those on the back of the door.

She examined herself in the mirror, wearing nothing but matching red lace lingerie, complete with suspender belt.

Emily had always been proud of her willpower, her ability to resist temptation—the temptation of dessert, the temptation of a third glass of wine, the temptation to sleep in, to cut class, to skip the workout. Then she discovered that her husband had been lying to her for their entire relationship, and that flipped a switch in her. A few different switches.

This studio was what it looked like when her switch was in the on position.

If there was one thing she would've wanted to change about this unit, it would be to add a shower, so she could wash up fully before leaving. But a shower would make it a living space instead of the professional one it was zoned for, and she didn't want to start dealing with illegal renovations, under-the-counter payments. She didn't want to open herself up to any additional problems.

Emily did not put on the canvas jumpsuit. Nor did she put on the dirty tennis shoes in the bathroom. Instead she stepped into a pair of heels she kept here. These shoes weren't in great condition, but that didn't matter.

She opened the convertible, which was already dressed in those busy florals that hid all manner of sins. People talked about thread counts of six hundred, eight hundred, a thousand, linens you could buy from some guy with a folding table out on Broadway. But compared with D. Porthault's four hundreds, those supposed luxury linens felt like sandpaper. Thread count wasn't really a measurement of anything. Measurements often missed the point.

The doorbell rang.

Emily looked at herself in the mirror. She pushed her breasts together, straightened her thong.

She pressed the button for the intercom, and heard the click of unlocking, then the sound of the door opening, closing.

Footsteps in the hall. Slow, measured.

Emily didn't know how these things ended; it wasn't discussed. But from the very beginning, she'd already been preparing for the end, anticipating that sooner or later the edifice would collapse under the weight of duplicity and secrecy and guilt and fear, and all those negatives would eventually outweigh the positives, and it would become clear to one or both parties that what you were doing was indefensible, or reprehensible, or simply not that fun, not anymore, not fun enough. You could see it laid out in front of you, all the reasons why this was going to end.

What you couldn't see was when. It could be any day. It could be today.

She'd purchased lingerie specifically for the occasion, a trip to a downtown boutique, which in itself was an erotic experience, pre-foreplay. Buying lingerie was half the pleasure of lingerie.

If today turned out to be the end, Emily wanted him to remember her like this. It's how she wanted to remember herself too.

"Wow," he said, standing in the doorway.

This was the other half of the pleasure: the look on his face, right now.

"My goodness."

Part Three

THIS EVENING

CHAPTER 25

APARTMENT 11C-D.

"Oh," Emily said, the waves crashing over her. "Oh my god."

This was probably the appeal of hard drugs, wasn't it? Feeling the type of good you hadn't known existed. This was Emily's heroin.

"Oh god you're so good at that."

She wanted to be liberal with praise, she wanted him to know what he was doing right, not just because she wanted him to do more of it, but because she wanted him to feel good about it, because in the abstract there was plenty to feel bad about. More for him than for her. He was not the one married to a villain.

"Please," she said. "I want you inside me." This was the dirtiest phrase she could manage.

He did not oblige. Instead he continued with his tongue.

"Please." Emily liked the sound of begging for it, and she knew he did too. He worked his way up her body, her abdomen, one breast, the hollow of her neck, he nibbled an earlobe, exhaled into her ear, his fingers continuing the mission of his tongue, another shiver down her spine.

She pulled him in, and gasped. "Oh good god."

If you think about sex too closely, it's ridiculous. What *is* this? Sliding a temporarily hard part of him in and out of a temporarily wet part of her. How can this be worth ruining your life?

There were a lot of things it was better not to think too closely about.

She came again.

♦ ♦ ♦

They'd met a dozen years ago, introduced by a mutual acquaintance who was always introducing everyone to everyone else, oh you simply must meet so-and-so.

"Ah! You're Emily Merriweather." He'd shaken her hand firmly, like a colleague. "I've been looking forward to meeting you. I hear you have an encyclopedic knowledge of art." They quickly fell into a conversation about everything, gliding from one subject to another. They were both unaccompanied at a party, accountable to no one for their choice of company.

Some men's flirting can immediately feel creepy, threatening even, sometimes before they say a single word. For others, flirting seems like nothing more than a type of entertainment. Rarely is flirting sexy, pure and simple. And just once in a blue moon, not so simple.

He was undeniably appealing. But he was older, back when Emily was interested only in young men, their energy, their passion, their promise. She had a romantic vision for her romantic life, nurturing a young man along with her own maturation, a scrappy little team. You can't conquer the world if you've already won. Plus he was married, and she was single. That wasn't a thing that interested her.

This was before Emily had even met Whit. Then she got sidetracked by her disappointing dating history, then by Whit and his money, by children, by this expensive, expansive existence. She slowly lost track of who she was, and what she wanted out of life, distracted by what she wanted out of today.

Emily had been such a good girl for so long, and had been feeling suffocated, not only by the rules but by her compulsion to follow them, to always be reasonable, responsible. She had the urge to smoke a cigarette, to eat a steak, to fuck a stranger in a restaurant restroom. She'd been stifling self-destructive impulses for years; that's what it means to be a grown-up. But as her children's schooldays extended into afterschool, and her free time stretched out, these urges grew stronger, and she began to wonder if they were really all that self-destructive after all.

Then she found herself seated next to him at a dinner in Miami, for Art Basel, the type of big party that makes it almost impossible not to fall into close conversation with one person. He'd never before talked much about himself, nor his business, always deliberate to direct the conversation back to her career, her interests, and later her art collection, her kids. He'd done a lot of parenting himself. He did the laundry. His wife earned more than he did, and he was proud of it.

"My husband wouldn't be able to tolerate that," Emily said. He didn't take the bait.

There were plenty of people in her life who threw around lots of lingo, people who amplified this and that on social, people who wore tee shirts with slogans, who signaled their virtue at every opportunity. But almost none of these people wanted to end legacy admissions to elite educational institutions, or to socialize healthcare, or to increase inheritance taxes, nor for that matter any other taxes, or even pay the taxes they fairly owed.

"The only thing I have against taxes," he'd said, "is that the people who should pay the most avoid paying anything at all. Like these people here in Florida, flying American flags on environment-ruining lawns maintained by undocumented immigrants who are paid illegally low wages, illegally. And they call themselves patriots." He shook his head. "I'm happy to pay my fair share. That's the only way society functions, isn't it?"

His smile was unabashedly earnest. Almost everyone in Emily's life was cynical, or ironic, or selfish. This man was the most earnest person she knew, aside from children. It wasn't until she took note of this sincerity that she realized how attractive it was to her.

The other dinner guests climbed into hired cars back to their hotels. He walked her back to hers, and they continued chatting in front, and with each passing second the urge grew stronger to invite him up, she was watching his lips but could barely pay attention to what he was saying, she was so distracted by the idea that in five minutes they could be in bed, all she needed to do was—

"Well," he said, "this was tremendous fun."

He leaned in and kissed her on the cheek.

"Good night."

Back in New York, it began innocently enough, or at least gave the appearance of innocence. But the innocence gradually sloughed away, like a molting animal, replacing its coat with something that looked outwardly similar, but was altogether different.

This evolution happened alongside the revelations of Whit's iniquities, drawing a stark contrast between two men who'd grown up in the same city at the same time with the same privileges, had attended the same sorts of schools, went to the same parties, they were even the same height. Superficially, they were very nearly the same person. Yet in many ways they were opposites. Unlike Whit he didn't pretend to be a tough guy, didn't want to be. He would never brag about his wealth, such as it was; he barely pursued money. He had a rare type of confidence that had nothing to do with dominance, with possession, the difference between a man who truly loved women and a man who simply loved having sex with them.

Of these two men, it was clear to Emily that one of them had been interested in her primarily because she was beautiful, the other perhaps despite it. One had tried to have sex with her as soon as possible, the other seemed to be avoiding it. One was fundamentally selfish in bed, and Emily was absolutely certain the other would be generous. It was something in the way he looked at her.

She contrived to have business with him, in a way that she hoped was a transparent invitation, without being explicit. She didn't think he'd say no if she propositioned him explicitly, but she also didn't think there was any way she could make a first move.

"Are you okay?" he'd asked one lunchtime at the Mark, putting down his fork.

"Yes." She blushed, and forced herself to meet his eye. She had tumbled again into a sexual fantasy. "I'm sorry, what did you ask?"

"I asked what you were like in your twenties?"

Emily was desperate to make him see it. "I was a lot poorer," she said, "and I wore sexier lingerie." She thought she was making herself abundantly clear, but still it took weeks more of hand-wringing, and procrastination, and masturbation, until she invited him to her apartment in the middle of the day, and stood too close to him, and licked her lips, and he finally—*finally*—said, "At the risk of making a fool of myself—or is it too late for that?—may I kiss you?"

"Please," she said.

And there they were in her entry gallery, at eleven A.M., making out like teenagers. Her children were at school, her housekeeper at the supermarket, her nanny taking a first-aid class, her husband in Khartoum. They stood under an ornate chandelier that Emily had purchased at the Paris flea market along with other light fixtures and pieces of furniture, a whole shipping container whose logistics cost a lot less than she was prepared to spend.

After a few minutes, he said, "I should go."

She couldn't hide her disappointment. "Oh?"

Their hands hadn't strayed far, but she could feel his arousal pressed up against her hip, her own too. She was on the verge of orgasm, just from kissing.

"I should give you time to think about this."

"I've already thought about this." She'd been thinking about it more or less nonstop. Especially at night, in bed.

"Well then, I guess I should give you time to reconsider."

"Why in god's name would you want to do that?"

He smiled. "Because this is a serious thing."

"Does it have to be?"

That made him laugh. "Maybe not. But even if it's not serious, it's still, I think, serious."

"Oh."

"Can we have lunch tomorrow?"

"Yes." Emily already had a lunch on the calendar; it wouldn't be the last time she canceled on Skye.

"I can't wait," he said, and kissed her again.

"Me too." She closed the door behind him, then stood in the hall and brought herself off in a matter of seconds. "Oh god," she said, amazed at herself.

Had this man appeared in her life at just the right moment? Or was he right because of the moment?

The downtown restaurant was packed with the usual assortment. Scruffy guys were doing their best to make sure everyone knew they were artists—paint-spattered boots, nicotine-stained fingertips, noontime whiskey.

Man-bunners on barstools swirled and sniffed biodynamic pét-nats with a vigor that suggested emergency. A tableful of Zoomer fashionistas were angling their wineglasses and their appetizers and their pouts just so, for their cameras, swaddled in the tan plaid and the red soles and the circular little badges. A trio of young guys—one white, one Indian, one Chinese—all stared at their phones, wearing different colors of lightweight hoodies, and sneakers, a United Benetton of tech bro-dom. A pair of skeletal ladies were lunching on chardonnay, dressing on the side.

The hostess greeted him by name, escorted them across the room. Along the way he shook hands with one guy, waved to a pair of doyennes dripping in diamonds. He had a particularly New Yorker-y way of interacting with people that was disarmingly intimate, as if we're all playing some sort of game. Playfulness was something Emily definitely didn't get out of Whit. It was something she missed. One of many things.

"You seem to know everyone here."

"Yes, it's my commissary."

A busboy whisked away the extra plates as they settled into a corner banquette for four, the best table in the house, in plain sight, and settled in to discuss having an affair as if contemplating starting a business venture—logically, soberly, enthusiastically. But they couldn't keep their eyes off each other, could barely keep their hands to themselves. Their knees kept touching, thighs, an electric current under the table. She almost couldn't bear it.

"I don't want anyone to get hurt," she said. "That's the most important thing."

Emily didn't know if this were true, or if it was just the right thing to say. It was occasionally hard to distinguish between what she thought she ought to feel and what she actually felt.

"If anyone gets hurt," he said, "I promise it's going to be me."

"How can you promise that?"

"Are you kidding?" His eyes were twinkling, crinkling. He almost always looked at least a tiny bit amused. "You're a heartbreaker if I've ever met one."

She was constantly blushing around him.

"Do you want dessert?" he asked, even though he knew she didn't. "Coffee?"

"What I want"—she put her hand on his thigh—"is to get out of here."

He signaled for the check.

"There are people at my place, almost all day, every day," she said. This conversation may have sounded rational, but that wasn't how she was feeling, not at all. She was feeling emotional. She was feeling, frankly, insane.

"Can we go to yours?" she asked. "Right now?"

Those first few weeks, she found herself getting aroused willy-nilly, just riding in a car, sitting in meetings. She'd never in her life felt so sexual. They whiled away afternoons in hotel suites. He brought her to orgasm in the back of a taxi, hand up her A-line. They fucked frenetically in the cramped basement bathroom of an out-of-the-way restaurant, like she'd fantasized, at once more arousing and more uncomfortable than anticipated. One evening he locked his office, hoisted her up on the desk. That was the most intense orgasm of her life. Plural. She felt weak afterward. Dizzy.

Part of the enjoyment was the pure betrayal of it, the revenge. Even though Whit didn't know what she was doing, she did, she had this hidden thing, this self-assertion. She took pleasure in the machinations, the assignations, the novelty of a clandestine relationship.

Arousal is situational. This apparently was a situation that aroused her.

She was also, always, afraid. Afraid of getting caught, afraid of it turning bad. Afraid of her husband, afraid of her lover, afraid of his wife, afraid of herself. Most of all, afraid of falling in love.

After that first reckless month, she started to panic about getting caught—about credit-card records, about surveillance footage, about cellphone location tracking, all the incriminating evidence a private investigator could coax out of bellhops and maître d's and drivers in exchange for hundred-dollar bills. That taxi driver! He'd snuck glances in the rearview. And Whit was definitely a person who'd hire a PI out of curiosity, just for the hell of it. Emily began to worry that he'd already done that, maybe even way back when he picked that fight about the starchitect. Maybe that was when Whit started building his case. Maybe he'd been having his wife followed for years.

Emily recognized that it was bananas to rent a painting studio for the express purpose of conducting an extramarital affair. She did it anyway.

And the sex, good god. They luxuriated in it, extravagant foreplay, every position, taking occasional breaks in the action—their sex had water breaks, *intermissions*—second rounds, thirds. One afternoon she lost count of her orgasms; it was double digits.

"You've ruined sex for me," she'd said after that. "I never want to do it with anyone else."

"Hey." Emily raised herself up onto an elbow, looked at him. "Are you okay?"

"Yeah," he said, but he didn't sound it.

"Are you sure?"

He nodded, and that too didn't seem genuine, but she decided not to press, and instead to try to make him feel better, about whatever it was.

"Gorgeous," she said, staring at him. "You know that, don't you? You're gorgeous."

"Don't be ridiculous. Passable is what I am."

"How can you say that? You seem to have done all right for yourself."

He grinned. "Yes, I suppose so. But not thanks to my looks."

"Oh no?"

"I'm charming."

She slapped his chest. "And modest!"

"You told me so yourself, didn't you?"

"I guess I did." Emily had rarely wanted a man solely because he'd been born handsome. And she never trusted a man who wanted her solely because of the same luck. "But I also told you that you're gorgeous."

"Yeah, well, you're biased."

"You bet I am." She kissed his chest. "I'm smitten."

"Me too." He stroked her skin. "I love lying here, talking to you."

"But I do most of the talking." He was the only man Emily had ever known who listened far more than he talked.

"Well, that's what talking is, isn't it? Listening."

They lay in silence. She nestled up against him. "Oh," she said, feeling him. "You really want me again?"

"I never stop wanting you."

"Oh good."

A bad marriage wasn't something Emily wanted to model for her children, so she'd been trying hard not to let it show. She wanted her kids to grow up with the type of wealth that opens all the world's doors—the education, the connections, the experiences, the social and cultural capital, the capital capital. She could not leave Whit, not until the kids were grown.

Admittedly, there were times when she worried that this sort of wealth didn't do anyone any favors, and maybe did harm. She also recognized the absurd privilege it took to contemplate that, the very idea that it was an option to have hundreds of millions of dollars but you *declined.*

Another irreconcilable tension.

A year ago, if you'd asked Emily what was missing from her life, she never would've answered this. She never would've imagined it. And as much as she relished the physical intimacy, it was the pillow talk she looked forward to most, the honesty of it, she was able to say things here that were otherwise unspeakable—about her ambitions, her frustrations, her disappointments. In the rest of her life she felt silenced, unable to admit any complaints, all of them laughable in the context of the world's suffering. But reclined here on those soft old sheets, Emily wallowed in her complaints, and it was delicious. She became dependent on this honesty, even while in the very act of profound deception. This was where she was the truest incarnation of Emily Grace Merriweather Longworth.

At first, they rarely mentioned spouses. Both were vaguely aware that there were third rails in a relationship like this, and husbands and wives were probably the highest voltage. Emily didn't want to lie around naked complaining about her husband. She'd staked so much of her identity on the hard-won territory of the moral high ground, and she didn't want to fritter it all away unnecessarily.

But as they grew more comfortable, she couldn't help herself. It turned out that the chief subject she wanted to be honest about was her bad marriage. And as she learned one awful thing after another about Whit, the affair's momentum gathered steam.

What did Emily want out of this? She wanted to be wanted, she wanted sex with someone who desperately wanted her, whom she desperately wanted. She wanted adventure, escape. She wanted to do something mischievous. She wanted to feel alive.

There was a lot she wanted. But she promised herself, over and over, that love wasn't what she was looking for. She didn't want to be in love, and she didn't want to be loved.

By the time both her children were in college, she'd be in her late forties. At that point she will have squirreled away somewhere in the neighborhood of twenty-five million dollars. Plenty of money, and plenty of time, to start a new life.

She could wait. Couldn't she?

"Oh," she whispered directly into his ear.

Today he'd been slower, gentler. He'd even stopped moving entirely for a minute, then two, still deep inside her, staring into her eyes, almost a contest. Finally she pushed herself up against him, and wrapped her legs around his back, and felt the intensity welling up within her.

"Please," she whispered, and he started moving his hips in little circles, no in and out, no thrusting. *"Please."*

Whispering could be so much louder than screaming.

Even while in the very act of doing this, she could scarcely believe it.

"Oh my god."

And then they were spent, and she rested her head against his chest again, and listened to the pounding of his galloping heart, hoping to synchronize their tempos. She couldn't tell whose was beating faster, just that they were out of sync.

"I love you," said Emily.

"I love you too," said Julian.

CHAPTER 26

FRONT DOOR

Chicky ran. One foot in front of the other, soles slapping. Breath-breath in, breath-breath out. Shoulders back, elbows up, hands loose. Focusing on his breath, on his footfalls. Trying not to think about all the things he had to think about.

Breath-breath in, breath-breath out.

During his years on day shifts he'd done his six miles per day in Central Park at predawn or thereabouts. In those wee hours he almost never recognized anyone. But with this new schedule he saw too many familiar faces in the park. Upper West Side moms. Bohemia residents. This made him feel as if he was intruding or pretending or something. It made him uncomfortable. In broad daylight the reservoir path didn't feel like his rightful territory.

So he was trying out the East River path. Down past the mayor's mansion to the Queensboro then back. The Upper East Side was not a neighborhood where he recognized anyone.

Breath-breath in, breath-breath out.

It didn't take a genius to imagine an inside job. Especially if you weren't going to be the inside man. Get ten half-assed gangsters together and add liquor and one of them was going to propose some employment-related crime or another. Guaranteed.

Most schemes had been easy for Chicky to decline. Sometimes he could even say, "Stop right there. I don't even want to hear it." Sometimes he had to hear it out. Many criminals believed that everyone else would commit crimes too if they weren't afraid of getting caught. The only reason people were law-abiding was lack of balls. Which could make it tough to say no. You had to accept looking like a coward.

El Puño's was one of the schemes Chicky needed to hear out. Needed to pretend to entertain. For a few seconds he believed and maybe even hoped that this guy might have an original idea. He was after all a successful criminal. Maybe his skills were transferrable. So Chicky had stood there, hemmed in by goons, nodding as he listened to this knucklehead. It became obvious that El Puño was a successful criminal not because of his brains but because of his balls.

"Yeah," Chicky had said. "I'll think on it."

That's what he was doing as he ran.

Breath-breath in, breath-breath out.

Chicky knelt in front of his white Amana range. Over the years he'd been in a couple dozen Bohemia kitchens. There were no white ranges in the Bohemia. No Amanas.

There was a mousetrap down there. A little mouse café that dispensed poison. Not a spring trap because Chicky didn't want broken-necked mice dying under his stove. In fact he didn't especially want the mice to die. Just go away. But it wasn't possible to reason with rodents.

He retrieved his new revolver from its hiding spot under the stove. He hadn't wanted to leave the thing anywhere in plain view. Nestor made no secret of his habit of coming and going into the units without necessarily asking permission.

Chicky put the gun on the table where he'd eaten twenty-five years' worth of family meals. Casa Diaz did not feature a dining room. He loaded one bullet at a time. He felt the weight in his hands. In his mind. Firing a gun was a heavy thing to contemplate. Chicky may not have known all the legal nuances between self-defense and manslaughter and different degrees of murder but he did know what premeditation was.

He didn't attempt to reconcile his sympathy with mice with his disgust at rats. Prejudice was something else that couldn't be reasoned with.

"Hey Chick what's good."

"Oh hey Alberto. I got a package for you."

"Yeah." The smell of weed wafted from Alberto's. Not a cloud of fresh smoke but maybe last night's. Or maybe the smell was permanent. "I was hoping that was you who signed. Thanks."

Chicky went inside and retrieved Alberto's box from the gear bag.

"Appreciate you." Alberto had headphones around his neck like a guy with one of those good union jobs out at LaGuardia. "You okay Chicky? Your face looks a little, um . . ."

"Yeah all good. But listen Alberto. I . . ." Chicky wanted to say something but if there's one enemy you don't want it's your neighbor. They'd never gotten around to having that beer. "I don't want to be responsible for holding your . . ."

"I know bro. I'm sorry. It's just I forgot this was coming."

"You *forgot*?"

Alberto shrugged. "But thank you Chick. Really. I'm gonna spend the whole week with this."

Chicky shook his head and turned back to the task of double-locking his door.

"What?" Alberto asked.

"It's . . . It's none of my business is what it is."

"You ever try it?"

Chicky turned around. "Huh?"

"I noticed you don't have any console."

Chicky squinted. "The fuck you talking about?"

"I'm talking about gaming." Alberto held up the package. "This is a beta. I'm a developer."

"You're a what?"

"A game developer. I code, freelance. Mostly for this one company down in Mexico City."

"You code?" Now everything made a different sense. "That's what you're doing in there?"

"Uh, yeah. What did you think?"

Chicky reached behind him. It seemed secure but what did he know about biking with a gun in his pants?

He set off. Riding through city streets was dangerous. It was entirely up to your physicality and concentration and reflexes to keep yourself alive, weaving in and out of cars and trucks and forty-thousand-pound buses, with car doors flying open and taxis jockeying for fares and pedestrians staring at their phones, with distracted drivers and speeding drivers and drunk drivers and plain-old bad drivers, all of them surrounded by metal boxes and life-saving airbags while you're just an exoskeleton exposed out there with nothing but your wits.

Plenty of guys cycled for exercise. You saw them with their six-thousand-dollar titanium rides and aerodynamic sunglasses and cleats and gloves and shorts and shirts. Cycling *socks*. Chicky had a battered old helmet and padded shorts for longer rides and gloves for the cold. Not cycling gloves, just regular gloves he'd bought from a guy on the street who sold hats and socks and phone cases and miscellaneous shit made in China. Chicky took care of the maintenance himself with secondhand tools. YouTube could teach you how to do basically anything.

Riding in the park by contrast was boring. But today Chicky was too distracted to trust himself in traffic. So he pedaled toward the park. Past the projects and past the corner bums and past Junior's where no one was at any tables yet but a few guys were already bellied up to the bar. It wasn't a tremendous leap of imagination for Chicky to see himself joining that sad-ass population.

There but for the grace of god. That was something Chicky had told himself plenty over the first half century of his life. But then the grace of god went and deserted him. Now it was just his own grace that was keeping him going. The supply was running short.

♦ ♦ ♦

It was for just a week or two every year when the foliage was like this. Fall was definitely the shortest season. Blink and everything is brown, muddy, cold, shitty. Fall used to be back-to-school and Riverside softball and pennant races and the first hopeful weeks of football before it all fell apart. Fall was street fairs and block parties and Halloween costumes and trick-or-treating. How awesome was trick-or-treating?

But then softball started hurting and the girls started leaving and his wife started dying and his life started going to shit. Now fall sucked.

People told Chicky not to make any big decisions in the wake of Tiffani's death. Things will get better, they said, or less bad, you'll become less sad. Don't solve a temporary problem with a permanent solution.

"Yeah." Chicky would nod along. "I hear you." Even though it was bullshit. Chicky's problems were not temporary. Not a single motherfucking one of them.

Fall. Even the word was filled with failure and sadness.

Chicky didn't like being this person. But it came with a certain liberation. It opened up different sorts of possibilities.

He climbed off the bike at the Bohemia's service entrance. Chicky made a habit of arriving a half hour early in case someone needed something, even if it was nothing more than the overnight guy wanting to go home already. Overnight was a slog. And the day guys too wanted to get home to their kids or wives or dinner. Chicky didn't have anything to get home to, or stay home for.

Today though he was nearly late. Chicky couldn't remember the last time he was actually late. Years. Decades?

"*Cómo están?*" he said to two women wheeling coolers down the sidewalk.

"*Todo bien,*" one answered. "*Y tú?*"

"*Todo bien,*" he lied. These women must be lying too. How could everything be good? Every morning they were driven in from Corona by Esteban in a beat-up beige Sienna whose passenger-side door had been replaced with a gray one and a rear window with a steel plate. Esteban made two trips every morning, three women apiece, each with her own cooler in the way-back packed with lunches prepared in a noncommercial kitchen by Esteban's wife and his sister-in-law. Tamales and tortas and empanadas and other portable foods with no sauces and no messes and no utensils and no license and no health code and no taxes and no documents and no English. Cash only.

Those tortas were delicious. Not exactly good for you though.

The women moved from one apartment house to another selling lunches to work crews and building staff. After lunchtime they'd set up on street corners near subway stations and try to unload whatever was left. In late afternoon they'd converge on a church to donate the unsold food for the needy. In exchange they were allowed to use the bathroom and have coffee and sit for the first time since midmorning while they waited for the Sienna to take them home to Queens.

Back in school everyone who'd served food had been Hispanic too. Every single lunch lady in every school Chicky had attended.

"*Hasta mañana*," one of the women said.

Chicky didn't speak all that much Spanish but enough. The old super Tommy O'Sullivan had been surprised at Chicky's lack of fluency.

"What can I tell you Boss? I'm a third-generation New Yorker."

They'd been at an old Irish bar in the previous millennium. Back then many of the guys drank at the city's various O'Whatever's with cigarette machines and phone booths and plywood doors for the women's toilet stalls and no doors at all for the men's. Anything you wanted to do in the men's toilet was going to be semi-public.

"My family came here just as legally as yours. Maybe *more* legally."

"That right?" Tommy asked, with a smirk. Tommy had a fresh beer every fifteen minutes. They'd been at the bar for two hours. "How you figure?"

The jukebox was Tom Petty and Guns N' Roses and "More Than a Feeling" every motherfucking night. Plus Diana Ross and Smokey Robinson and other Motown. Sad drunk white guys liked to listen to Black people sing about being sad. Maybe it made them feel better, that other people were sadder.

If there was one band that sounded like a white-guy bar, it was Boston.

"You know that Puerto Rico is a part of the United States, Boss?"

Tommy had looked at Chicky like he was pulling his leg. "Get the fuck out of here."

"My family didn't *immigrate* to New York. Just *moved* here. Just like from Iowa or some shit."

"Iowa." Tommy chortled at the idea. If there's one thing Irish New Yorkers and Puerto Rican New Yorkers and any other New Yorkers agreed on, it was that they didn't know where the fuck Iowa was, and didn't care.

There were as many American citizens living in Puerto Rico as in Iowa. Puerto Ricans got no vote whatsoever while Iowans got to choose the candidates for president. That didn't make any fucking sense.

Out in the world Chicky used a big lock for his bike. But here in the Bohemia's bike room there were no locks. Chicky didn't want to be the only one especially since his bike was without doubt the least valuable. In fact it had practically no value. But still it made him a little uneasy to just walk away from unsecured property.

Canarius was in the break room with a textbook and scratch pad and pen and graphs. Canarius did homework all the time and all of it looked hard. Chicky didn't want to interrupt. He also didn't want Canarius to pay him any mind as he moved the revolver into his uniform's jacket. The gun hung in there in a noticeable way. He'd need to find a better spot.

Guys used to play cards in here but now they mostly stared at their phones. Watching sports highlights and playing video games and chuckling at memes.

Chicky changed into his white shirt and gray pants with the satin stripe. He'd never been able to decide if these uniforms were dignified or ridiculous. There was no in-between. Chicky's opinion depended largely on mood but also on how people interacted with him and other things going on in the world. He could change his mind a few times over the course of one shift.

He went into the windowless bathroom to tuck the gun into the back of his pants. Then he put on the jacket and examined himself. There was definitely a bulge that would be noticeable if he was reaching and bending and carrying things. This was another temporary solution.

Which might as well be the story of Chicky's entire existence: it'll do.

Until it won't.

CHAPTER 27

APARTMENT 2A

"Listen," Julian said. He didn't want to bring this up, not now of all times, not here of all places. But he couldn't ignore the subject. He couldn't let her walk into tonight not knowing.

"Uh-oh."

"Yeah," he said. "The Rothko."

"Oh god." Emily rolled her eyes.

"I've offered to refund my commission, but he hasn't accepted, at least not yet."

She didn't say anything.

"I don't want you to intervene, not at all. I just want you to be forewarned, in case it comes up. He called this morning to yell at me."

"Oh god I'm sorry."

"Please. Don't apologize."

"Is he going to sue you?"

"I don't know. Yeah, maybe."

She sighed. "My husband is a real ass, isn't he?"

Julian laughed at her profanity; Emily almost never cursed. And Julian never joined the subject of Whit's horribleness, never piled on.

They stood in the short dark hall, kissing. They broke apart, stared, kissed again. Neither wanted it to end, today even more than usual. Tonight was going to be hard.

"Go," she said, with that lopsided grin. Emily had a lot of different smiles, but it was this crooked, unguarded grin that he'd only ever seen when they were having sex, or after. It was his favorite of her smiles. It was one of his favorite things in the world. He loved everything about her, which, he knew, meant that he loved her.

For a long time neither had uttered the phrase, which was a type of promise, one neither was in a position to keep. But you didn't need to say it to feel it, to know it. Then one day he'd let it slip, and she'd said it too, and then suddenly there they were: in love with people they weren't married to.

"Go now," she said. "Go before I drag you back to bed."

He didn't go for another minute. Was this their last time together? Their last kiss?

"I'll see you soon?" he asked. Her smile grew more crooked. God, that smile. He wondered if anyone else in the world ever saw this smile.

"You know you will."

They kissed again before he extracted himself and exited to the street, where cars were parked haphazardly on the sidewalk, others headlong into garage bays, a pair of men bickering in Urdu, others smoking cigarettes and others eating samosas, exhaust systems being tested, tires replaced with a loud *bzzz-bzzz*, all this busy industry out here, while in there Julian had just spent an hour in the ultimate luxury: the arms of someone you love.

Emily would follow in a few minutes, after cleaning up the studio, and cleaning up herself. She was fastidious about not looking or smelling like she just tumbled out of bed, and careful to make sure that the studio always looked like a place to make art, not love. She'd take a taxi home, for which she'd pay in cash, because she was also fastidious about not creating records. Emily was much more worried about getting caught than Julian was. She had a lot more to lose. Julian didn't know all the ins and outs of her subterfuges, and didn't want to ask. It was hard to decide where to draw the lines around the bounds of their intimacy.

This had started off as just a bit of fun, releasing the pressure valve of long-term monogamy, of encroaching agedness, a little escape from the everyday.

"If it gets too serious," she'd said, back in that brasserie, before they'd ever been to bed, "we have to stop. I won't leave Whit. I can't."

Now it had gotten every type of serious.

"Yes," Julian had said. "I feel the same way."

As with so many things, easier said than done.

"When do you want to see me again?" Emily had asked, after their first time together. Julian was watching her rearrange herself in the bathroom mirror, surrounded by his wife's toiletries.

"I've never done this before," he said. "I don't know how. Do you?"

She shook her head, and met his eye in the mirror. God, she was exquisite, he didn't even want her to leave now, he wanted to jump back into bed, and never leave. But he needed to get back to the gallery.

"I want to see you again tomorrow, but every day is probably not practical." Someone needed to erect guardrails, and Julian thought that's what she was asking for, because she didn't want to do it herself. "How about next week?"

"Sure," she said, and he could see she was disappointed. He could see, right there at the very beginning, how this would end. "What day is good for you?"

They compared calendars, and chose Thursday.

"Hey," Emily said, "look at me."

He did. In the following months, he came to believe that he'd never looked at anyone as closely as he'd looked at her.

"Please don't be cavalier with my affection."

"I won't," he said. "That's the last thing I'll be. I promise."

They never again went to his bed, and never once to hers. They went to hotels before she rented that studio. They met every week, had sex immediately, went out for lunch, returned to bed.

Had those afternoons been the happiest days of his life? "You are at your very best," she'd said, "when you're naked." That was hard to beat.

He'd told himself he wouldn't do this—he'd promised—but eventually he couldn't help himself: he tried to talk her into leaving her husband, without trying to talk her into it. "Nine hundred thousand dollars per year," he'd said. "It's not *nothing*."

"No, of course not."

"Plenty of people think that a million dollars is a lot of money. Especially per year."

He knew that Emily wasn't one of those people. She was wearing a cashmere sweater that was the softest fabric he'd ever touched in his life.

"The problem," she said, "is that I'm not even confident I'd *get* the nine hundred. Whit is such a vindictive person. He'd make my life hell, beyond the money. He'd go out of his way to ensure that I was miserable. Just for the sport of it."

This was how these discussions went: Julian made suggestions, Emily parried back. He wanted to help solve her problem; he wanted to *be* her solution. But he never mustered the nerve to say it, to propose it explicitly: "Leave him for me." It was something people did all the time, they fell out of love, into love with someone new, started new lives, blended families, coparenting, whatever.

Julian increasingly believed that his marriage had run its course, and he was no longer committed to trying to salvage it. Damn the gossip, he thought. Damn the consequences.

But Emily's situation was different. Her children were too small, and her husband's money was too large. Julian knew that her answer would need to be no, and asking would only break the magic seal, and the whole thing would eddy down the drain, and it would be Julian's fault for being greedy, for pushing too far. So he didn't push at all.

The relationship had always been on tenuous ground, and he'd felt it begin to fray at the edges as soon as it began. Emily took immediate umbrage at Julian's guardrails, she intimated that he didn't care for her enough, accused him of being withholding, his rules were arbitrary, mean. He believed the opposite. He was terrified of caring for her too much, of ruining their lives. He thought she was too touchy, and he got mad at her for being unfairly mad at him.

Plus there was self-loathing. Julian didn't want to be this cliché, this middle-aged man in love with a younger woman who wasn't his wife. He didn't want to be in love with someone he couldn't have. But you don't get to choose what you want. Or whom you love.

Or how you lose the person you love.

A couple of months ago, she was lying in that convertible, watching him dress, and she was seized by a fit of melancholy. He could see it on her face. “Hey, what’s wrong?”

She pulled the sheet up over her naked body. “I can’t believe this is my life.”

Julian sat on the edge of the bed, and stroked her shoulder.

“My most important relationship, and it’s not with my husband.”

He gathered her up in his arms, to try to comfort her, but this made her cry harder, and pull away. She apparently didn’t want to be comforted. Julian suspected she didn’t know what she wanted, but it looked like she didn’t want this sort of relationship.

Maybe she didn’t, truly, want him.

That was when Julian knew that he’d been right. It would indeed be his heart that ended up broken.

This affair was maybe the best experience of his life. But it was also the worst.

If it doesn’t hurt, it isn’t love.

CHAPTER 28

FRONT DOOR

"Guys," Oleksander said, "come in please. Have a seat."

Olek had a very thick neck. He never looked comfortable in his suit and tie. In the office he always took off the jacket and loosened the tie. Sometimes he rolled up his sleeves too but never when he expected residents. He didn't want them to see the tattoos.

He moved aside the complicated door-lock housing he'd been tinkering with. Olek's father had been a mechanic. He'd grown up learning to fix bicycles and typewriters and mopeds and cars. Anything. Then in the military it was guns and trucks and tanks. Olek had always taken things apart just to see how they worked then put them back together.

Chicky had learned something like this in the Marines. You repeat actions over and over to commit the motions to muscle memory. No thought. In an emergency you wanted to be automatic. Chicky suspected that Olek never stopped preparing for emergencies.

Mike Tyson summed it up pretty good: everyone has a plan until you get punched in the mouth. Olek always had a plan. Chicky was trying too. Trying to think through contingencies and responses and counter-responses. Examining his willingness to commit certain acts. Weighing the likelihoods of outcomes. But he also knew he might get punched in the mouth.

One emergency the super was not prepared for was any type of time-sensitive task on a computer. Every time this guy addressed his keyboard it looked like he'd never seen one before. Every single time.

"You know what my name means?" Olek had once asked Chicky. "Defender of mankind."

There were rumors of military service in Ukraine and prison in Siberia and an illegal crossing of the Northwest Passage. A year at a fishery in Alaska or two years or a commercial boat, in any case something rugged and miserable-sounding in the Arctic. There was something scary as fuck about Olek but also kindhearted and gentle despite the disturbing eyebrows and the prison-tatted arms.

A clean record was an employment requirement so none of the guys had done any time. Chicky suspected that the policy might be waived if your time had been served in Ukraine or Russia or whatever the hell Olek had gone through during the first however many years of his life. No one could agree on his age. Canarius thought late thirties. "Are you out of your fucking mind?" Zaire asked. "That guy's pushing sixty." Chicky thought the truth lay, as usual, somewhere between.

"The Goffs are having a party." Olek used one pointer finger to jab around. "The caterers arrive at five. Guests at six. Fifteen people. Names in the system. One guest with personal security." This was not unusual, Secret Service or bodyguards or entourages. Though less often now. There were fewer celebrities, residents and guests both. It was a letdown. "Senator Brock Martin. Of Arkansas."

Chicky did not follow politics but Martin was impossible to ignore. He was the most anti-immigrant racist of all of them. No wonder this guy was bringing security. And it figured he'd be the guest of Goff, who held the Bohemia's title for biggest racist. Though there was competition.

"Mrs. Frumm is again worrying about rodents." Speaking of. "She hears it in the night." Chicky sympathized. If a rat climbed out of his toilet he'd need to move.

The super glanced up. Rafael was seeing out a crew. Four o'clock was the end of contractor hours. Workmen needed to be out or the resident would incur fines and everyone would be pissed.

Olek managed two dozen people and all of them were men. All the outside vendors were men too. The contractors and subs who spent months or years on renovations. The architects and engineers and inspectors. The telecom installers and security consultants and pest-mitigation experts. Movers and carpet installers and furniture deliveries and rubbish haulers. FedEx and UPS and Amazon and USPS carriers. Garbagemen and firefighters and occasionally cops. Every year hundreds or thousands of people shook Olek's hand in the Bohemia's nerve center. Ninety-nine percent were men.

There'd been a female postal carrier but she'd retired. One of those good pensions.

There were also plenty of other people who worked at the Bohemia indirectly. None of these employees was a man. No one who lived at the Bohemia scrubbed their own toilets except Olek. Not only were all the housekeepers women they were all Black or Hispanic women. Plus the nannies and au pairs and babysitters and occasional night nurse. A few daytime maids who wore the whole getup. A rotating selection of home healthcare aides who were somehow all middle-aged West Indian women. Chicky could tell the new ones from a block away. They'd be wearing sensible shoes and clutching referrals and surprised to find themselves approaching one of the most famous apartment houses in the world. Am I really going to work here changing some old man's diaper? Yes she was.

For Olek these women were just names on lists. His was a world of men. He lived here in that world's basement, tinkering with shit. Getting ready for an emergency.

If there was one guy whose well-being Chicky worried about as much as himself, it was Olek. The super seemed awfully lonely and not doing anything about it. As if he'd accepted that alone was all he'd ever be, and shrugged, and started taking apart a vacuum cleaner or some shit.

"That is all. But listen guys: do you know anything about this march?"

Chicky looked at Canarius then back at Olek. "Don't know what you're referring to Boss."

"A Black man was killed by the police today. In Harlem."

Fuck. Those must have been the gunshots Chicky heard.

"And a Black man was also killed over the weekend. Which I think we all know about, yes?"

Chicky and Canarius nodded. Everyone knew about that.

"I am hearing that there will be a demonstration tonight, a protest, what you call it. So keep a lookout for . . ." Olek shrugged. *"Problems."* Olek shrugged a lot but never to communicate that he didn't care. "Do not hesitate to call me. Or nine-one-one. The worst the police can do is not come."

Chicky could think of plenty worse things the police could do, which was the point of the protest. But he wasn't going to be the one to say it.

Chicky found Zaire in the break room. "Hey Zaire? You know anything about this demonstration?"

"You mean tonight's protest against the killing of brothers by the police? Fuck yeah."

Chicky clipped a walkie-talkie onto his belt. "You going?"

"Damn straight."

"Any of the guys going with you?"

"That's not for me to say." Zaire had changed out of his uniform. "You asking because you curious? Concerned for your fellow workingman? Or you asking to report it to the boss man?"

All three would be the honest answer but Chicky gave none. Chicky and Zaire did not agree on much. Their relationship could easily become hostile. Chicky took responsibility for preventing that.

"I heard them talking this morning," Zaire continued, "about hiring *extra* security to protect them. I am so sick of these fucking people."

"What people?"

"*These* people." Zaire waved his arm to indicate the whole building on top of them. They were in the basement.

"Why do you work here? Why don't you get a job that doesn't make you angry all the time?"

"Because I don't want to be *anesthetized*, Chicky. I don't want to pretend that my oppression does not exist." Zaire rose. The bench had been sat on for so long that there were ass-shaped indentations in the wood. "'The future belongs to those who prepare for it today.'"

"Malcolm X?"

"That's right Chicky." It was an easy guess. Zaire quoted Malcolm all the time. "'Education is the most powerful weapon which you can use to change the world.' That's Nelson Mandela."

"Maybe," Chicky said, "but I barely finished high school. And you didn't, did you?"

"True education does not come from the white man's school. Trigonometry? Emily Dickinson?" Zaire sucked his teeth. "Fuck all that."

"Yeah," Chicky said, "okay." Chicky didn't want to have this conversation again.

"You're a blind man Chicky." Zaire sucked his teeth again. He sucked his teeth a lot. "You can't see the world in front of you. You can't see how it hates your motherfucking guts."

Maybe Zaire was right. "Maybe you're right."

"Damn straight. And we will see justice done Chicky. Maybe tonight."

That sounded specific. "What do you mean?"

"I think you know what I mean."

Chicky didn't know and didn't want to. "Just be careful," he said pointlessly. Zaire let out a snort of dismissiveness. He wasn't going to be careful. He wasn't going to take advice from Chicky.

"'I don't even call it violence when it's in self-defense,'" Zaire said.

Chicky had heard this one before so he was able to finish the line: "'I call it intelligence.'"

"That's right Brother Chicky." Zaire gave a big smile and his whole face lit up. It was a shame he didn't smile more. "That's exactly right."

Contractor hours were over. The staff had turned over to night shift. Olek sat through a supposedly urgent meeting among the building's architect, and Mr. Goff's architect, and the contractor about a kitchen renovation, with a brief appearance by Mr. Goff himself. As with everything involving Mr. Goff, the situation was adversarial for the simple reason that Tucker Goff was a fuckhead.

Olek closed his door. He flipped through his key ring, and used a small brass key to unlock the desk's bottom drawer. He glanced up to make sure no new visitors were arriving. This was the time of evening when residents were just getting home and might pop in to complain about pipes clanging, or water not hot enough, or Zaire's attitude, or those rowdy children who make a racket in the lobby every morning at eight-fifteen. Every single morning. Like it's a playground.

The old-fashioned desk's tall drawers had built-in dividers spaced three inches apart. The front sections contained personnel files in alphabetical order. The next sections contained recently ex-employees, guys who had quit or been fired or died.

Olek looked up again.

The rear-most section contained a handgun in a leather holster and a few clips of ammunition. Olek rammed home one of the clips.

He looked up again. Still clear. He strapped the holster around his left calf and ankle, inserted the Glock, pushed down his pants, all in barely five seconds. Olek had practiced this until he could do it in the dark, and under time pressure, stress, and mortal peril. If you knew that mortal peril might become a possibility, you could plan for it. Olek was, always, prepared.

Chicky's phone rang again. Another call he didn't want but had no choice but to answer. "Yeah Boss, what's good?"

"Just calling about that problem with that guy," Junior said. "Have you thought about my, um . . . solution?"

"Yeah Boss I'm gonna give that some thought. Most definitely."

Junior waited for a different answer but didn't get it so pressed on. "Puño is a serious motherfucker. The type of serious motherfucker who shoots people just for the fuck of it."

Chicky was climbing the stairs. He was holding his cap and holding his tongue and holding his temper. "Yeah Boss I understand."

"Do you Chicky? It don't sound like you do."

Chicky was now at the top of the central service stairs under a lightbulb encased by a metal cage to protect it from getting broken. This light reminded Chicky of school. His recollection was that every single light was caged but could that be accurate? There seemed to be cages everywhere in Chicky's life. Cashiers in liquor stores and dope dealers in fake bodegas and counters at the Chinese takeout. If it wasn't cages it was bulletproof glass.

"You have another solution Chicky?" Junior talked a big game about how he was all about family. *Mi familia* he was always saying especially when he'd had a few. But it was bullshit. Junior had already sold out Chicky. Maybe he'd set up the whole thing to begin with.

"Not yet Boss."

This was an impasse. Chicky needed to get off the phone and start his shift. But he could not be the one to say so. His hand was on the door handle to the lobby.

"All right then Chicky. Call me tomorrow?"

"Absolutely Boss. Absolutely."

Chicky pushed out to the gleaming marble and the shiny brass and the glow of all the wood, the soaring ceilings and the spotless rugs and the fresh flowers. It was hard for Chicky to believe that this was the world he lived in for eight hours per day. He silenced his phone to mute his other world. But it was still there.

Afternoons were getting shorter and nights longer. This was impossible not to notice if like Chicky you were out in it every day in every weather, wearing big raincoats and heavy topcoats and clear plastic covers for your cap, holding a giant umbrella to shelter residents coming in from the curb.

The sun had already migrated well past Chicky's field of vision. It was now perched somewhere over Jersey. Chicky's shift no longer included a single minute of sunshine falling on his sidewalk and wouldn't again till spring. And by then who knew if he'd even be alive.

As Chicky took up position on the sidewalk—his sidewalk—he was acutely aware of the gun tucked into the back of his pants.

CHAPTER 29

APARTMENT 11C-D

As soon as she stepped into the apartment Emily could feel the tension emanating off Tatiana, like an electrical current arcing between wires. Emily made a beeline to the den, where Hudson was with Cecile the French tutor. *"Ça va bien, Hudson?"*

"*Oui!*" he said, with his typical excess of enthusiasm, leaping up for a hug. Emily knew she had only a few years left of this type of unbridled affection. Bitsy was already beginning to resist.

"Je m'appelle Hudson!"

"Très bien, Hudson." She kissed him on both warm cheeks. *"À toute à l'heure."*

It felt almost like a deliberate act of elitism to teach children French in a city that was one-third Hispanic. But the kids were already picking up plenty of Spanish from the household help, just by osmosis, and Emily liked the idea of both. She'd consulted Whit, and as expected he was pro-French and anti-Spanish, but he also acknowledged that this was completely her call.

Tatiana was lurking in the hall, arms crossed.

"That woman," Tatiana said, referring to Yolanda. Over the years it had become obvious that Tatiana, a light-skinned Colombian, was an unabashed racist who could not tolerate any suggestions, requests, comments, or certainly orders from the dark-skinned Dominican nanny. At the barest hint that Yolanda was trying to tell her what to do, Tatiana would lose her mind.

At the moment, Yolanda was chaperoning Bitsy for tennis lessons on Randall's Island, a place Emily went only rarely, to have a passing familiarity. For a while she'd had trouble keeping track of the East River islands, which all began with R: the one with the jail, the one with the tram, the one under the Triboro Bridge where sports happened for New York's youth, at the far end of traffic-choked rides reminiscent of the arduous overland journeys that people never stopped talking about in LA. Randall's Island had once been the site of an insane asylum and a hospital for indigent immigrants and a school for juvenile delinquents and a burial ground for the hundreds of thousands of bodies that had been exhumed from graveyards at Bryant Park and Madison Square, a hodgepodge of industrial-revolution misery out of a fairy tale. Hundreds of thousands of bodies!

"My parents are coming soon to pick up the children. It's fine for you to leave now, Tattie."

The housekeeper clearly wanted to get something off her chest, but Emily couldn't deal now. After Jules had left the studio, Emily had stayed in that bed for ten minutes, sobbing. She hadn't yet recovered. She was worried that she never would.

"Whatever it is, let's discuss it tomorrow, please? I need to get ready for the evening."

"Yes miss. Of course."

Emily hadn't grasped the extent of the Tatiana-Yolanda issue until last spring. Chicky had come up to 11C-D with a delivery, and heard sounds of distress. The Bohemia's thick walls were filled with sand—a fad among eighteenth-century builders to dampen sound, to make apartments seem as luxurious as houses—so it needed to be a lot of anger, a lot of fear, a lot of something that produced such a volume. Chicky rang the bell, and no one answered. His contacts included a phone number for every apartment. For 11C-D, it was Emily's cell.

"Hello?" she'd answered, from down in the basement of New Hope.

"Hi Mrs. Longworth, it's Chicky from the front door. Sorry to bother you. But, um . . . is everything okay?"

The children were thankfully at school. Emily's imagination jumped to physical disaster, flood, fire. "What do you mean?"

"I heard a, um, commotion from your apartment."

"Oh, I'm sorry, but I'm not home. What sort of a commotion?"

"It sounded like maybe someone yelling. I was worried it might be you."

Emily knew it had to be Tatiana and Yolanda, at each other's throats. "Okay, Chicky, thanks for letting me know. I'll look into it."

"Very sorry to have bothered you, Mrs. Longworth."

"No bother, Chicky." Her worry spiked again as something scampered across her consciousness, but she didn't mention it. "Thank you for your concern, Chicky. Thanks for calling."

Emily took a scalding shower to wash away any traces of her afternoon, and some of the anxiety that was building up.

She stepped into the bedroom-sized closet, and let her fingertips trail across the cashmeres, the silks, the Sea Island cottons. Emily used to care a lot about what she wore to galas, which dress, shoes, jewelry. She'd get her hair done, mani-pedi, try on a half dozen lipsticks. Makeup alone would take an hour. Getting ready for an evening could be a full-day endeavor.

Not anymore. Emily no longer wore a different dress for every party, no longer shopped for new shoes, bags, earrings, anything. She streamlined the operation into a one-woman pit crew with herself the race car while listening to public-radio news, which last month Whit announced he could no longer abide, finally driven over the edge by a story about someone who self-identified as a queer Vietnamese storyteller, who'd grown up never seeing any stories about folks who looked like them.

"How is this *news*? And what does *folks* mean?" Emily knew Whit didn't want to have a conversation about this. The only thing anyone wanted with this subject was to tell other people how wrong they were. "I'll tell you: *folks* are people who are not white."

NPR wasn't the sole object of Whit's ire. It was the *Times* too, *The New Yorker*, all the media Emily consumed. Whit had never been a paradigm of progressive compassion to begin with, but was now on the precipice of something ugly. Emily remained the household's Democratic wing, as with many families whose husbands prioritized corporate earnings and asset protection while the wives donated to charities, and volunteered, and social-signaled their support for various left-wing or -adjacent causes. At the ballot box, the two wings canceled each other out. Though in truth Whit didn't vote all that often. "What's the point? New York is never competitive."

"And now to New York City," the newscaster transitioned, "where the protests against Liberty Logistics are growing louder."

Emily froze, holding a ruby teardrop to her face. It was this or the diamond-and-ruby clusters. In truth she was in the mood for emeralds, if it was possible to be such a thing, but she'd already put on a red dress, and didn't want to look like a Christmas tree.

"For two decades Liberty has been a *major* defense contractor. They don't make missiles or fighter jets or other big-ticket items, right? Liberty makes *body armor*."

Emily hit speed-dial. Whit answered, "Yes?"

"Are you listening to NPR?"

"Oh god, you know I'm not."

"Well this is about you." Emily turned up the volume, held her phone toward the speaker—

". . . to so-called *bad actors*, organizations or nations that engage in illegal activities such as terrorism, even *genocide*. This began to emerge two weeks ago, with the leak of an internal memo that sorted Liberty's profit margins by clients. This data revealed that the very worst actors are exponentially more profitable than stable state regimes. Which means that not only does Liberty sell to unsavory clients, the company is price-gouging those clients, right? Profiteering."

Emily was impressed by how clearly the reporters saw the problem, explained it. Maybe it wasn't nearly as nuanced as she'd imagined.

"And I understand there are protests outside the company's headquarters?"

"That's right. Right now *hundreds* of people are on the street, calling for an investigation into the company's business practices, and for the Pentagon to cancel its contracts. They're also calling for Logistics' CEO Whitaker Longworth to resign, and even to face a *criminal* investigation."

Wow, Emily thought. That was awfully fast.

"Thanks for your reporting. And now, to other news: this isn't the only protest in New York. A march is just getting underway against what some are calling a *murder* by the police of a Black—"

Emily turned down the volume. "Well," she said, then couldn't think of how to continue. She was tempted to gloat, after a fashion, but that would be counterproductive.

Whit didn't say anything for a few seconds, and Emily worried he'd hung up. "Whit?"

"I think," he finally said, "we might need to leave the city."

Emily took the call off speaker. "What do you mean? And go where?"

"Southampton, maybe. Or the islands."

"The *islands*? What are you talking about?"

"Just for a few months. Until this dies down."

"A few *months*?" This was never going to die down. "Where would the kids go to school?"

"The schools can't be worse than the radical-liberal indoctrination we're now paying for."

Last week the fifth-graders had sung "Lift Every Voice and Sing" in American Sign Language. Whit hadn't attended the recital, of course, but Bitsy had mentioned it over dinner. "Singing? In *sign* language?" he'd later asked. "What the actual fuck?"

There was also a burgeoning movement to rename the school, which had been founded by a rich landowner in the eighteenth century who was now being accused of racism. "Sure, but weren't *all* rich landowners in the eighteenth century racist?"

Whit had been making noises about yanking the kids, but what he didn't understand was that all New York schools were in the same grip. "They *all* call themselves progressive, Whit. It doesn't *mean* anything, really." Even the traditional Saint this and Saint that, boys in blazers and girls in those pedophile-entrapment skirts, were trying to keep up with the Joneses, and these days the Joneses' main priority seemed to be performative social-justice advocacy.

"Oh yes they can, Whit. The schools can be much, much worse. And what *islands* are you even talking about? Are we going to live on more than one?"

"We'll talk about this later."

"We're not fleeing in shame to any *island.* That is not an option."

"We may not have a—" He stopped, seethed.

Emily took a few beats to try to calm down, but couldn't.

"You could have done *anything* with your life," she said. "And you chose a career where you root for *wars* to break out."

"That's ridiculous."

"Couldn't you have invested in wind turbines? Or, I don't know, *luggage*?"

A friend of theirs had done the financing for a suitcase brand that had blown up.

"That's not the way the world works. You get the choices that are put in front of you—yes or no, yes or no. Liberty was what was put in front of me. I said yes. And is it really so horrible, where you find yourself? In the apartment you'd always dreamed of? And a beachfront mansion?"

"I didn't ask for any of that." This wasn't true; she had in fact asked for the Bohemia. She'd practically demanded it.

Whit didn't bother to contradict that part of his wife's argument. "What did you think? That I could afford a private plane from wages at a soup kitchen? You're not naïve."

He was right. Emily just hadn't appreciated it would be this bad.

"I've gotta go," he said. "I'll see you at the thing."

She hung up, stared at the TV, shopkeepers covering windows with plywood, armed guards at boutiques, a phalanx of police. Preparing for the worst.

Then she opened her voice-memo app, and checked that the recording she'd just made was audible. If she ever needed to prove that her husband was an unfit parent, here was a compelling piece of evidence. Whit might be building a case. So was she.

"Hi Daddy." Emily kissed her father on the cheek. "Mom."

"Darling." Emily's mother was swathed in mauve, taupe, puce. Someone had apparently once told Blaine that bland was the same as elegant, and she'd arranged her whole life accordingly. All her homes looked like Ritz-Carltons.

Hudson came bounding down the hall, threw his arms around his grandmother. Bitsy arrived more slowly. If only Eve hadn't bitten into that goddamned apple.

"So," Griffin said, "what's going on with your husband?"

Emily's dad had never especially cared for his son-in-law as a human, but he respected the hell out of the guy's money.

"Oh that?" Emily waved it off, literally. "That'll blow over."

"Will it?"

"And how are you doing, Daddy?"

"Okay, I suppose." Griff had a lot of complaints, about everything, but he was still sane enough—mostly—to not enumerate all of them all the time. He still had manners.

"You kids all packed?" Blaine asked. "Elizabeth? Hudson?" Emily's mom did not care for nicknames, which was maybe why Emily was adamant that her kids have them. "The car is waiting."

Yolanda was off to the side, holding the overnight bags and Hudson's teddy. "I'll bring these down," the nanny said. "Excuse me."

"The place is looking nice." Blaine looked around. "Is that a new Hopper?"

"No." Emily felt herself blush. "I think it was getting reframed last time you were here."

"So, for tomorrow." Blaine was back to business. "We'll drop the kids back by dinner?" Blaine was not eager to feed grandchildren any unnecessary meals. Food was something else that Emily's mom did not care for especially. For decades her diet had consisted largely of gin and Merits, but recently that had become an unfashionable lifestyle. So she'd taken up pickleball, and kale. She wore visors.

Emily's fundamental goal in life had been to be nothing like her mother, to have a real career, be a different mother, marry a different sort of man, have a different marriage. But her marriage was not nearly dissimilar enough.

"Whatever's best for you," Emily said. She kissed Hud, then Bitsy. "Love you both."

"Me too Mommy okay bye-bye." Hudson was on his way out the door. When it came to coming and going, that kid was all business.

"Wait," Emily said. "Come back."

She needed a real hug from Hudson, from Bitsy too. She squeezed them tight. The love was always there, but sometimes it leaped to the fore, like a 3D movie, shocking in its insistence, overwhelming. "I love you so much."

"I'm very sorry to have bothered you, Mrs. Longworth," Chicky had said, the next time she saw him after his call about the ruckus.

"No bother! That was just Yolanda and Tatiana, having one of their disagreements." Emily didn't want to overshare, but she did want to give Chicky some clarity. He seemed legitimately relieved, which made her wonder, again, what he'd been so worried about in the first place.

"Chicky? Why did you call me?"

"Oh"—his eyes darted away—"no particular reason."

"Come on." She smiled. "What did you think you were overhearing?"

Chicky shrugged. He clearly didn't want to have this conversation, but also didn't want to lie. "It was a woman screaming, you know? That could be serious."

"Did you think that the woman was me?"

"I didn't know what to think."

"Did you have any reason to *believe* it was me?"

"No."

But Emily could see right through him. Chicky was lying. And she needed to know why.

CHAPTER 30

FRONT DOOR

"*Hasta mañana*," Chicky said to Delmy who cleaned 5B. Then to Carmen who cleaned 3D. And to Sandro the Bohemia's handyman and to Oswaldo the daytime doorman from a building around the corner.

Then, "Good evening Mr. Onderdonk. Mrs. Onderdonk. Can I get you a taxi?"

Almost no one ever said yes anymore but still Chicky asked: can I get you a cab Mr. Blankenship? Taxi Mrs. Frumm? Now it was almost always Ubers unless people were getting into their own cars driven by their own drivers. Chicky missed running into the street with whistle blowing and arms waving. It felt great to do something for two people at once and neither was him. It made him feel valuable and valued. It was a small thing but more than nothing.

"No thanks Chicky."

The Onderdonks went to Carnegie Hall or Lincoln Center a couple of nights a week. They walked unless the weather was bad. Tonight it was perfect but still Chicky had to ask about the taxi. It was acceptable to be wrong only one way.

"Mr. Onderdonk? I was wondering if I could ask for some advice. Maybe tomorrow?"

Art Onderdonk was the only resident Chicky knew for certain was a practicing lawyer. Other Bohemians had gone to law school but as far as Chicky could tell none worked as lawyers. There was an investment banker and a COO and a housewife. Those three had all gone to Harvard Law.

"What's it about Chicky?" Onderdonk's head was cocked.

"I've got some, um, issues related to my wife's healthcare."

"Well that's not really my area of expertise."

"Oh sure." Mr. Onderdonk was being less gracious than Chicky had hoped. But not expected. "Very sorry to bother you."

"No bother Chicky. I hope your wife is okay?"

Mrs. Onderdonk was looking antsy as hell and Mr. Onderdonk clearly couldn't give less of a shit. These people didn't want to hear about any dead wives.

"Again very sorry to bother you. What are you seeing tonight?"

"*Figaro.* Do you know it?"

"Can't say that I do sir."

"Mozart was a genius Chicky. An absolute genius."

"Yes sir."

Chicky had seen that movie in middle school. Actually *in* school at that point in June when some teachers could no longer be bothered. They'd pop in VHS tapes that were supposedly educational. The Mozart flick was for—what?—history? It took a whole week to get through. That Mozart seemed like an annoying guy but there was good nudity in the movie. It used to be a challenge to find video of naked women. Now almost nothing was easier.

"Have a great evening Mr. Onderdonk. Mrs. Onderdonk."

Some residents were still coming home from work while others were going out. Cars were dropping off and picking up. Household staff departing and food deliveries arriving. The sidewalk was packed with passersby and joggers and commuters and seemingly every dog on the Upper West Side. It was easy to tell those who were trudging home from those heading to the park. The golden retrievers in particular all looked as if they were making a prison break.

And here was Mrs. Longworth striding out the door. Chicky had seen more than his fair share of beautiful women on Central Park West. Movie stars and models and even some no-name trophy wives who could knock you out. But he'd never seen anyone more glamorous than Emily Longworth. Maybe that was because he also saw her with her kids and her neighbors and she was always nice and kind and patient. Day in and day out. Chicky believed he knew her. He believed she was just as beautiful inside as out.

"Mrs. Longworth. You look dazzling tonight." Sometimes she was even more perfect.

"Thank you so much Chicky. Are you doing okay?"

The front door closed slowly on a spring mechanism to ensure that it didn't inadvertently slam on someone's hand. A big heavy door like this could ruin a life.

"Yes I am. Thank you. And you?"

"I'm keeping it together Chicky." Her big high-watt smile was amazing but it was this small gentle smile he liked best. "Thanks for asking."

He walked her toward an Escalade with a guy in a black suit behind the wheel. The Longworths owned at least two other vehicles but Mrs. Longworth didn't seem to drive.

Chicky heard a shriek and spun to see three young women hustling up the sidewalk. "Oh my god!" one yelled. "Alexandra Daddario!"

"No," Chicky said. He put up his hands protectively. "She's n—"

"Oh it's okay," Emily said.

"Can we get a photo?"

"Sure."

The women closed around Mrs. Longworth with phones angled this way and that. The whole thing took ten seconds. The women said thanks and giggled up the block.

"Why'd you do that?" Chicky asked.

Mrs. Longworth smiled and shrugged. Chicky offered his arm and stared off the driver, who nodded, go ahead dude. It was a big step up into the truck and her dress was long and tight and her heels tall and skinny. Just helping her climb into a car was a thrill. Just touching her.

"Thank you Chicky. Have yourself a safe night."

"Thank you Mrs. Longworth. You too."

♦ ♦ ♦

After the hotel incident it had taken a few days before Chicky laid eyes on Mr. Longworth again.

"Give us a minute," Mr. Longworth had said to DeMarquis. Then to Chicky, "I've been meaning to thank you for all your help these years."

"Oh Mr. Longworth please. There's no need."

"This"—extending a small envelope—"is in appreciation of your hard work."

"Mr. Longworth. That really isn't necessary."

There was a good amount of foot traffic around them. Chicky didn't want to accept this envelope too readily or at all. But he also didn't want to make Longworth spend much time in full view of Central Park West trying to buy someone's silence.

"And for your discretion." Longworth extended the envelope another few inches.

"Your family always takes good care of me, Mr. Longworth." Each December Mrs. Longworth walked around shaking hands and looking guys in the eye. She handwrote personalized cards that were nicely printed photos of the kids. She filled the envelopes with multiple hundred-dollar bills. The cards were signed WHIT & EMILY LONGWORTH but it was only one person's handwriting.

"Very good care."

Mr. Longworth smiled as if at an idiot. Then he shoved the envelope into Chicky's pocket.

"Please Mr. Long—"

This exact thing happened to Chicky at least once per year: some guy would pat Chicky on the chest in the same condescending way and say the same condescending thing: "I insist."

The next day Mr. Longworth stopped at the front door again.

"I feel like we may not have completely understood each other."

DeMarquis was again ten paces up the block.

"Sir?"

Mr. Longworth looked Chicky firmly in the eye. "I can *ruin* you."

Chicky was shocked by the shift in tone. But then again he wasn't. If you're surprised by the nastiness of people like Whitaker Longworth you have no one to blame but yourself.

"Not just get you fired Chicky. But anything bad you can imagine happening to you? I can make that happen."

The envelope contained ten thousand dollars. Chicky needed the money and he needed the job. He was at Longworth's mercy.

"Do we understand each other now?"

Chicky knew that Emily Longworth was at this asshole's mercy too. In some way or another everyone was at the mercy of men like this.

"Yes," Chicky said. "Completely."

That was when Chicky decided to tell Mrs. Longworth about the beat-up hooker. Partly for her safety. Partly to ease his conscience. Partly out of revenge.

But he couldn't just blurt it out. He needed the information to be pried out of him. Chicky knew that the nanny and housekeeper were always at it. That it was just a matter of time until he'd witness something that would be a defensible excuse to say something vague that would make Mrs. Longworth wonder. Something that would make her ask for specific information. He'd deny it but she'd press. He'd be unable to resist.

"Chicky I need to ask you something." Sure enough she'd sought him out midmorning when the sidewalk was quiet. "It's delicate."

"Of course Mrs. Longworth. Anything."

"When you heard yelling in our apartment, why were you worried about me?" She looked around. "Were you worried that my husband was hurting me?"

Chicky took a breath but didn't say anything. He was waiting for her to make it impossible to stay silent.

"I need to know *why* you were worried. Maybe you don't want to tell me. Maybe you feel like it would be a betrayal of some professional code. You think you can't reveal this . . . *whatever* about my husband. You're an honorable man and you believe people are entitled to privacy. I agree. And I appreciate it."

He opened the door for Mrs. Frumm and that yappy dog. They were headed to the park.

"I'm not asking you to reveal some petty . . . indiscretion. I wouldn't say that I don't care about that, exactly. But in truth?" Mrs. Longworth shrugged. "I don't care about that. But if I need to worry about my safety? My *kids'* safety?"

There it was.

"That's what I need to know Chicky."

CHAPTER 31

APARTMENT 2A

Julian pulled closed his brass doorknob, and stepped into the short hall that his apartment shared with the Petrocellis', separated by a demilune table with a Ming-style vase for dried flowers, and two mail trays. There was a similar setup at every landing. There were fresh flowers in both lobby wings and at the desk. The Bohemia's annual budget for flowers was eleven thousand dollars.

Massimo Petrocelli had been a famous opera singer, and music was always on when the Petrocellis were home, like the Royal Standard that flies when the Queen of England is within. When Julian was growing up all his friends played music. The woodwind kids had chapped lips from sucking on reeds, the string players calloused fingertips, badges of honor in households filled with Schubert and Brahms, Mozart and Beethoven, and above all Bach. Bach had been practically a religion on the Upper West Side. Parents pushed their children toward music, and discouraged sports. Now it was the other way around. Dartmouth offered far more admission slots for football than for violin.

Those were also the days when people like Julian's parents—an academic and a therapist—could afford a big apartment on the park, and send their kids to private schools, and expect to retire on a pension with comfort. It was a very brief moment, wedged into the middle of the last century, when it looked as if egalitarianism would become the natural state of human affairs. The rest of the history of human civilization presented incontrovertible evidence of the opposite.

"Hey Chicky," Julian said, out on the sidewalk. "How's it going?"

"Oh I can't complain, Mr. Sonnenberg. You?"

Chicky was wearing his uniform, Julian his. Both had satin stripes down the sides of the pants.

"Me either," Julian lied. "I'll see you later."

"Nice tux," the bus driver said. "Welcome to the M72."

"Glad to be aboard," Julian said. "Thanks for having me."

Way back when Julian toured prospective colleges for himself, he'd watched two students run across an Ivy League quad wearing tuxedos and carrying Champagne, and he'd thought: yes, please. Julian himself never did end up running across any campus in tux with bottle, but he never forgot the gift those boys had given him. Not a promise, but a possibility, which was even better. An unmet possibility is an everyday disappointment. A broken promise is horrible.

As a rule Julian took public transportation whenever he wore black tie. The A train to the various Ciprianis, the E to Midtown ballrooms, the crosstown bus to the East Side clubs and museums. Someone would always say something complimentary, or clever, or just friendly, making his life a little better. On the other hand, wearing a tuxedo in the back of a hired Suburban made him feel like a schmuck.

Some people were always trying to look as if they had more money than they did. Not Julian. He sat in the back of the bus, staring at nothing except his problems. He was worried about having open-heart surgery, or dying before the surgery. He was worried about the IRS audit of his business, worried about that business dissolving, worried about Whit suing him. He was worried about his finances, worried about his marriage, worried about his distant children, worried about his dying dog. He was worried about the strife on the Bohemia board, the murderous police, the demonstration tonight, the horrible state of political affairs at home and abroad, the climate crisis.

Julian Sonnenberg was worried about everything.

Everyone else on the bus was staring at their phones, and Julian realized this was yet something else to worry about: he'd neglected to charge his phone. Midafternoon was normally when he plugged in the thing, but today he'd neglected it. The phone was going to die soon.

The bus approached his stop, and Julian could see a disturbance out there, a dozen protesters with placards—BLOOD MONEY NOT WELCOME and LIBERTY LOGISTICS = CRIME SYNDICATE and LONGWORTH FOR WORST MAN OF THE YEAR. A couple of cops were nearby, neither looking especially vigilant. One of the protesters was standing a safe distance away, filming, hoping for an overreaction, an altercation, anything that could go viral.

A squad car bleep-bleeped through choked traffic, then turned and accelerated, lights flashing, off to something more urgent than a face-off between a mini-mob of counterculturals and a black-tied alpha capitalist. There were plenty of bigger problems in this city. Or maybe not necessarily bigger, but more potentially violent. These millennials in their jumpsuits and bucket hats were not an imminent threat to public safety.

As Julian climbed the steps his attention was caught by a few Black men walking down Fifth Avenue. Black men did not tend to cluster on this stretch of Fifth at night, nor for that matter during the day. Sometimes it seemed like America has come so far. Sometimes it seemed like nowhere at all.

This nineteenth-century palace had been built for one of the original robber barons, and was filling tonight with modern-day robber barons and the artists who bowed to them for patronage, and a smattering of courtiers like Julian. The structure had now been a cultural institution for far longer than it had ever been a residence. It was like a citadel of money, populated by the moneyed, for the purpose of safeguarding money, propagating money, shuffling money around to mutual advantage.

At parties like this Julian felt like a supplicant, sometimes even an employee. He had a harder time imagining himself with a billion dollars than in the backyard smoking joints with the ballerinas-in-training and the aspiring actors, filching mini-quiches and truffled arancini, inhaling enough purloined canapés to maybe—hopefully—qualify as dinner, washed down with random swigs of someone else's pinot grigio from half-empty glasses.

He collected his seating assignment, a thick ecru card, hand calligraphy. He shook hands with his half-friend, half-enemy, half-client Carter Horton, who'd recently come to a dinner at the Sonnenbergs' and announced that he was thinking of running for mayor, and Julian had nearly failed to not laugh at the presumption. Carter worked in some obscure corner of finance where he'd been hugely successful at the very limited endeavor of making himself rich, which he apparently thought qualified him to run a sprawling bureaucracy that employed tens of thousands of civil servants.

"Dahling," Carter's second wife, Elisabeta, said, "*so* good to see you." Like most of Donald Trump's wives, Elisabeta had immigrated to America from Eastern Europe under an arrangement that, at its most generous, would be called sketchy. She had a thick accent.

"And you, Elisabeta. You're looking lovely." These days Julian rarely felt comfortable complimenting women, except Europeans. They had different standards.

"I meant to tell you"—Elisabeta kissed Julian on one cheek—"your cock"—then the other cheek—"was *spectacular*."

Julian felt as if he'd been knocked sideways. What did Elisabeta know about his cock? Was it possible that he had at some point had *sex* with this beautiful Serb? And somehow *forgotten* it?

"I enjoyed it *so* much."

That was when he realized she was talking about the coq au vin he'd served. Other people hired caterers.

"Thank you," Julian said, disappointed. For a brief instant there, he'd enjoyed being a man whose cock had been appreciated by Carter Horton's wife. There was something about jackasses that made you feel as if you had to compete with them, even if you didn't want to.

Julian made his way through the vast hall, marble floors and classical statuary and colossal floral arrangements, hello-how-are-you, shaking hands, kissing cheeks, let's grab a drink, grab a lunch, get together with the wives, the dogs in the park, yes, yes let's, let's find a date, love to. Julian had no intention of following up on any of these pseudo-plans.

At the far end of the room he turned back to survey the crowd. Not quite all the men were wearing tuxedos. Some were still in business suits, too professionally important to waste the time with a wardrobe change. Though some of the non-tuxedoed were obviously artists—shaggy beards, canvas sneakers. The artists being honored tonight were emerging ones, the sorts who didn't own dinner jackets.

All the women took the dress code seriously—jewelry, makeup, hair. Some towered above their dates, in heels on top of a height advantage to begin with. These taller women tended to be significantly younger than their husbands, and far better looking. The guys with the most stunning Amazonian wives were almost always roly-poly trolls, triple chins and bovine jowls, pear-shaped and ham-assed, beady eyes and male-pattern bald.

The more moneyed the population, the better looking the women and the worse looking the men. An inverse relationship.

Julian's eye was caught by a red dress. She was a powerful magnet, a force beyond his ability to resist. He wondered, not for the first time, if she knew this.

"Julie," Ellington said, suddenly at his side. El was resplendent in a purple velvet jacket. He could pull off things that most men could not. "You ought to pick your jaw up off the floor."

Julian felt himself flinch, and hoped it was just emotional, not physical. Not visible. He hadn't realized it was that obvious. El receded into the crowd before Julian could come up with a defense, leaving behind a lingering chill.

The cocktail hour was drawing to a close, and the catering staff were trying to shoo guests into the ballroom. "The program is about to begin, please," with arm extended. "This way, please." Almost no one was in any rush for the program to start. Most people were here for the cocktail-hour chitchat, not the awards, and certainly not the speeches.

Julian couldn't help but glance again at Emily. She was not with her husband. Maybe Whit was not coming? That would be a relief. Most people in Whit's situation would shy away from the public eye, but Whit was not most people. He looked forward to confrontations. Being combative was one of many ways he exploited his privilege: he didn't need to accommodate anyone. The very definition of an asshole.

Emily seemed to float through the room, laughing alongside a helmet-coiffed East Side matriarch, the president of one of the clubs. Julian couldn't hear Emily's laugh through the din, but in his head he could, and the imaginary sound made him smile.

Now Julian noticed that Jen too had finally shown up, just under the wire. He made his way against the flow, excuse me, pardon me, and kissed his wife on the cheek. He'd already decided not to tell her about the doctor's bad news, not here. Maybe when they got home. Maybe tomorrow.

"How was your day, Jules?" Jen asked. "You do anything fun?"

Was there something suspicious in his wife's question? Something accusatory? Did he care?

"Lunch with a douchebag. Does that count?"

"Hmm." Jen had little interest in this New York population, the intersection of art with socialite with a sprinkling of chattering media. This was her husband's pool, into which Jen waded only when specifically requested, and was sometimes resentful, and occasionally late, which Julian halfway suspected was purposeful. More than halfway.

The ballroom was packed with eight-tops, Chiavari chairs in silk sleeves, gold-tone chargers and glass votives, densely packed red roses in low vases that wouldn't interrupt anyone's view of anyone else. The table decor wasn't imaginative, but it was definitely expensive.

Julian located their table exactly where he expected, at the center of the room, in front of the dais, where the donor class is always seated, in prime position to be observed wearing couture while making showy tax-deductible contributions to worthy causes. Julian himself would be obliged to donate tonight, though on a much smaller scale. He was still debating how much. Tax write-offs were compelling, but only if you had profits to balance. Only if you were alive to file your taxes.

"Here we are." Julian guided his wife toward the table. "This is you."

"Christ," Jen said, noticing the name next to hers. "I should've come down with a migraine."

"Sorry," Julian said. His own place was on the far side of the table. "I owe you one."

"Much more than one."

"Jennifer, nice to see you." Ellington kissed her on the cheek. "You remember Tripp?"

Tripp Hubbard had moved into Ellington's meticulously renovated Sugar Hill brownstone three years ago, but supposedly neither man wanted to marry. Jen and Tripp immediately dove into animated chitchat about the new season—Tripp was a dancer. Jen could turn it on, when she wanted. Julian wished she'd want to more frequently.

The four of them remained standing behind their chairs, as if playing tight man-to-man, waiting for at least one of their hosts to arrive. What they were guarding was their politeness, or their obeisance. At a party like this, it was always clear to Julian who the most important people were. It wasn't the people getting the awards, nor the people providing the entertainment. It was the people with the most money. The whole thing was a facade constructed to elicit donations, and to bestow recognition on the largesse. Like the pyramids: all that work, just to bury a king.

And here she came, the queen. My god, Julian thought, just look at this woman. She literally took his breath away, he couldn't seem to get enough oxygen. But this time he had the presence of mind to hide it. Or try.

Emily kissed him on both cheeks, and Jennifer too, then shook hands with Ellington, with Tripp, and introduced herself to the table's sponsored artist, and her plus one, both of them Black, both wearing locked hair, both discernibly queer.

When Whit arrived a minute later, Julian could see him assess the table he'd paid for. "Precious?" Whit asked the plus-one. "Is that what you said your name was?"

"That's right."

Whit smirked. Julian could see immediately which sort of trouble was brewing.

"Sonnenberg," Whit said, extending his hand.

"Hi Whit. Thanks so much for having us."

"Our pleasure." Whit smiled tightly, with his mouth but not his eyes. The two men were apparently going to pretend, for the sake of propriety. But not all that much.

A waitress arrived with amuse-bouches, little plates with little potatoes with little dollops of little beads of caviar. Whit placed his phone on the table, screen up, making it clear that there was a finite amount of attention he was planning to pay. Like Jennifer, Whit was here as a reluctant spouse. He looked around with obvious disdain before his eyes alit on Julian's, and stared in challenge. Julian stared back. Julian knew he'd lose this game of chicken, but he waited a beat, which he thought would salvage some measure of dignity. It felt more like the opposite.

♦ ♦ ♦

The appetizers were cleared, salads delivered. Servers made sure wineglasses never fell empty; the mandate was explicit to get the guests drunk. Whit was the only one at their table who was obliging.

"Another whiskey."

Julian glanced again at Emily, her mouth, her lips, it was almost unbearable. Which is exactly what he'd suspected when she'd proffered this invitation, months ago. Before anyone was calling into question the "Rothko," before anyone had leaked Liberty's reports, before anyone was protesting Whit. Before Julian had started seriously considering ending his marriage.

"We're benefactors," Emily had said.

"Of course you are."

"We need to fill a table. This is an art party. It makes all the sense in the world."

The Longworths and the Sonnenbergs had seen one another plenty, but mostly in passing—in the Bohemia's lobby, on the sidewalk, at cocktail parties. Julian and Whit had interacted a lot, professionally, but the two had never been social friends. The women had never had any conversation much beyond hello. This foursome had never shared a table.

"Don't you think it will be hard?" Julian asked.

"Sure," Emily agreed. "But it can also be fun."

"Oh yeah?"

"We'll be sitting there, surrounded by all these people." She kissed his chest. "Picturing each other naked." Her mouth continued to his stomach. She kept going. "You," she said, "will be picturing this." She took him in her mouth. And now that was exactly what he was picturing, torturing himself. He reached under his napkin, and shifted himself, thickening—

Stop it!

Julian forced himself to pay attention to the woman giving the speech, who'd arrived up there with index cards, always a bad sign. "In work that explores the devastating legacy of inherited trauma in powerful narrative imagery that reflects the fierce urgency of now."

Nothing snuffed out an inconvenient hard-on quicker than index-carded remarks.

An Inconvenient Hard-On: a good title for a presidential memoir, a companion volume to his vice president's.

". . . the lived experiences of BIPOC and queer folk. We need to do more to celebrate the *innumerable* times that Black women have *literally* saved this country."

"Oh for fuck's sake," Whit muttered. *"Literally?"*

Ellington glared, and Emily shifted uneasily, and suddenly Julian could no longer sit here. "Excuse me," he said to no one in particular, folded his napkin, made his way amid the clinking of silver on china. Or rather flatware on porcelain; there was neither silver nor china in here.

"I want to thank my mother. God rest her. Perfect. *Black.* Soul."

This was delivered as a standing-ovation line, observed at first by mostly Black people, but then none of the white crowd wanted to be seen sitting while Black people stood, so the whole room rose, clapping for . . . what? That this woman had loved her dead mother? This standing ovation wasn't even guilt, it was just a charade, the type of cynical performance that made a mockery of actual progress. Julian was hit with another wave of desolation.

He walked through the mostly empty hall, a half dozen people waiting for drinks from a beleaguered bartender. As the ballroom hubbub receded behind Julian, the sounds of the street came to the fore. It seemed to be more than the usual idling engines and honking horns and the clicking-clacking of high-heeled shoes. He checked his phone, in low-power mode. No important messages.

"How many people are out there now?" Julian asked the security guard, whose hands were clasped over his crotch, like a soccer player guarding a free kick.

"Last time I looked, about thirty."

"Any trouble?"

The guard narrowed his eyes, maybe trying to figure out who Julian was, why he thought he was entitled to this inquisition.

"If you don't mind me asking," Julian added.

The guard took a beat before answering, making it clear he didn't owe Julian anything. "Don't think so. But I haven't been out there in a while." This guy exuded a malevolent competence, as if he maybe couldn't read proficiently but was expert in how to rip out fingernails with needle-nosed pliers.

Julian pushed open the door, stepped through the vestibule, and the outer door, to the landing above the steps that separated private property from public sidewalk. It wasn't a hard, secure border. The doors weren't locked. The guard didn't seem to have a gun.

Elisabeta was out here with a cigarette. Julian had never really been a smoker, just a bummer of other people's cigarettes. She extended her pack toward him.

Why the fuck not? He accepted. God, that felt good, the nicotine rush, a thing to do with your fingers, the excuse to watch a woman's mouth, it's all so sexy. Julian wondered if Elisabeta knew exactly what she was doing with that mispronunciation of *coq*. Maybe she wasn't altogether dissimilar from Emily, who'd also known what she was doing, even if Julian at first didn't. Sexier lingerie.

The anti-Whit protesters were still being overseen by the same cops who were still paying the same minimal level of attention. These days a lot of cops seemed to spend their shifts staring at their phones, something that doormen at the Bohemia were forbidden to do.

Julian also noticed a different commotion. He took a few steps across the landing, to get a better angle, and could see some Black marchers holding placards. All the protesters here were white. So were the cops, who now took notice. Then Julian saw a third crowd coalescing, people streaming toward the avenue from the side street, a dozen, two dozen. All men. All white. One of these white men was carrying a baseball bat.

"Oh fuck," Julian muttered.

There was a lot of dissatisfaction converging here. The white mob stood on the corner, watching the Black marchers approach the white protesters.

Julian was standing on the steps of this mansion as if he owned the damn place. This would be a horrible thing for someone to notice, or god forbid take a photo of.

"That does not look good," Elisabeta said.

"No," Julian agreed, "it—"

The *pop-pop* of distant gunfire cut him off.

CHAPTER 32

APARTMENT 11C-D

Emily felt the fear flood the room. The strife out there was separated from the extravagance in here by nothing more than velvet drapes and breakable windows.

Maybe you tell yourself: no, not in America. It can't, as Sinclair Lewis said, happen here. The uprising will happen in a crueler place, triggered by greater inequity, greater iniquity, a more stratified economy, more repressive politics. Americans can rest assured on a quarter-millennia's experience, and evidence: it hasn't happened yet, and things used to be so much worse.

But, as they say, past performance is not indicative of future results. Maybe it's not the harshest conditions that will create the uprising, but the opposite. Maybe it's the incremental improvements, the small doses of empowerment, that will prove the viability of large-scale upheaval, and embolden the revolution. Maybe what's happening now isn't the culmination of anything, but the instigation. Maybe Emily will look back on today and chide herself: *of course*, it was so *obvious*.

She heard another *pop* out there, and a collective gasp in here, and her spine went rigid. How could you feel safe in this room, tuxedos and gowns, diamonds and gold, Champagne and caviar, while out there are so many grievances, and so much anger, and so many guns?

The emcee tapped the mic. "Ladies and gentlemen, please remain calm." He waited for the hubbub to die down. "Our next presenter needs no introduction."

Was this really going to continue? Maybe there wasn't any choice.

Between entrées and dessert, the program paused for the customary chit-chat interlude, which a lot of people were using to check their phones, looking for news, for warnings.

Not Whit. "What do you think the odds are that a white man is going to win something tonight?"

He was looking down at the program, the descriptions of the awards, the nominees. The Emerging Artists Fund's mission was to help creatives who didn't have access to the traditional paths to success.

"Are any white men even *nominated*?"

"Yes," Emily answered quickly, trying to shut this down. This was one of the boards on which she served, and she knew that three of the nominees were white and identified as male.

"Really?" Whit looked up at his wife. "Do they happen to be gay?"

He was not wrong. Every single one of the award winners in recent memory had come from historically marginalized backgrounds, and that would be true tonight too. At the first gala meeting, the chair had pronounced, point-blank, "We need to center people who use they/them pronouns." Emily knew that at least a few people in that meeting disagreed with this knee-jerk litmus test, but no one was willing to make the objection aloud.

"Hmm?" Whit wanted to be proven right, and he wanted Emily to be the one who needed to admit it.

"Black women," Whit continued, "account for something like six percent of the American population. White men are thirty. So if things are *equitable*, five white men will win for every one Black woman."

"Oh Jesus," Ellington said, not quite a mutter.

"And it's still Black right? We haven't gone back to African-American?"

This had been one of Whit's most recent diatribes. "People used to demand to be called African-American," he'd said. "It was a whole thing. Then it became black lowercase, then it became Black uppercase, then people were talking about communities of color, about BIPOC. Though doesn't people of color sound an awful lot like *colored people*?" He'd shaken his head in mock offense. "Can you tell me that this evolution isn't designed to ensure that some people are always kicking toward the wrong goal, guaranteed to miss, and get canceled for it? People like me. And people like you too, Em."

Whit was leafing through the program, and Ellington was glaring at him. Emily knew that Whit was not going to back down. The whole point of launching into this was to not back down. The whole point of Whit.

"Do I misunderstand what *equity* means?" Whit continued. "Or is *reparations* a more accurate description of what's going on here?"

Emily thought that Ellington might punch Whit, but at that moment they were saved by someone bustling to the table, and Emily looked over to see Skye, arms and mouth wide open.

"Emmie! I was hoping I'd see you tonight."

The last time they'd seen each other had been by happenstance in a Hell's Kitchen café, months ago. Emily had been with Jules. "My god, Emmie," Skye had said at the barista counter, "you look *amazing*." This was one after-nooner, barely fifteen minutes after Emily had orgasmed on the tip of Jules's tongue. She was still glowing, and the compliment made her blush even more. She was flustered as she introduced Jules. "He's a gallerist," she'd sputtered, "we live in the same building. We ran into each other." She was explaining too much, too fast.

Skye hadn't given any wink-wink, but Emily could see suspicion in her very restraint.

"Skye!" Emily exclaimed now, standing for a careful embrace. Neither wanted to disturb either's hair. "You look fantastic. That dress!"

Whit stood too. "Skye," he said, with an air-kiss, "nice to see you."

Emily's mind was spinning over how to handle Jules. If she introduced him as if the café had never happened, that would be an admission of guilt. And possibly disastrous if Skye responded with something like "You've introduced us before." On the other hand, if Emily got out in front of that café meeting, it might beg the question of when it had been, and where, and why exactly, and—

"Hi. Skye." Jules was making the decision for her. "Julian Sonnenberg, I think we've met."

Skye glanced at Emily, who was trying her best to remain impassive.

"Hi Julian. You don't remember seeing me, do you?"

He blanched. Emily's stomach churned.

"I, um . . ." Jules was panicking. Emily thought she was going to throw up.

"This morning, we saw each other in the park," Skye said. "With our dogs?"

"Oh my god! That was you? Of course it was. Sorry. This is my wife, Jennifer."

Emily felt as if her execution had just been commuted, already strapped into the chair.

"Hi Jennifer, nice to see you. I'm Schuyler Walker."

"Your name is Skye Walker?" Jen asked. "That's the best name I've ever heard."

Whit was now examining Jules with drunken hostility. "How do you know Skye?"

"Oh, I don't know," Jules said. The ballroom lights flickered. "Just around."

Skye seemed to digest this, while Emily's wheels spun: Jules has just admitted it, hadn't he? With a tacit plea to Skye to keep the secret?

Yes, that's exactly what had just happened. And Emily could see that Skye got it.

"That's right," Skye acceded. Now Skye would also understand why Emily had been avoiding her. A lot had just transpired, in the space between words. "Just around." Sometimes that's true.

Now Jennifer was paying closer attention too. Emily felt her chest getting tight. This was back on the verge of catastrophe. Emily tried not to look at her husband directly, but she couldn't help herself. Whit was wearing an unusually smug smirk, even by his standards.

The lights flickered again. "Ladies and gentlemen"—the emcee was back—"I hope you're enjoying your desserts. We're ready to present the evening's final awards."

"It's been *way* too long," Skye said. "We have a lot to catch up on. *Obviously.* Call me tomorrow?"

It took all Emily's strength to maintain her equanimity. She'd foreseen many potential problems, but this hadn't been one. "Of course," she said.

♦ ♦ ♦

In her moments of more critical self-examination, Emily wondered if she'd overshared with Julian deliberately, to create an excess of intimacy as a manipulation, a dynamic she was fashioning to make something happen. Her first questionable revelation had been about her prenup. "It wouldn't be *poverty*," she'd admitted. "I haven't *completely* lost my mind. But I'd have—what?—*one* percent of our net worth?"

She'd been toying with Jules's chest hair. He didn't respond.

"What would be fair? I honestly don't know. I didn't earn hundreds of millions of dollars. And *earn* is slippery. It suggests merit."

She was building her own case, to herself. Maybe to Jules too.

"People do all sorts of things for money," she continued. "They sell drugs, sell their bodies, sell out their values, their integrity, their communities. People put up with every indignity, they betray their friends, break laws, break trust, lie, steal. And this isn't even the exception, is it? This is the rule. Maybe everyone does things for money they're not proud of. I sure have. Clearly."

Jules, like Emily, had not predicated his career on pursuing wealth. She'd stumbled into wealth, and Jules had stumbled around it. This was a choice they'd both made, which itself was an unearned luxury. This was a subject on which Emily and Jules saw eye to eye.

"Is this really so bad? What we're doing?"

She wasn't asking an honest question, and she didn't want an honest answer. Jules knew this. "No," he said. He kissed her. "It's not bad at all. It's wonderful."

The second questionable admission had been about the choking.

"It's how he . . . um . . . *finishes*."

"Oh," Jules had said, taken aback. "Choke in an enjoyable way? Or not?"

"Not enjoyable for me, no. For a while, it didn't really bother me. But then it started to hurt, and it was, frankly, disturbing. And scary. I had to ask him to stop."

This revelation had felt like a more intimate act than the sex they'd just had. More of a betrayal. It was also a little humiliating.

"After that, our, um, *frequency* fell off dramatically. He seemed to stop wanting me. Then I discovered he'd been finding other women to choke. Escorts. He's also hitting them."

"Wow, that's awful. How'd you find out?"

"Chicky."

"Chicky *Diaz*?"

"Do we know another Chicky? And if all that isn't bad enough, he hires escorts who *look like me*. That's who he wants to choke, and hit. That's his fantasy."

"Oh Jesus Em. I'm so sorry."

"That's what turns him on." This was, Emily knew, coals to Newcastle. "Beating his wife."

Nothing stokes hatred so much as being hated. This is true for fans of sports teams, it's true for sectarian conflicts, it's true for racism, it's true for warring nations. It's true for one person at a time, hating one other person.

Emily saw her phone light up, and pushed open her bag to check. "Oh," she said. "I'm sorry, excuse me." She rose. "Daddy? Everything okay?"

As she left the table she saw Whit knock back the last of a whiskey, and beckon a waiter.

"No," her dad said, "everything is definitely not okay."

"The kids? What's wrong?"

"The kids? No, the kids are fine. But do you know what's going on out there?"

"Well, that depends on what you mean, Daddy."

"The police have ceded all control. *All* control. Rioters are marauding down Park Avenue."

"Marauding?" Emily didn't know the precise definition, and she suspected neither did Griffin, and that whatever marauding was, it was not going on. Also *rioter* was probably inaccurate. And the police had not ceded control of the Upper East Side. Her dad was wrong about everything.

"What exactly do you mean, Daddy?"

"I can see them out the window, walking *in* Park Avenue, as if they *own* it. They're going to come in here, I just know it. They're going to storm in."

"The doormen won't let that happen."

"The doormen? The doormen are *Black*. Whose side do you think they're going to take?"

"Oh Daddy. Really?"

Griff Merriweather, like his daughter, had always been a Democrat. He'd voted for Obama, twice. But then he'd told a dirty joke at work, got called out by a young woman of color, canceled, bought out of his partnership, career over, and suddenly he was watching Fox News day and night. Emily recognized that her dad was being pushed away from the left more than he was being pulled in by the right—it wasn't the port that was appealing, it was the storm that terrified Griff Merriweather, not to mention Whit Longworth. Men like her dad and her husband were becoming terrified animals, backed into the corner, lashing out in the same way. Being rich and powerful and white and male doesn't prevent anyone from being scared.

"We're going to get out of here before it's too late. Driving up to Westport."

This seemed like not only an overreaction, but a terrible idea. Emily had a vision of their Mercedes surrounded by a mob, the Connecticut plates, the prep-school and golden retriever stickers, like a bright blinking neon sign of white affluence, one of those mobile ads cruising around.

"Daddy, it's not a great time to be driving around the city. Streets are closed. You might get stuck, somewhere you don't want to get stuck." She didn't need to stoke Griffin's fears of racial violence. That bonfire was already lit, with plenty of fuel. He understood what she was saying, without her being specific. "My event is almost over. Then I'll stop by. Okay? Please sit tight."

"Hi Gareth," Emily said. "You're looking swell tonight."

"Oh hi Emily. *Hi.*" He was so grateful it made her want to cry. Emily had seen the clip—everyone had—in which Gareth had said, "I promise that we're *always* going to put on all the greatest hits by all the greatest dead white guys." He'd been trying to reassure a conservative board that was pushing back on the opera's diverse-voices initiative, at the expense of Mozart. A young board member had recorded the meeting, hoping for exactly this sort of hot-mic moment, then blasted out Gareth's comment out of context, with her own snark, to two million followers. Gareth was fired immediately, disinvited, disgraced, ostracized, a toxic meme with no hope of redemption.

"But I'm marginalized!" Gareth had been born at a time and place when being gay meant being ridiculed every day, and it was a good day if ridicule were the full extent of it.

"Well, I've got to get back in there," Emily said, giving Gareth's arm a reassuring squeeze. "But it's really good to see you."

Ellington was standing with Jennifer, who was watching Emily approach, appraising her, now beckoning her. "Emily, please join us. Ellington was just telling me about his old Jaguar. How old did you say it was?"

"Fifty-five years? No, fifty-six."

"Goodness!" Jennifer turned to Emily. "Older even than my husband. Yours too, right?"

Emily felt as if a bomb of bile had exploded in her stomach. She nodded.

"Aren't you worried about taking responsibility for something that old? I mean, you can't know what problems the car might have had, what accidents. It must be a lot of maintenance too, repairs, parts. For all you know, the thing might die tomorrow. Is it worth all that?"

"Well, I do love that car."

"Ah, love. Of course." Jennifer turned to Emily. "Do you think you'd do that, Emily? Take someone else's . . . car?"

Jennifer and Emily were staring at each other, just a couple of feet apart, surrounded by a thousand people. Emily's head was spinning. Should she pretend that she didn't know what Jen was talking about? Would that be worse? She decided to defend herself.

"Well, if the owner didn't want it anymore? It would be a shame to let something so wonderful just sit around, unused. Unloved."

Jules was standing on the far side of the table, watching this interaction while chatting with someone else, but there was no way he could hear it. Whit wasn't paying any attention at all.

"What's the point of life," Emily continued, "if not love?"

Jennifer stared at Emily for a second before she opened her mouth, reconsidered, then said, "There are a lot of different types of love. I mean, it's not as if Ellington has *sex* with that impractical car he loves. Do you, El?"

"What in god's name are you talking about?"

The women continued to stare at each other. Ellington glanced from one to the other.

"We're talking about impractical love. Aren't we, Emily?"

When Emily had told Jules that she didn't want anyone to get hurt, that hadn't been entirely true. She'd wanted Whit to get hurt. But suddenly it looked like Whit might be the only one who'd dodge it.

"And to present our final award of the evening, for Emerging Artist of the Year, please welcome to the stage last year's recipient of Gallery of the Year, Ellington Toussaint and Julian Sonnenberg, of the Sonnenberg-Toussaint Project."

Emily watched Ellington climb the steps up to the portable stage, followed by Julian, both of them dashing. Ellington was beaming, but Julian wore an uncomfortable smile, as if he were ashamed to be up there. "I don't want to be the old straight white guy," he'd told her this afternoon, "bestowing my blessing on some young queer artist of color."

"You're not old. You're young."

"Well thank you. But that's not the point." He sighed. "I used to feel good about things like this, being in front of people, giving out an award, or accepting one."

"You should."

"Well thank you again. But now every time I'm in front of people it seems like a chance for people to resent me. To hate me."

"Not only are you young, you're incredibly virile."

He'd chuckled, half-hearted, like his smile now, standing off to the side while Ellington gave remarks about representation, and advancements, and so much more work to be done. Jules was collapsing into himself up there, and Emily's heart hurt for him, for the sadness that had been overtaking him, today more than ever.

"Are you sure everything's okay?" she'd asked, still in bed. His love-making hadn't been the only thing that had been subdued. He swallowed, and nodded. She knew he didn't want to say it aloud, whatever it was. She didn't press him. She let him have it, his secret.

This would not end up being the single thing she regretted most, but it was awfully close. As she watched Jules on that stage, she realized she'd never loved any man so much. What a waste.

There was only one thing she ended up regretting more than allowing his silence: keeping her own.

"On behalf of everyone at EAF, I want to thank all of you for coming out to celebrate this fierce, brilliant, richly diverse class of artists."

All the evening's winners were arrayed on the dais.

"Richly diverse?" Whit asked. "Really?"

"Let's give these folks one more hand."

Julian and Ellington had returned to their places at the table, and stood there, applauding.

"So," Whit said, "I count one, two, three, four, five, six, seven winners. Seven *folks*."

"Oh Whit give it a break."

"What? I'm not entitled to count the award winners? That's too much *entitlement*?" He took another sip. He was, obviously, drunk. "Am I *surprised* that none of the awards went to white men? No. White men don't have the proper *lived experience*. White men are not *diverse*."

The honorees were filing off the dais, shaking one another's hands.

"I believe a couple of grants were specifically earmarked otherwise, weren't they?" Whit consulted the program again. "Yes. One for a creator of—I quote—Indigenous, First Nations, or Latinx heritage. And another for—again, quote—artists of the African diaspora."

"Whit, that's enough."

"Oh lord," Precious said, under her breath in a way that was meant to be heard. "Let's go."

"You're welcome!" Whit called after them. "I'm so glad you were able to join us!"

Very few people were in a rush to leave the sanctuary. Who knew what was happening out there? People in here were looking at phones, checking news, summoning drivers. No one in their right mind was going to stand out on Fifth Avenue, in formalwear, and try to hail a taxi.

Whit shot the cuff of his seven-thousand-dollar bespoke tuxedo, and checked the time on his thirty-thousand-dollar wristwatch. Emily had once heard Whit admit, reluctantly, that yes, straight white men had clearly enjoyed a good long run of it, but that was over. Whitaker Hamilton Longworth had been born a generation too late.

"According to Twitter," Ellington said, "shots fired in the vicinity of Park and Seventy-first."

Whit shook his head. "It must be 740." Possibly the most exclusive apartment building in the world, which wasn't all that far away. Not nearly far enough.

"Well, another fun night of shelling out five figures to get scolded by Black women. Or was it six figures?" Whit took another sip. "And now we can go out there and run for our lives."

Whit remained seated with legs crossed, holding his nearly empty glass.

"Maybe next year I'll underwrite an award specifically for an artist of European descent. What do you think, Em? Do you think the European *diaspora* can be called a community? Or is *community* applicable only to communities of color, or the LGBTQRSTUV community?"

Ellington stood. "Dude, are you serious right now?"

"Ellington," Emily said, "I'm so sorry, I think my husband may have been overserved."

"Don't apologize for me, Emily. We have nothing to apologize for."

"Oh really? Nothing?" Ellington asked.

Whit was wearing an arrogant smirk, and Emily could see there wasn't anything she could do about the impending train wreck. She just needed to stay out of the way.

Now Julian too was standing. "El, this is not the time."

"No, Julie? Then when *is* the time?"

Whit stood, languidly, not a care in the world. "You and I have a problem, Toussaint?"

Tripp decided it was time to insert himself. “Come on, El, let’s go home.” Ellington glared at Whit, making it clear that he wasn’t backing down, just giving in to reason. Then he turned away.

“Well well well,” Whit said, and Emily could tell he was about to say something horrid. He had a specific look on his face when he was being extra-vile.

“Saved by the twink.”

That was when Ellington spun around and punched Whit in the face.

CHAPTER 33

FRONT DOOR

This job gave you plenty of time to think. Too much time. Especially on nights. Recently Chicky had spent a lot of it trying to figure out where he'd gone wrong. His wife got sick and his kids need schooling. That was it. Where was the mistake? Was three kids too many? Should he have bought some shitty house out in Jersey so he could stop paying rent? Or moved to a smaller apartment as soon as the girls started college? A one-bedroom or a studio was all he really needed. But how would he see his girls? Would they sleep on the floor? Get hotel rooms? And they'd, what, meet for *brunch*?

Though that's what everyone got. If you were lucky. You hoped your kids didn't need you but also didn't hate you. You hoped they were willing to visit. Have brunch.

Should Chicky not have borrowed money from that loan shark? Of course not. But how else was he going to pay last year's back rent?

Should he have avoided working for Junior? Maybe. But isn't family the obvious answer?

Should he have quit being a doorman? Found a better paying job? Like what?

Should he? Should he? Should he?

Way too much time to think.

♦ ♦ ♦

A guy with a whole bunch of shit was taking a seat against the stone wall of the dry moat.

"No, uh-uh." Chicky hoped this was loud enough but not too loud.

If the guy heard he didn't respond.

"Hey," Chicky said to Canarius, "I gotta go to the corner. Homeless guy."

Canarius came out from behind the desk to watch. After what had gone down twenty years ago the building had a protocol for situations like this: one of the doormen would take care of the problem while the other stood by as a witness.

"My friend," Chicky said to the guy. "I'm sorry. Not here." Chicky's personal protocol was to be extra-careful. Wary. Of them, of course. But also of himself. That had been his mistake.

"*Por favor*," the guy pled.

"You can't be here my friend." Chicky didn't want to speak Spanish. He didn't want that connection. "I'm very sorry."

This guy didn't have the messy look of drug addicts or drunks. He didn't look crazy and he wasn't dirty. He was just a middle-aged guy with his stuff and nowhere to go. A guy no one wanted.

"I'm sorry," Chicky said. "Believe me."

Chicky was not far from being evicted himself. And evicted was awfully close to homeless. And homeless was one bad-luck shelter away from being on the street. From being this guy.

Just because you had a good union job and worked your whole life didn't mean you weren't going to end up on the street.

This guy had a piece of fresh gauze on his arm. Blood had seeped through it.

"I can't let you stay here, my friend."

Sometimes Chicky really fucking hated this job.

Olek sat on his sofa, phone in hand, scrolling. Mostly swiping left, occasionally right. But he would not be meeting anyone tonight. This was just a way of distracting himself.

His television was tuned to the local news. A good-looking Asian man was reporting from the Fifty-ninth Street Bridge, which counterprotesters had just crossed onto Manhattan. The caravan was mostly large pickups with flags on their tailgates. American flags and thin-blue-line flags and at least one Confederate flag, MAGA hats on dashboards, TRUMP bumper stickers. At least a hundred vehicles that ended in a swarm of motorcycles, motors rumbling.

Olek returned to the endless supply of flesh on his phone. This never stopped awing him.

When Oleksander Ponomarenko was growing up in Ukraine in the eighties and nineties, it was unacceptable to be gay, despite the supposed decriminalization of gay sex in 1991. This was especially true in the army. They would beat the shit out of you, then never talk to you again. And that was the best case. It was also possible that they'd concoct a situation in which you died. Shot during a training exercise, would be the report. Or fell out of a helicopter. These incidents were investigated, and everyone knew exactly what happened, and the conclusion was always the same: accidental death. If anyone needed to be faulted, it was the dead man. Always.

Just a few months after Olek's military service ended, he was arrested in an underground nightclub. After a brief unwinnable trial he was sentenced to five years for the crime of public indecency. The public aspect was a private club. The indecency was being in a room filled with men.

Even when he moved to Alaska, Olek remained in the closet. One hundred percent of his sexual encounters in Alaska were furtive, and more than half were anonymous. Alaska had not been the right choice. It had not been a choice at all. Alaska had been a necessity.

New York City was a revelation. Chelsea! Olek literally could not believe it. His mind could not process a paradigm shift of this magnitude. Here was a whole neighborhood—a *nice* neighborhood—where it was not just okay to be gay, it was practically required. The cafés, restaurants, bars, shops: every business of every sort was filled with gay men. Attractive gay men. Olek had a hard time believing that Chelsea was not an elaborate conspiracy to corral gay men, throw them in jail, and beat the shit out of them. That made far more sense.

Olek gradually accepted that for many men it was possible to be openly gay in New York. Proudly gay. Flagrantly gay. Not Olek. He simply could not. He did not want the residents to know, and in particular he could not bear the idea that the staff would know. None of the guys were gay, and the sense that Olek detected was often homophobic. Sometimes it was much more than a sense. *Faggot* was a word he heard regularly. *Faggot-ass motherfucker* was something Zaire said all the time. This was the person who was the most vocal about racism. About prejudice.

But Olek did not want to lecture anyone. He did not want to educate anyone. He did not want to change anyone's mind about anything. Olek had finite goals and low expectations.

So he kept his sexual life secret. He never brought men home. He never went on dates anywhere near the Bohemia, in this neighborhood where he did not feel like he belonged.

Olek was acutely aware that he knew practically no women, not to have real conversations. There had to be something wrong with such an existence. But other parts of his life were far better than he could have imagined. Hell's Kitchen and Chelsea and Greenwich Village, all these fantasies, were easily reachable on the subway line that ran beneath Central Park West, one, two, three miles away. Olek could swipe right here on his couch in one of the most famous buildings in the world, and fifteen minutes later be in a Chelsea bed.

But tonight he needed to remain here, vigilant. A night like tonight could be life-defining.

In most of the world, people like the Bohemia's residents lived in fortresses guarded by private soldiers, sometimes public ones. But American oligarchs weren't as careful, because they didn't think they needed to be. Americans were complacent, with their Miranda rights and public defenders, their supermarkets and free vaccinations, their Grindr, their Chelsea. Everyday luxuries make it hard to anticipate worst-case scenarios. Americans thought the world was ending if their electricity went out and they couldn't charge their phones to post on Instagram. They had no idea.

Extra security was always the right choice.

The senator left with his Secret Service team. Chicky went to the basement to oversee the catering crew carrying out glassware and dinnerware and big bags of linens. Then he double-locked the service entrance and set the alarm. Raul would be showing up soon for the overnight but he'd use the front. No one else would be coming or going through the service door till morning.

The rest of the shift would be quiet. Even all the dogs had been walked.

The Sonnenbergs and Longworths were still out but otherwise the house was full.

Sirens were not unusual but tonight was a lot. Like early covid when ambulances were nonstop and always meant someone was dying or dead. Those sirens had been a constant reminder that your life was in danger. Chicky hadn't missed a single day except when he actually had covid. Three times. Otherwise he was at the Bohemia with everyone else on staff but almost none of the residents. The building emptied out immediately and stayed that way for six months. Nearly all these people had bigger and safer homes to live in for a month or two or six or forever. Places with outdoor spaces and easier social distancing and more available medical care and less death.

Corona where the lunch ladies lived had been the single deadliest neighborhood in America. Spanish Harlem wasn't far behind.

Chicky was suddenly aware that Olek was standing next to him. For a big guy Olek could sneak up awfully quick. This was one of the things that Chicky found scary about the super.

"Things are okay out here Chicky?"

"So far so good Boss."

Olek nodded. The super was comfortable with silence in a way that most people weren't. Chicky had a hard time not talking. But talking was often not what Olek wanted.

"I am hearing that the march is large," Olek finally said. "And violent." He sounded rueful. A lot of guys were eager for conflict to escalate. Especially knuckleheaded incels draped in camo and nativism posting about the storm that's coming, saddle up, lock and load. Guys who thought of themselves as men of action saving America or saving democracy or saving the world or whatever. Like they're in some movie. Chicky suspected all those guys were fraudsters. Olek was the real thing.

"Keep your eyes open Chicky. Let me know the first sign of trouble."

"You worried about anything in particular Boss?"

"Sure Chicky. I am worried about vandals. I am worried about attacks on you just for working here. Most of all I am worried about people using the distraction to do bad things." Olek cocked his head. "Did you hear that?"

"No," Chicky said. His hearing was beginning to fail. Along with the rest of him. "What?"

"Gunfire."

Bzzz.

An unknown caller again. What the fuck? This time Chicky answered. "Yeah?"

"'Bout time you answered."

This guy was talking like Chicky should know who he is. But Chicky didn't. "Who this?"

"Who this? Who the fuck you think?" It was El Puño.

"Oh hey," Chicky said, then grimaced at himself. Who was he, Taylor Swift?

"So that thing we talked about? Let's do that shit *now*. Cops all caught up in other shit tonight."

"Nah," Chicky said, "now's no good." He could almost hear himself explaining about the Secret Service and the super's heightened vigilance and how tonight was a bad idea. But that would just be putting off the inevitable. And suddenly Chicky was so damn tired of putting off the inevitable.

"Why not?"

Why not? Because Chicky has worked his whole life without doing anything wrong. It was never going to be a good time. And it was never going to be a good time to say so.

"Yeah, no, sorry," Chicky said. "I can't do that. I'll have to get you some other way."

The guy didn't respond. Chicky needed to get off this call. "Thanks," he said. Thanks? He rolled his eyes at himself and hung up.

Okay, he told himself, now you did that. Now you need to live with it.

His heart was a jackhammer.

CHAPTER 34

APARTMENT 11C-D

"Whit." Emily put one hand on her husband's chest. *"No."*

How many people saw the actual punch? More than zero. This could still get worse. This scene was now being watched by at least dozens of people. Emily's feet were planted, albeit in steep heels. Whit would need to shove her aside to get past; he'd need to knock her over.

"No." Emily was not going to raise her voice. "You *cannot* brawl here. Not tonight. Not"—she continued in a ferocious whisper—"with a *Black man*. Get a grip."

He didn't relent, but also didn't advance.

"Someone is filming whatever's about to happen, Whit. Which needs to be *nothing*." She could see him accept that she was right. Whit didn't actually want to get into a fight anyway. He didn't know how, he'd be humiliated. More humiliated. "You go home," she said. "I'll order a car."

"What? Why?"

"I have to stop by my parents'. My dad called, he's worried about the . . . protests, I guess. I'm afraid he's going to do something that'll scare the kids."

"Okay, fine. But don't order a car. I'll drive you." Whit of course meant that DeMarquis would drive. Emily didn't want to travel the quarter mile in a Maybach, which invited the type of attention she didn't want. On the other hand DeMarquis and his gun would deter trouble. Maybe the color of his skin would help too. Though maybe the opposite.

Emily turned away from her husband. "Jennifer," she said. "It was good to see you."

"Hmm," Jen said, tight-lipped. Hmm, Emily thought, giving Jen her warmest smile while receiving the coldest one. Emily had been dreading this, and here it was.

"Thanks," Julian said, "for having us."

"Good night Julian." Emily continued her performance. She was committed to not breaking. "Thanks so much, both of you, for coming."

If Emily had known that this was the last time she'd speak to him, would she have said something different?

Whit buttoned his jacket, steeled his jaw. Drunk as he was, he was still aware enough to know it was going to be bad out there. The howling started the moment he stepped outside.

"Murderer!"

"War criminal!"

The protesters had been waiting all night. They surged forward. But the police were ready, they'd finally put away their phones, and now they closed in, hands up, albeit without much sense of urgency. This wasn't a crowd that would bum-rush the joint.

"Fuck you, Longworth!"

Emily kept her eyes on her feet. Now would be a dreadful time to fall down the stairs. DeMarquis put his large body between the crowd and Whit as the three of them crossed the sidewalk to the car. Emily slid into the backseat, followed by Whit. DeMarquis shut the door behind them, walked around the vehicle calmly and menacingly, and settled behind the wheel.

"We're going first to my in-laws'," Whit said.

DeMarquis pulled away carefully. Some of the protesters were in the street.

Emily looked over at her husband, and felt her eye drawn to his lap. "Oh Jesus. What in god's name do you think you're doing?"

"There's a lynch mob out there."

"Since when do you carry that thing around?"

"And the person they want to lynch is *me*."

"Is it loaded?"

"Of course," Whit said.

Whew, Emily thought. He didn't know.

A Black man was weaving among the traffic-jammed cars on Madison Avenue, glaring through windshields. DeMarquis shook his head slowly, a warning: not this car.

"This is not a *lynch mob*, Whit. These are protesters."

Emily was shaking her head, and he noticed.

"What?" he asked.

"Nothing."

"What?"

She wanted to end it, right now. She wanted to say, I'm through with you.

She couldn't do it.

A policeman was blocking the street, holding up his hand. DeMarquis lowered the window.

"Street's closed," the cop said.

"We're just going to the building on the corner of Park."

"What can I tell ya? Can't get through here."

"It's fine," Emily said. It was just one short block. "I'll walk."

"No you won't," Whit said.

"Don't you dare tell me what to do. Don't you dare."

"I'll come," DeMarquis said. He pulled to the curb, climbed out, opened Emily's door.

"Give us a minute," Whit said. DeMarquis shut the door with a soft click, and stood sentry. "What with the leak, and all this press, these protesters. I've gotten messages from the *FBI*. Even that goddamned painting . . ."

She almost pitied him. This was the most genuine she'd seen him in years. Yet their marriage wasn't on his list of things falling apart? Had he even noticed? She didn't get all the way to pity.

"Are you going to come home?" he asked. "Later?"

"We'll see." She leaned over to kiss her husband's cheek. "Thanks for the ride."

And this? Would she have said something different to Whit too, had she known?

Emily accepted DeMarquis's arm. "Thanks."

These days people often responded to thanks by saying no problem, or sure thing, or you bet. Not DeMarquis. "You're welcome" is what he said, always.

Up ahead Emily could see stragglers in the middle of Park. She didn't see any placards, banners, signs. She couldn't hear any chants. It didn't seem like a protest anymore.

A couple of people had paused at the corner. They were joined by a third, a fourth, all of them facing Emily and DeMarquis. They were backlit by streetlights, and Emily couldn't tell anything about them, just the general shape: big men. One turned to another, said something, and both nodded. They started walking in Emily's direction, and the others fell in step behind them.

"Damn," DeMarquis muttered.

"What?" Emily knew what, but wanted to pretend she didn't. She was terrified.

"Just keep walking." DeMarquis guided her to his other side, away from the street. "If anything needs to be said," he continued, "I'll be the one who says it."

The approaching men were twenty feet away, and now Emily could see them clearly. "Oh," she said to herself, understanding what was happening in a different way. "Oh no."

"Yo," said the guy in the lead.

The cop who'd blocked the street was nowhere in sight. The four men were forming a semicircle at the curb.

"Yo!" One of these men was planted in the middle of the sidewalk. "What's up, *my brother*?"

CHAPTER 35

APARTMENT 2A

"You're a fucking idiot."

Julian and Jennifer were standing among dozens of people, everyone looking around for their cars, peering at license plates, back at their phones, beckoning spouses, hustling into backseats.

"What?"

"I can't—" Jen shook her head. "Emily Longworth? Really, Julie? She lives *in our building*."

Julian couldn't have this conversation now. He just couldn't. "What are you talking about?"

"Oh don't give me that shit. I have to *see* this woman, Julie. In the *lobby*."

He swallowed but didn't say anything, which itself might be an admission of guilt.

The Suburban arrived. "Don't even think of getting in this car," Jen said, and slammed the door. The whole black-tie scrum could have witnessed this. But everyone had their own concerns.

"Hey, man." Ellington was standing next to Julian. "We should talk. Tomorrow?"

Julian sighed. "Yeah." No sense putting off the inevitable. "Sure."

Ellington patted him on the arm, in a way that felt like pity. Another important part of Julian's life appeared to be coming to an end. It all seemed to be falling away, at once, right now.

♦ ♦ ♦

Jen opened the window to get some air. The Central Park transverses were mostly below grade, with sooty stone walls that made her claustrophobic, and curves that often made her nauseated.

Well, she thought, mystery solved. Now she knew the source of that black hair she'd found on Julie's flannel jacket a few weeks ago. How do you get someone else's hair on your lapel?

Years ago, Jen had made a certain peace that her husband might have an affair. Or affairs.

"What I want is for him to not fall in love," she'd admitted to her therapist. "What I want is for him to not leave me."

"Because?"

Jen had given this a lot of thought. "I don't want to grow old alone."

"Do you love your husband?"

"I do, yes. Not the same way I used to. But it's definitely love. A companionable sort. Which is enough for me. But I don't think it's enough for Julie. I doubt it."

"You don't feel like this is something you can talk about?"

"Well. I *am* talking about it."

Dr. Simon smiled.

Jen shook her head. "We don't talk about things like this. Sex. Love."

"Why not?"

They just didn't. "I guess I'm worried that if we have this conversation, we might conclude that we don't have a future."

"Would that be so bad?"

"Do you know what it's like out there, for women my age, dating?"

"Do you?" Dr. Simon never revealed anything about herself.

Jen had heard plenty. She had divorced friends, and friends who'd never married. College friends, law-school friends, colleagues, moms. Attractive women—physically, intellectually, professionally—who'd waited too long, who'd wanted their kids off at college before fleeing bad marriages. These women ended up on all the apps, dating fat old guys with comb-overs and erectile dysfunction. Their standards collapsed, along with their dignity, their self-esteem. Some gave up, embraced celibacy, vibrators, book clubs, waited for grandchildren. Others were tottering around Manhattan in ludicrous heels and ripped jeans and aggressively colored hair, trying to look like teenagers while also toting around Viagra, condoms, lube, little mobile sex shops in their Goyards. These women had once been pursued all over town. It was a harsh comeuppance.

"It's awful."

"It sounds like you've already decided you can live with your husband's infidelity."

Jen didn't condone an affair, exactly. She didn't *want* Julie to cheat. "Yes. I guess I have."

But Jesus, how *stupid* could he be?

On the other hand: good for him. Emily Longworth was a spectacular woman, intelligent, charming, and although not the same age as Julie, the gap wasn't degrading. In fact, Emily Longworth was pretty goddamned perfect, wasn't she? Jen realized that she was perversely proud to be married to a man who could attract Emily Longworth.

But a moment later Jen realized that Julie would fall in love with this woman, wouldn't he? Of course he would. Maybe he already had.

Oh fuck.

On the other other hand: would Emily fall in love with Julie? Probably not.

And regardless, there was no way Emily would leave Whit for Julie, who was not only older than her, but—much more saliently—substantially poorer. Julie could never afford Emily. He could barely afford new shoes. It was Jen's income that kept the Sonnenberg household afloat.

Maybe Emily Longworth wasn't so bad, after all. This affair will run its course, as affairs do. Emily will break Julie's heart, and he will be grateful to have a wife to return to. So maybe someone as unattainable as Emily Longworth was for the best.

The social justice warriors were breaking up into small groups, some peeling off, others milling around, placards on the ground. These protesters had been prepared to be harassed by police, maybe even looking forward to it, they were privileged young white people, they weren't afraid of any NYPD; they weren't the people who'd get shot. But now their antagonist was gone, and the police were leaving too, and the SJWs were aware that there were many other protesters out in the city, and counterprotesters, and jumpy cops, and it was late, and who the hell knew what was going to happen? Julian could see it in their faces, in their skittish movements: they were nervous.

Another pair of police cruisers whizzed down Fifth Avenue too fast for the synchronized lights, so the drivers had to slam on the brakes at each intersection, failing to learn the same lesson again and again and again, all the way down the avenue.

Julian unlocked his phone, to try to beckon another car, or check the bus schedule, but the device died immediately. Home was a twenty-minute walk through the park. He started walking.

Then he noticed the mob.

It was fifty people, walking in Julian's direction. This seemed like the same crowd he'd seen before, but there were more now, more baseball bats. All were white men, a lot of them wearing tactical vests and combat boots and caps that were camo or MAGA or LET'S GO BRANDON. Some were also wearing face masks, not in a covid-safety way, and a few balaclavas. A couple of actual helmets. The guy bringing up the rear carried a flag on a pole. DON'T TREAD ON ME.

"Hey Antifa punk!" one of these guys yelled at one of the protesters. *"Fuck you!"*

This mob was now streaming into the avenue, interrupting traffic, their pace quickening as they smelled blood. Maybe not exactly the blood they were looking for, but maybe they weren't all that discriminating when it came to the targets of their hatred. They had plenty to go around.

The last of the protesters dropped their placards and fled. Some of the mob gave chase.

Everything was happening fast. Julian was frozen in place, wearing a tuxedo, standing in front of a limestone mansion.

"What the fuck do you want?" This was directed at Julian by a burly guy in a NO MERCY tee. A half dozen men were surrounding Julian, a couple in Boogaloo Boys–style Hawaiian shirts, another in full tactical gear with helmet and vest with a profusion of bulging pockets.

"I said: what the fuck are you looking at, *pussy-ass motherfucking Jew*?"

Julian didn't want to get beat up. Nor did he want to back down. He raised his chin, heart hammering in a way that felt newly perilous. He could, after all, get scared to death. Now.

"Hey!" Everyone turned at the shout: a cop. "What's going on here?"

"Just helping keep the peace, Officer," said a guy in a desert-camo cap with the silhouette of an assault rifle. A peace-lover, for sure.

"Your services aren't required here," the cop said, but the half dozen thugs didn't budge. "Let's break it up." The cop's hand was on his sidearm. *"Now."*

The standoff lasted forever in a couple of seconds before NO MERCY finally acquiesced. "Yes sir." He turned toward his right. "Stand down." His left. "Stand down. Move out."

The cop waited for the men to start moving, then turned to Julian. "You good?"

Julian nodded.

"You should get home."

"Yeah." Julian had never in his life been afraid of any policeman, not in America. Though he'd been wary of some cops abroad, in places where the police didn't look like him. "Thanks."

At the park gate, Julian glanced back at the flashing squad cars, and the white mob continuing uptown. Julian's interest in seeing what would transpire here was outweighed by his interest in not catching a bullet. Plus the need to get home and try to make amends with his wife. This wasn't how he wanted his marriage to end. Was it?

He walked into the empty quiet. The park seemed relatively safe now, out of the way of the skirmishes. But of course a city park was a dangerous place late at night, and Julian was hyperaware of his environment. His eye was drawn by movement, two people on a path that would intercept his. It looked like young men who were walking toward him, though maybe that was just an assumption. Two women wouldn't walk in the park this late.

Julian's heart was still pounding from the encounter with the mob, and it didn't take much for it to spike with fear. This reminded Julian of his childhood when no one in their right mind would've walked into the park at night, even in daytime it was dicey, especially if you were alone.

New York in the 1970s may have been famously run-down, but it was the '80s that was far more dangerous. The city's most lethal year, with 2,245 murders, was 1990. Last year, there weren't even 400. The '80s city was a universally dangerous place, the crack epidemic, violent crime everywhere, random acts of brutality. You knew how to avoid junkies and muggers, how to seek safety, you knew it was your own damn responsibility, police and parents and teachers couldn't do it for you, no one except maybe a doorman. You were always trying to avoid trouble, but you were also ready to confront trouble that couldn't be avoided. Which had happened to Julian on the basketball courts right near here, where one afternoon he'd caught an elbow to the face, a bloody lip.

"How you like that, motherfucker?" His opponent was all up in his face.

"Fuck you," Julian said. "That's how I like that."

This guy's name was Luke, or Kirk, something monosyllabic with a *K*. They'd never had a conversation, but they'd been on this court together a few times, and the guy was always a dick. He'd been hassling Julian all game. Looking to start a fight.

"What you say to me, white boy?"

You knew that if a first punch was going to be thrown, you wanted to be the one who threw it, because there often wasn't a second, and there were no bonus points for gentlemanly style. So without any preamble Julian hauled off and punched this K-guy right on the nose, bam, and he immediately went down to one knee, bleeding copiously.

"Oh shit!" the chorus rang out with unmistakable glee. Teenaged boys loved nothing more than a fistfight. Violence was a part of life—a broken nose, a cracked rib, a badge to wear, a story to tell. Julian's older brother had gotten into a couple of fights, his dad too. A rite of passage.

Julian did not gloat, did not stand over his opponent like Ali over Liston. He just turned away, walked to the top of the key, and said, "Ball," palms up to catch a pass. He was trying to play it cool, but he was terrified. He was, as usual, the only white kid on the court.

The K-guy found his courage, immediately after one of his friends started holding him back. "I'm gonna fuck you up!"

"Ball," Julian repeated, and someone obliged. Everyone was watching.

Julian barely had any idea what went on the rest of that game, couldn't keep track of the score, didn't give even the tiniest shit. He'd already won, and everyone knew it.

The two figures on the intersecting path disappeared briefly behind a stand of trees, then reemerged into a pool of lamplight, a hundred feet away. Now Julian could see them clearly. It was two young Black men, and Julian had no doubt about it: they were rushing toward him.

At him.

CHAPTER 36

APARTMENT 11C-D

"Can you run?" DeMarquis asked.

"Yes."

"Good. Let's run." And they did, with DeMarquis holding Emily's elbow. The other men's footsteps followed. The distance to Park Avenue wasn't far, and the entrance to her parents' building was just around the corner, but Emily could hear the men gaining, she could feel it, and suddenly her arm was yanked, and she stumbled, and one of her heels broke, and she lost her balance, and first one knee then the other hit the pavement, dress tearing, stockings ripping, pain shooting up her arm—

"Oh fuck ma'am I'm so sorry." This was coming from a man with a thick beard and a shirt that proclaimed ALL ENEMIES FOREIGN AND DOMESTIC. He was kneeling beside her.

"What the hell?" she yelled at him. She was lying on the sidewalk, leaning on one elbow. DeMarquis was scuffling with two of the other men, then spun away, and elbowed one in the face, and pulled out his gun, and everybody yelled all at once.

"Get the fuck back!" DeMarquis shouted. "Get the fuck away from her!"

For an instant everyone was too stunned to move. DeMarquis's gun was trained on the man kneeling beside Emily.

"Whoa, buddy," ALL ENEMIES said, putting his hands up. "You don't want to be doing this."

"*Doing this?*" Emily asked. "What in god's name are you talking about?"

"Is this man kidnapping you, miss?"

"Are you out of your *mind*?"

Now one of these men pulled his own gun. "All right, *my brother*," he said. "That's enough of that." This guy was wearing a cap with RWDS in giant red letters. Emily didn't know what that meant, but she had no doubt it was purposefully offensive.

"He's my *driver*, you idiots. *He's* protecting me. From *you*. Get the hell away from me."

Mouths fell open.

"Are you sure, ma'am?" Ma'am. This reminded Emily of Justin Pugh, a pantomime of politeness that serves to disguise the misanthropy and misogyny and racism lurking below. Emily wouldn't be surprised if Pugh too were in the city tonight, riding around in his oversized truck, with his oversized goons, looking to perpetrate hate crimes under the guise of law and order. This was exactly the sort of situation Pugh dreamed about.

"Am I *sure*?" Emily clambered to her feet. "Are you kidding?"

DeMarquis was sidling closer to her, with his gun still aimed at the armed man. "Are you okay?" he asked.

"Yes," Emily said. "Thanks."

Her broken shoes were more of a liability than anything so Emily took them off. She felt the cool sidewalk under her feet while she gathered the contents of her bag. Her phone was cracked.

The four white men were exchanging looks. "Uh," ALL ENEMIES said. "Sorry."

"Who are you apologizing to?" she asked.

"Um, you?"

"Apologize to him, you racist ass. You're the goddamned enemy here."

DeMarquis pulled the brass handle, but the front door didn't budge. "The f—?" He cut himself off, pulled again, and still the door didn't move, just shivered in its sturdy frame.

The doorman walked across the lobby, looked at Emily, at DeMarquis, at the gun. This doorman was Hispanic. "Help you?" he called out through the door.

"I'm going to the Merriweathers'," Emily said. "My parents."

The doorman looked at DeMarquis again, then back at Emily. "He with you?"

"Yes."

The doorman was obviously conflicted. "Put the gun away."

DeMarquis shot him a what-are-you-kidding look.

"We were just attacked," Emily supplied. "He's my, um . . . my bodyguard."

The door opened, and Emily stepped inside.

"You coming in?" the doorman asked DeMarquis.

"No." DeMarquis was looking around, holding the gun down at his side. He didn't want to be brandishing it, but he wasn't ready to put it away. He wasn't out of danger.

"Maybe come inside?" Emily asked. "Until those jerks disappear?" She could see DeMarquis consider this. He didn't want to show fear, but didn't want to get into a shoot-out on Park Avenue.

"Maybe there's a side door I can use?"

"Absolutely," the doorman said. "I'll bring you around."

"Thanks, DeMarquis," Emily said. "I'm so very sorry. That was mortifying."

"Not your fault." But it was, wasn't it? "I'm sorry," she reiterated. "I really am."

Emily was alone in the elevator. Both her knees were skinned, and she suspected she'd fractured her fifth metacarpal for the third time—a cycling accident, a skiing accident, now a racism accident.

Emily got a couple of sobs out of the way, then wiped her eyes, gathered herself, and stepped into her parents' apartment, holding her broken shoes in her bleeding hand.

"Hi Daddy," she said, with a smile. "Is everything okay here?"

CHAPTER 37

FRONT DOOR

Chicky could tell from the grille that it was a Navigator approaching. It was black. It sure as fuck looked like El Puño's vehicle. And this vehicle looked like it was coming straight at him. He knew he should reach for the gun but it's a big thing to draw a gun. Especially at your place of employment.

It's also a big thing to get shot.

Chicky couldn't seem to make himself reach for the weapon.

And then it was too late. The truck was directly in front of the Bohemia. And then it was past. And then it was gone.

Not the same rims. Not the same tinted windows. Not El Puño. Nothing to do with Chicky.

But damn he sure did choke. Next time, Chicky told himself, just grab the thing. Hopefully there wouldn't be a next time. But somehow Chicky was pretty fucking sure there would be.

Another big vehicle pulled to a stop. Chicky opened the backdoor.

"Welcome home Mrs. Sonnenberg."

"Thanks Chicky." Mrs. Sonnenberg looked like she'd been crying. Sounded like it too, sniffly and hoarse. Though maybe she was just tired. It was late. Chicky knew she kept an early schedule.

Canarius raised his eyebrows—where was Mr. Sonnenberg? Chicky shrugged—who knows?

Another unseen car gunned its engine. Or the same car. Chicky felt the same fear.

He rubbed his hands against the chill. September comes in hot and humid and summer as anything. Then the crisp September 11th weather arrives and nighttime temperatures start falling. The sun starts setting before dinnertime and the leaves changing. Then you're standing here wishing you had a coat, just weeks after sweaty shirts sticking to slick skin and shimmering sidewalks and fire hydrants spraying screaming kids, drenching them in happiness.

Very little in life will end up being as fun as an open fire hydrant with all your friends from the block, your brother and cousins too, and that time your dad made a guest appearance, pulling off his shirt and running through the spray while "Rapper's Delight" blasted from a boom box on a stoop. That moment when Chicky realized his pops was really going to do it? That was the closest he could remember to pure joy. Snow days were close, building forts beside stoops and using the tops of garbage cans like Captain America shields and lobbing snowballs like grenades. There was at least one big snowfall every winter, a foot, sometimes two, it snowed dozens of times per winter. Not anymore.

"You know why Chicky?" Zaire had asked in April when it was clear that winter was over and there'd been only one day with measurable snowfall. "Because the world is ending." Zaire tended to exaggeration but he usually wore a little smile that let you know he was kidding. This time Zaire was dead serious.

Chicky would not be around for the end of the world. He'd never been especially aware of his own horizon till Tiffani got sick but now he couldn't stop staring at it. Right there past the next bad choice or the next bad luck or the next bad diagnosis. Chicky suspected he had run out of good ones.

Olek made his final sweep. He checked the service door, its alarm. He turned out the lights in the laundry room, the gym, the bicycle room where none of the bikes were locked. He rode each service elevator to the top, walked down each service stair. Nine teenagers lived in the Bohemia, and they sometimes used these stairs to smoke cigarettes and marijuana and, Olek suspected, have sex. He did not want to interrupt these activities, or report them, or in any way try to prevent them. All he wanted to do was ensure that no evidence was left behind.

He rode each passenger elevator too, descended the front stairs of polished wood, gleaming brass, pendant lights. On the tenth floor, he could hear that the disagreeable widow Mrs. Frumm was watching what sounded like Fox News at rock-concert volume. On the second, the Petrocellis were as usual playing music loudly. Shostakovich, an unusual choice.

Otherwise, all was quiet. Back downstairs, Olek double-checked that his office was locked, then crossed the basement to his apartment. He had a craving for the good vodka he keeps in the freezer, but that was out of the question tonight. He needed to remain sober. Alert. Prepared.

Olek turned the television to local news. He unbuttoned his shirt, tossed it aside. He unlaced his shoes, removed his socks, put his feet up on the coffee table. The cuff of his jeans rode up, and for a moment he stared at the butt of the semiautomatic pistol peeking out of his ankle holster.

Ethel Frumm turned off the news. Everything was going to hell.

She couldn't hear the sirens outside. She couldn't hear the taxis or the trucks or the subway, she couldn't hear the elevator groaning or her neighbors moaning. She couldn't hear almost anything without her hearing aid, which since Abe died she no longer wore at night. Ethel has had trouble sleeping since the rat episode, and her insomnia was exacerbated by the nighttime clamor. She tried to remember to put the hearing aid back in when she took the dog out, but she often forgot. Hearing wasn't the only thing Ethel was losing.

On the other side of the bed, where Abe had slept for nearly sixty years, Ethel now kept a loaded Glock 9mm.

A candy wrapper blew by. Chicky noticed a cigarette butt too. He grabbed the broom and dustbin as he did dozens of times per shift. When it was windy, hundreds.

The subway rumbled below. During days Chicky had rarely noticed the train but at night it was unmissable. He could tell the uptown on the upper level from the downtown on the lower. The locals that stopped nearby made a different sound from the expresses that didn't. That express was nonstop for more than three miles, skipping the entire Upper West Side, the longest stretch in the transit system. Chicky hoped the motormen enjoyed opening it up. He'd loved it as a kid. Back then less attention was paid to safety. Everything used to be more exciting.

A familiar car was gliding down the avenue. Chicky girded himself as he crossed the sidewalk in four strides to the curb with right hand extended to grab the door handle. Chicky could do this with his eyes closed. Like stealing second base.

Chicky opened the car door but as usual Mr. Longworth didn't get out. He waited for DeMarquis to assess the environment. The driver squinted at movement a block away before dismissing it. Just a doorman admitting a resident. He nodded. That was when Longworth climbed out.

"Welcome home Mr. Longworth," Chicky said. Many residents were happy to chitchat with the staff, especially with Chicky. But not Longworth. He never said anything except to ask for or demand something. Or to complain. Mr. Longworth was not a proponent of thank-yous. Chicky suspected that Mrs. Longworth's extra politeness was meant to make up for her husband.

Tonight the guy's resting-asshole frown was supplemented by a wild look in his eye—drunk?—and—was it?—yes, a fat lip. It looked like someone had punched Longworth in the face. No doubt the guy had it coming but still it's surprising. Billionaires in tuxedos don't tend to get into fistfights. Though what did Chicky know about it? Nothing.

Chicky nodded at DeMarquis. One of the first things you notice about DeMarquis is that he has a left earlobe but not a right. DeMarquis seemed to hold himself above the staff or at least very separate. Chicky didn't know if this was intentional. It was also possible that the guy was under orders not to fraternize. Chicky wouldn't put it past Mr. Longworth. He wouldn't put anything past that guy.

DeMarquis couldn't afford to be as unfriendly as his boss but he didn't go out of his way to be nice. This was a type of guy Chicky remembered from the Marines. Not that different from gangsters whose main goal is to be hard as fuck with no soft spots.

Chicky shut the car door and hustled to grab the building's. He winced from that possibly cracked rib or two. He smiled as he held the door. Nastiness may be Longworth's prerogative but Chicky needed to continue to kiss the guy's ass. This humiliation felt like penance, almost biblical. Though Chicky didn't know what he should be atoning for. Certainly not by groveling to this guy of all people. If anyone should be atoning it was Longworth. But that's not the way the world works.

The men's heels clicked on the floor past the leather sofa to the north elevator into which the driver-bodyguard peered before his lord stepped inside. After the elevator closed Canarius met Chicky's eye. The younger man shook his head in disgust. Chicky nodded in agreement: what a dick.

It wasn't hard to imagine what Longworth was worried about. A man with that level of wealth who made his living in that sort of business. The guy definitely had reason to fear for his safety. More so today than ever. Hating Whitaker Longworth had just become a public activity.

By mutual agreement Canarius spent the shift in the lobby while Chicky took the sidewalk, sweeping litter and helping people into and out of cars and hailing taxis and holding the door while asking if anyone needed help, saying good evening and good night and always always *always* extra-polite. Drunk people were quick to take offense, tired people too, and rich entitled assholes who were drunk and tired were a minefield. With guys like Longworth you never know. Until you know. Chicky knows.

Canarius joined Chicky on the sidewalk. "Mr. Longworth seemed upset," Canarius said, stroking his beard. Canarius's beard was still new.

"Uh-huh," Chicky agreed. There was a lot unusual tonight.

"Mrs. Longworth is still not home? Late for her to be out without her husband."

It was late for her to be out, period. There weren't many nightlife types at the Bohemia. Mrs. Longworth wasn't one of them.

"You see that dress?" Canarius asked. "Longworth is one lucky motherfucker."

Canarius probably wanted to shoot the shit about Longworth's fat lip and disheveled bodyguard and missing hot wife. Most other guys might oblige. But Chicky did not gossip. Plus he was worried that people could see his crush and he didn't want to be mocked. He'd deserve it. Of the many lines that you don't cross, that was the brightest. It would be less egregious to rob the joint.

Canarius wasn't getting enough satisfaction so he returned inside.

Chicky was plenty familiar with the night shift's ebb and flow from when he first started working at the Bohemia. This time of night was often a flurry as the last of the well-dressed and well-mannered people got home by eleven, eleven-thirty. After that things got dicier for the overnight. Almost everyone who came home after midnight was inebriated. Occasionally stumbling and sometimes crying or maybe squabbling down the sidewalk. Or necking in the back of a taxi, occasionally in inappropriate company. Sometimes trying to slink in with red eyes or missing underwear or trailing a rank cloud of weed. Or with lost keys or lost wallets or lost shit. With drivers needing to be paid and bad dates needing to be rebuffed and muggers or rapists needing to be told, in no uncertain terms, to back the fuck off. Sometimes the police summoned or an ambulance or, more than once, an attorney.

The overnight had reminded Chicky a little of the Arabian Peninsula in a specific way: you're on a mind-numbingly boring patrol where nothing happens for hours and days and weeks at a time, months even. But then out of nowhere something does happen. And everything that happens is huge. So you might be bored out of your skull but you still need to stay alert. You need to stay prepared. Because something is always, maybe, about to happen.

CHAPTER 38

APARTMENT 11C-D

The kids had been asleep for hours. Emily's mom was asleep too, anaesthetized by what Emily suspected might be marijuana gummies. "Oh no," Blaine had disputed, "it's natural herbs and supplements. I get it from the club pro." Emily saw no reason to set her mom straight.

Emily emerged from her parents' bathroom with bandaged knees and palms. Her dad was peering out the window, looking like a sheriff at the saloon window. Griffin was too old to be willing to risk getting mugged again, and too reactionary to see it as an anomaly, so he'd put their pied-à-terre on the market. They'd received no offers yet, which Griff blamed on the radical-left politicians who were turning the city into a woke cesspool of crime and homelessness, instead of on the bland decor of neutrals and chintz in a unit that was overburdened with assessments to pay for things like multipurpose rooms that no one ever used, and elevator modernizations.

"Those people are a menace," he said.

"What people, Daddy?"

"*Those* people." He pointed at the window, in the direction of the marchers.

"It was white vigilantes who chased me and DeMarquis." The so-called patriots with their racial grievances, clutching their Second Amendment, their good old days. She'd googled the initials on that cap: Right Wing Death Squad. What was with these people? Moving through the world, telling people how much you hated them, hoping to start fights.

"They thought he was *kidnapping* me. Or something."

"Well, do you blame them?"

Emily didn't want to argue with her dad. Not tonight, of all nights. She almost—almost—didn't say anything, but then she did. "Yes," she said. "I do blame them."

She retrieved her phone, sent a text, then looked at her father again, in his tartan pajama bottoms, his monogrammed slippers, his YALE tee shirt. Griffin Merriweather's father had also gone to Yale, as had his grandfather before. All those Merriweather men believed they'd earned their good fortunes, and never seemed to ask themselves this: if everyone you know has achieved the same success, is that really success? Has it been achieved?

You make your own luck: that's something lucky people say.

Emily was tired of holding her tongue. "And I blame you too, Daddy."

"Me? What in tarnation do you mean by that?"

Emily wasn't going to convince her dad of anything; he wasn't her problem to solve. Whit, though, he was Emily's responsibility. She had stayed silent long enough. Too long.

It had taken five minutes to drive across the park from the Merriweathers' to the Longworths', where DeMarquis parked illegally at the fire hydrant where he always parked illegally, and accompanied his boss upstairs. Their standard protocol.

The apartment seemed empty. "The children aren't here?" DeMarquis asked.

"No. My kids are over there with my wife." My this, my that, my the other. "Come on, DeMarquis. Let's have a chat."

Oh fuck no. "Yes sir."

There were three rooms in this apartment that DeMarquis would call a living room, and Mr. Longworth strode into the nearest, where he poured a large portion of brown liquid into a heavy-looking tumbler. This guy obviously didn't need another drink, but DeMarquis wasn't going to say so.

"Get you something?"

"No thanks, Mr. Longworth."

"You don't want to have a drink with me, huh?"

"I don't drink, sir." This was not true. What DeMarquis didn't do was drink with his boss.

"Some water?" Mr. Longworth didn't wait for an answer. He opened the sideboard's door, and there was a little fridge there. He took out a small green bottle, twisted off the cap, handed the bottle to DeMarquis. "Please." He indicated one of the sofas. "I insist."

Of course he did. "Yes sir."

"What do you think of what's going on out there tonight?"

Oh sweet Jesus no. "Sir?"

"The, um, protest. Demonstration. Whatever. What do you think of it?"

"In truth I haven't given it much thought." This too was not true.

"You think it's justified?" Mr. Longworth took a swig. This guy used to be so controlled, but over the past years he'd clearly forgotten how to stop. Not just with the liquor. The girls in particular indicated a real problem with impulse control, and discretion, and anger. DeMarquis had been driving Mr. Longworth for more than a decade, he'd sat in the car outside the hotels where his boss was fucking hookers, he'd paid off hotel staff, he'd even paid a couple of the girls who'd obviously been through something unpleasant. Both those girls bore a striking resemblance to Emily Longworth.

DeMarquis took a healthy gulp of water.

"I don't think the protesters are wrong," Mr. Longworth said. "Does that surprise you?"

"No sir." DeMarquis took another swig. The sooner he finished this bottle, the sooner he could get the fuck out of here. "Sorry to ask, but would it be okay if I used the restroom?"

Mr. Longworth didn't answer immediately. He was the type of asshole who made you wait just for the fuck of it. "Of course. Powder room's right through there."

"Thank you. Excuse me."

DeMarquis did not need the bathroom. He just stood in there, staring into the gilt mirror, surrounded by wallpaper, porcelain tiles, brass sconces, crystal chandelier, fluffy towels. This was the fanciest room DeMarquis would be in this month, and it was the fucking powder room. He flushed the toilet, ran the water, shut the tap.

"Can I help you with anything else, sir?"

DeMarquis didn't want to seem insolent, but he really wanted to go home. He'd already been working for fourteen hours, and he had to be back here in eight, and he was still at least thirty minutes from bed. Every minute he stayed here was a minute of sleep he wouldn't get tonight.

"Thanks, DeMarquis. See you in the morning."

Whit gazed out to the park, strung with necklaces of lights along the footpaths, and black holes at the lake and the reservoir, the welcoming twinkling over on Fifth Avenue.

What a fucking disaster. People really hated him, all of a sudden. Or was it all of a sudden? Maybe people have hated Whit for a long time, and he was just now becoming aware of it.

He never intended to be a bad guy. He wasn't insane, he wasn't a psychopath, he wasn't evil. What he was, admittedly, was greedy. But wasn't greed *the* core principle of capitalism? The dominant ethos in America? People talked about racial reckoning, about social justice, climate justice, *menstrual* justice, for Christ's sake. Distractions. All justice was some form or another of economic justice. And as long as people were up in arms about pronouns and capitalization and representation, they were keeping their own selves down. These trendy issues were like any other fad—a new social-media app, a dance craze, fashion, pop music. They come and go.

Not greed. Greed was the national sport, always had been. And Whit had been spectacularly good at it. Now he was being pilloried for that success. Canceled.

Yes, admittedly, it had been risky to engage in practices that some people might call profiteering. But wasn't that exactly what John Pierpont Morgan had done too? And IBM? That's one of the ways you get rich in America. When the brass ring comes into view, you reach for it.

Emily had been one of those brass rings, shiny and perfect. Maybe it was time to bring that union to an end.

He would give her half, of course, regardless of the prenup. After all, she'd be the one with primary custody, a lifestyle to maintain for the kids, he didn't want any of them to be needy, that would be horrible, and he'd look horrible. Plus he didn't need all that money anyway. No one did.

Whit didn't pursue money because he needed money. He pursued money because he needed something to pursue, and he already had everything he wanted.

Money was infinite.

Emily pushed open the den door. This was the only room that wasn't swathed in neutrals, but looked as if it had been extruded from a Ralph Lauren catalog, leather and plaid and gilt-framed paintings of horses and dogs, the sort of art Emily deplored. The hallway light cast a bright triangle across both her kids' little bodies, sprawled next to each other in the convertible sofa. She kissed the tops of their silky heads, breathed in the warmth of their innocence.

She felt a pang at the idea of a convertible. If her parents knew. If her *children* knew.

Christ, what the hell was she doing?

What is a person in this world, moving among other people? The economy, the media, capitalism will all tell you that you are the things you love—the cars, the clothes, the sports teams and indie bands and beauty brands, the vintage kitsch and reality-TV personalities.

No. Emily knows that life is people. You are who you love, who loves you back. Who you choose to love. Who you love despite yourself.

It's also, she knows, who you hate. It's what you do with that hate.

For a while Emily had managed to convince herself that there was nothing all that wrong with sneaking around, buying lingerie, spending afternoons in bed with a man who wasn't her husband. But it was clearly shameful, because she was ashamed.

Even if she ended it with Julian, she still needed to leave Whit. Her marriage would be unbearable without her lover.

Her phone dinged: DeMarquis had finished dropping Whit at the Bohemia, and was returning to the East Side to collect Emily. He'd be here in ten minutes.

Of course she and the children will be fine without hundreds of millions of dollars. *Of course.* What good was a fortune if it made you hate yourself?

You only live once. This can't be her life.

CHAPTER 39

APARTMENT 2A

Julian reviewed his mental map of the park, the lake and transverses he'd need to get around, the gates of escape out to the avenues, the death traps of the vaulted tunnels, the sanctuary of the park's precinct house, which wasn't on his route, but could be.

Yes he could run. Though of course running itself might kill him.

Out of the frying pan.

Along with fear, Julian was hit with shame. He did not want to be a white man scared of people just because they happened to be young and male and Black. But he also did not want to get racial-profiled himself, did not want to get beaten—or worse—because of the color of his skin.

"Hey!" one of the youths called out.

The only chance Julian would get was to run, and only if he did it now.

Maybe he'd been deluded all along. Maybe his behavior all these years hadn't been motivated because he was not racist. Maybe it was because he was. Maybe his racism just looked different from some other forms.

Their paths would converge in twenty feet.

"Hey, mister!"

Mister? That scrambled his thinking. "Uh," Julian called back. "Yeah?"

"Excuse me. There's a police station in the park, right?"

Julian didn't understand what was happening. "Um, yeah."

"Do you know where, exactly? My friend needs medical attention."

Now Julian looked at the other guy, who was clutching his abdomen, which was sopping red. Blood was plopping onto the path.

"Oh shit." Julian rushed over. "What happened?"

"Some dudes chased us into the park."

Julian bent to examine the wound, a gruesome slash through a BLACK LIVES MATTER shirt.

"Oh fuck." Julian put his arm around the injured guy, and realized he was just a kid, fifteen or sixteen years old. "The station is up this way."

Both of these kids were younger than Julian's youngest child.

"I'll take you."

Central Park was designed to look like aboriginal landscape. The bodies of water, the rock outcroppings, the hills and dales and twists and turns, the fields and meadows and cascades tumbling over boulders, it all seems like nature had been cordoned off, preserved, in the middle of this island.

That's not what happened. The park was entirely man-made, sculpted and molded by twenty thousand workers planting nearly three hundred thousand trees, building ponds and lakes and waterfalls, fields and meadows, paths that snake up gentle rises and down again, a set of six steps here and three there, Julian keeping a fast pace, growing fatigued. This trip home had taken far longer than he'd anticipated, with the detour to the precinct, the interaction with the cops.

"Good luck," Julian had said to the kids. "Thank you," the bleeding one said, "for your help."

There was just one final hill before the exit, and then this stage of Julian's night would be over. He wasn't looking forward to the next.

Jennifer had never expressed much interest in what Julian did with his afternoons, so he hadn't needed to lie much. Now he would. He was committed to blanket denial. He wasn't confident that his wife was going to believe him, but he also didn't think this would be a marriage-ender. She'd be furious for a few months, and maybe she'd never completely get over it, but she would push past it. She wouldn't walk away. They would still grow old together.

Julian didn't want to play the open-heart-surgery card tonight; that felt wrong. But not telling Jennifer tonight also felt wrong, closing a door. This was not something you withheld from your life partner.

It was a hard choice, one he couldn't make now.

A rat scurried across the path right in front of him. "Fuck!" he yelled, jumping out of the way. It was a very big rat.

"Okay," he reassured himself. "Okay." He resumed trudging up the hill, glancing at the shrub into which the rat had disappeared. The exit was right up ahead. The path was well-lit.

It would be just a few minutes more, at most.

CHAPTER 40

FRONT DOOR

Chicky heard an e-bike that sounded higher pitched than normal. The battery was on fire.

"Hey!" Chicky ran across the sidewalk with both arms waving. "Hey!"

The rider squeezed the brakes and came skittering to a shaky halt. He jumped off and let the bike fall. He took a couple of steps away and watched for a second. Then he grabbed a handlebar to drag the bike toward the curb.

"Hey, you okay?" Chicky asked.

The guy was staring at the bike. Probably wondering if the thing was going to be salvageable or if he was watching seven hundred dollars combust next to a pile of dog shit. He yanked at the insulated pack but it was still strapped to the rear rack. The straps were very near to the flames.

"Be careful please," Chicky said.

The guy managed to unclip the strap. He dragged the bag away from the flames and unzipped it and checked that the food was intact. He pulled out a slip of paper and extended it toward Chicky with his eyebrows raised. Chicky looked down. Mexican food. Chinese delivery guy. It could just as easily have been the other way around.

"Yeah." Chicky pointed. "That building is right up there." He held up two fingers. "Two blocks."

The guy nodded his thanks. He slung the pack over his shoulder and started trudging away to deliver the food with only a quick glance back at his burning bike.

Chicky did a few sets of toe raises. Partly to keep warm and partly to work off nervous energy and partly because he tried to do some isometric at least once every hour. Fitness was getting harder and he hadn't yet given up. He still remembered Mrs. Longworth complimenting him just after she moved in. Chicky had been carrying a case of wine for Mr. Blankenship who cared a lot about wine and made sure everyone knew it.

"My goodness," Mrs. Longworth said, "look at you. Like it's nothing but a box of feathers."

Emily Longworth had been surprisingly friendly from the get-go. "Were you in the military, Chicky?" He was surprised she knew his name. There were many staff names for residents to learn. Most new arrivals didn't make much of an effort. Some, none. But for the staff it was required. You needed to learn everyone's name even before they moved in.

"Yes ma'am I was."

Out in the world people sometimes mistook Chicky for an off-duty cop. This happened a lot on subways. He could tell by the way passengers looked at him and by the way knuckleheads sidled away. Chicky liked to play it up by crossing his arms and staring people down. He had no weapon and no authority but he took satisfaction doing this bit. Making the good citizens feel safer and making the bad guys think twice.

"I can tell," Mrs. Longworth said. "It's the way you hold yourself. Your, I don't know . . ." She curled her arms and let out a giggle. "You know how to handle yourself, don't you?"

That giggle, Jesus, it was a drug. Chicky was hooked. He was pretty sure Mrs. Longworth was manipulating him. It wouldn't be the first time he'd been manipulated by a beautiful woman. Chicky was willing to be manipulated by the right person. Or for the right reason. Mrs. Longworth was both.

Longworth's driver strode out of the lobby like a man on a mission. He jumped into the Maybach and sped away faster than Chicky thought was respectful in his boss's quarter-million-dollar sedan. Then all was quiet again.

Sometimes the late-night silence felt peaceful. Sometimes it felt creepy as fuck.

To the north a teenaged boy was walking an unruly-looking golden-doodle on the park side of the street. Otherwise there were no pedestrians. Just a few doormen. Other tired guys like Chicky who were counting the minutes till they could go home and crack a beer and put up their aching feet, *ahhh*. A block to the south Pedro was tidying his own stretch of sidewalk with a broom and dustbin. Pedro was a few years younger than Chicky. He'd moved to the Heights from the DR as a child and graduated high school and got a union job and did it well.

There were thirty thousand doormen in New York City and plenty of buildings where you could do the job. The apartment houses on this stretch of Central Park West were the Major Leagues. The Bohemia team had won the World Series.

Chicky looked downtown and back up. Not a moving car in sight.

The only thing he could see moving was a big rat across the street. Chicky would remember this, later, this final creepy second of stillness before all the shit started. Then things unfolded like he could've imagined.

Except the end.

Chicky would never have seen that end coming, not in a million fucking years. Though once it did happen, it wasn't a surprise. Not at all.

Part Four

TONIGHT

CHAPTER 41

FRONT DOOR

Chicky can tell immediately that he's outnumbered by overwhelming force. Two men are coming on foot from uptown and two from downtown. Both the truck's passenger-side doors are flying open and two more men are emerging from the vehicle. So in total it's six guys coming from three different directions and every one of them is holding a gun.

Fuck.

All these guys are advancing quickly and deliberately with weapons secure in both hands and bodies angled sideways to present the smallest possible targets. They're dressed entirely in black including caps and face-masks and gloves. They're all wearing mirrored glasses. Chicky can't see even a tiny patch of skin.

This is no amateur smash-and-grab. This is no crime of opportunity created by the protests and distracted police. These are trained soldiers. This is a well-organized operation. Which is reassuring on the one hand but alarming on the other.

"Get inside," says one of these guys. Not loudly enough to draw any unnecessary attention.

Chicky opens the door. Canarius looks up. The lead guy says, "If you press the panic button you're going to die. Put your fucking hands in the air."

Canarius's newspaper flutters to the floor.

"Phone?"

Chicky hands over his device. Behind him one of the invaders is locking the building's front door. Another guy is rushing around spray-painting security cameras.

"Walkie-talkies?"

A third guy is yanking the landline's cord out of the wall while a fourth aims his gun at Canarius from a safe six feet away. These guys know what they're doing.

"I need you to slowly reach into your pocket for the keys. Very slowly. Unlock the drawer that holds the spare keys." These sets are here so the staff can get into apartments to take care of repairs and admit tradesmen and deliver perishables. Also in case of fire or flood or other emergencies.

"Get 6C and 8D and 10C and 11C-D."

If you work in a building like this you know without thinking who lives where. You know plenty about them.

In 6C: Henrik Van der Luyden grew up in London and came to America for business school and tech. He splits his time between Mountain View California and New York New York and Jackson Wyoming. He'd been an early investor in NFTs which was something that didn't make any sense to Chicky no matter how hard he tried. Marie Van der Luyden is a skeletal ex-model twenty years younger than Henrik and the most jewelry-dripping woman Chicky has ever met.

In 8D: Jack Maxwell was descended from Maxwell Manufacturing which closed in the 1970s after creating a fortune so big and diversified and fortified that it would never ever run out. Jack attended Yale and Yale Law before spending forty years managing the Maxwell Foundation where his job was to give away money to what's now called the Global South, a phrase that had been completely unfamiliar to Chicky until he'd discovered it on the foundation's website. Mr. Maxwell's collection of fine timepieces was documented in a magazine article about him.

In 10C: Abe Frumm had been a mergers-and-acquisitions lawyer with a sideline in theatrical producing. One of Mr. Frumm's angel-invested hits from the 1960s had been adapted into a Hollywood blockbuster that generated revivals and adaptations and soundtracks. Chicky doesn't know anything about residuals or royalties but even he's heard of this show and it was older than him. Abe's wife, Ethel, had been a homemaker whose three children all attended Ivy League colleges and then worked in finance and now had children of their own who'd all attended Ivy League colleges and now all work in finance. Abe and Ethel Frumm have a famous collection of seventeenth-century Dutch paintings.

In 11C-D : Whit and Emily Longworth. Their wealth has just become infamous.

These four apartments are all served by the northeast elevator. They all face the park. They're all immense. Those are extremely rich families though with Frumm it's hard to fathom because she's so cheap. But her apartment is like a museum. Most of the Frumm paintings have those little lights above them.

"Which of those people are home?"

"6C is out of town," Canarius says. "I think."

"You *think*?" The invader turns to Chicky.

"Yeah," Chicky confirms. "6C is in Corsica." There are a handful of Bohemia families who live in a few homes that they shuttle among as basically their occupation, towing fancy luggage and small dogs.

"Are any children home in any of these units?"

Longworth is the only family with kids and those kids left hours ago. "No," Chicky says.

"Okay"—pointing with a gun—"you go in there."

Chicky walks to the north lobby where leather sofas face each other across a coffee table with a large vase of tall flowers. Chicky has sat on these sofas only a handful of times for a few seconds apiece. Once to fix a bunched-up sock. Twice to replace Band-Aids. Another time it was to catch his breath when he had pneumonia and then again when he had covid. During covid he sat a few times though he doesn't remember precisely. It was early in the pandemic and it was hard to get tested so he kept coming to work until he passed out and needed to be hospitalized.

The only exception was when he killed that guy and Chicky sat on this sofa for at least an hour with cops. That had felt less like resting than having his movements restricted.

"Here is how this is going to work. You are going to stand at the desk as if everything is normal. My colleague is going to be with you. If you do a bad job he is going to kill you."

As promised one of the men sits on the floor with his gun aimed at Canarius.

"If anyone who lives here shows up—Hey, are you paying attention?"

"Yes."

"If anyone shows up, you will unlock the door for them. Is anyone going to show up?"

"Um . . . maybe? There's still a couple people haven't come home."

"If you do something stupid? That will be the last thing you do. You"—turning to Chicky—"are going to come upstairs. We are going to ring each doorbell. You are going to announce yourself. What is your name?"

"Chicky."

"*Chicky?* What the hell kind of name is that?" Chicky shrugs. "Okay Chicky. You are going to say, Sorry to bother you, there is a gas leak, an emergency, is it okay if you come in to turn off the valve? Tell them it will only take a minute. When they open their door, step aside. We will enter and subdue them and take care of our business. We will exit each unit within two minutes."

"Subdue them."

"Correct. If they do not open their door voluntarily we will use the keys. We are not planning to hurt anyone including you. But we are prepared to. So the same warning goes for you about stupid behavior. Do either of you have any questions?"

"No," Chicky says.

"No," Canarius says.

"This will be over before you know it. No reason to be a hero."

CHAPTER 42

APARTMENT 2A

Julian is mostly but not entirely hidden behind the park's stone wall. If the SUV driver looks carefully in this direction, he'll be able to see Julian. The driver is probably serving as lookout, and one of the things he's looking out for is witnesses. If Julian continues to stand here, he'll eventually be seen.

He is, of course, worried about his children, about his wife. But in the rational part of his brain he knows that whatever's happening at the Bohemia can't involve them, or him. If this is a robbery, it's not his apartment being robbed. If this is a kidnapping, it's neither himself nor Jen, and certainly not the kids. Is murder a possibility? If anyone in this world wants to murder Julian, it's Whit Longworth, and he wouldn't go about it like this.

What Julian should do, now, is nothing. Whatever this is, he should wait it out. It's not his responsibility to try to solve every problem he encounters. Sooner or later—probably sooner—the gunmen will leave with whatever they came to get, and then Julian will be able to go home without incident, without risk.

What he should do is call Jen to warn her, then call nine-one-one, and stay the hell out of the way, and out of sight. Yes, that's what he'll do.

Julian flips up his satin lapels to hide the white of his formal shirt. He starts to sidle away. His eyes stay glued to the Suburban. If the driver opens the door, or moves the car, or anything, Julian is going to sprint into the depths of the park. He takes another step, and another, careful not to trip, not to stumble on the downward slope. He arrives at a tree trunk that's behind a bush that's behind the park wall, and now he can no longer see much of the SUV, nor much of anything. He can no longer be seen.

He takes out his phone, presses the home button, nothing. He hits the button again, still nothing, and presses the power switch, more nothing, then he remembers: his phone died.

"Fuck."

He looks around, but doesn't know what for. A solution? He glances again at the Bohemia. It looks like a fortress, but he knows it isn't, because he just witnessed the breach.

Then he comes to the sudden and sickening realization that no, he cannot wait this out. Because although it's not Jennifer who's in danger, it most certainly is Emily.

Julian grabs a handful of pebbles and rushes to the gate and exits the park, in full view of the SUV. He walks up the park side of Central Park West, in the indirect light under the cover of the trees, across from the Bohemia and from the driver who's sitting there watching for suspicious characters, for problems. Julian is trying not to look like either. Just a guy in a tuxedo walking home.

He sidesteps another rat.

"Fuck."

When Julian arrives at the corner he crosses the street quickly but hopefully not so fast as to draw attention. He fails.

The driver's door is swinging open, two legs coming over the side, black boots, tactical pants—

Julian sprints.

CHAPTER 43

FRONT DOOR

Chicky and the invaders board the elevator. The first one in spray-paints the security camera.

"Okay," says the guy who has done all the speaking. "Six."

Chicky turns the key and presses the button for the sixth floor. The Bohemia's passenger elevators have ornate wood paneling and gleaming brass fixtures and beveled mirrors and little benches upholstered in sky-blue velvet. Not the service cabs. These are bare bones of metal walls and metal floors. It can't be ruined if it's shitty to begin with. Like those trailers in the yard of the Luisa Moreno Leaders of the Fucking Future School. Pre-shittified.

The Bohemia was one of the last buildings in the city to replace manually operated elevators with automatic ones, years or decades after most other buildings. There used to be fifteen thousand elevator operators in the city. When those guys went on strike the city basically shut down. Which is what would happen today if those Amazon teams and UPS drivers recognized their strength.

But the elevator-operator strike extracted just a few short-term concessions. At the same time it convinced landlords to hasten along the operators' obsolescence. What the strike accomplished was the extinction of the entire profession. Labor power is a dangerous weapon to wield. It can really backfire.

The Bohemia's elevator project cost six million dollars. Money that was diverted from wages that had been paid to mostly Black and Hispanic union staff and instead disbursed to private contracting outfits that were all owned by white men. This was called modernization.

One of the invaders drops his backpack to the floor. He removes folded-up pieces of nylon and disburses them to his companions. They all fluff these packets open into large duffels.

So: this is definitely a robbery. Chicky is relieved. He'd come up with worse theories. He's relieved too that these are trained guys who know what they're doing and not El Puño–type knuckleheads who shoot first and ask questions later.

The elevator stops and Chicky turns the key and they all step off.

The code to the Van der Luydens' alarm is taped to a fob. Chicky punches in 1234 and the panel beep-beeps and the light turns green. Half the codes in this building are 1234 or 1111 or something like it. Codes that presume their own irrelevance. That presume impenetrability.

The talking guy waits in the kitchen with Chicky while the others rush away. Chicky can hear the clanging of metal on metal. One man returns quickly with a duffel bulging with what looks like boxes. Another follows carrying a large canvas that he leans against the elevator wall.

"Okay move out." The robbery of 6C took a minute. So this whole thing might take, what, five minutes? Five minutes is nothing. A half inning of a ball game.

But this first apartment is unoccupied. The others won't be.

"Now eight."

Chicky turns the key and presses eight.

"Here," the guy says. "Take this."

Chicky looks at a roll of duct tape. What choice does he have? None.

Chicky stands in front of 8D. The four intruders are off to the sides and out of sight.

Most buildings use digital cameras and fish-eye lenses and whatnot. But at the Bohemia it's just old peepholes with scratched glass you can barely see through. The building prides itself on not making modern improvements. Part of the charm. Which was why the elevator modernization was put off for so long.

It takes a while for someone to answer at the Maxwells'. "Yes?" It's Mrs. Maxwell.

"Hello ma'am it's Chicky Diaz—" Before he can even get out his excuse she opens the door. More presumption of safety. No one in Chicky's tenement would dream of opening a door at this hour without first getting a really airtight explanation.

Mrs. Maxwell gasps and her eyes bulge at the business end of a gun and the masked man who's holding a single finger up to his mouth—*Shhh.* She nods her understanding rapidly and without stopping. The intruders flow into the eat-in kitchen. They're all carrying fresh duffels.

"Step back."

Mrs. Maxwell obeys. Two of the invaders rush away while Chicky stands numbly and dumbly in the service doorway.

"Tape her mouth," the guy says to Chicky. He knew this was coming. He's being made to look like he's the inside man. "Now tape her hands together."

From a few rooms away Chicky can hear Mr. Maxwell say, "Hey, what the—" Then silence.

"Take my friend to your jewelry," says the guy who talks. Mrs. Maxwell nods again or maybe she never stopped.

Chicky steps out of the way. In the middle of the massive marble-topped kitchen island is a two-foot-high vase packed with three-foot-high lilies. The scent is overwhelming. Chicky can't tell if that's what's making him feel like throwing up.

Seconds later the Maxwells emerge at gunpoint and are directed to sit on kitchen stools.

"This will all be over in just a few minutes." One of the men zip-ties the Maxwells' ankles together and also to the kitchen stools. These guys are adept at zip-tying. Chicky is grateful that he isn't being forced to bind the Maxwells to their furniture. But the damage has already been done. He looks like an accomplice. At the very least. The inside man might also be the mastermind.

"If you make any noise we will have to come back here and shoot you. Understand?"

Chicky recognizes this guy's voice. Not as a specific person but a type. It's an accent and intonation and cadence that he's been hearing his whole life. It's white guys from Jersey or the Island who wear cargo shorts and calf tattoos and backward caps. Cops and firefighters and plumbers and mechanics. Working-class guys who hate socialism but not their own trade unions or pensions or Medicare or Social Security. Guys who play softball and watch football and drink beer. Guys who served in the military. Guys who carry guns. Guys who are not so very different from Chicky when it comes right down to it. But also as different as can be.

These days most young people don't have accents. Working-class white guys from Long Island or Hispanic guys from Harlem are all starting to sound the same.

Chicky suspects that this ringleader is about his age. He's obviously fit but in a sinewy way that looks belabored. Which at a certain age is the only way to be fit.

None of the other guys have spoken a word. Chicky can't ID any characteristics behind the masks and glasses. But they all have the firmer bodies of younger men. They all move with the quick practiced confident movements of trained soldiers. And they are all wearing body armor.

"Listen," Chicky says as they board the elevator, "10C is an old lady. She's going deaf and doesn't wear her hearing aid."

Mrs. Frumm is an ornery inconsiderate racist bat. But Chicky does not want her to get beaten or gagged or zip-tied or murdered. She probably has at most a few years left in her, which is something Chicky has seen plenty of times after spouses die. But this isn't how it should happen to Mrs. Frumm. This isn't how it should happen to anyone.

"I'm sure you can do your thing without her even waking up." The elevator doors open. "She's old and she's frail and she's nervous as fuck. I'm afraid if you . . . if I . . . I'm afraid she'll have a heart attack."

They're standing in front of 10C's service door. The guy seems to be staring at Chicky but because of the glasses it's impossible to be sure.

"I ain't joking," Chicky continues. "You don't want this to be murder, do you?" Chicky knows that face-tattooed thugs may not give a shit about murdering civilians. But soldiers usually do.

"Understood," the guy says. "We will try it your way."

There are two locks. Mrs. Frumm has a security system but she can't be bothered to turn it on except when she leaves town, which she barely does since Mr. died. This is something else Chicky has seen before with old people. Even if they have all the money to go anywhere and do anything at a certain age they stop wanting to. Some of these people have already been everywhere anyway. They don't want to deal anymore. Chicky doesn't blame them. Everything is exhausting.

All of Mrs. Frumm's kitchen lights are blazing. The hallway lights and the butler's pantry too. Chicky assumes that all this light is because of the rat trauma.

After thirty seconds one of the guys comes back to the kitchen trying to stuff a huge fur into a duffel. It's that ridiculous ankle-length coat that makes Mrs. Frumm look like a giant rodent.

As in the previous apartments the guy who talks stays with Chicky in the kitchen. His job seems to be to communicate and to make sure Chicky doesn't fuck around. Which is not something Chicky is planning.

Chicky is still plenty aware of his own gun. This guy has already turned his back to Chicky twice. Just for a split-second each time but long enough. Chicky could have drawn the gun and squeezed twice before the guy could respond. Then he could've bolted into the elevator to the basement and out the service entrance. But if Chicky shoots this guy then his crew might feel the need to shoot the residents. That's not something Chicky wants to be responsible for. Also if Chicky pulls the trigger the odds go way up that he himself will get shot.

Plus he doesn't want to shoot anyone. These guys might deserve to be in jail but not in caskets. Death is not the penalty for robbery. Chicky has spent no small amount of time contemplating crime and punishment and proportionality. Not because he's a philosopher of justice but because he himself had once meted out disproportionate punishment. And he never got over it.

It was back when Chicky was working nights the first time. Back before he had kids. Back when he was young.

A drunk Puerto Rican guy had stationed himself on the corner to harass people. Asking for money and asking for cigarettes and asking for blow jobs. The guy was abusive and menacing and out of control. Chicky tried to run him off but the guy kept coming back. Chicky called the police who said they'd send someone but it didn't sound like a promise so much as a brushoff. Menacing bums were just part of the landscape. Everyone needed to deal on their own.

Something about the Frumms set this guy off. He followed them while hurling profanity all the way to the Bohemia's front door. To Chicky's front door. To the door he was holding for Mrs. while Mr. trailed a few steps behind. Chicky was planning to have words with this knucklehead once the Frumms were inside. Maybe Chicky would get a little rough. Enough was enough.

Out of nowhere this guy shoved Mr. Frumm from behind. A sucker shove. Mr. Frumm stumbled and fell and slammed his face into the sidewalk. Even as he was still falling Chicky was already regretting that he hadn't acted sooner. Maybe halfway down the block. He should have put his hand up and planted himself in this guy's path. You want to make trouble? Okay shithead but you're going to need to go through me.

He should have at least said something. Anything. But he hadn't. So now Mr. Frumm was bleeding from his forehead and Mrs. Frumm was screaming bloody murder and passersby were stopping with their mouths hanging open in that oh-shit-what's-happening look.

It was just instinct. Not a decision. Chicky stepped to this guy and threw a punch that connected squarely. This guy swung back in drunken fashion. But even a broken clock was right twice a day and Chicky wasn't going to wait around. So he hit this stupid-ass motherfucker a second time and a third. The guy reeled backward and lost his footing at the curb and was too inebriated to do anything to protect himself.

If it hadn't been for the fire hydrant the guy would've bumped against a parked car. But because of the no-parking zone there was no car to break his fall. Instead the back of his head broke his fall and hit Central Park West with a sickening thud.

That guy was in a coma for three days before his sister pulled the plug. Every witness corroborated Chicky's account. The police didn't spend all that much time investigating. "One spic offing another spic?" Chicky overhead the Italian cop ask the Irish cop. "Just another day in paradise, am I right?"

It wasn't homicide and it wasn't manslaughter. Death by misadventure is what happened to that bum. But just the same Chicky had killed that guy. It's a horrible feeling to end a person's life. Chicky never wants to feel that way again. He isn't carrying a gun tonight to safeguard anyone's property. All he wants from that gun is to keep his own self from getting killed.

All the robbers are filing through the kitchen carrying a half dozen of Mrs. Frumm's paintings, a few of them rolled up, sliced out of their frames. Chicky is relieved to pull the door closed behind him. Mrs. Frumm was the second most likely to create a problem.

But the most likely is next.

Mrs. Longworth isn't home so Chicky doesn't need to worry about her. And if these robbers decide to beat the shit out of Mr. Longworth? Chicky's cool with that. But Chicky knows that DeMarquis carries a gun and wouldn't be surprised if Longworth has his own. This is a man who came home smelling of booze and having been hit in the face. Which means on the other side of the Longworths' door is a drunk angry asshole who might have a gun and probably no idea how to use it.

Chicky steps into the elevator and turns the key and presses eleven.

No reason to be a hero.

CHAPTER 44

APARTMENT 2A

The SUV's door slams, footsteps follow, but Julian doesn't waste time turning to look, he's sprinting in his leather-soled shoes and pants that have gotten tighter since he last wore them, the jacket too, his pumping arms straining at the fabric, feet flying, soles smacking against the pavement. This isn't a pace he can keep much longer; this is barely a pace he can keep another step. Thankfully he arrives to the corner and can slow now that he's out of view from his pursuer, at least for a few seconds. Ten seconds? Not much time. He still needs to hustle.

Julian's apartment is just above this sidewalk, this is the view from his windows, this is what he has seen for the past fifteen years: the Art Deco apartment house on the corner, the row of Beaux Arts town houses next to it, with their postage-stamp front yards with small trees, shrubs, potted plants arranged on tall stoops. Julian knows this block by heart.

He knows exactly where he's headed. The wrought-iron gate at No. 3 is open, as usual, and he pivots around the far side of the fence into the little yard, and drops to his knees behind the wooden hut that holds garbage cans and recycling bins. He kneel-walks toward the stoop, where he knows there's a small gap between the stoop's masonry and the hut's carpentry. He can look through this gap to the street while staying hidden.

Julian is acutely aware of his racing heart. How much strain is lethal? Dr. Ramirez said valve failure would be instantaneous. That, at least, is a blessing. He wouldn't need to writhe around in pain, his family wouldn't need to face excruciating questions about whether to pull the plug. He'd just die.

The driver has arrived at the corner, standing in the middle of the street, head turning carefully. There are a lot of things for someone to hide behind, parked cars, stoops, trees, doors. These aren't good hiding spots forever, but this guy can't look forever, he probably can't afford to look at all. His job is to stay with the getaway car, ready to flee from whatever crime is being committed. This guy can't waste time searching for harmless witnesses.

This specific peril will be over in seconds. Julian feels the urge to hold his breath, but also needs to catch it. Sprinting is hard, even for a couple hundred feet. Like legging out a double, you see those guys panting on TV, you wonder how professional athletes can get so winded so fast, pulling hamstrings, rupturing Achilles'. Human bodies are not made for sprinting. Especially not fifty-year-old bodies.

The driver's gun is against his thigh, a black gun in a black glove against black pants, hard to notice. This guy hasn't yelled any threats. He doesn't want to draw any attention. He swivels his head again, slower. His head comes to a stop, staring straight at Julian.

No, Julian tells himself, there's no way this guy can see him. How long does the driver stare? Probably not even a second before he gives up, turns away, jogs back to the corner, disappears.

"Holy fuck," Julian mutters. He clambers up, and creeps out of the little yard, looking around. He trots across the street to the Bohemia's fence above the dry moat. He looks down to eight basement-level windows. Two of those are in the break room. Two are in the meeting room. The other four are Olek's apartment. A light is on behind one of Olek's windows.

Now that Julian is standing here he realizes that this isn't going to be as easy as he was imagining. The iron fence is in his way, the angle is bad, the windows have security bars. It's hard to break into the Bohemia. Unless you have the nerve to walk straight through the front door with a bunch of guys with a bunch of guns.

Julian grabs a pebble from his pocket, steps back, throws. The pebble gets through the fence fine but his aim is off, and the little rock hits impotently against the brick wall. He tries again, misses by inches. His third attempt caroms off the fence. His fourth attempt manages to hit the window, but with nothing more than a quiet little clink. That pebble was too small, his throw too timid.

"Hey!"

Julian spins at the shout behind him.

"What do you think you're doing?"

Oh what the fuck is this? Some bro in flipflops and basketball shorts walking a golden retriever. Julian recognizes this guy. He wears shorts all year round.

"Trying to get the attention of my super."

The bro is nonplussed, but Julian isn't going to argue. Let the guy call the police. In fact—

"Hey, can you call nine-one-one? A robbery is in progress here. My phone is dead."

Julian turns back to the Bohemia while grabbing a whole handful of rocks, which he lets fly like buckshot just as the blinds rise in the lit-up window, and Olek recoils as one of the rocks cracks the glass immediately in front of his face.

The bro is on his phone. "Yeah, I think a robbery is in progress at the Bohemia?"

Olek raises his giant eyebrows, takes a beat to assess the situation, understands enough. He points to the west, toward the service entrance, and Julian points the same way, nodding.

"Yeah, um, this dude in a tuxedo said so?"

CHAPTER 45

APARTMENT 11C-D

On the drive home Emily composes the bare outlines of her script: she doesn't love Whit anymore, she knows he doesn't love her either, staying together for the sake of the kids is an unfair burden on children, she doesn't want them to grow up thinking this is what it means to be married, even though Emily has become convinced that this might be, in fact, what it means to be married.

She's not going to mention the prenup, not tonight, not ever. She's going to maintain the high ground while her slimy lawyer asks Whit's slimy lawyer to reconsider. Whit has in essence an infinite amount of money, so withholding it from his children and ex-wife wouldn't benefit him in any way, it would be nothing other than punitive. Is that really who he wants to be? Is that something he wants on his conscience?

Either way, Emily will be fine financially, the kids will be fine. What's the worst that can happen? They'll fly commercial, they'll play basketball and softball instead of riding horses and skiing, the kids will eventually get summer jobs, Emily will work too, she'll commute on the subway, the bus, she'll pay attention to the cost of things generally, but will never have to worry about wasted onions.

Plenty of people who commute on city buses are happy. It's people who are married to villains who are the unhappy ones.

Yes, she tells herself, I can do this. I will do this.

♦ ♦ ♦

As DeMarquis pulls up to the Bohemia, Emily sees a man climbing into a black Suburban that's parked at the hydrant in front of the building. So DeMarquis double-parks the Maybach alongside an aged mint-green Mercedes wagon.

Emily spent the better part of one magical summer riding around the Vineyard in one of these old Mercedes wagons—broken AC, all the windows down all the time, the smell of saltwater, the radio tuned to oldies, Carole King and Steely Dan, while Em and Skye cruised from beach to clam shack to bar to late-night bonfire. It's only in hindsight that you can identify when everything was as close to perfect as it would ever be.

These days nearly all of Emily's driving is done on Long Island in a luxury tank with children in back, all the latest safety features, amenities, uncountable cup holders that never seem to be quite rid of Goldfish dust. Emily would gladly trade any of her family's late-model cars for this old wagon. But she can anticipate all of Whit's reasons for rejecting the idea. Trying would just be starting a fight she's certain to lose.

DeMarquis puts on the hazards. "I'm sorry," he says, "would you mind waiting a sec?"

For years Emily felt intimidated by her household's employees, especially those who'd preceded her, like DeMarquis. But eventually she accepted her role as boss, or boss's wife, and she stopped being scared, or stopped acting like it. But there are still times when she regresses to her old insecurities, or manners, or deference, whatever slurry makes her obey people whose jobs are, in effect, to obey her.

Now is one of those times. "Sure," she says.

DeMarquis climbs out. He locks the car, which injects a fresh dose of fear in Emily, on top of the lingering anxiety from the East Side fracas. He must've locked up for a reason, and Emily looks around, and finds it: on the next block downtown, three men are headed this way. They're spread out to take up the whole wide sidewalk, a formation that suggests aggression.

Also, there's something missing from the front of the Bohemia: the doorman.

CHAPTER 46

FRONT DOOR

This is one dangerous situation. Chicky is trying to control his racing heart but failing.

The elevator opens. "Go."

Chicky rings the doorbell. It's a loud chime but this is a big apartment and who knows how far away Longworth is. Who knows if he can hear. Who knows if he's even awake.

Should Chicky warn these robbers that Longworth might be armed? These guys don't deserve to die. Though they are the ones who made the choice to carry guns in the commission of a robbery. So they've put themselves in a position to be murderers. They don't *not* deserve to die.

"Ring again."

Chicky does. Still no answer.

"Is he definitely in there?"

"He definitely came home a little while ago. I don't know where else he'd be."

"Okay. Open it up."

The next couple of seconds could be very fucked-up. Chicky hates that he's the one being forced to enter every space first. He turns the lock. He can hear the click of the mechanism. He tries to hide behind the door as he begins to pull it open.

He pulls more.

And more.

And now it's fully open and no shots have been fired yet.

No one is in the kitchen. Three of the robbers rush in with weapons held in front. The fourth lags behind Chicky. "Go in," he orders.

The kitchen is dimly lit from under-cabinet lighting that makes everything look extra-luxurious. Most kitchens at the Bohemia have stainless steel everywhere but not the Longworths'. Here it's marble and brass and glass that's all spotless and gleaming. Woodwork that seems to glow from within. The shiny stove is blue enamel with tons of brass.

This is the type of apartment that you can tell in one glance is the home of insanely rich people. You can see it just in the cabinet hardware and in every inch of fabric. Every single thing. Even the light somehow looks rich. No bulbs are visible anywhere.

Chicky saw the invoice back during the last stage of the renovations so he knows: this stove cost forty-five thousand dollars. A *stove*.

To Chicky's right is the huge pantry filled with household cleaning supplies and kitchenware and storage bins and crates of glasses and dishes. Chicky has deposited deliveries in there. It used to be a maid's room but live-in staff is no longer considered a good look. So it's been a few years since anyone at the Bohemia employed a live-in. These days the only resident staff are childcare providers. Chicky would have expected that the Longworths would be one of the families with a live-in nanny but no.

That dark pantry is definitely a place where Mr. Longworth might be hiding. Chicky holds his breath as one of the robbers takes responsibility for clearing the space. Any moment could be when everything goes FUBAR but some are more likely than others—

The light clicks on. Nothing.

"*Call out to him*," the ringleader whispers.

"Mr. Longworth!" One second. Two. Three. No response. "It's Chicky Diaz!"

Still no response.

"Go to the hall. Try again."

Chicky walks past the henchmen who've taken positions on either side of the door. This is how you clear a house with possible hostiles. "Mr. Longworth! Sorry to bother you!"

Still nothing. Longworth not answering is bad. It means he's aware that there's a problem and he's hiding. Maybe hiding with a gun aimed at whatever doorway he's behind.

Chicky looks to the ringleader for guidance. These guys are still wearing balaclavas and reflective glasses so Chicky can't see their faces or eyes or anything. Chicky raises his eyebrows and shoulders: what should I do? The guy twirls his hand: keep doing the same thing.

"Mr. Longworth!" Chicky calls out louder. Two henchmen push past Chicky. They advance on the public wing of dining room and various living rooms and front hall. That's where the most valuable art is going to be.

"Mr. Longworth there's a gas leak!"

To the right is who knows how many bedrooms. That's where the jewelry is going to be.

"I need to turn off your gas!"

At this hour the bedroom wing must be where Mr. Longworth is.

"Mr. Longworth?! Are you here?!"

Is he in the toilet? The shower? Passed out in bed?

"Go." The guy gestures with his gun.

"Mr. Longworth?"

Chicky creeps past a doorway to a kid's bedroom on the left side and another on the right. Then past a den with sofas and a lounge chair and a television. Chicky has never seen such a large screen except in a ballpark. Not even a sports bar.

He hears a knife slashing through cloth from the other end of the apartment. A painting being liberated from its frame.

Chicky keeps walking. Near the end of the hall light is coming from doorways on both sides. On the left must be the master bedroom with a view of Central Park. What's on the right?

Two of the robbers are following Chicky at a safe distance behind. Chicky is first in the line of fire. He's not even worthy as a hostage. His only value is protecting the lives of other people.

Maybe that's all he's ever been. A human body shield.

Chicky looks left into the master. A tuxedo jacket is flung across a king-sized bed that's otherwise undisturbed. Chicky doesn't see pants or shirt or shoes. Longworth has not undressed in here.

"Go right."

Chicky steps into the doorway across from the master. The rest of this apartment is filled with color and fabric and woodwork and curves but not here. This office is all glossy white and right angles and the cool glint of metals. A white desk with a computer screen filled with a news story. "Liberty Chief Under Fire," a picture of Mr. Longworth.

Also on the desk is a glass tumbler. With a half inch of amber liquid. And a big ice cube.

Chicky is getting a terrible feeling.

"Go in."

Chicky takes a step into the office while the robbers linger in the hall.

"Open that door."

Chicky really does not want to do this. But he can't see what choice he has. It's that drink that really worries Chicky. The unmelted ice cube. One of those big cubes that's an actual all-sides-equal cube. Even the ice here looks rich.

This chair is where Mr. Longworth was sitting when the doorbell rang. Looking at this screen. Getting drunker.

Chicky takes a few fast steps and pulls open the door in the corner—

It's a little powder room with no one inside and no place to hide. Chicky turns around. The nozzle of the gun nuzzles him in the back. *"Go."*

Chicky holds his breath again as he steps across the hall into the master bedroom. There's a variety of upholstery and fabric in deep colors. A massive chandelier is dripping with colored crystals that glitter like jewels. The floors are covered with wall-to-wall emerald carpeting that's topped with area rugs of different sizes and patterns. There's a lot going on. It looks like something out of a different century. What you'd expect a room at the Bohemia to look like.

The ringleader's footsteps fall silent on all the carpet. At the dressing table he swipes up a few pieces of jewelry and slips them into his pocket. He turns back to survey the room slowly. He must be looking for something. What? The jewelry box. There must be at least one in here.

The ringleader nudges Chicky toward a door and points his gun at the knob. Chicky doesn't like this one fucking bit. He shakes his head.

"Open it."

Chicky feels the barrel of the gun shoved into the small of his back.

"Now!"

Chicky reaches forward. He puts his hand on the knob and says a quick little prayer in his head. It's not that he's suddenly found religion but why not. He holds his breath again as he pulls open another door.

CHAPTER 47

APARTMENT 2A

Every apartment house like the Bohemia has a service entrance, usually a plain door, no brass or glass or decorative anything, just a no-nonsense barrier to entry of heavy-duty locks, reinforced steel, security camera, alarm system. Service entrances are sometimes around the corner, often in an alley. The Bohemia's is both.

Olek is standing in the doorway wearing nothing but jeans. The guy's whole torso is covered in tattoos and deeply ripped muscles plus some disturbing scars that look like knife wounds.

"A few minutes ago," Julian says, "I was walking home, and watched as an SUV pulled up, and two armed men got out. They met four other guys already on the sidewalk. All of them rushed in. It looked like Chicky was a hostage."

Olek spins on his bare feet and strides through the big open space of the basement.

"The driver," Julian continues, trotting to keep up, "just chased me around the corner, but gave up when I hid. He has a gun."

The super unlocks his office and rushes to his desk.

"There's no doorman out front."

Olek's desk has three screens. One is a computer monitor. Another provides the status of the building's HVAC, water, electricity, thermometers, sprinklers. The third is the security cameras. Most of these live feeds show static scenes—empty elevators, empty doorways, empty roof. But a few windows are black in a way that doesn't look like darkness.

"It's the concierge desk, both lobby cameras, and the northeast service elevator." That elevator serves the C and D lines, which are the building's largest; that's where the richest people live. The northeast service is locked on eleven. Exactly where Julian guessed. Where he feared.

Olek highlights the blackened window of the front desk's feed. He moves the cursor backward through time until light reappears and frenetic reverse movement and then the video arrives at a static scene of Canarius sitting at the desk, five minutes ago. Olek drags the cursor forward through a jumbled rush of the gunpoint invasion and the disabling of cameras by spray paint.

"Let's call the police," Julian says. "My phone is dead."

"The police are very busy."

"Sure. But still."

"There is a screen like this at the front desk. So if one of these men is at the front, he has seen me let you in. He has alerted his associates. They will be leaving quickly, or even coming to find us. If this is a simple robbery, maybe we call the police and hide. But I do not think this is a simple robbery. This is Mr. Longworth."

Julian's heart is racing again.

"This might be kidnapping," Olek continues. "Or worse."

"Worse?"

"Now that I am thinking, Mr. Sonnenberg, yes, please call nine-one-one, as you suggest. It cannot hurt. Maybe the police will arrive."

That's when Julian notices movement on the screen. It's the camera from the exterior of the front door.

"Oh," he says, understanding what's happening. The worst-case scenario. "Oh fuck."

CHAPTER 48

APARTMENT 11C-D

Emily watches DeMarquis cross the sidewalk. He glances at the tinted windows of the SUV at the hydrant, then turns to the Bohemia's front door. He pulls the handle, but the door doesn't budge. Another fancy apartment building, another door that's locked to him.

He raps on the glass. After a few seconds the door opens, and Canarius's head emerges. The men have a quick exchange, then DeMarquis returns to the Maybach, again eyeing the SUV, and glancing at the trio of pedestrians who are now at the corner.

Back behind the wheel, DeMarquis turns so he can see Emily and the sidewalk and the front door and the approaching men all at once. "Chicky is in the bathroom," he reports.

"Um," Emily says. This seems like TMI. "Okay?"

"I don't want to leave the car without a doorman out front. Not tonight."

"Sure." Emily is more than happy to enter her building alone, as she does whenever she comes home without Whit, which is mostly. But she'll wait until these men have passed.

The pedestrians stare into the Maybach. They can no doubt see DeMarquis in the streetlight, though not Emily cowering in the dark backseat. She wants to blame her fear on context. It's scary tonight, borderline lawless, the protesters, the counterprotesters. She saw a vehicle at the Met that evoked a land war. Security can do much more to exacerbate fears than assuage them.

For a few seconds Emily watches the men walk away.

"Okay then."

She wants to pretend nothing just happened. DeMarquis knows better, but won't ever say anything. He knows who she is. He knows his job.

"Maybe let's wait for Chicky to return?" he offers. "Then I can escort you up."

"Oh no, that's all right." Emily doesn't want to appear any more scared. Any more racist. "But thank you, DeMarquis. I appreciate it. Everything. Tonight can't have been easy for you."

"Are you sure?"

"Yes. Good night, DeMarquis. And thanks again. So much. I'm sorry to have put you in such uncomfortable positions."

Emily climbs out of the car, her stockinged feet on cool pavement again. She walks alongside the old station wagon, and glances at the receding backs of the pedestrians. She looks at the Suburban too, but there's nothing to see, just a big car with tinted windows, ignition off, taxi plates, unremarkable. Yet something about this one is niggling at her consciousness.

Canarius holds the door, the key hanging in its lock.

"Thanks, Canarius." Emily sees him notice that she's not wearing any shoes.

"My pleasure," he says, and locks the door behind her.

Now Emily realizes what's bothering her about the SUV: very rarely do people depart from the Bohemia at eleven-thirty on a Tuesday. "Do you happen to know who that car is for?"

Canarius waits a beat before answering, "No, ma'am. I don't." He holds her eye. "Sorry."

Emily feels as if he might be trying to communicate something. "Is everything okay?"

"With me? Yes, ma'am. Thank you for asking."

"With something else?"

"It's just . . . you know." He swallows. "It's crazy out there tonight."

"Yes, it certainly is." Emily doesn't want to wade too deeply into this. Not with a doorman. Not with a Black man. "Thanks again, Canarius. Have a good night. Get home safe."

She presses the elevator button, steps inside. A large mirror is mounted to the rear wall, and she's appalled at what she sees. Her hair is in disarray, and her makeup is streaked; blood has trickled down her shins from the Band-Aids; she's shoeless and her stockings are torn; her red dress is wrinkled, and stained from something she slid across on the East Side sidewalk.

"Good lord," she mutters, and reaches up to retie her jumbled scarf, but what's the point?

As the doors close in the reflection behind her, she catches a glimpse of—could it be?—is that a person sitting at Canarius's feet? No, that doesn't make sense. That must be a bag.

The elevator starts to move.

CHAPTER 49

APARTMENT 2A

Julian stares at the little window of live footage. The camera is mounted to the molding under the cab's ceiling, so the video is a strange angle, the top of Emily's head, looking down the front of her dress. She seems disheveled. And is she—?

Yes. Emily Longworth is barefoot. And bloody. Julian wonders what the hell has happened in the half hour since he last saw her. But at the moment that might be the least urgent issue.

"Do you know if Mr. Longworth is at home?" Olek asks. He bends over, straightens up, and Julian sees the automatic now in his hand.

"I thought they were together," Julian says. "I *saw* them together, an hour ago."

The super is wearing a follow-up question or two, but seems to decide that the answers don't matter enough to expend the time. Julian looks around. His eyes land on a giant wrench leaning against the jamb, and a charging station mounted to the wall. "Do those walkie-talkies work?" Julie is already grabbing two.

"Mr. Sonnenberg, please, stay—"

"I'm coming with you." Julian gives a handset to Olek. He picks up the giant wrench.

"No, Mr. Son—"

"I'm coming, Olek." He says this definitively, brooking no argument.

The two men stare at each other, and Julian can see Olek understand something. Maybe everything.

Olek is wearing nothing but jeans, holding a semiautomatic. Julian is wearing a tuxedo with that kid's blood all across the white shirt, but his bow tie is still knotted. They are an unusual team.

"Here's what I think we should do."

CHAPTER 50

FRONT DOOR

Chicky pulls the doorknob. By the time the closet door is halfway open he's more than halfway convinced he's about to get shot. He has known a few people who've been shot. Most have survived. But these are close quarters right here. And this probably isn't going to be a single bullet. So this won't be the same as catching a stray in the thigh. This will be multiple gunshots to the chest or stomach or head or all of the above.

He holds his breath—

Pulls—

Nothing.

This walk-in closet is the same size as Chicky's living room. Maybe bigger. The walls are divided into sections by shelves and bars and doors and cabinets that hold hundreds of suits and coats and blouses and skirts and dresses and shoes and shoes and shoes. Maybe thousands.

There's furniture in this closet.

Chicky stands in the doorframe while the robber drops to one knee with his gun in front. He's looking under hanging clothes for legs. He doesn't see any. After a couple of seconds he gives up and gets up and shoves Chicky back out of the closet.

"Yes this is One. Go."

Chicky doesn't understand what this means. He turns to face the guy. "Huh?"

The guy holds up his hand and shakes his head at Chicky: no I'm not talking to you.

"When?"

The guy must be wearing earphones under that balaclava. He must be talking into a mic.

"Copy." His voice is quiet but there's an edge. Not panic but definitely tension.

"Three, proceed immediately to front door to intercept. Initiate Protocol Gamma."

Chicky knows what this must mean. His heart sinks. He has to find an opportunity to stop this. He can't simply wait for the end. Not if it's going to end the way he now suspects.

"Longworth!" the ringleader yells. This is the first time the guy has spoken aloud in 11C-D. Chicky is worried as fuck about this. Not unlike a kidnapper taking off his mask. It indicates a resignation about being identified.

"Your wife is about to arrive!"

The ringleader motions with his gun to another of the robbers. He's pointing across the room to another door. Must be the master bathroom.

"She's going to become our hostage, Longworth. So if you do anything stupid she will die."

The ringleader holds up a hand and puts up three fingers. He points at the door and closes his fist.

"It's time for you to come out."

Pointer finger up.

The other guy rushes to that bathroom door.

Middle finger also up.

Puts his hand on the doorknob.

Ring finger up too. Then the ringleader points and the other guy yanks the door—

Nothing. Again.

Where the fuck is Longworth hiding?

CHAPTER 51

APARTMENT 11C-D

How long has it been since Whit left her on Madison Avenue? Thirty minutes? Emily hopes he's still awake. She needs to have it out, even if she's exhausted and he's drunk. She girds herself. She's been avoiding this conversation for way too long. So although she hopes Whit is awake, she also hopes he's asleep. Because although she needs to have this conversation, she definitely does not want to.

Emily rummages around in her handbag, grabs her keys. The elevator comes to a stop. She takes a deep breath.

The doors open onto a short hall that was originally designed to accommodate two apartments, but now it's the Longworths' private landing. This is where Chicky Diaz had stood a few months ago, listening to Tatiana or Yolanda screaming, worried that it was Emily in there. Even Chicky knew that Whit was a goddamned villain.

She slides the key in the lock.

Okay, she tells herself, this is it.

She turns the key.

Her new life is about to begin. Right now.

Emily notices a few things all at once: the Hopper that hangs in the entry gallery is not hanging in the entry gallery; lights seem to be on everywhere; a big black duffel bag is sitting on the floor.

She shuts the etched-glass door, which rattles gently in its mahogany frame. She takes one step into the gallery, and another, staring at that duffel. Is it Whit's? Could he be *leaving* her? What a bizarre turn of events that would be. But he's taking the Hopper with him? *Tonight?*

No, that doesn't make any sense—

This is the last thing that crosses her mind before someone grabs her from the side. She begins to scream but a hand covers her mouth and a man behind her calls out, "Got her!"

Has Whit arranged for her to be abducted?

"Longworth!" someone calls out, from down the hall. "It's time for you to come out."

This man's voice is familiar. It's getting nearer. He's walking down the hall.

"You have ten seconds."

The accent too. Now he comes into view. He's covered head to toe in black, with a face mask and even sunglasses. Nothing about him is visible. But by the voice and the body and the gait she knows exactly who he is. Also by the circumstance. She's not even a little bit surprised.

He walks behind her, and takes over the hostage duties.

"Then I'm going to start shooting your wife."

CHAPTER 52

APARTMENT 2A

When Julian was a teenager, the service stairs were where kids went to smoke, drink, make out, fuck. You tossed your empty cans and used condoms directly into the garbage chutes, and it never occurred to you that the staff could see this evidence flying into basement bins, perched there atop cinched-up Hefty bags.

Teenagers used to be idiots. Are they still? It's hard for Julian to imagine that his kids' generation could be as clueless. They're so hyper-informed about drug dependencies, mental health, microaggressions, institutional racism. On the other hand, death by selfie is now a thing. Subway surfing too. Pharm parties, for Christ's sake. So maybe today's teenagers are even stupider, because they know better, but behave just as idiotically.

But who is Julian Sonnenberg to accuse anyone of idiocy?

Julian has seen the blueprints. He knows that sixty years ago, 11C and 11D were purchased by the youngest son of a prominent family, a black sheep who eschewed the East Side as an act of rebellion, albeit not rebellious enough to renounce his inheritance. This scion knocked down walls, living rooms became bedrooms and vice versa, a hallway was extended, one of the front doors was closed up, the second kitchen was demolished.

A few features of the newly seven-thousand-square-foot apartment remained constant through that initial combination as well as an unfortunate renovation in the 1980s and then the Longworths' more tasteful overhaul. Nearly all the original millwork, the marble fireplaces, the intricate parquet floors, those are intact. It can still look like the nineteenth century, if you squint.

Not only does every building like the Bohemia have a service entrance, every apartment does too. This service door is usually off the kitchen. The original 11C's kitchen was demolished, but that old service entrance wasn't bricked up, and a fireproof door still sits at the end of a long hall. It's hidden from within behind a decorative wooden door that's clad in the same wallpaper as the rest of the hall. Anyone looking down there would think it's a linen closet, a powder room, something like that. Emily explained this to Julian back when she gave him a full tour.

The invaders have laid siege to the northeast elevator and its service stairs, so Julian climbs the northeast passenger stairs, while Olek climbs the other service stairs, headed to that hidden door, whose key he's carrying. Duplicates for all the apartments are kept not only at the front desk, but also in the super's office. Julian is carrying the Longworths' front door keys.

In hindsight, Julian suspected that Emily ended the house tour in the master bedroom as a sort of invitation. Lingering there. On occasion he has wondered how much she'd premeditated, how much she'd deliberately orchestrated, and to what end.

It's a long climb. The building's ceiling heights are tall, and the basement and lobby levels are cavernous. It's nearly two hundred feet up to eleven, taxing the limits of Julian's endurance, especially at this speed. He can feel his heart straining. But he keeps making ninety-degree turns, four landings per floor, around and around, up and up, his breath growing shorter and his quads heavier and his heart beating faster and time, always, running out for the woman he loves.

He knows that this might kill him. He speeds up.

As Olek rounds the very first landing he catches a glimpse of movement at the next level above, someone running up the stairs, and Olek gives chase, gun in his right hand and walkie-talkie in his left, bounding up two stairs at a time, and he runs through a cloud of what's unmistakably marijuana smoke, which gives him pause, and he now understands that this has nothing to do with the invasion. This is just one of the Sonnenberg teenagers, getting high in the stairwell.

"Hey," he calls out. "Stop running. I don't care about the smoking."

The footsteps stop. Olek resumes climbing, no longer at a sprint. He rounds the next corner and sees that it's the girl, a half flight above him.

"I'm sorry," she says.

"I don't care. Go home, now. Fast." Olek continues climbing.

"What? Why?"

He is now on the same level as Oona Sonnenberg. "There are armed robbers here."

"What?"

Should he tell this girl about her father? No. That would only make her worry. There's nothing she can do to help, except stay out of harm's way.

"Get inside your apartment, and lock the doors." She doesn't move. *"Now!"*

She startles, and bangs into his arm, knocks the walkie-talkie out of his hand, which hits the banister, then goes tumbling down, down, down, and splinters fifty feet below, in the basement.

"I'm so sorry."

Olek turns to her. "Get inside right now."

Julian checks his watch: he still has fifteen seconds before his scheduled rendezvous with Olek. He allows himself a couple of seconds to catch his breath, then continues up the final flight.

The robbers had probably confiscated walkie-talkies from Chicky and Canarius, so talking on these things would be a mistake. Instead Julian clicks the button once, twice, three times. Then he waits for Olek's response while he inserts the key into the Longworths' front door.

And he waits.

And no answer comes.

Okay, now what? Without Olek, opening this door is probably a suicide mission.

Would that be the very worst thing? Maybe that's an explicit trade that Julian would make, one life for another. But maybe it's folly to think it would work. Maybe it would be suicide but without any useful mission.

Sooner or later, everyone confronts this question: what do I exist for? Julian's daughter, Oona, wondered this very thing when she was only four years old—what are people for? Fifty-year-old Julian has been unable to stop asking it. What have I done with my life? What still remains for me to accomplish? What will I be remembered for?

It's a rare luxury to be able to choose the time and place and manner of your death.

Julian once learned that this is how suicide often happens. Not a long-term plan, just an instantaneous answer to this question: what if it all ends, right now?

That's what he's thinking when he hears Emily scream.

CHAPTER 53

FRONT DOOR

The ringleader yells, "First we're going to shoot her in one leg!"

Chicky doesn't understand why these guys should need to find Mr. Longworth. They shouldn't. All they should need is to not get ambushed. And now that they're holding Mrs. Longworth hostage that doesn't seem like a rational worry.

"Then the other leg!"

No. These robbers shouldn't need to find Longworth at all. Not if they're just robbers.

"Ten!"

Chicky is being marched down the hall. Still a human shield.

"Nine!"

There's a guy in front of Chicky who steps into the den's doorway and clears it.

"Eight!

The guy behind Chicky holds him in place by the shoulder.

"Seven!"

The guy in front of Chicky emerges from the den.

"Six!"

When things are spinning is when people start making rash decisions. Lethal decisions.

"Five."

They've now arrived at the kids' bedrooms. One of the guys reaches into a room and Chicky hears a click but no light goes on and another click but still no light and Chicky realizes what these clicks are at the same moment that the robber realizes and squeezes his trigger and squeezes again—

The two blasts are thunderclaps and the flashes lightning and Chicky leaps to the side and tumbles out of the line of fire into the den. He hits the floor and continues to roll. As the ringing in his ears begins to subside Chicky can hear Mrs. Longworth's muffled screaming from the front of the apartment.

Chicky scrambles to his feet and grabs his gun and scampers out of the den through the double doors into the dining room. He pushes himself into a dark corner.

What are his options?

Option one is to flee. Chicky can jump into the hall and make a few quick steps into the kitchen and around the island and out the service door and down to the basement and out to the street. But first he would need to navigate through the hall where there's at least one guy with a gun in one direction and at least one other guy with another gun in the other direction. Chicky can't see both directions at once. So the hallway is likely a kill zone. So no. He can't escape.

Option two is to try to rescue Mrs. Longworth. Though now that they've shot Mr. Longworth why should she need rescuing? What good is it doing these guys to keep holding her hostage? Or to harm her? None. They came here to rob the building and maybe kill Whit Longworth. Now they should just need to get the fuck out of here as quickly as possible.

Option three is to get himself into the safest possible defensive position and wait and shoot anyone who comes looking for him.

Three is the only option that makes any real sense.

Light is leaking from the hallway and through the windows from the streetlights. One whole wall of the dining room is filled by a massive painting. Chicky didn't witness this painting's arrival but he heard about it. This canvas came into the building via crane. The sidewalk needed to be closed as well as one lane of traffic and a few parking spots vacated. There were permits. *Police.*

The gun feels warm in his hand. Chicky worries that his palm will get sweaty but he needs to keep his finger on the trigger. That sort of safety is not an option here.

The painting looks to Chicky like just some big pieces of color. Something a child would paint. A young and not especially smart child. Chicky has seen plenty of art like this at the Bohemia. Splatters and dots and scrawls and simple-looking figures. Pictures that Chicky would be ashamed to hang in his living room but he knows that they're among the most valuable objects in the Bohemia. Ten or fifteen or twenty-five million dollars.

Chicky creeps to the arched double doorway. He leans forward to peek into the living room. Light is glinting off the grand piano. There's no one in here. He makes his way around a sofa and a reading chair and a standing lamp. He kneels behind the sofa and peers around the side to the front hall.

He can see the situation clearly. It's bad. One of the robbers is holding Mrs. Longworth as both hostage and shield. This guy's gun is aimed down the hall.

Chicky has no angle for a shot. But again he tells himself that he shouldn't need one. If these guys wanted to kill Mrs. Longworth they'd have done it already. They're going to let her go. So all Chicky needs to do is wait this out. Probably a matter of seconds. It will be over very soon. He settles into his crouch.

The front door flies open and someone comes rushing in swinging something—is it Mr. Sonnenberg? with Olek's giant wrench?—and the robber spins toward this danger and fires with a tremendous boom but gets kneecapped by the wrench before he can get off a second shot. The robber tumbles to the ground and redirects his gun and fires again and Chicky can see very clearly where this bullet hits. It looks fatal.

Chicky feels himself rushing forward without realizing he made the decision. He sees that Mr. Sonnenberg is not moving. Mrs. Longworth is screaming her head off. The robber is on the floor in obvious pain but still in possession of his gun and Mrs. Longworth is still in his line of fire.

Now the guy catches sight of Chicky and starts to redirect his aim—

Chicky squeezes and adjusts and squeezes again and knows immediately that both his shots landed. One in the chest and one in the face.

The guy is motionless. Maybe not dead immediately but soon. Chicky advances with his gun in front—

Pop! Pop pop!

This gunfire comes from down the hall. Chicky doesn't even look. He just grabs Mrs. Longworth by the arm and pulls her out of the line of fire. He waits a few seconds then cranes his head through the double doorway. There's a figure lying on the ground at the far end of the hall. It's a shirtless man whose body seems to be covered in tattoos. And what looks like a bullet wound.

Fuck. It's Olek. He's not moving.

Chicky hears rustling and banging. This noise must be the robbers exiting through the service door. Chicky waits another few seconds with his gun aimed down the hallway.

Dead silence. No movement.

He hustles over to Mr. Sonnenberg. Puts two fingers to the guy's neck.

"Is he okay?" Mrs. Longworth asks.

Chicky moves his fingers to a different position.

Mrs. Longworth is walking toward him.

"Stay there!" Chicky yells.

Chicky scoots to the robber and confirms that this guy is dead. His gun is lying a few feet away. It occurs to Chicky to collect this weapon but he doesn't want his fingerprints on it. He kicks it away.

"Is Jules . . . ?"

"Please don't come here!"

Mrs. Longworth doesn't listen. She collapses onto Mr. Sonnenberg. Chicky gets out of the way. She drapes her whole body across Mr. Sonnenberg with her head on his chest. She lets out a heart-piercing wail.

Oh, Chicky realizes.

Oh wow.

He catches movement from down the hall. Someone is emerging from a doorway. Chicky raises his gun again.

"Don't move!" Chicky yells. He's on one knee halfway between two dead men and a wailing woman. He has four bullets left. "Don't!"

It hurts like hell to hold the gun up. Those damn cracked ribs, the bruises, the pain is getting worse by the second.

"Chicky," the guy says. "It's me."

Chicky peers into the darkness and sees it's Mr. Longworth emerging from the kid's dark bedroom. Chicky thought Longworth was dead but he doesn't even seem injured. As he walks past a hallway sconce Chicky can see two obvious bullet holes in the guy's white shirt but no blood. None.

Holding the gun up is really fucking painful. Chicky lets his arm fall.

Of course: body armor. The thing that made Mr. Longworth rich also just saved his life. Chicky looks over at this guy's wife who's sobbing over Mr. Sonnenberg. Her whole body shaking with it. She's sprawled next to the gun that killed him.

That's when Chicky realizes it's his right side that's so painful now. But it was his left side that was beaten by El Puño.

CHAPTER 54

APARTMENT 11C-D

Emily is sitting in the front parlor with the cops. Although she'd wiped the blood from her hands, still she's covered in it, her arms, her legs, her dress, there's even blood on her face, smeared across her cheek, spatters on her forehead, in her hair.

"You're positive?" asks one of the detectives, a puffy red-faced Irish-looking guy, a dwindling breed of NYPD.

"Yes, his name is—was—Justin Pugh. He used to do business with my husband, but they had a falling-out."

The detective raises his eyebrows: and how. "What about the other intruders?"

"I never saw any of them. They were all hidden under masks and sunglasses."

There's a knock on the door that leads to the dining room. "Yeah?" the detective asks. The pocket door slides open. It's Emily's father, looking blanched after walking through a hall filled with bodies and blood. Blood on the floor, blood on the walls.

Emily is aware that she's ruining this green velvet sofa. Blood all over everything.

"I'm Griffin Merriweather. Emily's father." He looks around at the cops in uniforms and suits, and the EMTs who are standing by in case Emily changes her mind about needing medical attention. No one wants to be blamed if she changes her mind. Not with a woman like this.

Griffin hugs his daughter, then turns to the cops. "I'd like to have a private word with my daughter." Not a question. "We're going to step into the dining room."

The two detectives glance at each other, then Irish says, "Sure."

"You saw all those people get shot?"

Emily nods.

"I'm so, so sorry, sweetheart. I can't imagine how awful this must be."

Now she's crying again. Or maybe she'd never stopped?

"You don't need to talk to the police anymore tonight. You shouldn't. And you obviously can't stay here. So you're going to come home with me, and we're going to leave now. Right now. Okay?"

The desperate hours pass in a narcotic daze. Dawn peeks over the eastern horizon, accompanied by the chirping of a few birds. Not many. There aren't a lot of trees here. Over on Central Park West, dawn is cacophonous.

Has Emily slept at all? She can't tell. She stares out the window at Park Avenue, where doormen and porters are cleaning the sidewalks, the gutters, the floral malls in the middle of the avenue, picking up trash, broken bottles, discarded placards. By the time the residents leave for work, and school, and dog walking and exercise classes and recreational shopping and extramarital affairs, Park Avenue will bear no evidence of the protests and counterprotests.

Almost everything will be back to normal, for almost everyone.

Not for Emily.

She turns on the small television on the kitchen counter. Not a lot of cooking goes on in her parents' kitchen so they're willing to sacrifice counterspace for a screen.

The local news reporters are already on the story, on the scene. One of them is doing a stand-up in front of the Bohemia, surrounded by the swirling lights of emergency vehicles. "At least three fatalities, but names haven't been released yet."

Nothing will ever be back to normal for Emily, ever again.

Part Five

TOMORROW

CHAPTER 55

APARTMENT 11C-D

Griffin walks into his bland chintzy living room with a man Emily has never met, wearing a suit and tie, neither particularly nice.

"Sweetheart, this is my old colleague Eric Aronsky. Eric is a criminal-defense attorney."

Emily's mouth falls open. "Oh, Daddy."

"This is purely for your protection," Aronsky jumps in. Emily knows that his job is not only to provide counsel, it's also to bear the responsibility of the necessity.

"My *protection*?"

"I'm going to leave you two alone," Griffin says, and retreats.

"May I?" Aronsky indicates a chair, but doesn't wait for an answer before he sits. "I hate to be insensitive. But honestly I'm paid to be insensitive."

"Okay."

"Your husband may have been the victim of a homicide last night."

It was a robbery gone awry, but Emily doesn't want to voice that objection.

"If that turns out to be the case, it's almost inevitable that the police will look at the spouse."

Emily puts her hand over her mouth.

"We'll discuss all the details in the future. Finances, disagreements. Relationships."

She remains silent. She understands that this lawyer needs to warn her, strongly, and needs to make sure she understands, clearly.

"For now, the most important thing is this: do not say anything. To anyone. Especially not to the police. Not another word. The only thing you can accomplish by talking to the police is to create additional problems for yourself. So if the police contact you, Mrs. Longworth? Refer them to me."

He puts a business card on the coffee table. "Of course, you're free to use an attorney other than myself. I'm here as a favor to your father, who's a legend. But you don't know me from Adam. I won't be offended if this is the last time we speak. But any attorney will give you the same counsel. Do. Not. Talk. To. Anyone."

Emily takes her kids, parents, and nanny out east where they can hole up at the beach, bunkered behind twelve-foot-high privet and a gate that would require tactical battlefield weaponry to breach. Away from nosy neighbors at the Bohemia, away from nosy school parents, away from nosy friends, nosy acquaintances, nosy reporters. Emily is young and rich and beautiful, and her husband has just been killed after being revealed as an international villain. The tabloid press is having a field day, gossip sites, social media. Emily needs to be invisible.

She calls the hospital for updates on Olek and Chicky, but the staff won't give her any information. "We can't," the nurse says. "HIPAA rules." For the briefest instant Emily considers saying something about how she's paying the bills, but that's not only a losing argument, it's also a repugnant one. She doesn't want to be that person. "Thank you," she says, then sends more flowers.

Aronsky makes the drive out east with a couple of young colleagues. They set up in the dining room. The house is filled with massive bouquets. The florist will be sending her kid to college on Whitaker Longworth's condolence arrangements.

"As far as I know, you're not a suspect of anything," Aronsky assures Emily. "But we need to make sure there's nothing that makes you look like one, or be ready to explain anything that does."

She nods. She knows that it's his job to defend her no matter what.

But to do his job effectively he needs to know whether she's guilty of something. They review the day's chronology. Emily tells him that she spent a couple of hours at the studio, sketching. Aronsky doesn't so much as look up from his yellow pad. He doesn't begin to really probe until she mentions the call from her dad. "When exactly was that?"

"Ten?" She checks her phone. "Nine-fifty-one. He was concerned with the protest, and I was worried about him scaring the kids. I didn't want him to turn it into a scarring experience."

It certainly turned out that way. No one needs to say this aloud.

"When you decided to go over to your parents', was your plan to spend the night?"

Did she deliberately construct an alibi?

"No."

"So your husband was expecting you to come home?"

Did Whit think he'd be alone?

"Yes."

"Did you ask him not to arm the alarm?"

Did you set him up?

"No," she says. "We didn't discuss the alarm."

Three men were killed during the demonstration and four dozen demonstrators were hospitalized, all of them Black. To the extent that the culprits have been identified, they were all white vigilantes, or white cops.

One police officer was treated for a sprained knee, and four others for injuries sustained when one patrol car crashed into another while speeding down Fifth Avenue. All those policemen were treated at the same hospital, on the Upper East Side, and released.

"So, let's talk about this apartment where you sketched."

"Sure." Emily had hoped, irrationally, that they wouldn't return to this subject. "Though I wouldn't call it an apartment. It's a painting studio."

"And why is that you have it?"

"I wanted my own space where I could go to be creative."

"You don't have room for that at the Bohemia?"

"Physical space, maybe. But not the mental space, not with children around—"

"Aren't they in school?"

She glowered at the interruption. "And the housekeeper, nanny, deliveries, repairs, people coming and going all day. It's hard to concentrate. For years I've wanted to get back to painting, but haven't. And I thought maybe the problem was not having a dedicated space. I took that studio as a kick in the pants. I'm there once or twice per week."

"And what is it you're painting?"

"Color fields, mostly."

Emily can see that Aronsky doesn't really know what that means, and doesn't care. "Have you tried to sell any of these paintings?"

"No, that's . . ." She swallows. "This isn't a commercial endeavor. This is a hobby."

Emily halfway expects the lawyer to want to see the studio, and the paintings, and is a little disappointed that he doesn't.

"So, moving on."

Emily has come to understand that when Aronsky begins a sentence with "So," he's about to bring up a potential problem.

"That morning, your husband called Julian Sonnenberg. Do you know what that call was about?"

"No. Whit didn't mention it."

"If you had to guess?"

"Oh, it could've been many things. Julian is an art dealer who's done business with Whit. And with me. That's how we know—um, knew—each other. That's why we were together at the gala. Julian and Whit could've been talking about the gala, or a piece of art, or something to do with the Bohemia. Julian is on the board."

Aronsky's colleague has been scribbling furiously, and he gives the young woman a few seconds to catch up. "So, was there any issue between your husband and Mr. Sonnenberg."

Any issue? Every issue.

"Well, I don't think they *loved* each other. And Julian was on the board that rejected our initial renovation plans. Or rather, Whit's original architectural plans."

"What does that mean?"

"My husband and I don't agree about everything. Didn't."

"And what ended up happening with that disagreement?"

"Whit had to change the plans. We ended up renovating the apartment in a style that was pretty different from his original intention."

"Was it more like yours?"

"Yes, you could say that."

"Any other issues between your husband and Mr. Sonnenberg?"

She wills herself to stay calm. "Not that I'm aware of."

Emily can tell that this was all a warm-up. Here it comes.

"Do you spend a lot of time with Mr. Sonnenberg?"

She never stops worrying that the other shoe is about to drop. She knows it's just a question of when, and who, and how horrible it's going to be. Maybe it's now.

"Well, I *did*."

There's a narrative she needs the lawyer to construct, to pursue, to confirm.

"Julian is—was—very . . . political. Some might say *woke*. My husband certainly used that word. And when the information leaked that Liberty was . . . well, you know. Julian was condescending about it, in a way that seemed unkind. I felt like I ought to distance myself from him."

It makes her nauseated to say this, but she has no choice.

"And that leak?"

Emily is amazed—and relieved—that the lawyer is moving on from the subject of Julian.

"What about it?"

"Do you know who might have done it? The details that were leaked were pretty high-level. It's hard to imagine a person who'd have access to that sort of info who'd also benefit from its disclosure. Those seem mutually exclusive."

The inspiration had come from a combination of Morgan Lipschitz's boasts about manipulating public opinion plus that real-estate agent who'd suggested the leak of the Bohemia purchase. It wasn't a revelation to Emily that the controlled exposure of sensitive information could be useful. But it had never occurred to Emily that it could be useful to her, if it was orchestrated by her, which turned out to be far easier than she'd imagined.

"No," she said. "I know very little about my husband's business. I've met some of his colleagues, of course, some of the senior people, but only socially."

"And you? Did you know?"

"About his client roster? Not until the leak."

"Were you angry?"

"Angry? No. Disillusioned, maybe."

"It got you kicked off the museum board."

"Yes, that was unfortunate. But not surprising." In fact she'd been one hundred percent positive it would happen. "These are the times we live in."

"So, Mrs. Longworth. Your husband's gun. It was apparently not loaded. Do you know why?"

"Well, I hope it was because Whit didn't keep a loaded gun lying around a house with children. He promised he wouldn't. I guess he didn't have time to load it."

"Where did he store the gun?"

"In a safe in our walk-in closet."

"But that safe was found closed."

"Yes, so I've heard."

"Why would your husband lock the safe after removing the gun?"

"I have no idea."

"Do you know if he kept the ammunition in the safe with the gun?"

"I assumed the ammunition was in the safe, but it's not as if I checked. Or asked. The only thing I had to do with the gun was to tell Whit that I didn't want it around."

"So you never touched it?"

Her heart races. "The gun? No."

"So there's no way your fingerprints would be on it?"

"I don't think so." Now it feels as if her heart has fallen all the way through her stomach. "Why are you asking all this about the gun?"

"Just to know the answers. In case it comes up."

"Oh," she says, unsatisfied. More than unsatisfied: terrified. "That goddamned gun."

She'd once had a conversation with Camila about gun safety. Gun unsafety. "Guns are the leading cause of death for American children," Camila said. "Car accidents are second."

"That can't be true. Is it really?"

"Followed by other injuries, then congenital disease, then cancer. Three times as many kids die from guns as from cancer."

They were breaking down cartons. Box cutters were the thing it was illegal to carry around.

"Owning a gun doesn't make you safer, this is well established. Owning a gun makes you more likely to get shot. And more likely to die by suicide. Even though gun owners aren't any more depressed than other folks, they're much more likely to attempt suicide, and much more likely to succeed."

Emily had recently learned that Whit had broken a lot of promises; his promises no longer meant anything. So after that conversation with Camila, Emily decided to check the safe. She kept the safe's security combination with other codes in a small notebook in her desk, along with checkbooks, and passports. This was an obvious place. Emily wasn't concerned that other people would find this info, but that she'd forget where it was kept.

Emily punched in the safe's code, and opened the door.

"Suicide is especially common," Camila had said, "for kids who have access to guns."

The gun wasn't in there.

It took Emily barely ten seconds to find it, and she sat there, staring at the thing, enraged. It was one thing to hate his wife, to humiliate her, to cheat on her. That was horrid, sure, but not unique, and not criminal. More problematic was paying prostitutes to enact sexual fantasies about inflicting violence upon her. That was awful. And the deplorable way he made his fortune, the way he rationalized it. Plus his increasingly appalling politics.

Every day, there was more and more to hate about Whitaker Longworth.

But there was still all that money, and the prenup. Plus Whit was not a demonstrably bad parent, at least Emily hadn't thought so. Not until she discovered that he kept a loaded gun in exactly the type of place where a curious kid would find it: in his bedside drawer.

That notebook contained not just Emily's security codes and their joint codes but some of Whit's private codes too. Codes to his computers. His tablets. His phones. And within all this hardware, documents were accessible. Sensitive documents such as the executive-summary spreadsheet of Liberty Logistics' financials, and the memo about earning categories—a cornucopia of damning information.

Maybe Whit was building a case against her. She could do the same thing.

The hard part was figuring out which document would do the most damage, the quickest. Which revelation would elicit the most unsympathetic response from Whit. Which response of his would give her the best excuse to leave, and the best argument in court. Not necessarily in a court of law, but in the court of public opinion, which was the one Emily truly cared about. She'd be well off no matter what. The important thing was to be well regarded.

"None of your neighbors has been specific about the sequence of gunshots."

"That's understandable. The walls are filled with sand. To dampen sound. And directly below us, Mrs. Frumm is nearly deaf. Next door, well, you know what happened."

Gareth Blankenship's body wasn't discovered for six days. No one was home in the Longworth household, so there were no immediate neighbors on the eleventh floor, no one to notice the smell except whichever porter brought up the mail, but that guy was on the landing for only a few seconds, not even enough time for the elevator door to close behind him. Gareth had swallowed a few dozen pills with a chocolate milkshake. He hadn't left a note.

"And above you?"

"There's no one above us." Emily doesn't intend the double entendre, but she notices it. The lawyer does too.

"And are you positive about the sequence of the gunfire?"

"Positive?" She rolls her eyes. "Have you ever been in a gunfight? In the midst of it I wouldn't have even known my *name*. I'm not positive I'm remembering *anything* accurately."

Her first instinct had been to confront Whit about the loaded gun, but instead she slept on it, and then again. When he was out on one of his late-night excursions, she went into the kitchen, and collected a pair of the housekeeper's yellow gloves. She returned to her bedroom, put on the gloves, grabbed the weapon.

Emily had never before handled any firearm.

She knew she shouldn't google anything on her phone, nor on her computer, nor on anything that could be traced to her. So she'd gone to the library in Harlem to research how to load and unload an automatic handgun. How to ensure that there wasn't any round left in the chamber.

Emily had been growing more careful every day. More crafty. She was deliberate about what information to leak, and careful about how she leaked it. She hadn't thought there was any way anyone could ever trace the leak back to her, but that was before it crossed her mind that anyone might be looking in the context of a murder investigation. Murder changes everything.

She awakens in the middle of the night, every night, drenched in a cold sweat, worried about the last thing Whit said to her before he died.

How did he know?

CHAPTER 56

FRONT DOOR

During Chicky's formal interview he comes to understand that the cops don't suspect him. If they're looking for an inside man or an enemy of Longworth they don't think it's Chicky. They're not asking about his movements that day or his life or his problems or his possible motivations. They're not asking about Junior or El Puño or Tiffani's bills or back rent or credit-card debt. The cops don't give a shit about Chicky.

"And do you know where your colleagues were that night?"

Chicky looks over at his lawyer, Mr. Gennaro, who'd been referred by Mr. Onderdonk. "Don't worry Chicky," Onderdonk had said, "we'll take care of you." Chicky didn't know who exactly *we* was or what he meant by "take care of you."

Gennaro nods: okay to answer.

"Just Canarius and Olek," Chicky says. "The guys who were working with me."

He's in a private hospital room courtesy of a Bohemia resident who wishes to remain anonymous. But Chicky knows who it is. And the resident knows that Chicky knows.

"What about Zaire Diggs?" This is the white detective asking. His name is something with a lot of syllables, maybe Polish. Again Gennaro nods. Chicky and the lawyer had discussed this already. Which Bohemia guys were going to be suspects and what Chicky did or did not know about their activities and motivations and alibis.

"I think Zaire went to the demonstration. At least he told me he was going to."

"But you have no direct knowledge that Mr. Diggs attended the protest?"

"No sir."

Chicky knows that cell phone movements can be tracked but that proves only the whereabouts of the phone not the person. Just like red-light cameras can prove that a vehicle broke the law but not who was driving it. Just like other evidence can be incomplete or disputed or negated. There are many ways to create reasonable doubt.

"And how would you describe Mr. Diggs?"

"What do you mean?"

"A happy person? An angry person?"

Chicky isn't going to help if the cops are going to try to pin this on Zaire. "Zaire's a good guy."

The Black detective takes the unlit cheroot out of his mouth. "And why are you carrying a gun without a permit?"

Chicky can't remember this guy's name either.

"I moonlight as a bouncer at a bar. The other night I had a . . . problem. With someone who's well known to be violent."

"Oh yeah? Who's that?"

"I'd rather not say."

The maybe-Polish cop looks at Chicky as if this is a personal affront.

"Okay gentlemen . . ." Mr. Gennaro stands. "If you don't mind. My client needs rest."

The detectives glance at each other then one of them slides his business card onto the little swing-armed table. Chicky looks down at the card. Detective Lou Kozlowksi. Chicky can never see a Polish name without thinking about all the jokes guys used to tell about Polish people. In middle school and high school and the Marines. Dozens or maybe hundreds of minor variations of the same joke. Polacks were so stupid they couldn't change a lightbulb. Chicky had no idea why anyone believed Polish people were especially stupid. It was probably just a question of recent immigrants whose original language made it harder to learn English. There are a lot of types of prejudice and they all amount to pretty much the same thing.

"And here's mine." Gennaro hands a card to each detective and collects theirs. There will be a gun charge for Chicky to contend with but the lawyer doesn't seem concerned about it. "If you need anything further please don't hesitate to contact me directly."

There also used to be a lot of jokes premised around a trio of guys—one white and one Asian and one Black—whose punch line revolved around the Black guy having a much bigger dick to the delight of a very stupid white woman.

The cops leave the hospital room.

"Is that it?" Chicky asks Gennaro.

"I don't know," the lawyer says. "Maybe. Maybe not."

Chicky wishes so much that he'd had the chance to go over the story again with Mrs. Longworth. He's almost positive he remembers what they agreed upon, but not one hundred percent.

And in that margin might be the difference between freedom and jail.

For both of them.

CHAPTER 57

APARTMENT 11C-D

"So." Aronsky is leafing through his pad. "I don't want to ask this, Emily. I really don't."

"Go ahead," she says. "Whatever it is, I understand."

He meets her eye. "Would people say you had a *good* marriage?"

She can't help but notice the wording. He isn't asking about the actual state of her marriage, but what other people would say about it.

"Yes."

"Would anyone be aware of any issues?"

Again, he's asking about witnesses. About evidence.

"In general, no. But recently, because of the disclosures about Whit's business, I've been . . . let's say *disenchanted*. I've expressed this to a few friends."

"This verifiable anger: has it been at Whit? Or at the leaker? Or at the public response?"

"I didn't say *anger*. But yes, all of the above. I was disenchanted with my husband, and I mentioned that to some people. I wouldn't be surprised if they mentioned it to others."

"Could I get their names?"

"Sure. Morgan Lipschitz. Nicole Becker." Emily writes down their phone numbers.

"Did you and your husband have any disagreements in public?"

Emily and Whit had often disagreed in public, but not in a way that would've been visible to anyone. But again this question is about verifiable evidence.

"No."

"And . . . I'm sorry, but . . ."

"No need to apologize. Go ahead."

"Is it possible that anyone might come forward about an extramarital relationship?"

Emily inhales sharply through her nose. She needs to express her distaste for this subject, but she doesn't want to be a ham about it.

"It's not *im*possible. But no, none that I was aware of."

Aronsky taps his pen on the paper. She knows he has to ask the follow-up. "And you?"

"And me, what?"

"Come on, Emily. You know what I'm asking."

If he already knows the answer, he's being an asshole, and she doesn't think he's that type. She doesn't need to say anything.

"Here's the thing," Aronsky continues. "When there's a homicide, the police always suspect the spouse, at least a little, because the spouse is often guilty. This is especially common when the murdered spouse had been conducting an extramarital affair. More common when the surviving spouse had been."

Emily's mouth is now hanging wide open. She needs to be appalled.

"So, again—and I'm not asking for details, I'm just saying—if there *were* any extracurricular relationships? The police are going to find out. Because no one is ever as careful as they think they are. And the police are going to look for such relationships, because they have to."

The truth is she'd never in her entire life cheated on anyone, not once, not until she took up with Jules. And then she cheated all the time.

The thing that's been waking her up at night is this: there's no way Whit figured it out on his own. Which means there's no way the secret died with him.

Emily maintains eye contact with her lawyer, but still says nothing. She has been practicing this for years: not volunteering information.

Aronsky keeps his eyes locked on hers. "You know your movements can be tracked, right?"

"Movements? What movements?"

"All movements. Everywhere you go, whenever you're carrying your phone. Which I'm assuming is all the time, or nearly."

"No, I didn't know that." Of course she did. "But I have nothing to hide."

Emily has hired a few local high-school kids to tutor hers. Bitsy's and Hud's lives will never again be completely normal, but this immediate crisis will end, and they will return to the city, to school, to existences that will be very different yet look similar. She doesn't want her children to have fallen too far behind.

They're in the pool house, which is serving as school for now. When they need a break, the kids play Ping-Pong.

Emily informs the lawyer that she's paying for all of Chicky's and Olek's medical care, as well as the balances on Chicky's wife's healthcare.

"Oh Jesus, really? I don't think that's a great idea."

She uses the same smile that she always uses in situations like this. It's something she practices in the mirror, trying to perfect it.

"I'm sure you know that this money isn't meaningful to my overall financial situation."

Whit's life insurance will pay out quickly. Not that Emily needs this money, per se, but it will simplify cash flow. The disposition of Liberty Logistics is going to drag on for years. Up until a month ago the company's valuation had been somewhere north of thirty billion dollars, but with the recent press who knows. She'll sell all of Whit's share, as soon as possible, but without being anyone's sucker.

"I'm in a position to help people I care about, to improve their lives immensely, and it essentially won't cost me anything. Why in god's name would I not do that?"

"Because they're *witnesses* to your husband's murder, Emily. It might look like you're bribing them."

"Be that as it may," she says. "It's the right thing to do."

CHAPTER 58

FRONT DOOR

It all happened in the course of maybe sixty seconds. That time span is the only difference between what Chicky told the police happened and what really happened.

A lot can happen in a minute. It began when Chicky noticed movement at the end of the hall. He could see Olek unmoving and possibly dead just inside the old service entrance. Chicky believed that Mr. Longworth had already been killed so he assumed this movement had to be one of the robbers. He was wrong. It was an unharmed Mr. Longworth who called out to Chicky. Who walked down the hall. Who arrived at the front hall holding a gun by his side.

"Are you hurt?" he asked his wife. Mrs. Longworth was lying across Mr. Sonnenberg. She was sobbing with her whole body.

"Why is my gun unloaded, Emily?"

She looked up at her husband but didn't say anything. The dead robber's loaded gun was lying just a few feet away from her.

Chicky still can't decide if it would have been better if he'd picked it up and removed it from harm's way. Further harm.

Better though is not objective. Better for who?

"I could've been *killed*," Mr. Longworth said.

Mrs. Longworth still didn't respond.

"Did you set this whole thing up?"

Jesus is *that* what had just happened? Chicky couldn't believe what he was hearing.

Mrs. Longworth looked up at her husband in utter disgust at his accusation.

"Get up," Mr. Longworth said. "You're making a fucking fool of yourself."

Chicky thought: I shouldn't be here for this.

"What? You think I didn't know?"

Longworth was speaking to his wife as if Chicky weren't even there. Which he shouldn't be. Chicky should go check on Olek. He should leave this married couple alone.

Chicky was still kneeling. He began to push himself up but it was a lot harder than expected.

"Of course I knew about your little love nest. Your pathetic lit—"

The explosion took Chicky by complete surprise. He tumbled to the side and banged against the wall and knocked into a picture whose glass broke into large shards that shattered on the floor.

Mr. Longworth was suddenly lying on his back with both hands clutching his neck. Blood was pouring through his fingers.

Mrs. Longworth was holding the dead robber's gun. It was literally smoking.

Mr. Longworth's neck wound looked bad but it hadn't been an immediate kill shot. It seemed unlikely the guy would survive but not impossible.

Chicky understood instantly that Mrs. Longworth could not risk her husband surviving. Did she too understand this?

"You know what needs to happen," Chicky said. "Don't you?"

Mrs. Longworth looked over as if surprised to find Chicky there.

"Can you do it?" he asked. "Or do you want me to?"

Chicky's Magnum had four bullets left but he wouldn't use that gun. Instead he'd take the semiautomatic from Mrs. Longworth's hand. Then afterward he'd place that gun in his pocket as if he'd seized the thing for the sake of safety. This would be a rational course of action. It would also explain his fingerprints and gunshot residue. Yes. That's what he would do.

"Mrs. Longworth?"

That story would track. It was just a question of adjusting the sequence a tiny bit.

"Mrs. Longworth?"

She looked at her husband. He was kicking out his legs and his eyes were darting around. She turned back to Chicky and her mouth fell open.

"Oh my god Chicky?" She was staring at his midsection.

Chicky looked down.

Red and blue lights swirled against the wall.

CHAPTER 59

APARTMENT 11C-D

Emily doesn't trust herself to drive, so she asks DeMarquis to come out to the beach and get her. All her family's cars seem wrong for this, but the SUV is probably least wrong. It can be mistaken for a hired car.

They drive in silence. Emily has never spent much time in this backseat. The Goldfish dust is palpable. After ninety minutes, as they close in on the Bohemia, Emily begins to shake. At first she thinks it's because she's cold. She reaches for the thermostat but it's already at seventy.

When she sees Canarius on the sidewalk, in Chicky's spot, she starts to cry.

DeMarquis parks at the hydrant and accompanies Emily inside, and up the elevator, and into the apartment. The police have processed the crime scene, and Tatiana and her cousin have cleaned.

Emily's walk-in closet is similar in size to the studio she'd lived in for a decade. She still has the same pencil sketch, hanging above her vanity, that she'd once hoped would convince visitors she was a serious person.

She chooses a modest black skirt and jacket, an ensemble purchased specifically for this general sort of circumstance, though not this exact one. She doesn't add any jewelry. She carries the simplest, smallest handbag, filled with not much more than lipstick and a couple of handkerchiefs.

The sun has set, but Emily puts sunglasses over her puffy red-rimmed eyes. She certainly looks the part of a grieving widow. Maybe too much, considering that it's not her dead husband's service she's going to.

As the elevator doors are opening to the lobby, Emily can see her nightmare waiting. She reaches her hand to press a button—any button, just get away from here—but changes her mind. She needs to face this. Whatever happens here, now, she has it coming.

What can Emily say? It was indefensible. Emily did something indefensibly selfish, and it got this woman's husband killed. It's unforgivable.

"I'm so sorry." That's all she can say, isn't it?

Jennifer Sonnenberg is also wearing all black, and sunglasses. Jennifer's cheeks are streaked with tears, but because of the sunglasses Emily can't see her eyes. Can't read her expression.

"Are you waiting for your children?" Emily asks.

Jennifer takes a couple of beats before answering. Emily wonders if she's trying to decide how civil to be. How uncivil.

"They're already there," Jennifer says. "I needed a few minutes."

The memorial chapel is only a few blocks away, but this isn't something a widow walks to. Emily looks outside, and sees paparazzi out there. Just a couple of them, on the far side of the street, with their gigantic lenses, their camera bags, their manic air. There might be others Emily can't see, lurking nearby, ready to spring into action.

"Do you have a car coming?" Emily asks.

"Uber."

"Can I . . ." Is Emily really going to suggest this? "Can I give you a lift? Please?"

Jennifer takes off her sunglasses, and turns to Emily, who uncovers her eyes too. The two women stare at each other for a few seconds before Jennifer asks, "Did you love him?"

Emily doesn't know what the right answer is. There's the truth, but the truth is not always right. The right answer here is whatever is going to lessen this woman's suffering.

She prepares herself to be slapped. "Yes," she says. The truth. "Yes I did."

Jennifer doesn't respond for a second, and another. Her tears are flowing freely. She turns away, and puts her sunglasses back on.

"Good," she says. "Me too."

CHAPTER 60

FRONT DOOR

"Thank you guys," Chicky says. "I appreciate you. Every one of you."

It's just after four, the shoulder between the day shift and night. Nearly everyone is packed into the break room. The day guys are on their way out and the night guys in. Except Canarius who's at the front door alone. Someone always needs to be there no matter what else is going on. Whether a party or a pandemic or a paramilitary invasion, a doorman is always at the Bohemia's front door in the path between the residents and any inconvenience or any danger or anything else they don't want.

"I can't tell you how much I appreciate this." Chicky makes a fist and pounds his heart while holding up the greeting card in his other hand. Chicky himself was the one who purchased this card. It came in a box of ten that's stored in a cabinet along with the first-aid kit and the food-delivery menus.

A dozen residents are also here. Mrs. Longworth isn't among them. Chicky knows she can't be seen at any type of party. Chicky notices that Olek has retreated to his office. Now it's time to say goodbye to him too.

"Come in Chicky my friend. Come in." Olek is wearing a restrained smile, the only type he has. Chicky clutches the card with the check inside. Eight hundred dollars. No one was able to think of a specific gift. Chicky doesn't blame them. He too would have failed if he'd been tasked with choosing a present for himself. The things he wants cannot be bought.

"There is something I must tell you," Olek says. He looks serious. This is the first time Chicky and Olek have been alone since that night. It will likely be the last.

"I heard everything."

Chicky knows immediately what Olek means. His heart sinks.

"I saw everything."

The super's door is wide open. Anyone can walk in. Anyone can see in. Chicky doesn't know what to say. So he doesn't say anything.

"I have not told anyone," Olek continues. "And I will not."

Chicky doesn't know if he should respond. Olek has already been interviewed by the police. So what could he want? Is he going to extort Chicky?

"Why are you telling me this now?"

Olek shrugs. "I do not want you to have to wonder. To worry. I know it is a terrible thing to have to worry about secrets being exposed."

Chicky doesn't say anything.

"Chicky, my friend." Olek stands, extends his hand. "I wish for you only the best."

Now Chicky understands: Olek is repaying all the favors Chicky granted over the years. Coming in early and staying late and swapping shifts, anything Olek asked and plenty that he didn't need to. Olek is repaying it all by not ratting Chicky out as accessory to murder. That's pretty big compensation.

"Thank you Boss. I'll be back." And who's to say otherwise? But after life-threatening situations people change their minds all the time.

"Sure you will Chicky."

Chicky was wrong: a restrained smile isn't Olek's only type.

"Sure you will."

Chicky limps up to El Puño's building. That Navigator is idling at a hydrant in front.

"Yeah," Chicky says to the Tree, "how you doin'."

Chicky nods at Face Tattoo. Both these guys are bundled up against the cold.

"He around?"

The Tree sucks his teeth. A window of the SUV lowers. It's El Puño in there.

"Hey," Chicky says. El Puño answers with the tiniest of nods. It's going to be like that.

"All right." Chicky reaches into his pocket. The Tree freaks and Face Tattoo pulls a nine. "Chill," Chicky says. "It's an envelope."

Chicky extends the envelope toward the window but El Puño turns away. He won't even stoop to take money from a doorman. Like Whit Longworth, El Puño occupies a higher plane of existence.

There are plenty of very different-looking guys in this world who are actually the same exact type of asshole.

Face Tattoo is still holding his gun. The Tree snatches the envelope. The envelope is sealed. Chicky is hoping that this dissuades anyone except El Puño from opening it. What's inside is a thousand dollars in twenties, so it feels like a big stack, with a note: *Sorry for your inconvenience. This should cover your expenses.* If for some reason El Puño had needed to use a bail bondsman to spring his posse, the expenses could've added up to, at most, a grand. Chicky gave the guy the benefit of the doubt and rounded up too. To be polite.

If El Puño is the one who opens the envelope it'll be only El Puño who knows what Chicky paid and the guy will be able to save face. Chicky hopes that'll convince him to let the matter drop. Saving face is important to guys like El Puño. To guys like Chicky too. Maybe to everyone.

But Chicky isn't going to be the inside man for anyone's Bohemia heist. He'd always suspected it was a horrible idea and now there's evidence all over the goddamned place.

And Chicky isn't going to pay a penny more. What's this guy going to do?

Chicky has already been shot.

Fuck it.

CHAPTER 61

APARTMENT 11C-D

Emily was pressing both hands against Chicky's gunshot, with her phone on the floor, on speaker.

"Nine-one-one what's your emergency?"

"People have been shot! At least one is still alive with a gunshot to his abdomen. Please send ambulances to the Bohemia, apartment 11C-D."

Emily ended the call. The color had drained from Chicky's face, and his back was against the wall, directly under the spot where the Hopper was supposed to be hanging. The first thing you see, when you enter. A painting of a working-class man, dressed in his uniform, taking a break. Emily had thought it was awfully clever, when Julian found it for her. She'd thought it was perfect. That was when she began to think that Julian too was perfect.

"Does it hurt a lot?"

"It's not so bad," Chicky said, an obvious lie. Then, "Listen Mrs. Longworth."

"Emily. Please."

Chicky smiled weakly and briefly. "Is that nine-one-one call definitely over?"

She pressed the screen, which didn't respond. "Yes." Now the screen was smeared with blood.

"We don't have much time. So let me, um, refresh your memory of what just happened."

Emily didn't understand what Chicky meant.

"The robber who shot Mr. Sonnenberg, that's the same person who also shot your husband."

Emily met Chicky's eye. He was clearly in immense pain, but he didn't seem delirious.

"It happened just like it happened. This guy shot your husband the first time as he came into the hall then finished him off point-blank when he was lying on the floor. Just like it happened, except for the person pulling the trigger."

Chicky's and Emily's faces were a foot apart. She heard him gulp down his pain.

"Right after that second shot is when I came through the living room door. I shot the shooter twice while he shot me. And now here we are, you calling nine-one-one, tending to me."

Emily could hear sirens. Chicky leaned to the side, groaned, and collected the semiautomatic. "I picked this up to keep it away from . . . whoever." He pocketed this gun. "I have gunshot residue on my hands. I fired my weapon. How many times?"

He was quizzing her.

"Twice."

"That's right. But so do you. You have gunshot residue on you plus plenty of blood, my blood, your husband's, Mr. Sonnenberg's. It will make sense for you to want to clean yourself off, all this blood. *Go do that right now.* Before the police run any tests on you. Before they take any samples. Go get towels or something for my wound, and wash your hands while you're in there."

The sirens were very loud. The walls in the Bohemia may be thick and filled with sand but the windows are old and single-pane. Emily refused to replace them with modern windows, which just aren't the same.

"Your husband never said a word before he died. There was nothing for me to hear. I don't know anything about . . . anything."

How did Whit know? Maybe he did hire a detective, just as Emily had feared. Maybe there were records, a dossier, a case Whit had built against his wife, a file that was going to make it look like Emily had plenty of motivation to want her husband dead. Because she did. And now he was.

"And I never"—Chicky winced—"I never told you about that girl in the hotel."

Emily's mind was hurtling forward into the logic problem of this narrative. Was this something that could simply be never mentioned? She nodded.

The sirens had arrived. The cops were here, or ambulances, both. Emily took off her scarf, and used it to wipe the blood off her hands.

"I also never told you about the, um, commotion I heard from your apartment."

Yes, that too. No reason to bring the bickering-help storyline into it.

"What I *had* to witness, though, was that your husband's gun wasn't loaded tonight, when he tried to fire. But I have no idea if *you* knew anything about his gun being empty. I strongly suggest that you too did not know. Whether his gun was loaded, or unloaded, for whatever reason . . ."

Now she understood. "Oh my god, Chicky. I didn't *do* this."

"Sure. Course not."

Emily couldn't tell if he was being honest or not.

"The police, though," Chicky continued, "they might go looking for evidence. For motivation."

Evidence.

Motivation.

Emily could hear a commotion on the far side of her door.

"But I don't know anything about any of that, Mrs. Longworth. All's I know is that the person who shot your husband is dead."

That was when the cops burst in.

"Hands up!" a cop yelled. "Don't move!" The type of conflicting instructions that seemed designed to get you killed.

Then Chicky passed out.

After the service, DeMarquis accompanies Emily upstairs. She's going to change her clothes before they drive back out to the beach.

"Mrs. Longworth?"

"Yes, DeMarquis?"

He reaches into the pocket of his black overcoat, and removes a large manila envelope, folded in half.

"What is this?"

"I, um . . ." He clears his throat. "Maybe you should just open it."

Her heart plummets into the pit of her stomach as she undoes the metal clasp. Lifts the flap. Reaches in. Her skin is dry, and she can't find purchase on the paper.

She licks her thumb, tries again.

The top of the first page says it all: an image of Julian stepping through the door of her painting studio.

Emily gasps.

So here it is, she thinks: finally, that long-awaited shoe. Well, at least now she has the answer to a question that's been gnawing at her.

"This is the only copy," DeMarquis says. "I destroyed the originals."

"You destroyed the investigator's files?"

"I was the investigator."

Emily doesn't understand what's happening here.

"No one else knows," he continues. "Now that your husband, um . . ."

Is this a negotiation? An extortion?

Emily swallows. "What do you want, DeMarquis?"

"Nothing."

"Nothing?"

"Well, I guess I want to keep my job."

The tears start gushing—tears of relief, tears of grief, Emily can't tell—and she drops the dossier to the floor, throws her arms around DeMarquis, and sobs against his chest. It takes him a couple of seconds to return her embrace, then she weeps yet harder, and the two of them stand in the entry gallery, this interstitial space where so much of her life seems to happen, death too, beginnings and endings, everything.

CHAPTER 62

APARTMENT 11C-D

Chicky had been correct: very little in the narrative needed to be adjusted.

Emily had been on the floor, surrounded by bloody bodies. Dead robber, dead lover, shot doorman, shot husband. That was when Chicky offered to be the one to finish off Whit.

She looked over at her husband, bleeding from that first shot of hers. His neck wound certainly looked serious, but what did she know? If he somehow survived, Emily would be spending a large chunk of her life in prison for attempted murder.

No, that was not acceptable.

If Chicky finished off Whit? That would ensure Chicky's silence about Emily's first shot, as well as about any other damaging details the doorman might know about Emily's relationship with Jules, about her motivations for wanting her husband dead. But murdering Whit would haunt Chicky for the rest of his days. Or worse.

No, this was not something a doorman could take care of for her, like carrying groceries, hailing a taxi.

She was still holding the robber's gun.

No, this wasn't really a choice.

Emily Grace Merriweather Longworth rose, and stood over her husband, and looked him in the eye, right there in his own home.

Boom.

CHAPTER 63

FRONT DOOR

All the leaves have fallen. The bright colors have turned to browns and the greens to grays. The sky is low. The lake's glassy reflection is broken up only by ducks gliding toward the Bow Bridge, their triangular wake.

Chicky waits at the drained fountain but doesn't sit. He's too nervous to sit plus it would be too cold on that stone.

It won't be warm again for months. The Bohemia struggles in this type of weather. The building has an energy-efficiency rating of D. Mr. Sonnenberg used to refer to this as a scarlet letter of shame but for a nineteenth-century structure it was not unusual. Old buildings were built before plastics or fiberglass insulation or PVC piping or high-efficiency windows. Before global warming.

It isn't reasonable to hold such old things to contemporary standards. Which is what old people say to defend themselves. But that doesn't mean it isn't true.

Chicky watches Emily Longworth come around the bend. She smiles when she sees him.

"How have you been Chicky?"

"Oh you know." Chicky shrugs. He doesn't want to get into all of it. He's wearing a catheter. "And you Mrs. Longworth?"

"Please Chicky. After everything? Please call me Emily."

"I'm sorry," he says. "I don't think I can."

She laughs. God, that laugh. She rubs his arm. "Hmm. Not as firm as it used to be."

"I haven't exactly been able to hit the weights."

"I hope you can get back to it soon. I hope you can get back to everything."

She opens her arms and steps forward and pulls him in for an embrace. Chicky has never before hugged one of the residents. Not once in three decades as a doorman.

"We will all miss you Chicky. I hope you know that. The place just won't be the same."

"I'll miss you too."

She hands him an envelope. It's sealed. "Please open it," she says. "If you don't mind."

Chicky needs to take off his bulky glove to get a finger under the flap.

"It must've been rough when you were a kid with that name? My goodness. No wonder you go by something else."

Chicky can feel his cheeks burn despite the cold. "Yeah. But it was also the president's name, you know?"

"President?"

Mrs. Longworth apparently doesn't know. She's too young.

"Nixon," Chicky says. "That's what people called him."

"Oh right."

Chicky unfolds the page.

"Here. Allow me." She leans forward to share possession of the piece of paper. "That number at the top? That's your account number. And down at the bottom on the right? That's your balance."

"Jesus." It's more money than Chicky ever dreamed he'd have. Mrs. Longworth has already paid for his healthcare and Tiffani's bills. Now Chicky will be able to wipe out his credit-card balances and the past-due rent and the other late-notice bills. He's never going to become a person with a good credit rating. He'll never get a mortgage. He's never going to be a legitimate type of rich. But he'll be able to set aside money to pay for the rest of his girls' schooling and for his own health insurance and his retirement. A retirement that's starting right now.

"Thank you," he says. "Thank you so much."

"You're welcome." She gives him that reluctant little smile that he knows she uses for accepting compliments and thanks. “And thank *you* Chicky. You saved my life.”

“No I didn’t.”

“Of course you did.” She looks around then meets his eye. “If not for you I’d be spending the rest of it in prison.”

Maybe the first gunshot could have been explained away. Mistaken identity. Finger spasm. Confusion.

But not the second.

There was no way to explain away rising and standing over a bleeding man and executing him with a point-blank shot to the head. That’s murder.

“I hope you’ll come back and visit us?”

“Definitely. I definitely will.”

The alternative narrative had been Chicky’s idea. Mrs. Longworth had not objected. They both knew they were making a deal. This deal. But there had been no number attached to it. Not until now.

Chicky puts the bank statement in his pocket.

“Okay Chicky. I should get going. Please take care of yourself.”

“You too Mrs.—”

She levels a gaze that’s both challenging and playful.

Chicky doesn’t work at the Bohemia anymore. He’s no longer the help. “You too Emily.”

Ten million dollars in a numbered account in the Cayman Islands. Chicky could never have imagined this would be the turn his life took.

She gives him one final smile before she turns away. Chicky stays at the empty fountain in the middle of the park in the middle of the city where he has lived his whole life. Millions of people think of New York as theirs, and they’re all right. If you think it’s true, it’s true.

The sun will set any minute. Then the rats will start to come out.

Chicky looks up at the Bohemia’s famous silhouette. You see it all the time in TV shows and movies. It’s in tourism guides and art-photography books. It’s in the private photo albums of millions of people, maybe tens of millions, tourists from all over the world, New Yorkers too. It’s a landmark. It’s also a place where people live and work. It’s a place where people die.

Emily Longworth turns a bend around the lake and out of his sight. Out of his life.

The doctor told Chicky that walking is the only exercise he should do for the time being and he should do a lot of it. He turns his back on the Bohemia and sets off toward home, three miles northeast. Past the lake where people rent rowboats but not Chicky, not once in his life. Past the Great Lawn where he used to play ball and the reservoir path where he used to run. Past the museums on Fifth Avenue that he never visits. Past the mansions of Carnegie Hill and the private schools. Past all the things he used to do, and the things he never does, and the things he'll never do.

Life can look like a series of foregone decisions, both the good and the bad, all the non-choices that create a predictable path, inescapable, inevitable, here is your home, here is your family, your friends, your job, here's how you'll grow old and here's how you'll die, each of us the hero of our own inconsequential little story, all of us eyewitnesses and unreliable narrators, each of us just as wrong and just as right as anyone, all of us flung together, the housewife and the gallerist and the doorman, you are who you are, until you're not.

ACKNOWLEDGMENTS

This novel is set largely in a famous apartment house on Central Park West in New York City. I live in a famous apartment house on Central Park West. My real-life home and this novel's made-up building are not the same place. I've never attended any of our board meetings, I'm not aware of any conversations about sensitive issues such as the ones in this novel, and all the details about the Bohemia are deliberately divergent from reality—the architecture, the security, the shifts, the office, everything in this book is made-up, and most especially the characters. These people are all fictional, not based on anyone.

Except the titular Chicky, who was inspired by longtime doorman Johnny Irizarry. Not Johnny's life experiences, but his mannerisms, his way of speaking, the Mets. I began inventing this novel out there on the sidewalk, but just as I was starting to actually write the book, Johnny got sick. After emergency hospitalization and treatment and recovery, he returned to the front door as soon as possible, and for the next year and a half he came to work, dying. Before his illness, Johnny and I had stood out there talking about softball, and the weather; now we were talking about the meaning of life, and death. Johnny came to work until a couple of days before he died, and he was buried in his full uniform, plus a Mets pin. He would have loved the 2024 baseball season.

I'd like to thank all the other guys who've worked at this building while we've lived here: Terry Armstrong, Brandon Aviles, Jeffri Batista, Joe Bello, George Black, Mark Borenstein, Deron Chu, Tom Connolly, Tito Cortez, Steven Garcia, Rodrigo Gomez, Joshua Horne, Kensley Jn-Baptiste, Roberto Marra, Angelo Martinez, Armando Martinez, Irving Martinez, Javier Martinez, Nestor Massari, Amur Mathura, Morris Montoya, Brian O'Shea, Amaurys Perez, Michael Postiglione, Edward Preiman, Richard Purcell, Justin Rivera, Christopher Roberts, Osire Safont,

Chris Saminath, Dennis Santiago, Anand Singh, Christopher Torres, and David Vasquez.

Thanks to everyone who provided notes, criticism, and encouragement on early drafts: Amber Cortes, Ellen Coughtrey, Rupert Friend, Rebecca Gardner, Suzanne Gluck, Meaghan Leahy, Sandra Mora Leahy, Alex McIntosh, Chris Parris-Lamb, Molly Ringwald, Jennifer Breheny Wallace, and Anna Worrall.

Thanks to editor Sean McDonald and everyone else at MCD, FSG, Macmillan, and WME who helped to turn a manuscript into a book and launched it into the world: Gretchen Achilles, Mitzi Angel, Benjamin Brooks, Hank Cochrane, Ken Diamond, Brianna Fairman, Nina Frieman, Jonathan Galassi, Justine Gardner, Debra Helfand, Spenser Lee, Tracy Locke, Alex Merto, Guy Oldfield, Sheila O'Shea, Bri Panzica, Sylvie Rabineau, and Chandra Wohleber.

Thanks, as always, to my wife, Madeline McIntosh, and to my agent, David Gernert.

Thanks to anyone who has gotten far enough to read this sentence.

Final thanks to anyone who has written to me over the years to say something nice. It means so much. If the impulse ever strikes to drop a kind note to anyone who has created anything, I urge you not to fight it.

A NOTE ABOUT THE AUTHOR

Chris Pavone is the author of *Two Nights in Lisbon*, *The Paris Diversion*, *The Travelers*, *The Accident*, and *The Expats*, for which he won both the Edgar Award and the Anthony Award. His novels have appeared on the bestseller lists of *The New York Times*, *USA Today*, and *The Wall Street Journal*; are in development for film and television; and have been translated into two dozen languages. Pavone grew up in Brooklyn, graduated from Cornell University, and worked as a book editor for nearly two decades. He lives in New York City and on the North Fork of Long Island with his family.